ARABELLA NIGHTSHADE
&
THE CURSE OF
BLACKTHORN MANOR

BY J.D Brown
First edition 2025

Prologue

The wind howled through the broken halls of Blackthorn Manor, rattling the shutters and stirring the heavy drapes like restless spirits. Beneath the ancient stones, something stirred, a memory, a curse, a name long forgotten by time but never erased. Arabella. Her name was once whispered in these halls with love, then with fear, and finally with silence. Those who dared to speak it said she was a beauty like no other, with hair dark as midnight and eyes that shone like glass under the moonlight. A bride-to-be, standing on the edge of a life that never came to pass. The manor bore witness to everything. The stolen moments. The broken promises. The final, shattering scream. Now, it waits. Watching. Listening. Some say the house has a heart of its own, and that it beats only for her. Tonight, new footsteps cross the threshold.

And the house stirs once more, hungry for memory, desperate to be heard. Arabella is waiting. She always has been.

ARABELLA IS WAITING

CHAPTER ONE
THE NEW FAMILY OF BLACKTHORN MANOR

1800

"Arabella! Arabella! ARABELLA!" Maid Fawns cried out in a frantic, worried tone from across the room. "Arabella! You shall be late if you do not hurry!" Arabella awoke, still floating in the glow of the most delightful dream, a dream in which she was marrying the love of her life, Sir Edward Blackthorn. He was a tall, slender man of striking handsomeness, with long, wavy blonde hair that fell just past his collar. Eyes that shimmered a stormy blue-grey, so piercing that they seemed capable of cutting through the hearts of any lady with a single glance. And he was hers; no one could take him from her. But as her eyes fluttered open and reality slowly crept in, a chilling thought struck her, ice-cold and unforgiving. The remnants of a dream lingered in the edges of her consciousness, hazy and disjointed, yet something about it felt wrong, too vivid, too real. She could not shake the feeling that she was not alone, that something was waiting, just beyond her reach, ready to unfold in ways she could not yet comprehend. Was it only a dream... or had something far darker begun to unravel?...

present-day

"I really cannot understand why you did not take that left turn. It would have saved us from getting lost in the middle of nowhere." Isabelle promulgated, her face a picture of 'I told you so.' "Calm down, love. This is the way My Maps is taking us." Henry responded with a reassuring smile, his fingers drumming lightly on the steering wheel. "It might not look right, but hey, when has technology *ever* made things simple?" He cast a quick glance at the road ahead, then back at her with a wink. "Trust the satnav... and your charming husband." Their daughter, Chase, who was about to turn eighteen, sat in the back, absorbed in her audiobook, *The History of Women in the Victorian Era*. She loved anything related to period pieces, especially the struggles women faced and their fight for rights. She had little in common with her parents. Even her appearance set her apart, her mother had bright blonde hair and brown eyes, while her father had hardly any hair at all, with the same brown eyes. Her parents were the epitome of normal, a typical middle-class couple. Isabelle, a charity fundraiser with a law degree, had never pursued career law, despite her parents pushing her towards it. The idea of defending clients in court had never held the same appeal as working for causes she was enthusiastic about. Though her parents had insisted it was a more secure and prestigious path, Isabelle had always found herself drawn to helping those in need, an impulse that led her to the world of charity. The law, with its rigid structure and cold logic, seemed a world away from the emotional satisfaction of making a difference, no matter how small. Isabelle found fulfilment in helping others, though the shadow of their expectations lingered. Henry on the other hand, had been an A+ student back in his day, and he took immense pride in his career as a teacher. It was not just a job for him; it was a calling. In contrast, Chase had a self-contained presence that seemed both grounded and out of step with the world around her. Her mahogany brown hair framed a symmetrical face dusted with freckles, features that might have been called pretty if she ever tried to be noticed. But Chase didn't care for that. She wasn't the kind of girl who sought attention; she was the kind who watched everything, listened carefully, and kept most of her thoughts to herself. Her eyes were a clear, striking blue, a shade made more vivid by contrast with her dark hair. There was a stillness in them, something observant and distant, as if she were always half-tuned to a world others couldn't partly see. Not cold, but calm. Thoughtful. Her style was her own: relaxed, thrown together with intention but without vanity. Chase wore worn-in Doc Martens and a faded denim dungaree dress, usually layered over a soft, oversized jumper. A vintage-style hat, wide-brimmed slightly and leathered, often sat atop her head shading her eyes and giving her the look of someone who had wandered in from a different era. There was a kind of gentle defiance in how she moved, a calm confidence in her refusal to blend in. Most people didn't negligibly know what to make of her, But Chase had never minded being hard to define. Nevertheless, Chase loved her parents deeply and would do anything for them, but there was a silent emptiness in her heart, something she could not to the max put her finger on, a feeling she could not name, but that lingered, nonetheless. "We're here." "Oh my, that is incredible! I feel like we have just arrived at a royal castle!" Isabelle exclaimed; her voice filled with awe as she gazed at the grand estate. The size and beauty of the home left her utterly gob smacked. "How did you find this place?" "It was on 'FindMyDreamHom.com.' It has been unoccupied for about seventy-five years." Henry replied, his face lighting up as they pulled onto the long, winding driveway. How had he managed to find such a magnificent, well-preserved home? Blackthorn Manor had once been a symbol of untold wealth and power, standing tall in the heart of the untamed wilderness. Constructed by the visionary Sir Howard Blackthorn and his elegant wife, Lady Catherine, in the early 1800s. It was a testament to their legacy. The manor was nestled within an expansive six hundred acres of lush, untapped land, surrounded by towering forests that whispered with secrets of the past. The sprawling estate boasted immaculate gardens that bloomed year-round, their vibrant colours a testament to careful cultivation and timeless beauty. Serene ponds with their surfaces perfectly still, mirrored the sky above, reflecting the everchanging hues of dawn and dusk. Majestic willow trees lined the water's edge, their branches swaying gently in the breeze. The stables, fit for royalty, stood at the far end of the grounds, elegant yet functional, housing prized horses whose coats gleamed like polished marble. It was a place of hushed opulence, where every corner seemed to whisper of history, wealth, and power. Their only son, Edward, grew up amidst this magnificent empire, unaware that the splendour of Blackthorn Manor would one day be lost to time. "Dad, Mum, is this it?" Chase's voice wavered with excitement. "It is amazing! Can I explore? I bet there is all kinds of historical treasures, secret rooms..." She grinned mischievously. "...Maybe it is even haunted." Her laugh was light, but there was a chilling edge to it, her eyes glinting with a strange, playful darkness. She stepped forward each step getting slower, heading toward the towering ten-foot oak doors. The wood was worn and weathered, deep cracks running through its surface. Two rough, black steel knockers, twisted into thorn-like shapes, hovered ominously at the centre, daring anyone to enter.

1800

Arabella sprang from her bed, her eyes at once drawn to the tall, freestanding clock in the corner of her bedchamber. "Seven o'clock!" she exclaimed, her voice betraying her surprise.

Turning to her right, she froze, startled to see her own reflection. She stood there in nothing but her nightshift, her long black hair flowing straight down her back, save for a single braid to the left side. At just eighteen, Arabella was the very picture of beauty her complexion pale and smooth, with a hint of rose to her cheeks, and lips a deep, vivid red that contrasted starkly with her dark, obsidian lashes and hair. Though she was petite, barely five feet tall, there was an undeniable grace in her posture, a dead confidence that stretched her presence beyond her small frame. Every movement she made was fluid, and deliberate, as though she was always aware of the space around her. Her head held high, shoulders back, she walked with the kind of poise that made her appear taller than she truly was, almost regal in her bearing, as though she belonged to a world far grander than the one she inhabited. It was a quiet strength, the kind that did not need to be loud to command attention. "Come in!" she called, her voice carrying through the room. Miss Fawns entered promptly, her expression one of practiced composure, though the slight tightening around her eyes betrayed her urgency. "Lady Nightshade." She began, her tone firm yet caring, "We must see to your bath and attire at once. Sir and Lady Blackthorne are soon to arrive, and you shall be late for the rehearsal if we delay any further." She moved briskly toward the washbasin, gathering fresh towels. "The morning is slipping away, and first impressions are not so easily mended." miss fawns added giving Arabella a friendly glare. Lady Blackthorn and her husband had been in Scotland on business for the past three months, but their return was imminent, and Arabella could not afford to waste time. She cast Miss Fawns a look, one interweaved with arcadian frustration, her eyes briefly flashing with a mix of impatience and unspoken words. The weight of the moment pressed down on her, but she swallowed it, masking the storm of thoughts swirling in her mind. With a slight nod in acknowledgment, she set aside her annoyance, forcing a calmness to settle over her features, at least outwardly. The last thing she wanted was to show weakness in front of Miss Fawns, no matter the frustration that simmered just beneath the surface. Arabella's relations with Lady Blackthorn were far from cordial. The older woman had always looked down upon her, convinced that Arabella was unfit to be the wife of Sir Edward, her son, who stood as heir to both the manor and the Blackthorn estate. Had it been left to Lady Blackthorn, she would have chosen a wife for her son based on status and wealth alone, with little regard for the affections of either party. Love, in Lady Blackthorn's eyes, was but a secondary consideration in the arrangement of marriage; a mere luxury, if it should happen at all. "Come now, Lady Nightshade, we must attend to your toilette." Miss Fawns insisted, her voice gentle but demanding, guiding Arabella toward the bathing chamber. Miss Fawns had served the Blackthorn family for over twenty years. She knew Lady Catherine Blackthorn well, or rather, she knew the cruel, calculating nature that lay beneath her composed exterior. Miss Fawns had seen the signs over the years, the way Lady Catherine could turn even the most innocent conversation into a subtle power play and the coldness in her eyes, when she thought no one was watching. It was not the loud, obvious cruelty that one might expect from a villain, but something much more dangerous: the kind of hushed manipulation that left no marks, no scars, yet left people feeling like pawns in her carefully constructed game. All Miss Fawns could offer Arabella was her sympathy, for she knew the young woman was trapped in a world where love and choice were luxuries too rare to hope for. But that was not the case for Arabella. She and Sir Edward shared a love that was pure and true, and tomorrow, they would be united in marriage.

CHAPTER TWO
DISCOVERY OF ARABELLA

Present day

Isabelle and Henry began unpacking the car. They had not brought much; they both wanted a fresh start. The few bags they carried were light, just the essentials. It was not about material things, not anymore. What they looked for now was something far more intangible: a chance to leave behind the past and build a new life. Their old home had been an apartment: two small bedrooms, one bathroom, and a living room that flowed into an open-plan kitchen with a breakfast bar. Cozy and compact, overlooking the city park, offering a touch of nature in the middle of urban life. Originally, it had been Henry's apartment, but after six months of dating and with Isabelle three months pregnant, they decided to move in together. The apartment, once a simple bachelor pad, became their sanctuary. A space where they could lay the foundation for their life together. For the next twenty years it was the heart of their family, holding within its walls the laughter of their child, the soundless hum of everyday life, and the overload of countless memories. It was a place of comfort and familiarity, each corner telling the story of their journey as parents and partners. Chase wandered through her new home, a chill creeping over her skin as she lost track of time in the labyrinth of rooms and corridors. It was like something straight out of a horror movie: vast, empty, and unfamiliar. The silence seemed to stretch for miles, the kind that filled every corner and weighed on the air. The rooms, once bustling with life, now felt cold and distant, their emptiness only highlighted by the dim light filtering through the windows. Every creak of the floorboards, every whisper of the wind outside seemed to echo louder in the stillness, as if the house was waiting for something to happen. She only knew the essentials of a home: a bedroom, a kitchen, a bathroom, a living room but this place was different. Her life had expanded in ways she could not fully comprehend. *'Thirty rooms? Who needs thirty rooms?'* she thought, feeling a shiver run down her spine. Every hallway seemed to stretch on forever, doors standing open like dark mouths, waiting to swallow her whole. The more she wandered, the more she felt like a lost child in a strange and dangerous world, a place that did not feel right. She could not shake the thought *'How lucky am I?'* She had never imagined living like a princess, yet here she was in a house grander than any Disney fantasy.

'Was it really luck?'

'Was something darker unfolding around her?'

'What kind of person would she become in this place?'

'What would waking up every day in a mansion like this feel like?'

These questions swirled in her mind, and though her imagination raced, a deeper, more sinister feeling gnawed at her. Something about this house felt alive… watching…Waiting…

Isabelle and Henry finished unpacking, their movements slow and intentional as they removed the dusty white sheets that had been draped over the old furniture for years. With each piece revealed, the air in the room seemed to grow heavier, as though the house itself was waking up. Stirring from a long, uneasy slumber to reveal its secrets. Shadows clung to the walls a little tighter, and the creak of old floorboards beneath their feet sounded more educated, more alive. It felt as if the house had been waiting for this moment. Watching

silently all along, and now at last it was ready to
speak. Isabelle coughed, the thick dust tickling
her throat. "All this dust... we need to open a
window." She muttered, brushing a hand over a
tarnished side table. Her eyes scanned the
room, a subtle unease creeping over her.
"Henry, could you pass me the hoover?" Henry
handed over the vacuum with a smile, though
something about his expression seemed off. His
usual cheerfulness was there, but it felt a little
forced, like he was trying to hide something.
His eyes lingered on an old, intricately carved
chair near the corner of the room, a piece that
seemed out of place among the more modern
furniture. For a moment, his gaze softened as if
lost in thought, before he quickly turned back
to the task at hand, his smile returning to his
face but not perfectly reaching his eyes. As he
continued uncovering hidden pieces of
furniture, the floor creaked underfoot, as if the
house were reacting to their presence. Isabelle's
fingers brushed against a faded family portrait,
the faces in the painting appearing too lifelike
as if the painted eyes stalked there every move.
The temperature in the room seemed to drop,
but neither of them mentioned it.

1800

Arabella had finished getting ready and made her way down the grand staircase, a sense of bittersweet happiness washing over her. The preparations for the wedding had brought her immense joy, a rare lightness that lifted the dimness from her heart. Each detail, from the lace on her gown to the scent of the blooming garden, filled her with hope for a future she had once believed impossible. But as swiftly as joy had come, so too did fear, creeping in like a cold draught beneath a closed door. It whispered doubts into her thoughts, curled itself around her chest, and reminded her that happiness in this house was often fleeting. She soon remembered the long day ahead with Lady Blackthorn her mother-in-law. Arabella shook off the thought and continued, stepping outside into the front gardens, where she would greet the Blackthorns. The day was beautiful; the warmth of the sun kissed her face as she looked up to find nothing but an endless sky, a soft cascade of blue. Just a little further down the garden path, a vast driveway stretched ahead, flanked on either side by lush greenery that swayed gently in the breeze. Towering hedges and ancient trees cast dappled dullness across the gravel, and the air carried the faint scent of jasmine and earth. It was the kind of path that seemed to lead not just to the gates, but to another world "They're here." Arabella whispered to herself. As the carriage approached, Arabella caught sight of a stunning black and gold vehicle, its enormous wheels seemingly made of iron, drawn by two perfectly white horses with vibrant saddles. As the carriage drew nearer, the sound of galloping hooves grew louder and louder pounding like thunder against the earth. The rhythmic clatter echoed through the trees each beat quicker than the last. Arabella's heart skipped. Suddenly the sound stopped, and Arabella looked up to see the carriage right before her. With the help of a footman, Lady Catherine and Sir Howard Blackthorn stepped down from the carriage, their presence commanding the space. Arabella could not help but admire their rich, imposing style. "Welcome home Sir. Lady. I trust your journey was pleasant?" she began, her voice soft but polite, a practiced warmth in every word. "Shall we have tea in the drawing room? I would love to hear about your…" Arabella's offer was cut off sharply, the sudden interruption slicing through the air like a blade. The polite smile faltered on her lips as the irritation in the air shifted, her words now hanging in the space between them, unresolved and dangling. She blinked, her composure quickly restoring itself, but the moment of uncertainty was enough to leave an unsettling feeling. "Maid Fawns." Lady Catherine said, her tone cutting through the air, "Please ensure that our luggage is taken in. It has been a most tiresome journey. Sir Howard and I shall retire to the drawing room. Tell the cook to bring us a choice of sandwiches and hot tea yes hot tea will do" Without further acknowledgement, Lady Catherine went ahead into the manor, leaving Arabella standing there invisible to the blackthorn's eyes, a mix of emotions swirling within her.

CHAPTER THREE
THE REHEARSAL

1800

The drawing room was the heart of the house, second only to the grand ballroom. It was the most often used room in the manor, fitting for any occasion: morning readings by the fire; mid-afternoon tea with sweets; family gatherings; and after-meal cheese and wine. However today, it served a much more important purpose. The drawing room, with its opulent furniture and portraits of long-dead ancestors, was no longer merely a place for idle conversation or afternoon tea. Today, it would bear witness to something far more significant a gathering that would change the course of everything. The Blackthorns' only son's wedding rehearsal.

The vibe in the room was unsettlingly settled. Arabella thought she could focus on sounds that would usually be drowned out in a gathering like the clink of a teaspoon as milk swirled into the tea, the soft flick of pages as a book was turned, and the crackling of the open fire in the middle of the room. She had always loved the sound of the fire; it brought her a sense of calm, watching the flames dance and flicker, as though they were alive. Arabella jumped slightly at the sound of Sir Howard's deep cough. In a way it was a relief, an excuse to break the silence. "Has your body not in whole gotten used to the country air?" she joked, offering him a smile. The room fell quiet for a moment, just long enough for the silence to stretch, thick and uneasy, like it might never end. All eyes shifted, breaths held, as though the walls themselves were listening. Before Sir Howard could respond, the door creaked open and Maid Fawns stepped in, her voice steady but urgent. "Sir Edward Blackthorn has arrived." She announced, her presence breaking the spell that had settled over the room. Arabella's head snapped up. "Edward, darling." She exclaimed, her voice bright with affection as a radiant smile spread across her face. Her hands clasped in front of her as she took a graceful step forward, the soft rustle of silk underscoring her delight. For a moment, the formality of the house melted away, and all that remained was the warmth of her joy at seeing him. But just as she was about to step forward and greet her love, Lady Catherine slammed her teacup down onto the coffee table with a clawlike click, effectively stealing the moment. "Edward, dear, come give your mother a kiss." Lady Catherine called, her voice smooth and commanding. Edward glanced at Arabella; his eyes filled with apology. The intimated message was clear *'I am sorry love, but I cannot ignore my mother.'* "Ah son, I am most glad to see you." Lady Catherine continued, her tone softening as Edward approached her. "I have a question about the villagers." Sir Howard spoke over lady catherine he and Sir Edward left the room to discuss business, leaving Arabella alone with Lady Catherine. A wave of anger surged through Arabella, her small frame trembling with frustration.

'This was supposed to be my wedding.' 'Mine and Edward's.'

'How could they take that away from me?' The words almost escaped her lips, but instead, she forced a smile and asked, "When shall we start the rehearsal?" Lady Catherine's gaze swept over her, devious and appraising, making Arabella feel as though she were a child about to receive a lesson from a stern teacher. "And why would we need a rehearsal child?" Lady Catherine asked with a mocking laugh, her eyes glinting with disdain. "We Blackthorns have hosted more weddings than I can count.

Everything has been arranged for our son since the day he was born. You-” she waved a dismissive hand, “-are merely the final piece. All that is required of you is to smile prettily and say 'I do.' Nothing more.” Lady Catherine leaned back in her chair, a lingering, satisfied smile on her face, as if she had just delivered a final verdict. Arabella froze, struck speechless, her heart aching with a stabbing blend of humiliation and sorrow. Lady Catherine's words rang in her ears, cruel and echoing, as if the room was mocking her. She lowered herself into the nearest chair, her movements slow and mechanical, as though the air had grown heavier. A dull roar filled her mind, and for a moment, she felt not like a bride to be, but like a stranger in her own story, an afterthought in a life already written by someone else. Just then, Maid Fawns appeared again. “Dinner is served, ma'am.”

Present day

It had been a long weekend for the family. The moving, the cleaning and the constant redecorating. Though they still had plenty of rooms left to tackle, the basics were mostly done. Henry spent most of his time plastering over cracks in the walls, smoothing over years of wear as if trying to make the manor forget its age. He worked in calm concentration, filling every fracture with care. He also sanded and polished the wooden doors and shutters until they gleamed, though the real struggle had been the plumbing. He had only managed to get the kitchen and one bathroom working, the rest a tangle of pipes he had not yet dared to touch. Isabelle, meanwhile, tackled the decorating, shifting furniture into place the way she liked it. Her vision slowly transforming the house into something that felt, at least in part, like home. Chase helped here and there, though more often than not, she just got in the way. Her attention span was too short for the slow, steady work, and she would abandon a task halfway through, distracted by a creaking floorboard or a half-open door. Chase had other things on her mind. She was not interested in the decorating or the unpacking; she wanted to explore the house more thoroughly. She remembered seeing a tower when they first pulled up to the manor. It was on the left side, and she was determined to find it. She wandered through the hallways of the third floor, but there was no sign of an entryway to a tower just empty rooms that her parents had not yet gotten around to. Frustrated, she huffed and turned to leave, but something caught her eye. A wooden slat was coming loose from the wall, its edge jutting out just enough to catch the eye. The wood looked old and brittle, as though something on the other side had been pushing its way out. "What do we have here?" she growled, drawn to the strange detail. She approached, curious. With a half-hearted tug, the plank came off, revealing a small keyhole hidden in the wall. "Gotcha." She whispered, a spark of triumph in her voice. Chase sprinted through the halls, leapt down the grand staircase, and ran straight to her father. "Dad？" she called out, her voice breathless. Henry looked up from his work, his brow furrowed in concentration. His protective goggles were covered in dust, perched halfway down his nose, giving him a slightly comical, dishevelled appearance. He wiped his hands on his shirt. "Yes, Chase?" his voice was steady, though there was a flicker of concern in his eyes as he pushed his goggles fully off his face. He straightened up, still wiping his hands on his shirt, his attention now fully on her. The dust settled around them. "Do you have a master key for all the doors in the house?" she asked. Henry paused, thinking for a moment. "You mean a skeleton key?" He nodded. "If so,

you're in luck. It's hanging up in the kitchen."
Henry blurted with a smirk, nodding toward
the doorway. "Right where I left it." With that,
he adjusted his goggles and went back to his
task. "Thanks!" Chase barely paused before she
dashed off toward the kitchen. When she
reached it, she stopped in front of the wall
where a collection of keys stayed. There were
so many, all different sizes, shapes, and ages.
How was she supposed to know which one was
the right one? Just as the frustration began to
build, something caught her eye: a large, black,
rusty key with the letters **B.T.** etched into it.
'That has got to be it,' Chase thought, a spark of
certainty running through her veins, as if
everything had led to this exact moment. With
trembling fingers, she slid the key into the lock
and turned it. The faint sound of the key
creaking echoed in the stillness, sending an
involuntary shiver down her spine. Before she
could take a breath, the door groaned open on
its own, a soft, eerie creak that seemed to
stretch on forever. A rush of freezing air swept
through the crack, carrying with it a whisper of
something, something that felt just on the edge
of her understanding. "That wasn't creepy at
all." She muttered, trying to ease the tension
with a little small talk, though the words did
not make her feel any braver. As she stepped

inside, she realized the staircase was a spiral. She had always wanted to climb one in a tower, and now she was about to do just that. The thought sent a thrill through her, a mix of excitement and nervousness swirling in her chest. It felt like a childhood fantasy come to life, a chance to see the world from a height she had only ever imagined. The further she went, the darker it got, but the dim light that filtered through the small, pointed windows in the roof helped guide her. When she finally reached the top, her eyes adjusted to the faint light. On the right, she spotted a rope dangling from the ceiling. She pulled it. And with a creak, a large window shutter swung open, flooding the room with light. Now she could see the space clearly. The dim light from the tower window cast long darkness across the room, revealing the forgotten corners and dust-covered surfaces. Every object told a story. The room was small, cluttered with cobwebs and old, stained boxes. She scanned the area, her eyes falling on more old furniture, dusty chairs and tables that looked as though they had been forgotten for decades. The bedding was torn and rat-bitten, its once-soft fabric now nothing more than a shadow of its former self. The curtains too, had long since lost their colour, hanging limp and faded like a ghost of their former vibrance.

There was no sign of life here, only the slow decay of time, but one box caught her eye. It was black, just like so many other things in this house. Curious, she opened it. Inside, there were photos, jewellery, and a tiny, clear bottle with a small cork screwed tightly in place. As Chase sifted through the photos, most of which appeared to be of the original family of Blackthorn Manor, one photo stopped her cold. It was of a young woman visually stunning, even though the photo was old and faded. But it was not just her beauty that grabbed Chase's attention. There was something else, an intensity, an almost otherworldly grace that made everything else seem to fade into the background. Her eyes, dark and knowing, seemed to pierce through the noise of the room, locking onto Chase with an unsettling familiarity. It was not the kind of gaze one could easily ignore. It was as if she knew something, something that Chase could not yet put into words. It made her skin crawl with a mixture of awe and apprehension. As she looked at the woman's image, she felt something else a strange wave of sadness, heartbreak, and an overwhelming sense of what she could only describe as death. The air seemed to grow heavier, thick with an unseen presence that pressed against her skin. Chase's breath caught in her throat, each inhale depthless, as if the very atmosphere were conspiring to suffocate her. Her hand trembled, the photo slipping from her grasp, falling to the floor with a muffled thud. Panic surged through her veins, hot and cold at once. She scrambled backward, her feet stumbling against the cold, unforgiving floorboards as she made her way to the door. Without thinking, she slammed it shut with a force that made the walls reverberate. For a long moment, she stood frozen at the bottom of the spiral staircase, her heart thundering in her chest, each beat a frantic drum in the lull.

CHAPTER FOUR
A GLIMPSE OF HER

1800

"Your mother can not stand me. She speaks to me like a maid, worse than a maid… a peasant." Arabella whispered, her voice barely audible, as she discreetly raised her fan to shield her face from the prying eyes of the dining table. Her eyes darted nervously to Lady Catherine, who sat across from her, regally inspecting the silverware as if it were beneath her notice. "Shhhh, she will love you once she gets to know you dear." Edward's tone was soothing, but his smile carried a touch of something more, maybe pity, maybe amusement. He leaned toward Arabella slightly, his hand brushing the back of hers, but the gesture was brief and quickly masked by the clatter of plates and glasses being set down before them. The footmen entered, gliding silently across the room, their polished shoes hardly making a sound. The silver trays they carried gleamed in the candlelight, their polished surfaces catching the flicker of the flames, erupting soft, shimmering reflections across the walls of the dining hall. The servants moved in mute synchronization, their footsteps light but purposeful, as though they too were aware of the invisible strain that held everyone in place. Arabella's eyes covered the trays, though her focus was elsewhere, lost in thoughts too complicated to voice. She took a long sip from her glass, the amber liquid burning a path down her throat, but it did little to dull the cold knot of unease that had taken root deep within her stomach. Every glance exchanged between Lady Catherine and Edward felt calculated, as though they were playing a game she was not meant to understand. For the starter, delicate, glistening oysters sat nestled on crushed ice, their salty aroma mingling with the rich scent of shellfish soup; creamy and opulent, twisted with the unmistakable tang of the sea. A whiff of freshly ground black pepper made its way through the air, teasing the senses before the first spoonful was even tasted. The sharp, earthy scent mingled with the aroma of roasted meats and delicate herbs, a perfect prelude to the meal that was about to unfold. Yet despite the lavish spread before her, Arabella could not seem to focus on the food. The main course followed: a plump roasted game bird, a pheasant perhaps, or partridge browned to perfection. Its skin crackling slightly as it was carved. Beside it, roast potatoes and tender vegetables, carrots and peas glistened with a sheen of rich, flavourful gravy. The deep, savoury aroma filled the room, so thick it seemed to hang in the air, inviting every guest to indulge in its warmth. For dessert, the spiced plum pudding was brought out, rich and dark, crowned with a soft cloud of whipped cream. It was drenched in a potent brandy sauce, which flamed briefly in front of everyone's faces around the table, before it was extinguished leaving only the faintest smell of brandy. The scent of the brandy mixed with the spiced sweetness of the pudding, creating an aroma that was both comforting and intoxicating. The meal went down like a treat, each bite a moment of indulgence. A luxury the table savoured with eager pleasure. Conversations flowed like wine between Howard and Edward; their voices rich with the confidence of men who had everything in hand. Their words swirled with talk of politics, investments, and developments, each subject more distant and impersonal than the last, as though the estate was their only concern and the world beyond was nothing but a backdrop to their ambitions. Lady Catherine however, seemed to grow increasingly uncomfortable with being left out.

She quickly seized the opportunity to dominate the conversation, her voice sharp as she regaled the table with tedious tales of her travels to Scotland. Her words were drowned in the soft clink of silverware and polite murmurs, but no one bothered to interrupt her. Meanwhile, Arabella sat quietly at the corner of the table, the solidity of inarticulateness pressing heavily upon her. Edward inquired after her well-being every ten minutes, but the words felt rehearsed, offered out of duty rather than true concern. His eyes never lingered long; they flicked past her like a passing thought. She lowered her gaze to the wine glass before her, watching as the deep red liquid caught the flickering light of the candelabras, swirling like the unease in her chest. It felt like she was vanishing, inch by inch, beneath the glittering polish of a life that no longer seemed to be her own. Excitement bubbled in her chest each time the footman came around with another round of complimentary wine, a delicate sherry, or a sweet port to pair with the rich dishes. She would sip, not out of genuine thirst but because it offered her a brief escape from the oppressive weight of the conversation. The wine was rich and dry, catching slightly in her throat, yet she welcomed the sting, it grounded her, reminded her she was still present, still real. She

wondered, not for the first time, whether
anyone would notice if she simply stood up and
walked away. Every so often, her eyes would
flicker to the servants, her gaze following them
as they moved around the room. They seemed
so at ease in the presence of wealth and
grandeur, so used to the rituals of this life. Yet
she could not shake the feeling that she too,
was just another servant in the grand scheme of
things. Even more so than the staff who glided
silently around the room, unnoticed, doing
their work with purpose and precision. At least
they had roles clearly defined, duties to fulfil,
tasks that gave them identity. Arabella, despite
the silks on her back and the ring on her finger,
Arabella felt like a ghost drifting through
someone else's story. Ornamental, voiceless,
expected only to smile, to look beautiful, and to
obey. She envied the quiet dignity of Miss
Fawns, who carried herself with assurance.
Arabella's world, by contrast, was one of
performance. Every word she spoke had to be
carefully chosen, every emotion masked
beneath layers of politeness and control. In this
moment, surrounded by opulence, she felt more
like a caged bird than a bride-to-be. Her cage
was not iron, but expectation, and its bars were
carved from traditions and duty. Her fingers
tightened around the stem of her wine glass,

and she reminded herself to breathe. But in the quiet moments between refills of wine, when the conversations shifted or fell into an uncomfortable lull, Arabella's thoughts grew darker. *'Was she simply the guest here?'* After indulging in a stomach warming meal, the family retired to the drawing room. The fire was crackling softly in the hearth as the wine and bourbon began to flow freely. Lady catherine reclined in her usual chair, her posture perfect, her lacerating eyes surveying the room. Sir Howard and Edward had resumed their discussion from dinner, their voices getting louder with each sip. Arabella seated near the fire, but not mainly in its warmth, held her glass tightly in both hands. The atmosphere shifted, becoming more relaxed until Lady Catherine, still perched as stiff as a pole, broke the silence. "Is it nightshade?" she asked, her voice cool and purposeful, as she sipped from a long-stemmed sherry glass, its polished surface catching the dim glow of the chandelier. Her posture, perfectly erect, uncompromising, radiated authority, and despite herself, Arabella found her own spine straightening, mirroring Lady Catherine's poise. There was power in stillness, and Lady Catherine wielded it like a blade. The question rested in the air like smoke; fragrant, poisonous, and impossible to ignore.

Arabella hesitated, unsure if it was a jest or a test. Her mouth opened, but no words came. She could feel the snappy gaze of Lady Catherine cutting into her like glass, weighing her every breath. *'Was this a warning? A provocation? Or something far more sinister?'* The sherry glass met the table with the faintest clink, yet the sound rang through the room like a gavel. Lady Catherine did not blink. "You do know the properties of such a plant, don't you?" she added, her tone dipped in mock sweetness. "It's mostly… effective, when used with the right intention." Arabella nodded stiffly, though her hands trembled beneath the table. Every word from Lady Catherine seemed dipped in veiled meaning, every glance a riddle. "It is ma'am, answering your first question." Arabella replied, her throat tightening as the words passed her lips. She sat a little taller, her hands folded tightly in her lap, the need to meet Lady Catherine's exacting standards of poise and propriety almost reflexive. "My family owns the Nightshade Quill Ink company." she continued, voice carefully intended. "My father was a quill maker in his youth, crafting each one by hand in a tiny shop just off the village square. He used to say that every line drawn carried a piece of the soul, and that true ink should bleed with intention." Her tone softened, a trace of warmth sneaking through the weight in the room. "It was always his dream to own his own ink business, and when the opportunity finally came, he named it after our family. 'Nightshade', it sounded noble, he stated. Memorable." A small, wistful smile flickered across her lips. "He believed names held power, and that ours would give the business an edge." She paused, the smile fading as quickly as it had come. The pride in her voice had barely settled before she noticed the flicker of something unreadable in Lady Catherine's eyes, curiosity perhaps, or disdain. Arabella could not tell which, and that uncertainty tightened like a cord in her chest. The silence that followed was cold and witting. as though Lady Catherine was weighing every word, every syllable, against some invisible scale. Lady Catherine raised an eyebrow, but her expression remained cold. "Yes dear, I am well aware of the ink business." She said, her tone dripping with mock sweetness. The corners of her mouth curled into a smile, but her eyes remained cold, unamused, keen as the tip of a quill. "It was completely the novelty some years ago. I recall receiving a letter written in that very same ink… the colour bled terribly." Lady Catherine set down her glass with a delicate clink, the sound more pointed than any raised voice. "Though I suppose." She added, tilting her head ever so slightly, "such ventures must feel like grand accomplishments when one comes from… simpler beginnings." Lady catherine continued to poke Arabella "I recall it didn't sell too well once your family became involved in that scandal." Arabella's heart skipped. The casual cruelty in Lady Catherine's words was daggerlike and deliberate. But Arabella, fuelled by the frustration and isolation of the evening, felt the words rise in her chest, a sudden rush of defiance. "Yes, my family was involved in a scandal." Arabella said, her voice Shakey but firm. "But that does not erase my father's hard work or the legacy of his business. And it certainly does not define me." A hush fell over the nearby conversation, subtle but noticeable. Lady Catherine arched a single brow, clearly amused by Arabella's sudden spark of defiance. "How brave." She commented lightly, swirling the remnants of her sherry. "And how quaint, to speak of legacy as if it is something one builds with calloused hands and sentiment." She leaned forward slightly, her voice lower now intimate, yet barbed. "In this house dear, legacy is not earned. It is inherited. And anything… tarnished… is best left buried." Arabella drew in a breath, her voice gaining strength. "With all due respect I love your son, and we shall be married tomorrow, with or without your blessing. I will be the new lady of the manor, and if you are still willing to live here in wealth and style, you will start treating me like your daughter." For a heartbeat, the room fell silent. Arabella's pulse thundered in her ears. *'Had she breathed that aloud?'* The wine, the feeling of humiliation that had been building all evening, the desperate need to be seen it had all spilled out in one swift declaration. Her cheeks flushed, and she quickly averted her gaze to the floor, wondering if she had gone too far. The weight of Lady Catherine's words lingered in the air, sharp and bitter. Arabella's heart thudded in her chest; defiance now tangled with doubt. *'Had she crossed a line? Or simply drawn one?'* Lady Catherine, her face unreadable, took a slow, deliberate sip of her sherry, as though Arabella had not spoken at all. The candlelight flickered against the crystal, irradiating whetted glints across her expression. A smile still curved on her lips, poised, and practiced, yet it never once touched her eyes. She placed the glass down with a soft, controlled clink, the sound seeming louder than it should in the silence. With a languid grace, she tilted her head just slightly and raised a single, perfectly arched

eyebrow, a presumed question, or a challenge.
Her composure remained unnervingly intact, as
if nothing Arabella said could possibly interest
her enough to disturb the mask of polite
detachment. The moment stretched, taut as
piano wire. Arabella could feel the heat rise in
her cheeks, uncertain whether she was being
dismissed or examined. In Lady Catherine's
presence, words were rarely needed to exert
control. The silence itself was a tool; sharp,
cold, and entirely hers with a peacefulness.
Lady Catherine reached for the silver bell
beside her and gave it a single, elegant ring. The
sound was soft. "Miss Fawns." she called, her
tone cool and devoid of warmth, as though
Arabella were no longer present in the room.
"It has been a long evening. I shall retire to my
bedchamber. Tomorrow will be a busy day."
She did not rise immediately, instead sitting
perfectly composed. Arabella sat frozen, her
words still lingering in the air, unanswered.
The rejection was not loud or cruel, but it was
cutting in its precision. She had offered a piece
of herself, her family, her history, and Lady
Catherine had cast it aside with a smile and a
bell. And Arabella, for all her pride and
upbringing, could do nothing but sit there, her
hands clenched in her lap, trying not to let the
sting reach her eyes. She turned, her

movements graceful, as though nothing had happened, and with a slight nod toward Arabella, Lady Catherine exited the room without another word. Arabella stood motionless for a long moment, the words she had just spoken echoing in her mind. She felt drained, the stress of the evening pulling at her. The tension that had gripped her chest seemed to dissipate only to be replaced by a cold emptiness. She left the drawing room wordlessly and made her way up the grand staircase. Her mind was still spinning, but when she passed the library door, she paused. She gently pushed the door open, leaving a small crack. Through the crack she saw Edward, sitting by the fire with a book open in his lap. It looked like he was reading something about the French Revolution, but his expression was distant. A warmth spread through her as she watched him. Her heart swelled with an emotion she could not predominately name, a mix of hope and uncertainty. She gave a soft, heartwarming smile, the first genuine one of the evening, and continued her ascent. Next time she would come up these stairs, she would not be alone. She would be hand in hand with her husband. That was how she had always pictured it, her fingers wreathed with Edwards.

Chase lay awake in the darkened room, staring at the ceiling, her mind racing. The manor was as silent as ever, but that residency was suffocating. She could not escape the nagging feeling that the house was watching her, waiting for her to make a mistake. Every faint draft seemed projected, as if the manor itself were observing her, judging her. It was as though the walls were pressing in, coaxing her deeper into its secrets with each passing minute. The old floorboards creaked as if the house was shifting, trying to catch her attention. She thought again of the photo, the girl with the hollow eyes, and the chill that still clung to her bones. *'How could a single image stir such raw, unshakable emotion?'* She could not explain it. Every time she closed her eyes; the woman's face was there. The sadness. The terror. The unsettling, fragile beauty of it. It was not just haunting, it was consuming. It felt less like a memory and more like a warning. A whisper from the past, begging to be understood. Chase wrapped her arms around herself, suddenly aware of how cold the room had become. Suddenly, a loud knock shattered

the stillness. Her body jerked upright, heart
pounding against her ribs like a drum. Sweat
beaded on her forehead. Her breath caught
somewhere between a gasp and a scream. The
knock had been so sharp, for a fleeting second,
she wondered if it had come from the walls
themselves, an echo from something buried
deep within them. She shot out of bed, tangled
in her blanket, and fumbled for the light
switch. Her fingers slipping as they found it,
and with a soft click, the pale-yellow glow of
the lamp flickered to life. But the light brought
no comfort. The shadows only seemed to shift
further into the corners, curling along the edges
of the ceiling like smoke. The knock came
again, loud, and insistent. "Who's there?" she
whispered into the dark room, her voice shaky.
She was alone. Of course she was alone. Or was
she? With her pulse racing, she moved toward
the window, careful not to make a sound. The
ancient house groaned under its own weight,
like it had secrets it was eager to share. Chase
reached for the curtain and pulled it back; her
breath held tight in her chest. It was a branch.
A small, thin branch, tapping gently against the
window, swaying in the wind outside. She
exhaled sharply, relief flooding through her,
though the eerie feeling still clung to her like a
fog. Chase let out a soft, nervous laugh. "Stupid

girl." She muttered, shaking her head as she pulled the curtains shut. She turned off the main light and settled back into bed, trying to shake off the persecution that had gripped her. The room was dark now, Chase pulled the cover up, curling into a ball getting herself comfortable. But it would not leave her. The feeling, it clung to her. She grabbed her laptop, desperate for a distraction. Her fingers hovered over the keyboard before she typed in the Blackthorns' name. The flickering screen casting a ghostly glow in the dim room. She scanned through the results: old family portraits, faded newspaper clippings, snippets of gossip from the manor's long history. Each slide she clicked on sent her further away. Then she saw it. A family photo, taken on the grand steps of the manor. The very same manor she now called home. The family was smiling, standing together, too perfectly. But there was something missing. The woman. The woman who had haunted the corners of her mind since that first moment she had seen her in the tower. The woman whose eyes, despite the passage of time, seemed to call out to her. Chase felt a shiver crawl up her spine as she stared at the photo. The family looked warm and normal but there was no sign of the woman. Just a plain portrait of a jovial family. No trace of her beauty, her fright. As if she had never been there at all. The hairs on the back of Chase's neck stood on end. It could not be a coincidence. The woman. The manor. The photograph. It was all connected, somehow, she could feel it deep in her chest, like a thread pulling tighter with every passing hour. And yet, a part of her hesitated. She did not know if she was ready to find out how. Some truths, she sensed, did not stay muted once uncovered. The manor creaked again, as if in response. Chase rolled onto her side, pulling the blanket tighter around her shoulders, trying to shut out the chill in the room. She closed her eyes. The haunting image of the woman's face still lingering behind her eyelids, but she did not push it away. Not this time. "I will find this mysterious woman." She whispered softly to herself, the words barely above a murmur, but each one deep with resolve. The promise premised in the air like a pact; an unspoken vow sealed in the piped down solitude of her room. She could not explain it, why she felt this unshakable pull, why she could not just let it go. But there was something inside her, something deeper than mere curiosity, that tugged her forward. It was not just the woman; it was the truth. The pieces of a puzzle scattered across time and space, waiting to be put together. And somewhere in the silence of this old house, she knew that if she did not uncover it, it would never leave her. She had to know who she was. What she wanted. Why, despite the years between them, the woman's image felt so... familiar. As if they were tied together by some invisible thread. As the dark of the night pressed in, the house settled around her with its usual creaks and groans, as though it were acknowledging her words. The feeling that the manor itself was watching her returned, unsettling and suffocating, but this time, Chase did not flinch. She could not. She was not going to run from whatever haunted this place anymore. No, she was going to confront it.

CHAPTER FIVE
REFLECTIONS OF JEALOUSY

Present day

Henry moved around the kitchen, humming softly as he prepared breakfast. Cooking had always been his domain; Isabelle was far too busy to bother with it. And when she did attempt to make a family meal, it usually ended in frustration, followed by the all-too-familiar call for takeaway. But Henry did not mind; it was simply how things had always been. "Morning love." He said, glancing up from the stove. Isabelle entered the kitchen, looking every bit the professional in her stropped suite. Her heels stood high on the ground, the steam from her coffee flask mingled in the air with the smell of fried bacon and eggs. "You look wonderful. Big meeting today? Excited to start your new job?" Isabelle gave a smile, adjusting the strap of her handbag. "Excited yes. Nervous? Also yes. It has been a while, but I am glad to be going back to work." Henry plated her breakfast and slid it towards her on the counter. "You've earned it." He insinuated warmly. "They're lucky to be having you join the team." Isabelle leaned over to kiss him on the cheek. "Thank Hun. Let us just hope I do not spill coffee or eggs on me before I even make it through the door." Henry went on and on about how beautiful Isabelle looked in her outfit and Isabelle gave him a look half affectionate, half pleading for him to stop. It was the look she wore when nerves began to get the better of her, though she would never admit it. "I've got a meeting with the town council." she replied, her voice lightening as she spoke. "They want me to organise some charity events." Isabelle said, her words slightly muffled as she chewed a piece of crispy bacon. She dabbed at her lips with a napkin, already reaching for her coffee with the practiced efficiency of someone used to multitasking under pressure. "Something about rebranding the organisation, making it feel more 'modern and inclusive. whatever that means." She added, rolling her eyes just enough to betray her irritation, though a hint of curiosity lingered. Her eyes lit up for a moment, her enthusiasm for the work she'd missed palpable in the air. Henry smiled, pleased to see her excited again. He, on the other hand, did not start his new role as head teacher for another three days, so for now, he had the house to himself. Isabelle would be out for most of the day, and with Chase leaving for college this morning, the house would be halcyon than ever. He would have time to get more work done on the place, though whether that meant fixing broken fixtures or repainting peeling walls, he was not quite sure yet. The silence after the morning rush felt almost unnatural. He stood for a moment in the middle of the kitchen, spatula still in hand, listening to the ticking clock and the low hum of the refrigerator. No Chase thundering down the stairs, no Isabelle rifling through her briefcase for forgotten papers. Just stillness. Henry exhaled and scratched the back of his neck. The list of repairs was long, but he figured he would start in one of the rooms upstairs, or maybe downstairs, he could not be sure. The house had needed repairs for years now. Despite this, there was something else about the house, something less tangible that unsettled him. As he had spent more time here, fixing things, he had begun to feel that the house was watching him. He did not believe in ghosts, but the house... it had a presence of its own. The creaks of the old floorboards, once easy to dismiss, now seemed to echo with a strange insistence. At night, when the world outside had gone still and everyone else was fast asleep, faint sounds filtered through the halls. Soft knocks, distant shuffles, the occasional whisper of movement that had no clear source. It was all starting to get under his skin, gnawing at his nerves, and leaving him wide-eyed in the darkness, ears straining for the next unexplained noise. Isabelle hardly noticed the oddities anymore. She had long since grown accustomed to the house's age and quirks, but Henry had always been more attuned to such things. And now, with the house empty for the day, the strange feeling lingered. There was something about this place... something that made him feel as though it was holding its breath, waiting for something to happen. Henry asserted his goodbyes to both Isabelle and Chase, giving Chase a few notes for lunch and pressing a quick kiss to Isabelle's lips. Chase, ever the teenager, scrunched her nose in mock disgust, a mix of embarrassment and amusement crossing her face. Henry and Isabelle both laughed at her reaction before he closed the door behind them, the speechless settling in. Standing in the now-empty manor, Henry looked around at the old, creaking walls, the peace pressing in. For a moment, he just stared, thinking of what to do next. He made his way upstairs to retrieve the toolbox he had left in one of the bedrooms he had not started on yet. Each step up the old staircase groaned beneath his mass. Dust hovered in the air, catching the light from a nearby window, and the wooden banister felt rough beneath his fingers. The bedroom door creaked as he pushed it open, revealing a space untouched for decades, peeling wallpaper, a cracked mirror leaning against the wall, and his toolbox sitting exactly where he had left it. As he passed down the hallway, something caught his eye; a hole in the wood on the wall, cracked out of place. Henry narrowed his eyes. "What do we have here?" he muttered under his breath, bending down to examine it more closely. His fingers brushed against the wood. It had looked as if it had been pried open recently, judging by the faint scrape marks along it. He pressed down on the sides, heart thudding faster. Henry wedged his fingers beneath the edges and slowly lifted the remaining loosened plank to reveal a hidden door. Chilly air seeped from it, carrying the unmistakable smell of dampness. Henry leaned in closer, his breath misting in the frigid air. The smell grew stronger, and the sense of something odd and unsettling washed over him. There before him, was a narrow set of spiral stairs, dark and uninviting, winding up into the unknown. A chill ran through him, knifelike and immediate, as though the very air had

shifted. Still he did not back away. His hand
hesitated for only a moment before continuing,
his fingers brushing against the cold wood. He
told himself it was just an old house, just his
imagination, but deep down, he knew there
was more. Something about this place did not
want to stay hidden. And despite the unease
curling in his stomach, his determination to
uncover the truth, to understand what secrets
the manor held, pushed him forward. He
climbed the stairs, each step colder than the
last, the air growing heavier with each turn.
Finally, he reached the top and stepped into a
small room, bathed in the light of the sun
filtering through a high window. It seemed like
just another room that needed work. But there
was something about it that unsettled him. The
only thing that caught his attention was a black
box, already open on the floor. Neither dusty
nor aged, like everything else around it. Henry
was able to work out some of the objects,
several yellowed photographs. His instincts told
him to leave it, but curiosity won out. He
picked up the box, its surface cold to the touch,
the chill seeping into his skin as though the
wood itself remembered things long buried. A
strange unease settled in his chest, but he shook
it off and turned to descend the stairs. As he
made his way back down, a strange sensation

pricked at the back of his neck, a feeling as though someone or something was watching him. Or following him.

1800

"Miss Fawns, might I ask for your thoughts on Arabella?" Lady Catherine inquired, her voice enweaved with a quiet, controlled curiosity, as Miss Fawns carefully removed her hairpins, preparing for the evening. "Lady, if I may." Miss Fawns began gently, her voice steady yet deferential, "I believe she is a sweet young woman, earnest and kind-hearted." She offered a warm, almost wistful smile as she adjusted the folds of the coverlet, pinpointing a fleeting glance toward Lady Catherine through the reflection in the age-speckled three-way mirror that stood sentinel beside the bed. "There is a sincerity about her… something rare. She brings much happiness to your son, and she is, without doubt, a most beautiful woman." "I see." Lady Catherine replied, each word wrapped in the chill of intentional restraint. She did not look up, her gaze fixed on a small blemish on the lace cuff of her sleeve, as though it required far more of her attention than Miss Fawns's sentiment. Her tone bore no trace of warmth, only the kind of politeness that draws blood without ever raising its voice. "Yes, wholly... though I daresay beauty alone cannot be enough." - "No, beauty is not everything." Miss Fawns said cautiously, but with a new sense of resolve, her eyes briefly meeting Lady Catherine's before lowering. "But, if I may speak freely, my lady." Miss Fawns formulated, her voice gentle but steady, "this manor, and the world beyond its gates are changing. The traditions we once held as sacred no longer carry the same weight, not in the eyes of the young. It is no longer enough to preserve the past; we must learn to live with what the future brings, even if it arrives wearing unfamiliar shoes. I believe a younger couple could benefit Blackthorne in these shifting times." Lady Catherine's eyes narrowed, her expression hardening with icy fury. "Are you suggesting that Howard and I have failed, Miss Fawns?" Her voice was a dangerous, controlled calm. "I shall be very disappointed if that is what you are suggesting." Miss Fawns heart dropped as the heft of her words sank in. She had not meant to cause offense, only to speak her truth, but now she could feel the storm rising in Lady Catherine's gaze. The shift was subtle: a tightening of the jaw, the way her fingers curled slightly around the armrest, the cool glint that replaced the feigned warmth in her eyes. Miss Fawns lowered her gaze instinctively, cursing herself for forgetting that even truth, when spoken gently, could feel like rebellion in a house built on control. "No, no, madam! I— I think you have done an astonishing job. Please, disregard me I am but a maid." Her voice faltered, and her face flushed with embarrassment. As quickly as she could, Miss Fawns fled the room, barely remembering to murmur a hasty, "Goodnight, my lady." She grabbed her lantern, her hands shuddery, and hurried down the corridors, taking the servant's entrance to escape to the safety of her quarters, her heart still pounding in her chest. Lady Catherine stared at her reflection in the mirror, a sneer twisting her lips as she took in the image before her. The candlelight caught on her high cheekbones and the fine silver threads at her temples, but it was not age that soured her expression, it was the jealousy toward Arabella stirring within her, fiery and sharp. *'Was she truly going to be replaced by a younger, more beautiful woman?'* A hussy in her eyes, one who sought vulnerable men with money. Henry, her only son, would be taken from her just like that. The thought coiled around her heart like a serpent, tight and unforgiving. She had spent years grooming him, shaping his future, securing the legacy of the Blackthorne name. And now, a girl with soft eyes and a trembling voice threatened to undo it all. How cruel, how careless the world had become, to let love- childish, fleeting love override duty. She turned away from the mirror, the rustle of her gown sharp in the silence. No. She would not surrender her son, not to sentiment, not to softness. Not without a fight. No. She would not allow it. Before the tears could even threaten to well up in her eyes, she turned her gaze sharply across the dressing table. Her hand swept along the surface, knocking over her perfume bottle. It tumbled to the ground with a soft, muffled thud empty. She picked it up without a second thought, inspecting it coldly, almost as though it were an intruder in her space. She turned her eyes back to the mirror, her face now cold and resolute. The anger that had simmered beneath the surface bubbled to the forefront, and with it, a plan began to form. Quiet, precise, and unstoppable. She would not allow this girl to ruin everything she had carefully built, everything she had controlled. The thought of Henry, so naïve, so caught in the web of his own emotions, made her stomach turn. She would remind him of his place. She would make him see the consequences of his choices.

No one could challenge the Blackthorne legacy
and walk away unscathed. She let out a breath,
one slow and deliberate, and gave a final glance
at her reflection. Her artificial smile flickered
for a moment before she blew out the candles,
the small flames vanishing in the darkness.
With a final, deliberate glance at the reflection
of her own image, she retreated to bed. The
silence in the room burdensome with the
promise of what was to come.

CHAPTER SIX
THE MUSIC BOX

Present day

Henry spent the entire day working on the manor, his focus entirely on the tasks at hand. He did not give much thought to the strange box he had found earlier. It sat on the kitchen counter, forgotten as he worked. By the time he had finished all his chores, most of his equipment had been piled up next to the box, effectively hiding it from his view. It was the kind of thing that a typical bloke like him would easily forget about, something insignificant, easily brushed aside. Out of sight, out of mind, as they say. He had let it slip from his thoughts, distracted by the demands of the day, always too busy to dwell on things that did not directly affect him. The weight of it, if he even noticed it at all, was light enough to ignore. As the hours ticked by, Henry made a few phone calls, reaching out to anyone who might be able to lend a hand with the manor. He was starting to realize that this was becoming a much bigger project than he and

Isabelle could manage on their own. Henry managed to find a company that would help with the decorating, and another that could oversee the plumbing. He chuckled to himself as he thought about it, he was just a teacher after all. He could not even figure out how to use a drill properly, fumbling with the power tool as if it were some kind of foreign object. The simple task eluded him completely, making him feel more than a little ridiculous as he struggled with something most people could do with their eyes closed. Buying a manor ten times bigger than his earlier home without any knowledge of basic skills was starting to feel like an absurd decision. It was getting late and the blackout in the room grew longer, creeping across the floor as the last traces of daylight faded away. Isabelle and Chase would be home soon. Chase had finished college a few hours ago but had decided to stop at a coffee shop with two friends she had met that day. Chase was always making friends, though not in the way most people might expect. She had a knack for picking the odd ones out, the private misfits or the ones who did not fit in with the popular crowd. It was not that she did not want to be part of that world, it was just that she found a certain kind of comfort in the fringes, where everyone else seemed just as lost as she felt

Henry loved that about her. He was proud that she was driven to be successful, rather than to fit in, even though she was an incredibly attractive girl. After a bit of difficulty, Henry finally managed to order Chinese food. The restaurant had no record of the manor's address, and it took a lengthy conversation to work out the details. Eventually, the food arrived, and Henry set the dining table with meticulous care, as if each plate, cutlery, and glass had its own place in the grand scheme of things. He moved with a quiet efficiency, placing each item in perfect alignment on the large surface. The soft clink of porcelain and silver was the only sound as he worked, his focus unvarying, even as the scents of the meal began to fill the air. He even brought out some old candlesticks, giving the table a blend of old-fashioned charm with a modern twist. "DAD! We are home!" Chase shouted through the front door. Isabelle realized that in their old property, shouting was not acceptable, as they had neighbours, and the walls were so thin. But here, the only thing they needed to worry about was disturbing the wildlife. "In the dining room!" Henry shouted back. Both Chase and Isabelle exchanged a look, their eyes meeting with a silent understanding. The raised brow from Isabelle suggested curiosity, while

Chase's expression was a mix of suspicion and intrigue. They had both seen Henry go off on his own little projects before, but there was something different about his behaviour tonight. They wondered what he had planned, and whether it would be another one of his unexpected surprises or something more serious. They opened the door to the dining room and were immediately hit with the warm glow of candlelight, the gleam of silverware, and the mouthwatering smell of Chinese food, neatly plated along the table. "Sorry, I think we've entered the wrong house." Isabelle said, her voice tinged with surprise. She took a hesitant step back, her eyes scanning the unfamiliar surroundings, as if trying to make sense of the situation. Chase piped up, a mischievous smile on her face. "More like we have travelled back in time to dine with Henry the eighth. No pun intended." They both laughed, the concern of the day melting away in the warmth of their shared humour. The family was having such a wonderful time chatting and eating around the table. "I've got a charity event coming up." Isabelle said between bites of spring roll, her voice a little muffled but her enthusiasm unmistakable. She swallowed and glanced up at Henry, her eyes gleaming with excitement. "The council caught wind of me moving to the manor and, well, they think this place would be perfect for it. They have been looking for a venue for this big charity event, something to raise awareness for historical preservation around the village, and since this manor is at the heart of it all, what better place to host it?" She paused, letting her words hang in the air for a moment, before continuing with a spark of pride in her voice. "Can you imagine, Henry? This old house, full of history and character, hosting an event that will bring people together, celebrate the community, and raise funds for the charities that keep our village's legacy alive?" She set down the spring roll, her eyes scanning the room as if she were already imagining the event unfolding in the space. "We have the grand ballroom, the gardens, the drawing rooms... all of it. It will be a perfect showcase of the manor's potential." Her hands moved with excitement, as if she could already see the event in her mind's eye, sparkling with energy and people milling about, the manor's long-forgotten grandeur revived once more. "That is amazing! When is it?" Henry asked, his voice full of interest. "Next weekend." Isabelle replied, her tone firm and matter of fact. She did not pause, as if the matter were already settled in her mind. Her eyes flickered over the room briefly before returning to Henry, a hint of determination behind her words. She was already mentally organizing the details, picturing how the event would unfold, and there was no room for disagreement. Henry almost choked on his drink at this, his mind racing. The house was not even people proof yet. He needed to get things in order quicker than he thought. "Chase darling how was your day?" he asked, trying to divert his thoughts. "It was fine." Chase replied. Her voice soft. "The college is small and basic, but nice. I met two new friends Emily and Hugo." Emily was a grade A student, intelligent and driven, with a passion for technology. She was about 5'9 and very slim, with natural brown hair cut to her neck and a slight wave. Her style was relaxed yet effortlessly chic skinny jeans, a hoodie, and chunky white trainers, as though she had just picked her outfit with eyes closed. Hugo, on the other hand, was originally from France, a country he often spoke of with nostalgia and a silent pride. His accent, although faint, still carried the essence of his homeland, and when he recounted stories of his childhood in the small village where he grew up, his eyes would light up as if he were reliving those moments. He had moved to England in year nine after his father's job transfer. Despite his good command of English, there were still certain words he struggled to understand. Hugo was studying fashion, which made sense considering he was born in the fashion capital. He stood around 5'5, slim, and had a bold style baggy shirt, oversized trousers, black boots with chains hanging from them, and a small chain around his waist. He also wore a cropped leather jacket with rips down the back, the worn edges giving it a rebellious flair, as if it had a story of its own. The jacket fit him snugly, accentuating his lean build, and the faded patches on the sleeves hinted at a time when it had seen far more adventures than he likely cared to admit. His short black hair was styled into a long fringe that swept across his forehead, the blonde streaks running through it like streaks of sunlight cutting through a stormy sky. The mix of dark and light in his appearance seemed to mirror the contrast within him, quiet and thoughtful, yet carrying an edge of unpredictability. "They're really funny and took me under their wings." Chase continued. "We went for coffee in town and just talked about life. They really want to see the manor, so I am planning to invite them over sometime." Isabelle cut her off, her tone shifting from excitement to practicality as she set down her fork with a soft clink. "Perfect.

You can invite them and their families to the charity event next weekend. But until then, we have a manor to decorate." she said, her voice firm but with an underlying hint of determination. She paused, making sure her words settled before continuing. "We cannot have people walking into a home that still feels... unfinished. I want this place to look as grand as it is meant to be, properly presented, every room dressed to impress. A grand event like this deserves a manor that matches its potential, don't you think?" Everyone finished their meals and started clearing the table. Chase and Isabelle were washing the dishes, the rhythmic sound of running water filling the kitchen as they worked comfortably in sync. The soft clink of plates and utensils clacking around in the otherwise subdued kitchen. It was a peaceful moment, a rare break from the usual hustle. But then, without warning, a loud crash shattered the calm. The sound came from upstairs, clawlike and unnerving. It echoed through the old house, mellifluous off the walls like something had been violently thrown to the floor. Both women froze, their hands still hovering over the sink. Chase's eyes widened. "What was that?" Chase whispered, her voice tight with uncertainty. Isabelle stood still for a beat, her mind racing. "I don't know." She prattled, a note of concern creeping into her tone. She wiped her hands on a dish towel and moved toward the stairs. But before she could take a step, Chase was already halfway up the landing, her steps quick. Automatically thinking it was Henry, they both darted upstairs shouting, "Are you okay?" When they reached the top of the landing, Henry appeared at the bottom of the stairs, looking equally confused. "What happened? I heard shouting." Chase looked at her father, then at her mother, her eyes darting between them, uncertain. The still in the room seemed to stretch, intensified with unspoken questions. She hesitated for a moment, the air thick with load. Then, her gaze shifted toward the dark landing at the top of the stairs, where shadows seemed to gather, cloaking the hallway in mystery. "We heard a loud bang upstairs." She alleged, her voice tentative but edged with concern. "We thought it was you." Her words poised in the air, a mixture of confusion and unease, as if she were seeking reassurance that there was a logical explanation to the unsettling noise. Her eyes flicked back to her parents, searching their faces for any sign of what had happened, but both remained conservative, their expressions unreadable. Isabelle's gaze was fixed on her daughter with an unflashy intensity in her eyes, while Henry with his brow furrowed in a mixture of curiosity and caution, glanced toward the staircase as though half expecting something, or someone, to appear. Chase swallowed, feeling the knot of unease grow tighter in her chest. There was something in the atmosphere of the house that did not sit right, a feeling that had only intensified since they moved in. "No, not me love." Henry replied. "Probably just a door shutting. It is a windy night, and we do have a broken window upstairs." With a sigh of relief, Isabelle headed back downstairs to finish the dishes. But Chase stayed at the top of the stairs, still unconvinced that the bang was just the wind. She walked to the end of the landing, her breath catching slightly as she reached for the handle and opened the door to one of the old bedrooms. One that, despite the years, still clearly bore the traces of a nursery. The wallpaper, once bright with playful patterns, had faded to a muted beige, curling at the corners. A small rocking horse sat in the corner, its paint chipped and one eye missing, staring into the room with eerie stillness. The light would not switch on, half the lights in the house did not work. Chase stepped inside and paused; her footfalls muffled by the dust-laden rug beneath her. Instantly, the air shifted, growing unnervingly cold. A faint, musty scent clung to the space, mixed with something sweeter and more unsettling, like old baby powder left open too long. Her heart began to pound in her chest. She could not move, could not speak. Her eyes squinted toward the corner of the room, where a music box with spinning horses sat. But no music was playing. Then, without warning, the spinning grew faster and faster. Chase could not look away, even though every part of her screamed to turn around, to shut the door and pretend she had never stepped inside. But morbid curiosity, dread, or perhaps something deeper, held her there, rooted to the spot. Her eyes fixed on the murkiness gathering in the far corner of the room. The room felt suffocating as the pounding in her chest grew louder. Then, with a jarring bang, the door slammed shut violently. Chase snapped out of her paralysis, scrambling to find the door in the pitch-black room. She screamed for help, but suddenly, music started to play behind her. She closed her eyes, not knowing why, but feeling a strange sense of safety in the darkness. The music grew closer and closer, until it sounded as if it were right in front of her. Delicate notes drifting through the air, far too clear to be a trick of the mind. It was not coming from a speaker or a phone; it was too old, too haunting. Each note

seemed chopped with sorrow, like it had
travelled through time just to reach her ears.
And then, everything went still. Chase opened
her eyes. Her heart thudding so hard she could
feel it in her ears. A white figure was emerging
from the wall. She could just make out what
she assumed was a woman, dressed in old-
fashioned clothing. The figure stopped for a
moment, staring at her, motionless, silent, as
though measuring her from across the room.
Then, with a chilling scream, it lunged at her.
Chase shot up in bed, gasping for breath. She
blinked, disoriented, and realized it was
daylight outside. Confused, she looked around.
'Was it all just a dream?' But it had felt so real.
She quickly got ready and headed downstairs to
the kitchen, where her parents were having
coffee. "What happened last night?" she asked,
her voice shaky. Isabelle laughed. "Okay Hun,
do not rub it in. I am late for work. See you
tonight." She kissed Chase on the forehead and
headed out the door. Chase turned to Henry.
"What was that all about?" she asked, her voice
interlaced with mix of frustration and
confusion. Henry looked at her, puzzled.
"Chase, have you banged your head? We played
some card games after we cleaned up the food,
and you demolished us. I did not know you
were so good at card games." Henry sheard,

"you've been holding out on us I see, well you definitely proved us wrong last night." Chase's mind raced. *'How was that possible?'* She could not remember any card game, let alone a whole night. The last thing she remembered was the bang, then darkness, then the woman... Yes, the woman. *'Was it a ghost?'* She swallowed hard, her mind spinning. Without another word, she slammed the door shut behind her and jumped into bed, grabbing her laptop along the way. It had not been a dream, she was certain of that, but she could not to the max understand why her memory dissolved into fog after that terrifying moment. The freezing air, the music, the figure in the doorway, it had all been so vivid, so real. And then… nothing. Just a hollow stretch of blankness, as if her mind had slammed a door shut to protect her from whatever came next. Her heart still raced when she thought about it, the details just out of reach, teasing her like hounds in the corner of her vision. Chase opened her laptop and began researching ghost sightings and their effects on people. She found nothing that seemed to fit, until she stumbled across a website titled *How Do You Know If You've Been Possessed? * Without hesitation, she clicked the link. She skimmed through the content, but one post caught her eye. She began to read:

*"When I was a young lass, I became obsessed
with this old tree house. My imagination was
vivid, wild even, and one day in the moderate
of my childhood, I made a friend who no one
else could see. To me, he was as real as the wind
in the trees. He had a name, a voice, and a
sorrowful smile that stayed with me long after
he vanished. I would speak to him for hours,
whispering secrets and stories, never
questioning His presence. The adults chalked it
up to loneliness, or creativity, but deep down, I
always knew there was something more.
Something... not utterly imagined. I called him
Pip. Every day I played in the tree house, and
every day I saw Pip. We were best friends.
When I went back to school, I made new
friends and one day invited them over for a
sleepover in the tree house. That night, when
everyone was asleep, Pip came to me, waking
me up with a soft whisper that felt like a breath
against my ear. At first, I thought I had dreamt
it. But the moment I opened my eyes, there he
was, standing at the foot of my sleeping bag, his
figure barely visible in the dim light from the
moon through the window. His eyes were
wide, glowing, full of a desperation I had not
seen before. He did not speak at first, just stood*

there, his expression haunted. I sat up, a chill running through me as I took in his unearthly appearance. It was as if he had changed somehow, his once gentle, friendly demeanour replaced by something darker, more intent. "What is it?" I asked, my voice barely above a whisper, trembling with fear. His answer came not in words, but in a single, bitter motion. he reached out, his hand cold against my skin, and in that moment, I knew something was terribly wrong. He was not happy with the two friends I had invited. I told him to go away. The next morning, I woke up to my mother's scream, a sound so stabbing and full of terror that it sliced all the way through the tree house. I jolted out of my sleeping bag, my heart thudding in my chest as I rushed to the ladders on the tree house and made my way down to the ground. Fear flooded my veins. I froze, my breath catching. There, hanging from one of the branches of the tree, was one of the children I had invited. She sagged limply, her body swaying in the wind as if she were the lighter than a feather. Shoelaces were tightly bound around her neck, knot so neat and secure that it could only have been done intentionally. Her small body dangled in the morning light, the scene so wrong, so utterly disturbing, that I could not look away. Her face was pale, eyes

wide open, staring into nothingness, as if frozen
in a moment of horror. I felt a wave of nausea
rise within me. How could this of happened?
After the police and the other child's family
had left, I overheard them speaking to my
mother: 'Your daughter's shoelaces are the ones
we found around her neck. There are signs of
struggle.' I could not believe it. They thought I
had done it. I tried to explain that maybe it was
Pip, but they thought I was crazy. I had so
much counselling after that day. When I turned
fifteen, I saw Pip again. It had been years since
I last laid eyes on him, years since the strange
occurrences that had plagued my childhood
stopped as mysteriously as they had started. But
there he was, standing at the edge of the old
oak tree in our backyard, just as I remembered,
his dark hair falling in messy waves around his
face, his eyes wide and unblinking, fixed on me.
I froze, my heart hammering in my chest. He
had not aged a day, not a single change in the
time we had been apart. The world around me
seemed to go still. "Pip?" My voice was hoarse,
disbelieving. He did not respond, but I could
see his lips move silently, as though he was
trying to say something. His hands twitched by
his sides, and I could feel the coldness of the air
around me shift, just enough to make me
shiver. I had tried so hard to forget him, tried to

*convince myself that he had been nothing more than a figment of my imagination, a dream I had outgrown. But here he was, as real and present as the tree he stood under. "You're real." I whispered, half to myself, half to him. He nodded slowly, and despite the emptiness in his eyes, there was something there now, something darker, like he had been waiting for this moment, waiting for me to understand whatever it was he needed to tell me. The silence stretched between us, thick and uncomfortable, until I could not stand it any longer. "What do you want from me?" But as I said that he vanished right in front of me. "I believe that on that dreadful night, I was possessed by something dark, something beyond my control, a force that made me kill my school friend. Pip was no longer the person I knew; he had become an evil spirit, consumed by jealousy and hatred. It twisted him, clouding his mind and turning him into something unrecognizable. I felt the malevolent energy creeping into me, urging me to do the unthinkable. I could not fight it, and I could not escape the horrifying truth that it was not truly me in control anymore. "**

Chase's breath caught in her throat as she read the chilling account. The fear she had been feeling only grew, intensifying with each word. Was something like that happening to her? Was she being influenced by some malevolent force, just like Pearl McDonald? The thought made her stomach twist with dread. Chase hurriedly got herself ready for college, feeling a pressing need for support. The morning seemed to move in fast forward, her hands fumbling as she grabbed clothes from her wardrobe and threw them on with little care for matching or neatness. She thought about the two people she had met just yesterday Emily and Hugo. It was strange, but it felt as if they had known each other for years, like an unspoken bond had already formed. She needed them now more than ever. They were the only ones who would not judge her, the only ones who might understand the strange things that were happening to her. As she made her way through the manor, her anxiety intensified. The vast hallways and towering ceilings felt suffocating, like the walls were slowly closing in on her. Chase continued down the hall, her footsteps quickening. The eyes on the old paintings on the walls were following her. It was absurd this was one of the largest houses she had ever been in, and yet, she had never felt more claustrophobic in her life. The manor had a presence of its own, pressing against her with each step. She needed to get out. Fast. She reached the front doors and pushed them open, the cool morning air greeting her like a long-lost friend. The relief was instant. Chase took a deep breath, inhaling the fresh air, trying to steady the racing beat of her heart. She turned back to look at the manor, its imposing silhouette looming behind her. The dark, weathered stone of the building seemed to stretch endlessly into the sky, as though it was reaching toward her. For a moment, she just stared at it, the dark windows like watchful eyes. She shuddered, but then with a renewed sense of determination, she whispered to herself, "This manor will not win." It was a quiet vow, but one that she hoped would help her face whatever it was that had begun to haunt her.

CHAPTER SEVEN
A BRIDE'S REFLECTION

1800

"Today is the day"

Arabella thought to herself as she lay in her bed, awaiting Miss Fawns gentle assistance to awaken her. She could not help but feel a surge of delight, a flicker of satisfaction blooming behind her composed expression. In just a few short hours, she would be wed and become the new Lady of the manor. Arabella Blackthorn. She mused inwardly, a soft smile touching her lips. Yes, the name suited her perfectly.

"Today is the day"

Lady Catherine thought, her mind swirling with schemes to halt the union. She paced slowly, her steps premeditated and deliberate, each one echoing softly across he polished floor. Her hands remained tightly folded in front of her, the knuckles paling from the pressure, betraying the tension simmering beneath her composed exterior. The silence of the room wrapped around her like a shroud, broken only by the rhythmic whisper of her footsteps.

Nothing, absolutely nothing would stand in her way when it came to her son's future, the manor's legacy, and her own position within the house. The thought of losing it all to this marriage filled her with quiet fury.

"Today's the day"

Edward thought to himself, his eyes scanning the morning paper, though his mind was preoccupied with the events ahead. By the end of the day, he would be a married man, and with that, the quiet assurance of having his wife by his side each morning, free from scandal, free from the whispers that had shadowed his every step. He smiled to himself, a rare moment of peace settling over him as he imagined what the future might hold. The uncertainty of the past seemed distant now, as if a fog were lifting and in its place, a new chapter was beginning, one that was his to shape. No more rumours. No more secrets. Just a life with Arabella. A life of quiet contentment and the security of a bond that would be public and permanent. He leaned back, folding the paper with a soft rustle, already feeling the weightiness of the day ahead.

"Today's the day"

Miss Fawns thought as she made her way to Lady Arabella's bedchamber. Yet despite the air of inevitability, something gnawed at her. She could not shake the feeling that today would not be a fairy tale, not in the way little girls dreamed of. There was a heaviness in her chest, a quiet unease threading through every breath she took. The gowns, the flowers, the lavish preparations all seemed like a veil, delicate and lovely, but too thin to hide the strange sense that something was just... off. She could not put her finger on it but the foreboding sense that things would not go as planned lingered in her mind. The Blackthorn wedding was the talk of the village and the manor, an event so important it had the entire household bustling with activity from dawn until dusk.

The servants rose before dawn, preparing for the grandest occasion the estate had seen in many years. Each member of the staff had their role, and every task was performed with the utmost care and attention to detail. The air was thick with contemplation, and there was a sense of urgency among them as they set to work. The kitchen staff had been hard at work since the first light of day, preparing an exquisite banquet fit for nobility. The scent of fresh herbs, roasted meats, and sweet pastries filled the air, drifting through the lower halls and into the courtyard beyond. Copper pots clanged, knives chopped with rhythmic precision, and the head cook barked orders with practiced authority. Every dish was crafted with care and purpose, stuffed game birds, warm bread rolls brushed with butter, and intricate desserts layered with cream and fruit, all destined to impress the finest of guests. There would be no room for error; not on a day like this. The smell made the servants' stomachs rumble in envy. In the corridors, the footmen polished the silverware, carefully cleaning each piece to a mirror shine. They inspected the fine crystal glasses, ensuring not a smudge marred their surface, holding each one up to the light until it gleamed. The slightest imperfection would not be tolerated. Footmen laid out the suits and uniforms in the grandest fashion, pressing every crease, straightening every button, and polishing shoes until they reflected the chandeliers above. Every garment was arranged with care on mannequin stands or draped neatly across canopied beds, awaiting the moment they would be worn. The whole manor was in a state of meticulous preparation; there was no time for slow working. The guests would be arriving soon, and nothing could be left to chance. The head butler, an impeccable figure in his dark tailcoat and pristine white gloves, was overseeing the final additions in the grand hall with an expression of composed authority. He moved with grace, eyes sweeping

over the polished mahogany tables, the fresh
floral arrangements, and the towering
candelabras that flanked the room. He paused
only to adjust a misaligned centrepiece or
instruct a footman to straighten a chair. Every
detail had to be flawless, this was no ordinary
day, and the honour of the Blackthorn
household depended on his precision. Even the
way the drapes fell or how the chandeliers
caught the light was under his scrutiny. He
directed the florists as they arranged baskets of
roses, ivy, and lilies in each corner, their
delicate fragrance filling the air. A long white
aisle runner was spread out, leading to the altar,
and arrangements of flowers cascaded down the
bannisters. Everything had to be in perfect
order. This was not just a wedding; it was a
statement of status, a public declaration of the
Blackthorn family's power. As the sun rose
higher in the sky, the manor seemed to shine
brighter, bathed in golden light, every corner
gleaming with the effort of those who had
worked so diligently. The servants moved
through the halls with responsibility, their
faces serious and composed under the
significance of the day's importance. Each step
was deliberate, as though the air itself was thick
with the expectations of the manor. Their crisp
uniforms shimmered in the flickering

candlelight, a stark contrast to the dark, polished wood of the floors beneath them. It was as if the entire household had fallen into an unspoken rhythm, one that reflected the gravity of the occasion. The clink of silver against fine China resonated through the air as trays were carried from one room to the next, and the faint rustle of linen as it was arranged on tables seemed to reverberate with alarum. They were all aware that today, nothing could go wrong. Every glance, every gesture, was a part of the grand design that would culminate in the most anticipated event of the year for them. This was not just a wedding; it reflected their loyalty to the Blackthorn family and the centuries-old legacy that this event represented. There was two faint knocks at the door "Arabella?" Miss Fawns called softly from the other side of the door. "Come in." Arabella replied, her voice a mix of excitement and nervous alarm. She smoothed the front of her night dress instinctively, her heart fluttering in her chest as footsteps approached the door. Every second felt stretched, charged with the strain of what the day would bring. Miss Fawns entered with a smile, carefully holding Arabella's wedding dress in her hands. The gown was a masterpiece, though its full grandeur was still hidden beneath the fabric's folds. "Shall we proceed lady Nightshade?" Miss Fawns suggested, her tone soft but pummelled with the energy of the moment. Arabella nodded eagerly, a flutter in her chest. "Yes, let us begin." Miss Fawns carefully helped Arabella slip into the gown, the fabric wrapped itself against her skin as it settled into place. Arabella straightened, feeling the weight of the dress settle around her like a second skin. She turned slightly, inspecting the way the gown fit, the soft sheen of the material reflecting in the light. The corset tightened around her waist, shaping her posture into the perfect, graceful silhouette. Miss Fawns worked quickly, adjusting the dress with an experienced hand, each movement done with precision. Arabella stood unpretentiously in the middle of the room, her heart pounding as the expectation of the day took hold. She did not yet dare glance at herself in the mirror. The emphasis of the moment gliding in the air, a tranquil tension that made her hesitate. Arabella could feel the fabric of the gown against her skin, cool and unfamiliar, the intricate design making her acutely aware of every detail. Her hands remained by her sides, trembling slightly, as if she could delay this moment just a little longer. It was not just the gown that felt foreign, it was everything that came with it. She was not sure if she was ready to fully embrace the change, the new identity that awaited her. *'What would it feel like to be Lady Blackthorn?' Could she live up to the legacy, the expectations?* Still, she wanted to wait to experience the final reveal when everything was set in place. "How do I look?" Arabella asked softly, the words escaping her lips almost without thought. Miss Fawns paused for a moment, her eyes scanning Arabella from head to toe, the faintest hint of admiration in her gaze. "You look… transcendent Lady Nightshade." she said, her voice filled with an unadorned reverence. Arabella felt a warm rush of pride at the words, though a knot of uncertainty still lingered in her stomach. The gown was breathtaking, and the transformation felt complete. Arabella smiled faintly, she looked at Miss Fawns, this?" she asked, her voice barely a whisper. Her fingers lingered on the delicate lace at the neckline, the fine artisanry too delicate to touch. Miss Fawns smile softened, and she stepped closer, her tone reassuring. "My lady, you have always had the strength within you. Today, you step into your new life, and there is no turning back. You are ready, more than you know." Arabella took in a breath, allowing Miss Fawns words to settle in her heart. But in that fit moment, as she stood still, half-dressed and surrounded by the scent of lavender and old wood, she felt transformed. Not just by the silk and lace, or by the delicate pins that held her curls in place, but by the gravity of what lay ahead. All she could think of was the life that awaited her. Soon, she would no longer be Arabella Nightshade, but Arabella Blackthorn, the new lady of the manor, with all its grandeur, expectations, and ghosts. "Are we ready for the results, Lady?" Miss Fawns asked, her voice soft but threaded with dread. She stood by the tall, floor-length mirror, an ornate antique from the late 1500s with clawed feet and intricate carvings curling along its gilded frame. Its reflective surface was still concealed beneath the ivory bedsheet Arabella had used the night before. Miss Fawns had insisted it remain covered, wanting to preserve the magic, the thrill, of seeing the final transformation all at once. Arabella took a deep breath, her heart fluttering. "Yes, I think I am ready." she replied, her voice steady but boxed with nervous excitement. In a swift motion, Miss Fawns pulled the sheet away, revealing Arabella's reflection. Arabella stood still for a moment, simply taking in the sight before her. She stared at herself, captivated, feeling both astonished and somehow overwhelmed by the image that looked back at her. The updo was perfection

Her long, dark black hair had been twisted into an intricate, elegant style, each coil placed with meticulous care. A few delicate lilies, their white petals gleaming against her dark locks, were tucked into the twists, adding a softness to the sharp elegance of the hairstyle. The flowers seemed almost otherworldly, their subtle fragrance filling the room with a sensible serenity, their simplicity enhancing the natural beauty of the hairstyle. Arabella reached up, touching the hairpins with her fingertips, feeling the prestige of the style settle on her head. The dress itself was exquisite. A stunning shade of duck egg blue, with soft white trimming along the edges, it seemed to capture the very essence of elegance and grace. The fabric flowed from her body like a gentle wave, moving with a practical fluidity that echoed the softness of a morning breeze. The long lace sleeves, which extended gracefully over her hands, were delicate and ethereal, the lace so fine that it almost seemed to shimmer, like spun silk. The pointed ends of the sleeves added a vintage air to the gown, as if it had been crafted centuries ago, yet somehow perfectly timeless. But it was the shape of the dress that truly took her breath away. The way it clung to her waist, accentuating her hourglass figure, and then flared out slightly to add just a hint of puff made her look like she had stepped out of a painting. Every movement she made seemed to bring the dress to life, the layers of fabric catching the light in subtle ways that made the gown glow softly around her. It was not just a dress, it was an experience, a vision of beauty and poise that transformed her, just as the life awaiting her was about to transform everything. Arabella could barely recognize the woman in the reflection, though it was her. The gown fit her like a dream, shaping her in a way that felt too perfect, too surreal. It was as though she were being prepared for something more than just a wedding, but for an entire new identity, one that would be defined by grace, by strength, and by the title she was about to claim. A diamond necklace rested delicately against her collarbone, the stones glistening subtly in the light. The diamonds, though not overly large, were impeccably cut, their facets sparkling like tiny stars against her skin. The necklace added a perfect touch of refinement, its understated beauty enhancing the overall grace of her look without overwhelming it. Arabella had always preferred simplicity, nothing too flashy, but the necklace was just enough to catch the eye without overwhelming her natural beauty. The heels were modest but elegant, offering just the right amount of height to make her feel taller and poised. They were a soft ivory, with delicate straps that wrapped around her ankles, holding her firmly yet comfortably. The heels themselves were thin, just high enough to elongate her legs without being overly dramatic, adding a graceful lift to her every step. As she stood, Arabella could feel the subtle shift in her posture, her shoulders pulled back slightly, her chin lifted just a fraction more. They were not shoes she would ever have chosen for comfort, but today, they made her feel like she could walk with the utmost grace, each step bringing her closer to the life she was about to claim. She stood there, mesmerized by the woman before her. Arabella knew in that moment, as she gazed at her reflection, that she was ready. She was ready to walk down that aisle, to take her place by Henry's side, to become Lady Blackthorn. She smiled at her reflection, a soft, satisfied smile that deepened the longer she looked. "I'm ready." She whispered to herself, the words carrying the heftiness of fitting determination. Today was the beginning of something new, an uncertain, glittering future that waited just beyond the horizon, and she was prepared to meet it with grace, poise, and unflinching resolve. Miss Fawns gave Arabella a graceful bow, the fabric of her skirt rustling softly as she dipped. The gesture carried more than duty; it held reverence, a silent acknowledgment of the transformation that had taken place. In that moment, it was as though Arabella were royalty. "I shall fix you stiff drink" Miss Fawns clad gently, her tone threaded with respect, as if even her words dared not disturb the fragile beauty of the morning. Arabella smiled warmly, offering her a grateful thank you. The words felt like a balm, soothing the nerves that had begun to stir within her as she looked at the woman who had helped her transform into this version of herself, someone new, someone poised to step into a new chapter of her life. The sincerity in her gaze matched the softness in her voice, the warmth of her appreciation filling the room. Arabella knew that it was not just the gown or the accessories that had made her feel different; it was the unnoticeable confidence that had grown in her heart, nurtured by the care and attention from those around her. Miss Fawns had seen her through this moment, and for that, Arabella was truly thankful. As Miss Fawns exited the room, Arabella turned her attention back to the mirror, her eyes taking in every inch of her reflection. She admired herself, savouring the beauty of the moment. This was her day, and she felt like the embodiment of everything she had ever dreamed.

Meanwhile, in the library, Lady Catherine sat with her cup of tea, her thoughts swirling with the growing urgency of the day. The walls, lined with towering bookshelves, felt like silent witnesses to her mounting anxiety. She flicked through a book absentmindedly, her eyes darting over the words but not truly reading them. When the butler, Mr. Brown, entered the room, she did not look up immediately. Instead, she set her teacup down with intended precision. "Ah, Mr. Brown." She said, her voice smooth but carrying a hint of frustration. "Thank you for coming so promptly. I have a dilemma." She paused dramatically before continuing. "My best ring has lost its glow. Do you have anything that could restore it?" Butler Brown, always composed, bowed respectfully. "Certainly, madam. I will arrange for it to be polished immediately." Lady Catherine's eyes narrowed slightly, a plan forming in her mind. "No need for that." She replied, her voice sharp with authority. "If you will simply fetch me the necessary polish, I am no stranger to a bit of arduous work. After all, you have a wedding to organize." She was adamant that she would manage it herself. There was a steely determination in her eyes, this ring was important to her, and she would not trust anyone else to fix it. Butler Brown hesitated for only a moment, his eyes briefly meeting hers as if weighing her resolve. Then, with a respectful nod, he straightened his posture. "Very well, my lady." He said evenly. "I shall retrieve the supplies at once." With that, he left the room, his footsteps echoing as he made his way down the hallway. Lady Catherine's eyes lingered on the ring, her thoughts darkening as she considered the upcoming wedding. It was a union she could not allow to happen under any circumstances. She would do whatever it took to see it stopped. Her son's future and the manor's legacy would be hers to control, no matter the cost.

CHAPTER EIGHT
THE SIT AND SIP

Present day

At college, Chase wasted no time trying to find her friends before class. The problem was she had only met them once, and now she had no clue where their usual hiding spots were around the place. She could barely remember the layout of the building, let alone anticipate where they might be lurking. It was a frustrating, yet strangely thrilling, kind of challenge. Maybe Emily's in the computer room, she thought, doing whatever she does on that squared machine. Or Hugo was somewhere outside, taking in people's outfits and sketching latest ideas for his latest fashion project. That seemed more his scene, comfortable, familiar, and effortlessly confident. For a moment, she almost envied the ease with which he navigated it all. Chase had not even thought to get either of their numbers. She had been too busy laughing and chatting to remember she had a mobile at all. Before she could start heading to any of the places she had imagined, she heard someone calling her name from behind.

"Chase… Chase… hold up!" She turned to see both Emily and Hugo making their way towards her. *'Thank God it felt like hours.'* "Hey girl." Hugo purred in his distinctly feminine tone. "You look like you've seen a ghost." "Funny you should say that" Chase started, a knowing smile tugging at her lips, but Emily cut in before she could say more. "I'm going to be late." She said quickly, already backing away. "Meet me at the library after college, yeah?" Both Hugo and Chase nodded, muttering their goodbyes before heading off in separate directions to their classes. During her history lesson, which focused on the events that had shaped the world they lived in now, Chase could not help the feeling that she was being watched. It was subtle at first, a creeping sensation at the back of her neck, like invisible eyes on her. But as the minutes ticked by, the feeling grew, gnawing at her, making it nearly impossible to concentrate on the lesson. She tried to brush it off, but the authority of it lingered, growing heavier with each passing second. The more the day went on, the more paranoid she became. Her mind raced, but before she could calm herself, someone in the class asked if she had a spare pen to borrow. The question made her jump out of her skin. Her heart raced. *'How embarrassing,'* she thought. She quickly stood up, eager to escape the prying eyes. "Just nipping to the toilet." She muttered as she passed the teacher. As she made her way down the empty corridor, she tried to convince herself it was nothing. Of course, it is empty, everyone is in class, she thought. But still, the sensation of being watched did not ease. When she reached the toilet, she stood in front of the mirror. Her reflection startled her. She did look tired, tired, and somehow… different. The girl in the mirror did not just look worn out, she looked like someone who had seen something. Something terrible. Chase turned the tap on, cupping icy water in her hands. She bent over the sink and splashed her face, the cold porcelain biting at her hands. Hoping to wake herself up but it did not do much to wake her up only leaving her feeling more unsettled. When she straightened up and looked into the mirror again, the lights flickered. And then, they went out completely. A small scream escaped her lips as she froze in the dark. The silence was deafening. "Not again." She whispered to herself, trying to calm her racing heart. Then she heard it. A soft creak, the sound of a toilet door easing open somewhere behind her. Silence followed, but only for a second. Then came the heavy footed, click of high heels striking the bathroom tiles. Sharp. Steady. Unmistakable. Someone was walking toward her, each step designed, as if they had all the time in the world. She turned around, facing the mirror as though it might shield her, though she knew it would not. And there, standing behind her in the reflection, was a woman. A white figure. The same one she had seen back at the manor in the nursery room. For a moment, the woman's image seemed … beautiful. Innocent, even. Her features softened, and the harshness of the previous encounter faded, leaving only an eerie calmness behind. But that fleeting sense of peace was short-lived. The longer Chase stared, the more she felt something was wrong. But then her face twisted, contorting into something monstrous. The pale figure screamed a shrill, deafening sound and lunged at Chase. Chase fell to the ground, her body reacting before her mind could catch up, an instinctive hope that the woman might vanish, even pass straight through the mirror. Her breath caught in her throat. But when she finally dared to look up, the figure was gone. No trace. Just the harsh, electric buzz of the overhead lights flickering back to life. They bathed the bathroom in a cold, eerie glow, illuminating nothing but empty stalls and reticence. Chase scrambled to her feet, feeling nauseous and unsteady. Her legs trembled beneath her, as if they might give out at any moment. This is not a dream, she thought, her heart pounding so hard. I am being haunted. But by what? Whatever it was it was not just a figment of her imagination, it felt real, too real. And worse, it felt personal, as if the ghostly woman or whatever it was, had chosen her for a reason she did not understand yet. Without a second thought, she rushed out of the bathroom, running back to the classroom. As she approached the door, she saw the last of her classmates spilling out into the corridor. How has the lesson finished already. The spirit… it had made her lose track of time again. She had to get to the library fast, with her legs have already started moving before the thought had fully formed, the need to be with her friends pushing her forward. The hallways blurred around her, whatever was happening she needed answers, her friends might be the only ones that could possibly help.

Chase finally reached the library, where she found Emily and Hugo nestled in the corner on brightly coloured beanbags, laughing at a joke that Chase had clearly missed. "Chase, come sit." Emily called out, patting the spot beside her on one of the free beanbags. Her face lit up with excitement. "How was today? Mine was formidable, I finally figured out how to separate text in Word! Total game-changer." Emily was cut off by Hugo, who dramatically waved a hand in the air. "Girl, no one cares about I.T." He said, rolling his eyes dramatically, his voice full of sass and mockery. He leaned back in his chair like he had just delivered some universal truth, a smug grin tugging at the corner of his mouth. Chase giggled, grateful to be back with these two crazy ones. They always managed to make her feel at ease, no matter how strange her day had been. "To be honest guys, I'm not having the best of days." She admitted, sinking into one of the beanbags. "Why not?" Emily asked, her eyes wide with concern. "What has happened? Tell us!" Chase hesitated for a moment, then took a deep breath. "Well… it's going to sound stupid and silly." She began, her voice barely above a whisper, "but I'm a thousand percent sure I'm being taunted by a dark entity." She paused, waiting for the laughter or eyerolls, but her face stayed serious. "I know how it sounds, but it is real. I can feel it." Emily and Hugo exchanged a long look, their expressions unreadable for a moment. Chase continued, her voice low and serious, the usual lightness in her tone completely gone. "Last night and today, I was greeted by a ghostly woman. At first, she seems... okay. Just standing there, watching. But then she screams at you. This awful, bone-chilling scream that rattles you to the core. And the weirdest part is I keep losing track of time. I swear I was only in the bathroom for ten minutes, but when I got back to class, two whole hours had passed." Hugo's eyes widened. "How is that even possible?" he asked, his French accent thickening with disbelief. "I do not know. That is why I need both of your help." Chase's eyes searched Emily's face, then darted toward the other. "Please, say you'll help me, even if you don't believe me." Her voice cracked on the last word, a tremble slipping through that betrayed the fear she had been trying so hard to keep buried. Emily gave her a reassuring smile. "Of course, we will help you! A ghost hunt sounds like an adventure, don't you think, Hugo?" "Dieu nous aide." Hugo muttered under his breath, his eyes wide with mock horror as he clutched at his chest dramatically. "God help us." He translated with a sigh, glancing around as if expecting the walls to start bleeding. "We're officially in a horror film now, aren't we?" The group made their way to the village's coffee shop; a cute little place tucked between a bakery and a florist. It was called the 'Sit & Sip;' a name Chase thought was cool, she was not sure about the place itself yet, but the smell of fresh coffee wafting through the door was definitely a good sign. They each ordered their drinks and snacks. Chase went for a double black coffee with one sweetener and a chocolate brownie. Emily, ever the sweet tooth, did not even glance at the menu before placing her order, a caramel iced coffee with extra cream and a generous drizzle of caramel sauce on top. She paired it with a chunky rocky road bar, loaded with marshmallows, nuts, and chocolate chips. "Breakfast of champions." she brought out cheerfully, unwrapping the bar like it was a prize. Hugo, always the health-conscious one, opted for a green tea with a slice of lemon and a ginger sponge cake. As they settled into their seats, sipping their drinks and indulging in their snacks, Emily leaned forward, eyes twinkling with excitement. "So, Chase…" her voice softer now, curiosity and concern mingling in her eyes. "When did this all start?" She wrapped her hands around her coffee cup, the caramel-sweet scent drifting between them as she waited for the answer. Chase could tell Emily was loving every second of this mystery. She set her cup down and began, "Well… It all started with this hidden tower room in the manor." She paused, glancing between Emily and Hugo before continuing. "I found a box there, with this creepy photo inside." Hugo, who had just taken a small bite of his sponge cake, froze mid-chew. His jaw dropped lightly open, the piece of cake forgotten as his face drained of colour. "Wait… what?" he said, voice muffled but rising with disbelief. "And you are just going to… what, piss the ghost woman off even more? That is your plan?" Chase let out a small sigh. "I do not think I have a choice. I need to see this through." She paused, gathering her thoughts. "I need to know why it's happening to me." Hugo sighed dramatically, looking like he might faint. "Okay, okay. Stop looking at me like that!" He threw his hands up in mock surrender. "I will help you, just stop with the eyes! But you owe me, big time." Chase beamed. "Thank you. You are the best. And you, Emily?" She turned to her other friend. Emily grinned, her eyes wide with prospect. "I am in. When do we start?" "Well." Chase said, "my mum is having a charity event next Saturday, so the house will be packed. How about you both come over tomorrow night and stay? We can plan." "Sounds good to me!" Hugo chimed in. "I'm in." Emily added enthusiastically, flashing Chase a reassuring smile. There was not a hint of hesitation in her voice, just the kind of certainty that made

Chase feel a little less alone. "If we're dealing with ghosts or demons or whatever this is, you're not doing it without me." The group settled on a time, agreeing to meet at The Sit & Sip for a "booster drink" before their ghost hunt. "Alright, great. I will see you tomorrow." Chase expressed, waving goodbye. Just then as she turned to leave the cafe, her dad, honked the car horn, drawing the attention of everyone in the coffee shop. Chase's face turned bright red, her cheeks flaming with embarrassment. Both Emily and Hugo burst into laughter, their shared amusement only making it worse. She slumped in the passenger seat, wishing for the ground to swallow her up. "Thanks, Dad." She muttered under her breath, rolling her eyes as she tried to shake off the awkwardness. As her friends waved goodbye, she could not help but feel the sting of their teasing, but at least it was a distraction from everything else.

1800

"Pardon my lady." The butler spoke, his voice breaking the wretched peacefulness as he entered the room. Lady Catherine had been waiting patiently, her posture regal and composed, but the foreboding hanging in the

air thick and palpable was incomputable for
Lady Catherine. Not in a bad way, in a frighting
psychopathic way, she had been expecting this,
and now that it had arrived the stillness felt
almost bliss. He stepped forward and with a
bow, passed the bottle of polish into her hands.
"Here you are, ma'am." "Thank you, Mr.
Brown." Lady Catherine replied, her tone light
but edged with retired authority. "And please,
keep this between us. I would rather not have
my husband think I am neglecting my duties to
do yours." "Very well, ma'am." he worded,
bowing again before turning to leave. Lady
Catherine's fingers curled around the bottle,
her grip tightening as she eyed it with growing
malice. The gleam of the glass reflected a dark
intent in her gaze, and a thin smile curled at the
corner of her lips. With a soft sigh, she rose and
made her way toward her bedchamber. As she
passed through the hall, her foot caught on the
hem of her gown, and she stumbled slightly,
only to find herself face-to-face with Miss
Fawns. Miss Fawn's eyes immediately flicked to
the bottle in Lady Catherine's hands. The
glance was subtle, but Lady Catherine noticed it
instantly. "Lady Catherine." Miss Fawns
greeted, her voice steady but with a hint of
respect as she stepped aside to let her pass. She
lowered her gaze slightly, a gesture of both

deference and habit, as Lady Catherine glided past, the rustle of her elegant gown almost drowning out the sound of her footsteps. Without breaking her stride, Lady Catherine tilted her head slightly. "Is the bride ready, Miss Fawns?" "Yes, my lady." Miss Fawns replied, her voice soft but filled with a drab admiration. "And what a bride she is." Lady Catherine's back remained turned, but the contempt in her voice was unmistakable as she muttered, "Yes, of course…" Her words trailed off, the air growing thick with the unspoken animosity between them as she persisted on her way. Lady Catherine finally arrived at her room, as she reached the door glanced cautiously around the corridor to ensure no one was watching. Once she was satisfied and sure that the coast was clear and she was alone, she rushed inside, closing the door behind her softly, and locked it with a swift turn of the key. In the solitude of the room she exhaled, her composure returning, at least for the moment. She took a deep breath, feeling the rush of secrecy and power. Striding towards the dresser, she paused only for a moment before picking up the empty perfume bottle she had carelessly knocked over the night before. Her fingers lingered on it, as if contemplating the events that had led her here. Opening the drawer beneath the dresser, lady catherine pulled out a small, elegant bottle of rose and lavender perfume. It was an anniversary gift from her husband many years ago. The glass delicate and etched with intricate patterns that had long since lost their sheen. She held it in her hands for a moment, the scent still lingering in the bottle. The mere smell of lavender made her stomach turn with disgust. She had never liked it, but she had kept it all these years, pretending for the sake of appearances. Now, it would serve a far more sinister purpose. With reasoned care, Lady Catherine poured half of the lavender perfume into the empty bottle, the thick liquid spilling with a soft, almost mocking hiss. Then, her gaze fell upon the bottle of polish, its dark liquid inside a stark contrast to the delicate perfume. The skull symbol on the label stood out, a clear warning that the contents were dangerous, to be handled with caution, to be used only as instructed. It was a curious thing to have in her possession. The faintest thrill ran through her as she read the label, her fingers tightening around the bottle. She could almost feel the power, an unsettling reminder of the risks she was willing to take for the sake of her pride. It would not be the first time Lady Catherine used poison to get her way. Lady Catherine glanced into the mirror before her, holding the makeshift concoction half perfume, half poison up to her face. Her reflection stared back at her, a woman cloaked in elegance and malice. She stood tall and proud, a side smile curling on her lips. looking at the bottle in her hands, the skull symbol, once a warning, now posed as an invitation and a mark of control, something she can command. She knew what she had to do. The weight of it settled in her chest, steady and unshakable. In that moment, it felt as if nothing could stand in her way, no fear, no doubt, no obstacle. It was as if the very air around her had cleared, leaving only a single path forward, and she was ready to walk it, no matter the cost.

CHAPTER NINE
Ghost vs villagers

Present day

The family sat down for dinner, which Chase
had helped her mum prepare. It had been a
hectic day for everyone, rushed, noisy, and full
of distractions. She desperately wanted to talk
about what she was going through. Her
thoughts clawed at her, begging to be let out.
However, Chase chose to stay quiet pushing her
thoughts to the back of her mind. She gave her
parents the floor to discuss their day. Now did
not feel the right time. Isabelle went first. "I
had a really stressful but accomplished day. I
have organized everything I need for the
charity event next Saturday." Isabelle had
always been good at her job; she never allowed
herself to fail. She always threw the best
charity events, and they always made the most
money. This charity event in their new town
would be no exception. It would be the best
that Blackthorn Village had seen. At least, that
was the plan. "That's great, Mum. I will help
too if you need." Chase offered, her voice soft

with affection. "Thank you, darling." Isabelle replied, her smile warm and appreciative. "I'm sure I could use your help somewhere." She reached out to gently squeeze Chase's hand, a rare moment of silent understanding passing between them, a shared sense of purpose that neither needed to put into words. Henry went next, his voice light and playful. "Well, my two favourite women of the house." He began, a grin tugging at his lips, "I've been rushed off my feet today. I have never made so many cups of tea and coffee in my life!" He chuckled, the sound warm and familiar, a reflection of his easy-going nature. He paused for a moment, looking around at the faces of his family, his eyes twinkling. "But someone's got to keep the caffeine flowing…right?" His humour was genuine, his way of lightening the mood despite the busyness of the day. "The house has been full of people all day, but I think the manor is coming along grandly." Henry said this with a proud, almost God like stance. He was pleased with how much work had been done, despite the chaos of it all. It had been a good day. The kind of day that felt like a small victory. The whole bottom floor was finally complete, and most importantly, it now had running water! Henry's grin widened as he gestured around the room. "It may not seem like much, but for us, this is huge." He breathed, the pride in his voice unmistakable. "No more carrying buckets up and down the stairs, no more worrying about leaks. We have proper plumbing now, and it feels like we have come a long way." He paused, taking in the space with a satisfied look, before turning back to the group. "We have all been so patient, but today, we have a little reward. The work's paying off." "Finally!" Isabelle sighed in relief. "So, what about you, love?" Henry asked Chase, turning to her. Chase hesitated, her heart racing as panic flashed in her eyes. She needed to think of something fast, something that would not set off alarms. Her mind scrambled for a way out of the awkward moment. "Umm... well, I invited Emily and Hugo over for a sleepover tomorrow night." She said quickly, the words tumbling out before she could stop them. She winced inwardly, knowing she had not asked first, but there was no turning back now. "I know I didn't ask first, but I just thought you wouldn't mind." She offered a smile, her shoulders shrugging in a half-hearted attempt to look casual, though her insides churned with uncertainty. It was not a lie, but it was not the whole truth either. She just hoped they would not question her too much. "That's fine, sweet, but next time, please let me or your father

know." Isabelle said, her voice calm but firm.
She softened her gaze as she reached out,
brushing a strand of hair from Chase's face.
"We just need to keep track of things around
here. The house is still being worked on, and
we don't want any accidents to happen." Her
words were not harsh, but they carried an
unmistakable sense of authority, a reminder
that even in moments of casual conversation,
her concern for safety came first. Isabelle's eyes
lingered on Chase for a moment, as though
silently urging her to understand. Chase
nodded, grateful that her parents were not
pressing her further. She knew Isabelle was
being serious, but she appreciated her mother's
calmness. It gave her a sense of relief, a fleeting
comfort that for now, she could keep her
secrets to herself. Chase let out a mousey breath
she had not realized she had been holding.
Chase retired to her room after a long meal and
a movie her dad had picked; something about
an alien coming to Earth and falling in love
with a human. As she shut her bedroom door
behind her, she flopped onto her bed and pulled
her phone out of her pocket. Earlier that day, in
the coffee shop, Emily and Hugo had
exchanged numbers with chase, immediately
creating a group chat and have been firing off
memes, theories, nervous jokes ever since.

Chase however, had kept her phone off all evening, trying to clear her head. So, she had missed a ton of messages. The group chat was called Ghosts vs Villagers, a playful name that suited the situation perfectly. As Chase finally turned her phone back on, she was met with a flood of missed messages, Chase skimmed through them seeing mostly banter, nothing too important, just their usual jokes and chatter. But then she spotted a message from Hugo, written in French. Chase paused, squinting at the unfamiliar words. She quickly opened a translation app, and the message read: "Tu es vraiment agacante, Emilie, arrête avec ces citations ridicules!" In English: "You're so annoying, Emily, stop with those ridiculous quotes!" Chase chuckled quietly to herself, picturing the playful argument between her friends. It made her feel a little lighter, as if despite everything going on around her, she could still find moments of normalcy.

[PHONE]

*CHASE: You guys are crazy. I cannot even
begin to read all this.
HUGO: Hehehe... :)*

*EMILY: It is Hugo. He cannot understand half
the things I say!*

*HUGO: Would you prefer I spoke only in
French? No? Did not think so.
EMILY: Calm down, Hugo.*

HUGO: Love ya, girl. XO

*CHASE: Right, it is getting late. I will see you
both tomorrow night.*

HUGO: Night, spooky squad.

*EMILY: Goodnight! Try not to get haunted in
your sleep. **[ghost emoji]***

Chase turned off her phone and placed it down
beside her bed. She turned off the light and
settled into bed, pulling the covers up to her
chin as darkness filled the room. Stillness crept
in around her, but the unease from earlier

clung stubbornly to her skin. It had been a lot to take in. Her eyes tiering, staring at the ceiling, but her mind refused to let her drift off. The images of the ghostly figure kept circling her thoughts... Chase woke up in the dead of night. Her eyes flicked open, and she groggily reached for her phone, turning it on and blinking against the dim light. It was 04:00 AM. A tired yawn escaped her lips as she squinted, one eye still half-closed from the lack of sleep. Her mind was still foggy, but at least it was not 03:00 AM the witching hour. She did not need that on top of everything else. Suddenly, a faint scratching sound broke the silence, coming from beneath her bed. It was like something, or someone was trying to reach her. Her heart raced and sweat beaded on her forehead. She froze, listening. The sound remained, a slow, intended scrape. With a tremor in her chest, she pushed the covers off and knelt on the bed, palms flat, bracing herself. Every instinct screamed at her to ignore it; to stay still and pretend she had not heard a thing. But curiosity and fear drove her forward. She took a deep breath, the pounding of her heart like the base of drum, thunderous in her chest. With one more glance around the room, her body tensed. Slowly, she lowered her head toward the edge of the bed, her breath even, her hair spilled over her shoulders just grazing the floorboards below. Her heart skipped a beat when her eyes scanned the dim space beneath the bed. She saw something: her hairbrush. The one she had dropped a couple of days ago. "That's where you are." She muttered to herself, relief, and dread mingling in her. Reaching for the brush, every inch felt like an eternity. Her fingers trembled hesitantly, but she gripped the handle. A bead of sweat rolled down her temple as she pulled it towards her, a small smile creeping onto her face. She had done it. But then she saw something else, something much worse. From the corner of her eye, a shadow drifted across the room. Stalling at first, almost lazy in its movements. A figure emerged, its feet and legs swaying unnaturally from side to side, as if floating just inches above the floor. It began to pace back and forth, each pass growing closer. Before she could even move, before she could scream or make sense of it, the figure leapt. It landed on the bed with a force that made the mattress jolt beneath her. Panic surged through her body like a lightning strike. In a reflex, she threw herself under the bed, her body crashing to the floor in a desperate scramble. She lay there, frozen. Her breaths shallow, her eyes wide with terror. Then came the voice. Soft, haunting, and chillingly close just above her head. "I smell the blood of a murderer." The words slithered into her ears causing Chase's blood ran cold. A sharp, primal fear surged through her; every hair stood on end. The fear locking her in place paralyzing, turning to ice. She did not dare move. Did not dare breathe. The voice, low, guttural, and far too close, cut through the silence like a blade. Each word struck her like a dagger, spiky echoing in her mind long after the sound had faded. It was not just the tone, it was the certainty behind it, the feeling that whoever, whatever was speaking… knew her. Shivers ran down her. Slowly, she became aware of something wet. She dared to glance at her hand, lifting it slightly to shine the light from her phone. Blood. Fresh, warm blood, pooling from a cut across her palm. It was as if someone had sliced her with a knife, but she had not felt it. Tears welled in her eyes as panic set in. Her mind raced. *How could she have been cut without even noticing?* She did not have time to process. She had to get help. Her fingers fumbled with the phone, shaking so violently that she could barely press the right numbers. The screen blurred as tears welled in her eyes, and her breath came in short, frantic gasps. She tried to steady herself, but the device kept slipping in her sweaty grip. The familiar sequence of her password suddenly felt foreign, like trying to solve a puzzle under water. Focus, she told herself, but the fear made it impossible. Then, without warning, something grabbed her by the ankles and yanked her from beneath the bed. She screamed, kicking out violently, trying to break free. The grip tightened, but then, as suddenly as it had started, it released her. Without thinking, she scrambled toward the door, her body moving on pure instinct. But before she could reach the handle, a sharp, unbearable pull jerked her backwards. Her hair. Her hair was being dragged, lifting her off the ground, as if someone were holding onto it like a rope. The pain was excruciating. Her neck strained, her scalp felt like it was tearing. Sobbing, choking on her own breath, Chase felt her strength slipping away. Her limbs trembled, powerless, as if the fear itself had drained every ounce of life from her. She tried to scream, but no sound came, only the spinning of the world. The sickening swirl of terror and pain overwhelming her senses. Then, with one final, desperate gasp, everything went black. She awoke with a sharp cry, her body crashing to the floor like a ragdoll. The impact jolted through her, and for a moment, she could not tell what was real. Her head throbbed with unbearable pain, a pulsing ache behind her eyes. Blinking rapidly, she tried to focus, tried to piece together where she was. Face down on the cold wooden floor, she lay still, the chill seeping into her skin. Every inch of her ached, as though she had been thrown, discarded like something broken. With effort, she rolled over onto her back, her vision blurry at first. As her eyes focused, she froze, terror flooding her veins. There, hovering inches above her, was the ghostly woman from before. She was suspended in mid-air, her long, ethereal hair drifting like smoke, almost brushing Chase's body. The ghost's dress rafted in a perfect, unnatural shape, as if it had been caught in the motion of standing stiff and hauntingly upright. Chase's breath caught in her throat. Her entire body trembled with fear. "What... what do you want from me?" she whispered, tears streaming down her face freely, her voice barely a breath wobbly on the edge of braking. She tried to crawl backward, but the significance of her fear kept her frozen in place. The ghostly figure stared down at her, its hollow, dark eyes seemingly piercing into Chase's very soul. For a moment, time seemed to stretch, the silence in the room leaden and suffocating. Then, in a voice that sent shivers through Chase's bones clear, chilling, and full of malice it spoke. "YOU!" The single word exploded through the room like thunder, reverberating in Chase's skull, but what superseded was even worse. The woman's face once pale and beautiful twisted into something unrecognizable, an unappealing, deformed visage. Her skin rippled and contorted, her features stretching into a demonic mask of rage and despair. Before Chase could react, the spirit fell forward, her body colliding with Chase's in a cold crushing embrace, pinning her to the floor. The pressure was suffocating, far heavier than it should have been, as if the ghostly women carried centuries of grief and rage in her form. Her weight unbearable. Her limbs useless. Chase screamed, but the sound was swallowed instantly. The ghostly woman's face was inches from her own, and all Chase could do is stare into eyes that clearly were not there. She could feel the coldness of the figure pressing against her, seeping through her skin, her heart hammering so hard it threatened to burst from her chest. Her mind reeled, and for a moment, all she could do was close her eyes, bracing for whatever nightmare would come next... When Chase woke up, she found herself tucked neatly in her bed, as though she had experienced a peaceful night's sleep. But there was nothing peaceful about how she felt. She stared at the ceiling, her mind racing, yet her body stringent and unresponsive. Every movement sent a wave of aching pain through her limbs. Tears welled in her eyes, slowly trickling down her cheeks and soaking into the pillow beneath her. She felt hollow, drained of energy so utterly exhausted, physically, and emotionally, that even the thought of getting up seemed impossible. But she could not lie there forever. The ghostly woman was still haunting her, still lingering in the back of her mind, and Chase knew she could not let it drag her any further down. Reluctantly, she dragged herself out of bed, the weight of each step making her body protest in agony. The shower was a desperate attempt to feel better, to wash away the fear that clung to her like stone. She stood motionless beneath the spray of water, arms wrapped tightly around herself. No matter how long she stood there the hot water did little to soothe her. It was as if the heat could not get through the stone. As the steam filled the bathroom, she noticed something strange on her hand, there was a faint scar, a thin, jagged line that had not been there before. She reached out to touch it, her fingers brushing over the skin, a barbed sense of dread settling in her chest. Chase turned to the mirror, wiping away the fog with the edge of her sleeve. Her breath caught the moment her reflection stared back at her. The face in the glass looked unfamiliar, a pale, washed-out version of herself. Dark circles clung to her eyes like bruises, and her expression was vacant, distant. She hardly recognized the girl looking back. The exhaustion etched across her face told a story she had not spoken aloud. Her eyes were hollow, dull, drained of the spark they once held. Her skin looked tight and drawn, like it no longer fit chiefly right. She looked like someone teetering on the edge of collapse. Someone who had been drained of whatever light they once carried. Even as she brushed her hair and watched clumps of it come away with the bristles, she did not flinch. She did not cry. She did not react. She could not. There should have been panic, or anger, or even fear. But all that remained was a numb, bottomless emptiness. A kind of fatigue that went deeper than her body, settling into her bones, her mind, her very soul. It was like watching someone else's life unfold from a distance, trapped behind the glass, helpless to do anything but observe. The mirror reflected a version of herself she hardly recognized; a pale, fragile girl who seemed to have lost her fight. But no matter how much she wanted to give in, she knew she could not. Not yet.

CHAPTER TEN
THE GIFT Of MALICE

1800

As Arabella sipped her tea, her usual poise was absent. She could not focus on the morning papers or any telegrams that had arrived. All she could think of was Edward, dear Edward, her love, the one she could not live without. Her mind drifted back to the moment they first met. It was spring of 1810, and Arabella had been attending a ball hosted by her father's friends. The venue was nothing short of stunning. As guests entered through the grand doors, they were immediately struck by the beauty of the place. A vast staircase, grand and sweeping, divided the room in two. The soaring ceilings seemed to stretch into eternity, while the crystal chandelier hanging its six tiers of sparkling diamonds, spewing a soft glow over the room. Every surface gleamed with refinement, velvet drapes descending in rich, dramatic folds, and intricate tapestries lined the walls, their colours vibrant yet muted under the glow of flames scattered in lanterns. Arabella

118

stepped into a hall fit for royalty. Footmen in crisp uniforms offered glasses of champagne and bourbon, while trays of canapés were passed around. The air was filled with the scent of fresh flowers and the sweet, heady perfume of ladies in attendance. The floral notes from the grand vases perched throughout the hall were rich and intoxicating, almost overpowering in their beauty. Whilst the subtle blend of jasmine and rose from the guests' perfumes added an almost ethereal quality to the air. Arabella, in her silver gown, stood out as a vision of youthful beauty. It was then that she crossed paths with Sir Edward. Their eyes met, and something shifted between them, a connection undeniable. He asked her to dance, and they spent the rest of the evening lost in the rhythm of the waltz, the music, and the magic of the night. It felt like fate, undeniable, as though every moment leading up to this had been conservatively guiding her here. It was not long before Edward came to visit her father's townhouse, and on his third visit, he arrived with a horse and carriage. They took a ride through the countryside, enjoying the peace of the evening, the way the fading light draped itself over the rolling fields, and how the wind whispered through the trees like an old lullaby. When they returned to her home,

Arabella turned to say goodnight, but instead she was met with Edward on one knee, his eyes filled with love and determination. "Arabella, will you marry me?" he asked, his voice full of sincerity. Arabella smiled to herself; the memory of that evening still vivid in her mind, as if it had only happened yesterday. She could almost hear the music playing inside her home, feel the soft brush of silk skirts against her legs, the wind blowing ever so slightly. A gentle flutter stirred within her, like the flutter of wings, and for a fleeting moment, the avoirdupois of the present vanished. The anxieties of the day, the exasperation in the air, all melted away beneath the glow of that cherished recollection. For a moment, she was simply a girl in love, caught in the magic of a night that had once felt endless. As she awaited further instructions about the wedding, Arabella began to twirl gently in the centre of her room, her gown flowing softly around her ankles. She hummed a melody she had just made up, letting the notes guide her steps as she moved through the serene room. Each soft note felt like a secret between her and the reticence, her feet almost dancing without thought, carried by the tune only she could hear. The music in her head filled the room like a daydream, one that made her feel light as air.

But the moment was broken by a sudden, stiff knock at the door. Knock. Knock. Knock. "Arabella, it is Lady Catherine. May I enter?" came the voice from the other side, sweet as honey, smooth and composed, the kind of voice no one would dare question. It was the sort of tone meant to soothe, to disarm, yet Arabella felt a familiar unease stir in her stomach. That sweetness was always bashed with something sharper, something that did not completely reach the eyes. Arabella paused mid-turn; her hands still delicately lifted as though caught in the middle of a curtsey. For a moment, time seemed to still, her posture frozen, her expression unreadable. She hesitated only briefly before replying, her voice steady but alternated with curiosity. "Yes, of course, my lady. Do come in." Lady Catherine smiled to herself before entering Arabella's chambers. The door creaked softly as it opened, and Arabella stood poised in alarum, her hands folded neatly before her. "Look at you." Lady Catherine blurted, her eyes trailing from head to toe, offering her best imitation of a warm smile. Arabella gave a graceful twirl, her gown flowing effortlessly as she moved, like ripples on water. For a moment, she felt weightless, untouched by worry, lost in the simple joy of movement. "I feel like a princess." She avowed brightly, a playful glimmer in her eyes. Then, with a pause just long enough to suggest careful thought, she added, "Lady, or should I call you Mother?" The word lingered in the air, light on the surface but weighted with meaning. As Arabella watched for the older woman's reaction, Lady Catherine's smile thinned. The warmth draining from her face, like sunlight slipping behind a cloud. Her eyes brilliant and unreadable. "Once you are wed, you may call me Catherine. Mother makes me sound old, and I like to think of myself as still youthful." Arabella nodded politely and stepped forward, taking Lady Catherine's hand and pressing a gentle kiss upon it. "Now, now, dear." Lady Catherine clothed, withdrawing her hand. "Let us get to the real reason I came to see you." From within the folds of her gown, Lady Catherine drew out a delicate bottle, small, glass, and glinting faintly in the light. Arabella instinctively reached for it, her fingers brushing the cool surface as she accepted it. She tilted her head, curiosity flickering across her face. "What's this?" she asked, the confusion in her voice soft but unmistakable. "As the groom's mother, I think it only right to pass down a gift." Lady Catherine said smoothly. "It would bring me such joy to know that when you marry my Edward, you'll be carrying a piece of me with you." She was always careful with her words, always knowing just how to cloak intention in charm. "Why thank you, Lady Catherine." Arabella said earnestly, cradling the bottle as though it were something precious. Her smile was genuine, if a little uncertain, and her fingers curled protectively around the glass. "I love Edward with all my heart, and I promise I shall never do anything to hurt him. I will be a good wife and if God allows it, a good mother." Lady Catherine turned toward the door, her expression unreadable. But just as her hand touched the handle, she paused and looked back over her shoulder. "We shall see." Those three words sliced into Arabella like a chill through lace. And then, she was gone. Arabella stood in the stillness of her room, the door clicking shut behind Lady Catherine like the end of a chapter. Moments ago, she had felt light, twirling, humming, imagining a life stitched together with laughter and love. But now, an invisible repute pressed against her, heavy and unwelcome. The warmth had drained from the room. She no longer felt like the heroine of a story, but rather a footnote. Unloved. Unwanted. A guest in her own fairytale. She walked slowly to the dresser, her silk skirts whispering against the floor. Sitting down, she gazed at her reflection. One single tear slipped down her cheek, and with urgency, she caught it on the back of her hand before it could ruin her makeup. Her breath hitched slightly as she blinked away the rest, forcing a smile to stay intact. This was not the time for tears, not when appearances meant everything. "I will not let that wretched woman put me down. Not on my wedding day." Her voice was a whisper, but it rang with unobtrusive defiance. Her eyes shifted to the bottle, Lady Catherine's so-called gift, resting like a curse on the edge of the vanity. Its delicate shape and floral design no longer charmed her; instead, it radiated something sinister. Without hesitation, Arabella snatched it up, her fingers tightening around the smooth glass. She yanked open the drawer and shoved it inside with a sharp thud, slamming it shut. She was not going to give Lady Catherine the satisfaction of feeling like she was part of the wedding. Not today. Not ever. "Sir Edward." One of the footmen said as he tried to adjust the groom's suit, struggling slightly with the stiff fabric. "I don't mean to sound rude sir." The footman said carefully, needle poised mid-air. "But I'd be able to finish much quicker if you could remain still." Edward looked down at him with a faint smile. "Pete, is it?" "Paul, sir." The footman corrected politely, his cheeks colouring. "Ah, of course,

Paul." Edward chuckled, his eyes bright with excitement. "Forgive me, I am a little distracted. Am I not the luckiest man alive? In mere moments, I shall call the most beautiful woman in the country my wife. It is slightly overwhelming." He paused, a genuine warmth spreading across his face as he thought of Arabella, the future he could already see unfolding before him. The footman glanced up, then quickly dropped his gaze again, doing his best to remain composed. But a smile tugged at the corner of his mouth, betraying his amusement. "I believe you may be sir." He said with hushed warmth. "The luckiest man, that is." "Then I shall do my best to keep still." Edward said with a boyish grin. His gaze softening as he looked down at the fine fabric of his blazer. Paul nodded and carried through with his duties, careful and efficient, as the groom stood tall and beaming, every inch the gentleman in love. Guests began arriving one by one, each more polished and refined than the last. The grand entrance hall gradually came to life, filled with the soft murmur of pleasantries, the clinking of glasses, and the delicate rustle of fine fabrics sweeping across the marble floor. Perfume lingered in the air, mingling with the faint scent of beeswax polish and fresh flowers, while every smile seemed rehearsed, every glance weighed with inconspicuous judgment. They gathered at the foot of the sweeping staircase, where silver trays were held aloft by poised footmen, each offering a complimentary glass of sparkling wine. Wrapped around the stem of every crystal flute was a single lily, tied delicately with a ribbon of white silk. Threaded through the silk in black stitching were the words: *Edward & Arabella.* The butler appeared through a hidden door nestled seamlessly in the wood-panelled wall, his entrance so smooth it was as though he had materialized from the house itself. His posture was impeccable, his hands clasped neatly in front of him. When he spoke, his voice echoed with formality and quiet pride, cutting through the ambient chatter like a bell tolling the next stage of the evening. "Sir and Lady Blackthorn." As the couple descended the staircase, all conversation in the room softened into hushed admiration. Lady Catherine, ever the image of composed perfection, drew every gaze like a magnet. For her age, she was striking, poised, commanding, and hauntingly beautiful. Dressed in a deep emerald gown embroidered with silver thread, her presence exuded both elegance and authority. There was something about her that made people stand straighter, speak softer, and watch longer. It was as if her very being held an unspoken power, one that demanded respect and admiration, yet also instilled a unadorned sense of unease. As she moved through the room, her eyes scanning the guests with practiced grace, it was clear that she was more than just the matriarch of Blackthorn Manor, she was its heart, its unshakable force. Every word she spoke seemed calculated, every glance a silent command. No one dared challenge her reign, and in her company, all understood their place. Sir Howard followed beside her, his posture proud. Though time had left its marks more plainly on him than on his wife, he carried himself with distinguished grace. His tailored suit of midnight blue and polished shoes marked him as a man still very much in control, still very much respected. Every inch of his attire was meticulously crafted, from the sharp lines of his jacket to the gleam of his cufflinks, a testament to his impeccable taste and invariant confidence. His posture, straight and dignified, suggested a man who had faced countless challenges yet remained unbowed. As he entered the room, there was an undeniable air of authority that followed him, the subtle but clear indication that he was someone who commanded attention without needing to ask for it. Though his age had softened the edges of his youth, there was no mistaking the sharpness in his gaze. Every movement he made exuded an elegance that was matched only by his power, his very presence reinforcing the legacy of Blackthorn Manor that he had spent his life upholding. Together, they were a vision; regal and unreachable. "Sir Edward Blackthorn." The butler announced, his voice ringing clear over the hum of conversation. At once, all eyes turned toward the future heir of Blackthorn Manor, a ripple of silent expectation sweeping through the room. Whispers flitted between guest, their gazes fixed with a mixture of curiosity and calculated interest, waiting for the next move in this delicate dance of power and position. Ladies tilted their heads, offering subtle smiles behind lace fans, their eyes lingering on him with a mixture of admiration and curiosity. They whispered behind their delicate coverings, aware that such a man held both power and intrigue, yet never fully revealing the depths of their thoughts. The gentlemen, though outwardly composed, nodded with restrained civility, their expressions schooled in politeness. Yet beneath their polished facades, a ripple of jealousy simmered. They resented his unshakeable position, his effortless grace, and the gentle dominance he commanded without so much as a word. It was a pressure they hid well, but one that was palpable to those who knew where to look, an undercurrent of rivalry, of tacit competition for a place in the world that seemed already secured for him. Edward moved gracefully through the gathered crowd, greeting guests with a warm, effortless charm. His suit was expertly tailored, the deep burgundy waistcoat catching the light with each step, and his jawline seemed jagged enough to cut through the fabric of the very crowd he passed. "What a man." whispered a lady standing near the back, her voice just low enough to only be heard by the few around her. They offered small, knowing smirks, but shot nothing aloud. Edward Blackthorn was the man of the hour, and everyone knew it. All that remained was the bride, and then the day would be complete.

CHAPTER ELEVEN
PUPPET ON A STRING

Present day

"Morning love." Isabelle called cheerfully as Chase entered the kitchen, grabbing a quick bite of toast and juice before heading to college. "I was thinking, would you and your friends like some pizza and ice cream for dinner? I can swing by the shop on my way home." Chase hesitated for a moment. "No, it's okay Mum." Offering a reassuring smile even though she felt a tight bit of guilt. "I will grab something from the coffee shop with Emily and Hugo after college. Thanks though." Her voice was steady, she did not want to worry her mother. Isabelle's gaze lingered on her daughter, sensing something amiss, but before she could probe any further, Chase was already out the door. "That was…odd." Isabelle breathed, narrowing her eyes as she turned to Henry with a faint frown tugging at her lips. "Did you notice anything strange about her this morning?" Henry looked up from his newspaper, eyebrows knitting together in mild confusion. He set the paper down on his lap, giving her his full attention. "What do you mean? Strange how?" Isabelle hesitated, unsure of how to articulate the nagging feeling she gazed at the door as she was trying to find the right words. "I do not know… It is just, well, something about her felt off. Like she was not there. Like she was going through the motions, but her mind was somewhere else entirely." Henry shrugged, still trying to process his coffee. "It is just the charity event weighing on you. You have been so busy love." Isabelle was not convinced. She leaned back in her chair, staring at the door through which Chase had just left, her thoughts far from settled. Something in her daughter's voice that felt wrong. "Maybe you're right." She sighed, but the unease in her voice was unmistakable. Henry, ever the optimist, perked up, his voice light and easy "she will be fine." He said "She is just growing up, that is all. A little independence never hurt anyone right?" his tone was warm "you know, why don't we take tonight for ourselves? It has been ages since we had a proper date night. You have been so wrapped up in everything, and we have hardly spent any time together. What do you say?" Isabelle's reluctance was evident in her pause, but eventually, she smiled. "I suppose you're right." She restated after a moment, her shoulders relaxing just slightly. She looked at henry "We could both use a break." Henry grinned, folding the newspaper and setting it aside with more enthusiasm than necessary. "It'll be nice to get out for a change." He uttered, the corners of his eyes crinkling. "A little time for just us, no distractions, no chaos. We could both use that." As they finalized their plans, Isabelle's mind could not shake the feeling that something was slipping through her fingers. She glanced back at the door, still unsure what was happening to Chase, and if she were the only one who could feel it. Chase arrived at college; the brisk morning air having done wonders to settle her mind. The solitude of the walk had allowed her to breathe for a moment, putting a little distance between her and the unsettling thoughts that had clung to her all morning. But as she hurried toward the classroom, she realized with a jolt that she was running later than she had planned. She slipped through the door just as the lecture began, and immediately, all eyes turned toward her. The disruption sliced through the quiet hum of the lesson, drawing every gaze in her direction. "I'm so sorry, I lost track of time walking here." She ventilated quickly, offering an apologetic smile as she tried to brush off the awkwardness. Her voice was a little louder than she intended, but she could already feel the eyes on her, and the last thing she wanted was to draw more attention. The teacher, a middle-aged woman with a faint air of discomfort, paused for a moment before replying. "No worries, miss…" She trailed off, suddenly unsure of Chase's last name. Chase stiffened, her mind racing as she searched for the right words. "I'm sorry, what's your last name again?" the teacher asked, glancing up from the attendance sheet. Without thinking, as if it were not her speaking, Chase blurted out, "Nightshade. Chase Nightshade." The words dropped in the air as the room fell silent. Chase's heart skipped a beat. '*What? Why did I say that?*' Her mind screamed, but before she could stop herself, the sentence was already out. Her face flushed with embarrassment. Her last name was not Nightshade. In fact, she had never heard the name before in her life. Confusion swirled inside her, but she quickly lowered her head, sinking into her seat, as if hiding from her own slip-up. She remained silent for the rest of the class; her eyes locked on the board though the words written there blurred into meaningless shapes. She was not really seeing any of it. Her mind churned with unease, replaying the moment again. *'Nightshade? Why did she say that? Where had it come from?* A heightened knot of dread sat in her stomach, like speaking again might trigger something strange, something she could not explain or control. So, she kept her mouth shut, terrified that more bizarre, unexplainable things might slip out. When the bell finally rang, Chase gathered her things slowly, her movements almost mechanical. She made her way to the library, where she was supposed to meet Emily and Hugo. The sensible hum of the space was a small comfort. She spotted them at one of the long tables near the windows and approached with a secret sigh, trying to shake the feeling that still clung to her. "Hey guys." Chase talked as she approached, her voice a bit strained, stretched thin by the effort of sounding normal. She forced a small smile, trying to push the weirdness of the morning out of her mind and act like everything was fine. Emily and Hugo looked up from the table where they sat. "Oh hey." Emily replied, offering a warm smile. Hugo glanced up from his phone, giving her a quick nod. "Hey." He added. Placing his phone back into his pocket. Chase sat down heavily, barely giving herself time to settle before the words came spilling out. "You're not going to believe what happened in class." She communicated, her voice low but urgent. "I was late, and when the teacher asked for my last name, I just, without thinking, said Nightshade. Like…Nightshade.? Why would I say that?" She looked between Emily and Hugo, staring at them for understanding. "It is not even my name. I have never heard it before. It just… came out. Like it was not even me saying it." Emily frowned, clearly puzzled. "You have no idea where that came from? No family member or something? Or maybe you read it somewhere?" Chase shook her head, feeling the unease creep back in. "I do not know. It just came out. It is so strange, and I do not know what to make of it." Emily looked thoughtful for a moment. "That's… odd" she said slowly "But maybe it is just a slip-up? You know, something random your brain pulled from somewhere, like a weird memory or a dream bleeding into real life." Chase glanced at Hugo, silently hoping for some guidance, anything to make this feeling go away. Hugo gave a small nod he usual reaction to things. Then he said with his voice calm and steady. "Alright, here is what we are going to do. We grab a few snacks from the shop, maybe a couple of drinks and head back to yours Chase. We will have a plain night in, no distractions, we will figure this out together, yes weird names, creepy vibes. Whatever it is, were not letting it mess with you alone." Chase felt a slight sense of relief at his suggestion. It was exactly what she needed to take her mind off everything, even if just for a little while. "Alright, that sounds good." Chase insinuated, her voice softer but grateful the tension in her body eased just a little. "Let's go." Back at the manor, Emily and Hugo stood at the foot of the grand entrance, their heads tilted back as they took in the full height of the manor. The sprawling structure loomed above them, its tall ivy, draped walls and weathered stone giving it a haunting kind of beauty. They both seemed a little overwhelmed. "Wow You live here?" Emily muttered; her voice tinged with disbelief. "You were not kidding. This place is massive." "Est-ce que mes yeux me trompent, quelle beauté!" Hugo exclaimed, his thick French accent adding extra flair to the words. "Are my eyes deceiving me? What a beauty!" Chase could not help but laugh at their reactions. With a playful roll of her eyes, she continued up the steps toward the front doors. "You guys coming in, or what?" she called out over her shoulder, her voice carrying a note of impatience, as if she were ready to move on from the awe-struck stares and get inside. After giving Emily and Hugo the grand tour of the house, which felt more like babysitting two overexcited toddlers at the zoo, Chase finally guided them into her room. Even that was enough to send them into a frenzy of excitement. Along the way Hugo had tried (and failed) to open at least three locked doors convinced there were secret passageways, while Emily could not stop marvelling at the antique portraits and soaring ceilings like she stepped into a period drama. "My god Chase, your room is three times the size of mine!" Emily exclaimed, her voice dripping with more than a little envy, and she made no effort to hide it. "Whee-wee, whee-wee, yes, yes, yes! This will be my modern design studio!" Hugo declared with a mischievous grin, but there was a hint of truth in his tone; if Chase let him, he probably would claim it as his own space for some wild designs. Chase raised an eyebrow, her expression a little distant as she surveyed the room with a faint shrug. "It is okay, I guess. I used to love it. But now… every time I walk in, I just see her." She explained quietly, her voice mixed with an undertone of discomfort. "I forgot to tell you both what happened last night." Chase began, her voice lower now, the playful energy from earlier replaced with something more serious. She glanced at Emily and Hugo, both of whom were now watching her intently, curiosity etched across their faces. The playful energy they had carried through the tour had faded, replaced by a quiet alertness as they sensed the shift in her tone. Chase hesitated for a moment, her fingers twitching at her sides before reaching down and gently pulled back the sleeve of her shirt. The fabric slid up to reveal the faint silvery scar along her hand. "It happened right here, in this very room." She continued, her voice now barely a whisper. "I was attacked. It was like… something was here with me. I don't even know how to explain it." The room grew blistering and thick. Emily and Hugo exchanged uneasy glances, both feeling the shift, not just in Chases voice, but the air around them, suddenly colder, as if the story itself had unsettled the very space. Without a word, they both gravitated toward the bed, sitting down as if the presence of the blankets might somehow offer protection. Neither of them spoke, but their eyes stayed on Chase, waiting. Not for the story, but for some sign that everything is still okay. That the scar, the cold, none of it meant what it felt like it did. But Chase changed the subject and moved towards the fact they are home alone. "My mum and dad are out on a date night, so we have the house to ourselves. We need to find clues." Chase commanded, determination in her voice. Hugo, however, glanced out the window at the darkening sky and sighed. "I was hoping to see the tower before nightfall." He piped up with a hint of disappointment in his voice. But the unpredictable winter weather had other plans. Thick clouds had rolled in fast, and the daylight was fading quicker than expected. The cold crept in around them like a warning; sharp and unforgiving. Still, they pressed on, determined not to turn back. The last traces of natural light vanished. With no other option, they switched on their phone flashlights, the narrow beams cutting through the darkness, as they approached the hidden door in the wall. Emily suddenly stopped, her feet frozen in place. "I can't go up there." She admitted, her voice a bit shaky. "There's something about spiral stairs I just can't deal with." Emily took another look towards the spiral staircase. Her jaw tight. "It is not just the height or narrow steps. It just gives me the creeps." She turned to Chase, her expression a mix of apology and firm resolve. "I'll stand guard." She said softly, her eyes scanning the around them. "Just in case anything happens. Better safe than sorry." Chase and Hugo exchanged glances, then nodded in agreement. It was decided. They would make their way up the narrow, spiralling staircase alone. The stairs creaked beneath their feet as they climbed into the pitch-black tower. When they reached the top, Chase reached into her coat pocket and pulled out a small candle. The wax was slightly worn, it was an old candle Chase found in one of the drawers in her room, Chase did not speak whilst she struck the match, shielding the tiny flame from a passing draft. The flickering flame brightened up the room just about. "Wow, this is not creepy at all." Hugo said sarcastically, his voice bouncing off the stone walls. Both Chase and Hugo began to search the room, their eyes sweeping over every corner, every shadow, as if the walls themselves might hold the answers they desperately sought. But the place felt off, empty, unwelcoming, and unnervingly still. "Guys! Everything okay up there?" Emily's voice echoed through the darkened hallway. It sounded so small, so fragile, in the vast drab that hounded. No answer. The silence pressed in around her. A cold knot of unease twisted in her stomach, tightening with each breath. The silence stretched on, suffocating, like a thick, damp fog that was slowly closing in around her. She strained her ears, but the only sound was her heartbeat, hammering in her chest, loud enough to drown out the rest of the world. Then a flicker. The hallway lights blinked, a brief, unsettling flicker. Emily's breath hitched, and she froze, her pulse jumping. "Chase?" Her voice was a whisper now, the kind that barely escaped her lips, barely enough to be heard over the oppressive quiet. No answer. "Hugo?" She repeated louder, but the words felt weak, swallowed up by the growing darkness. Her eyes darted around the hallway, flicking from shadow to-shadow half-expecting something or someone to leap from the shadows at any moment. The lights flickered again, this time lingering longer than before, as though hesitant, unsure. A brief stutter of light bathed the room in an eerie glow, only for it to fade into complete darkness. Then nothing. The room fell silent, the absence of light almost suffocating. A cold shiver ran down Emily's spine, her skin prickling with an instinctual fear she could not name, could not reason away. She stepped forward, trying to steady herself, trying to ignore the creeping sensation that the air itself was watching her "It's fine" she whispered to herself, "It's just a blackout it's just the dark". Emily swallowed hard, resisting the urge to turn back, to run. She had the overwhelming sense that if she did, something would chase her, and she would not see it coming. That is when she saw it. At the far end of the hall, barely visible in the dim light, was a puppet. Sitting on the floor, legs sprawled unnaturally wide, its head tilted at an eerie angle. Emily's blood ran cold. Her mind screamed something was wrong. Wrong. As if to confirm her fear, she noticed the strings. They were not hanging limply from the puppets limbs the way they should have been. No. They were suspending, floating, twisted unnaturally in midair, twitching and jerking in tiny, stuttering movements, as if guided by invisible fingers. Emily's stomach lurched. Her eyes unblinking. It was not supposed to move. The lights flickered again. Once. Twice. And when they came back on, the puppet had shifted. It was standing. Standing. Staring at her with its soulless, glassy eyes. Emily staggered back, her entire body wobbling. It moved. She did not know how, or why, but she was sure of it. Her heart racing in her chest. An unrelenting pressure building in her lungs. "Chase!" She screamed, her voice cracking with fear. "Hugo!" Her voice cracked, sharp, high, a desperate plea, an attempt to break free from the suffocating dread that was gripping her. But there was no answer. No hurried footsteps. No comforting voice. No familiar presence rushing to her side. Only the eerie invisibility. Not the kind that comes from emptiness, but the wrong kind. The kind that listens. That waits. From the corner of her eyes, she thought the puppet twitched again. She turned toward the spiral staircase, desperate to get to them. But before she could reach the door, it slammed shut. Slammed, with a force that rattled her bones. The sound echoed through the hallway like a death knell. The door was locked, immovable, leaving her trapped in the growing darkness. She spun back around, her mind racing. The puppet was closer now, its wooden joints creaking as it slowly shifted towards her, its limbs jerking unnaturally. Her breath quickened, panic rising in her throat. She had to move, she had to run, but her legs felt like lead, frozen in place. "Go away!" She screamed, her voice shrill, panicked, recognizable as her own. It tore from her throat with a raw desperation. But instead of retreating, the puppet moved faster now. Its limbs snapping into place with unnerving precision, jerking in that sickly, unnatural rhythm like a marionette, controlled by something with no sense of humanity. Wood clacked and creaked. The sound impossibly loud. The lights flickered violently, strobing in and out of existence. For a split second, she saw its head tilted, its mouth opened just a crack too wide. Then, endless blackness. Swallowing everything in its path. Emily's heartbeat roared in her ears, a thundering pulse that drowned out everything else. She could not see, could not move, her body frozen in place by the suffocating blackness around her. The air felt thick, pressing against her, as if the darkness itself were alive, coiling tighter with every breath. Then SNAP. A sharp, unsettling sound cut through the silence, like wood cracking under immense pressure, echoing in the stillness. The sound seemed to come from all directions, echoing off the walls, filling the space with an eerie, unnatural tension. The lights flared back on. The puppet was standing right in front of her. It is cold, wooden fingers curled around her head, digging into her scalp. The sensation was chilling, wrong in a way her body recognized before her mind could catch up. It was not just a touch. It was not even pressure. It was something deeper. A slow, seeping invasion that felt like it was crawling beneath her skin. Emily could not move. Could not scream. Her body was rigid. Locked in place by an invisible force as the air turned ice cold. The puppet's face loomed closer, its hollow eyes empty and yet full of something…something evil. Before she could even draw her breath to scream, it dragged her down the hallway, at terrifying speed. Her feet scraping against the floor. Her hands clawing at the air. But it was no use. The force pulling her was too strong. The strings pulled tighter. Lifting her. Dragging her along like a ragdoll. The lights flickered again, plunging them into darkness once more. Emily's body twisted, her limbs stiff with fear as she fought against the invisible grip tightening around her. Every muscle burned with effort, but it was like pulling against a wall of ice. Unmovable and merciless. The lights flickered back on, and the hallway was eerily empty. No puppet. No Emily. Just an empty landing.

CHAPTER TWELVE
THE OBJECT

1800

Arabella remained motionless in her bedchamber, her eyes fixed on the mirror, though she did not seem to see her own reflection at all. She simply stared, as if searching for something just beyond the glass. "Lady?" Miss Fawns called gently, stepping into the room without waiting for permission. It was improper, but the day was too important, and time too short for formalities. "Forgive me my lady." She added, her voice softer now, "but... is everything heartily all right with oneself?" Miss Fawns stepped closer; her hands folded anxiously before her. "My lady." She implied gently, "all the guests have arrived. Sir and Lady Blackthorn await you... and your future husband Sir Edward, he too is ready for the ceremony to commence." Miss Fawns stood silently, waiting with quiet intensity for Arabella to speak, her presence gentle but steady. At last, Arabella lifted her head and met Miss Fawns's eyes through the mirror. Her voice was barely more than a whisper, trembling with emotion. "Miss Fawns." She discussed, tears welling in her eyes, "I want to be a good wife to Edward… but how can I, when his whole family seems to despise me?" Miss Fawns stepped forward, placing her strong, weathered hand upon Arabella's shoulder. A hand shaped by decades of hard work and loyalty. "My lady." She said softly, "Lady Blackthorn is… a difficult woman. Cruel at times. But I honestly believe that once she sees how deeply Sir Edward cares for you and how well suited you both are to run this manor, she will come to see your worth." She gave Arabella's shoulder a gentle squeeze, the touch meant to comfort, to steady. Her smile was warm, genuinely so, despite the bind that lingered beneath it like smoke in the corners of the room. "Now then." She said softly, brushing a stray curl from Arabella's face. "Let's fix you up and get you to your wedding." Her voice carried a sense of purpose, of care, as though those simple tasks could somehow keep the unease at bay, even if just for a little while. Arabella gave a small, grateful sniff, wiping the tears from beneath her eyes. She turned to face Miss Fawns and gave her a quiet nod. "Thank you." She whispered. Miss Fawns worked patiently, her fingers deftly weaving Arabella's hair into a delicate updo. Each pin, each twist, was placed with practiced care. The silence between them was comfortable, reverent, broken only by the soft rustle of fabric. Arabella sat immovably, adjusting the lace on her sleeves. Her movements were slow and deliberate, as though the power of the day pressed upon every joint. Her eyes lingered on the edge of her reflection in the mirror, never mainly meeting her own gaze, as if unsure of the woman staring back. Miss Fawns paused for a moment, fingers hovering in Arabella's hair. "Almost done my dear." She said gently, her voice low and motherly. "You are going to take his breath away." Arabella offered a small smile whilst miss Fawns moved to the vanity and opened one of the drawers, retrieving a small, elegant bottle of perfume. She uncorked it gently and dabbed the scent along Arabella's neck, her wrists, and the bodice of her gown. The fragrance of lavender bloomed in the air sharp, clean, and floral. It struck both women at once, like a sudden breeze on a hot summer's day. Arabella inhaled deeply, closing her eyes for just a moment. "There, my lady." Miss Fawns uttered softly, her voice tinged with affection. "You are ready." Downstairs, the guests waited in hushed foreboding, the air thick with curiosity and confusion. A few whispered among themselves, throwing out glances toward the grand staircase. "Why is the girl taking so long?" Sir Howard Blackthorn asked, his voice low but plied with impatience. Lady Catherine offered the faintest of smiles, her expression carefully composed. If all had gone to plan, there would be no bride descending those stairs. "Don't worry dear." She announced, placing a hand lightly on her husband's arm. "I sent Miss Fawns to see to her." She knew full well that Miss Fawns would return with devastating news of the tragic death of Arabella. Shock would ripple through the guests like thunder, and Lady Catherine would play her part: the heartbroken mother-in-law, left to comfort her grieving son. With Edward shattered and vulnerable, she would remain the true Lady of the Manor. And soon, she could guide him toward a more suitable match, a woman of her choosing. But just as she relished the cruel sweetness of her imagined victory, a flurry of footsteps echoed down from above. Miss Fawns appeared at the top of the staircase, breathless but poised. She descended halfway, then turned to face the gathering crowd. The entire room fell silent, all eyes on her. *This is it* Lady Catherine thought. Her gloved hands clenched on her lap in anticipation, her knuckles was white as snow.

'*This is the moment.*' Miss Fawns raised her chin and called out, her voice ringing clear through the hall: "I now present… Lady Arabella Nightshade." The smile vanished from Lady Catherine's face like a candle snuffed out by wind. Gasps swept the room like a sudden breeze through tall grass. And then Arabella appeared. She stepped into view, poised atop the landing, her hands resting lightly on the polished banister, delicate and composed. Slowly, she began her descent. Her gown shimmered like moonlight on still water, catching the light with her every movement, graceful and planned. The hall seemed to breathe in unison; all eyes fixed on her in awe, transfixed. Arabella was radiant. The most breathtaking woman many in attendance had ever seen. Sir Howard offered her a warm, approving nod. Edward's heart swelled, his eyes locked on hers, filled with fierce, invariable love. But Lady Catherine… her expression soured like spoiled wine. Her chest burned with rage, her jaw clenched as she looked around and saw only admiration in the eyes of her peers. '*No, this was not how it was meant to be.*' Her thought hitting her like sharp glass. Yet she could not betray herself, not here. She was Lady Catherine Blackthorn, respected throughout the village. She could not afford a crack in her mask. When Arabella reached the marble floor, her heels clicking softly against it, Lady Catherine rose with premeditated grace straightening her spine, lifted her chin, and offered her daughter-in-law-to-be a smile; cool, composed, and practised to perfection. A smile that never reached completion, but the way Lady Catherine performed it was flawless, and you would not know it was all a lie. Behind that smile was calculation. Pride. Disapproval.

Present day

"Ughhh, it's useless I can't see a thing up here." Chase muttered to herself, squinting into the shadows of the tower room. Hugo sat perched on an old box, legs crossed, elbow resting on his knee, and chin in hand. He looked thoroughly unimpressed, bored even, waiting for Chase to finally admit defeat. "You know, I'm pretty sure there's nothing up here." He formulated flatly. "And if there was something, it's definitely gone now." Chase let out a frustrated sigh and flicked her hair over her shoulder, her patience thinning. "I swear the last time I was up here, there was a black box." Her brows rising, a flicker of uncertainty sweeping over her face.

"I'm not losing it, I know I saw it." The room offered no answers. "Well, I haven't got it." Hugo replied, holding up his hands defensively. Chase rolled her eyes not because she suspected him, but because he was the only one there to talk to. Her gaze lingered on him for a moment, just long enough to wonder what he might be thinking before her mind wandered to Emily. Emily. "She's still downstairs." Chase said suddenly, the realization hitting her. "She's probably getting bored waiting for us." Chase took a quick look at the door "we shouldn't leave her alone for too long, in fact lets go now." "Finally." Hugo groaned, springing to his feet. "At one point, I seriously thought I was going blind. It is that dark up here." Chase laughed, shaking her head as she shuffled through the cluttered space toward the stairs. "Come on." She spoke. "Let's get back before she starts googling how to ditch us politely." Hugo chuckled. As they made their way down the spiral stairs, the steps creaked beneath their feet, the narrow passage twisting downward like the inside of a seashell. Chase moved quickly, her focus on trying get down without injury. But that would soon change as Chase bumped straight into the door at the bottom, with a dull thud. "That's weird." She said, frowning. "Why would Emily shut the door on us?" "Maybe it wasn't Emily." Hugo said with a grin, eyes glinting with mischief. "Maybe it was the ghost." Chase shot him a glare, her hand still on the door. "Shut up Hugo. Not funny." Chase pushed the door open, calling out as she stepped inside. "Sorry Emily…" She stopped short. "Emily?" Her voice faltered. Her face dropped. "EMILY!?" Chase called out, louder this time, bouncing off the walls. Panic was beginning to creep into her voice. No answer. Hugo stepped forward, he glanced around, his earlier grin fading into something more cautious. "Maybe she went to your room?" Hugo passed squeezing past her into the hallway. "Could not blame her. This place gives me the creeps." Hugo tried to keep his tone light, but even he looked over his shoulder as expecting something. The room was still. Too still. Not the peaceful kind but the kind that hums in your bones, which presses against your ears like the moment before a storm breaks. Chase hesitated on the inauguration, her breath finite as her eyes scanned the space. No sign of movement. No sound. Just that terrible, unnatural restfulness. they moved quickly to Chase's bedroom, but the second they stepped inside, they both felt it, something was wrong. There was no sign of Emily. Then Hugo noticed something barely a sliver of movement. A gap in the wooden panelling of Chase's old wardrobe. "Chase." He whispered, voice tight and barely more than a breath. He lifted a finger to his lips, signalling for silence, then slowly pointed toward the cupboard in the corner of the room. Chase's mouth closed as she followed his gaze, her heart skipping a beat. The cupboard's door was slightly ajar. Hugo stepped slowly toward it, tightening every muscle in the room. The air felt thick and wearing, almost suffocating. He reached for the handle. Silence. Then, in one swift motion, he pulled the door open. Both Hugo and Chase gasped loudly. Curled up on the floor inside the wardrobe was Emily. Her arms were wrapped tightly around her knees, face buried, shoulders quavery with silent sobs. Her hair was tangled and wild, strands sticking out in all directions like she had been caught in a gale. Her whole body quivered, as if she had been left out in a storm and had not yet come in from the cold. "Emily?" Chase's voice cracked as she rushed forward, dropping to her knees beside her friend. She reached out, gently placing a hand on Emily's back, her heart pounding. "Hey… it is me. You are okay now. You are safe." But Emily did not look up. She just kept shaking. "What happened?" Hugo asked, kneeling opposite her. Emily slowly lifted her head. Her face was blotchy and swollen; her cheeks streaked with dried tears. Her eyes, red, raw, and unfocused, blinked slowly as if struggling to process the light, or even the moment itself. Chase gasped. There were strange bruises scattered along Emily's arms, dark and uneven, like something had grabbed her too tightly. And worse, pressed into the skin of her forehead, were faint but unmistakable marks. Finger-shaped. As though something had gripped her there… and held on. For a terrifying heartbeat, Chase could not speak. "Who did this to you?" She finally whispered, though she was not sure she wanted the answer. "Where were you?" she choked out, her voice hoarse. "I screamed… I shouted for you, both of you and no one came. No one came!" Chase's blood ran cold. A sharp shiver snaked down her spine. She leaned in closer, her voice low and urgent. "Emily… were you attacked?" She paused, locking eyes with her friend. "Did you see her?" Emily stared at her. Wide, unblinking eyes filled with terror. For a long, suffocating moment, she said nothing. Then slowly, as if each movement took immense effort, she nodded. Once. Deliberate. Haunted. Chase's legs buckled slightly. She stumbled, barely catching herself, and collapsed onto the bed. "She's real." She whispered, barely able to speak. "Oh my god, she's real." "I think I want to go home now." Hugo said suddenly, helping Emily to her feet. "I'm taking her with me." He added firmly, already guiding Emily gently toward the door. "She needs to get out of this house, you understand that. Right?" Chase nodded numbly, arms hanging at her sides, her mind reeling from everything that had just happened. The room felt too big, too undecorated now. At the onset, Hugo paused and turned back to her, his expression unusually serious. "You need to tell your parents. Or… someone. Real help, Chase. I mean it." His gaze lingered on her, searching for any sign that she had truly heard him. And then he was gone, the door closing softly behind them, leaving Chase alone in the room. Alone with the power of the truth. Thirty-two minutes had passed since Hugo and Emily left, and Chase was still sitting in the exact same spot, perched on the edge of her bed, staring blankly at the floor. Her phone buzzed beside her. She picked it up and saw a missed call from Hugo, followed by two messages:

[phone}
HUGO:

Hey girl, I am so sorry for leaving you. I had to get Emily home; she was shaking the whole way Is everything okay? XX

A few minutes passed. Then another message buzzed through.

HUGO:

You are not picking up; I am getting worried now. Please message me back, even if it is just a thumbs up or something.

Chase stared at the screen for a moment, her fingers trembling slightly before she typed her reply:

CHASE:
I am fine Hugo. Just a bit shaken up. I am so sorry for tonight. I hope Emily's okay. See you tomorrow. xo

She set the phone back down on the mattress beside her and exhaled slowly. The hush in the room pressed in again, deep, hardhanded, and watching. Far from the suffocating restfulness of Blackthorn Manor.

Isabelle let out a soft sigh and leaned back in her seat, the gentle hum of the car lulling her into contentment. "I wonder how Chase and her friends are doing." She mused aloud, glancing over at Henry as they drove back through the winding countryside roads. Henry, relaxed behind the wheel, gave a small smile. They were both still glowing from their lovely evening out, a rare escape from routine. The six-course dinner had been exquisite: sautéed mushrooms, a creamy shellfish risotto, perfectly roasted chicken, delicate fish in lemon butter sauce, for desserts. A decadent chocolate cake followed by the smoothest cheesecake they both had tasted in years. They had even splurged on a bottle of red wine, letting the evening stretch and swell with laughter and warm conversation. Henry had only allowed himself one glass, followed by a pint of beer as he was driving after all. Isabelle, on the other hand, had happily polished off the rest of the bottle without a care in the world. She even indulged in a shot of tequila with a couple she had met at the bar, a detail she planned to keep incredibly clear. "They're teenagers." Henry said confidently, drumming his fingers on the steering wheel. "They're probably telling ghost stories under the covers with flashlights." Isabelle shot him a look; one eyebrow arched in amusement. "Hun, they are nearly eighteen. It is not the 'eighties anymore. Flashlights under blankets went out with cassette tapes and jelly shoes." Henry chuckled. "Fine. Maybe it is phones under blankets now. Same idea, just brighter screens and worse posture." "They're probably just texting each other from opposite sides of the room." She added dryly. Henry let out a laugh, and Isabelle joined in, both chuckling at the thought of Chase and her friends texting from across the room. As they pulled into the manor's long driveway, the car jolted suddenly with a thud, making them both jump. "What the...?" Henry muttered, frowning. "What was that?" Isabelle asked, sitting up straighter, startled. Henry slowed the car down and threw it into park. "Probably nothing." He said more out of habit than certainty, already unbuckling his seat belt. "Stay here." Henry whispered as he climbed out. Isabelle watched him step out into the night, he disappeared around the back of the car, his footsteps crunching faintly on gravel. "Got it." he called out a few seconds later. He returned holding something in his hands. "Well?" Isabelle asked, curious. "What did you hit?" Without a word, Henry climbed back into the car and held the object up so she could see. 'A *puppet?*' A small wooden puppet, limbs limp, with a jagged crack running down the centre of its head. They both stared at it in stunned silence for a beat then burst into laughter. "You've got to be kidding me." Isabelle said between giggles, pressing her hand on her chest as she tried to catch her breath. "What is this, some kind of weird joke?" Henry shook his head still laughing. "Who the hell just leaves this lying in the driveway?" he implied. "Looks like it came straight out of a horror movie." "Or a teen drama with too much budget and not enough plot." Isabelle snorted. They were still laughing as they got out of the car, stumbling toward the front door, stopping every few steps to catch their breath. Isabelle opened the door, and before she could step inside, Henry swept her into his arms in an exaggerated romantic gesture. "Allow me, m'lady." he said putting on a mock-formal tone. She let out a surprised, delighted squeal, "Henry! You are going to throw your back out!" "That's a risk I'm willing to take for love." He grinned, just before stepping inside. Isabelle casually tossed the puppet over henrys shoulder. The door slammed shut behind them with a bump from his hip. The puppet hit the ground with a dull thud, landing right beneath the motion sensor, which flicked the spotlight on with a loud click. The beam cast a needle like circle of light across the gravel driveway. There it lay. The puppet. Cracked. Still. But upon closer inspection there was something disturbing. Red stains. Faint, but unmistakable. Smudged across the puppet's fingertips.

CHAPTER THIRTEEN
"EMILY!"

Present day

The next couple of days after that night when she had been with Hugo and Emily, things had been strange for Chase. She had not experienced any more terror from the ghost woman, which she was, of course, relieved about. But surely it was not over. She had seen enough horror movies to know that ghosts did not just disappear, they lingered. They waited. It never ended well. Still, the mildness was... manageable. College was a different story. Emily had not returned since the night she was attacked. Chase messaged her regularly, but she was always left on read. She still saw Hugo around campus. They shared the occasional brief conversation about how Emily was doing, about classes but she could tell something had shifted. Deep down, she knew Hugo could not bring himself to really talk to her. Maybe he was scared., maybe he blamed her for dragging both him and Emily into the whole ghost hunt. Maybe she did too. Chase did not push. She could not. Instead, she clung to those small interactions, like they were proof that things had not completely unravelled. But Chase felt isolated. It was like she had been abandoned by three people all at once Hugo, Emily, and even the ghost woman. Was she really that hard to be around? So much so that even a spirit had had enough of her? That thought made her smile a little. She was getting upset... over a shadow. Chase was sitting in her final lesson of the day, and she felt a wave of relief. The weekend was just around the corner. One more day to go, and then she could finally escape people and just be alone. Or… maybe not. She had almost forgotten her mu was throwing that big charity event on Saturday. Chase had agreed to help weeks ago, back when everything still felt normal. Back before the whispers in the hallways, the flickering lights, and the nightmares that did not end when she woke up. Back when she was still… herself. Still social. Still able to breathe, without feeling like something was watching her. Now, the thought of putting on a smile and making small talk felt almost impossible. Still, it was the weekend. '*weekends*' were supposed to feel good. It was almost a tacit law. On the walk home, Chase was by herself, like always. It had been days since she had walked with Emily or Hugo.

Lately, she just kept to herself. No detours, no talking. Just the usual route, head down, earphones in, world off. It was easier that way. No need to pretend. No need to explain the dark circles under her eyes, or the way her shoulders stayed tense. But today felt... different. She had not been to Sip and Sit in a while, and for some reason, she was suddenly craving one of their vanilla lattes and a cinnamon roll. Maybe it was the cold. Or maybe she just wanted something warm and simple, something normal, something familiar. The kind of thing she used to take for granted before everything went sideways. So, with a shrug to herself, Chase took a detour toward the café. Maybe a hot drink would settle the nerves she could not thoroughly shake. She stuffed her hands into her coat pockets, the cold biting at her fingertips as she crossed the street. Back at the manor, things were anything but calm. Isabelle and Henry had been running around nonstop, buried in charity event preparations and last-minute touches. The guest list had doubled, the flower arrangements had arrived late, and there had been a minor crisis over tablecloths that did not match. It had cost them an arm and a leg, literally draining their savings for the month, but finally, somehow, everything was ready. The lights were up, the furniture polished, the invitations sent. Now all they could do was hope it would go off without a hitch. They had left a few minor rooms untouched as they did not need to use all the rooms for the event. There was no rush. But the important spaces, the ones guests would see, were finished and looked incredible. The kitchen was a beautiful blend of modern and vintage. The cupboards and cabinets were painted a deep navy blue, while the countertops kept their original warm wood finish, now polished to a soft sheen. The old floorboards had been replaced with matte white tiles in a diamond pattern, giving the space a crisp, clean feel. The overall palette, navy, black, white, and natural wood, was tied together by the presence of leafy green plants scattered throughout, adding life and freshness. The dining room had been modernized too. The massive 20-seater table, now waxed and gleaming beneath a sleek glass top, commanded the room. The chairs were painted half black, half mustard, a bold compromise between Henry and Isabelle, who could not agree on a single colour. A large black rug anchored the space, making the table and chairs stand out. In each corner, towering six-foot vases overflowed with wild, cascading greenery, spidery yet elegant, adding a dramatic flair. Above the table rafted a stunning light fixture that stretched its length, with teardrop bulbs suspended at varying heights, casting a soft, cheering glow. The table was already set, each place meticulously arranged like a five-star dining experience, poised to impress. The main living area was breathtaking. Three plush sofas were arranged in a U shape around the fireplace, creating a space both intimate and grand. The old, imposing mirror that once hung above the mantel had been replaced with a sleek 95-inch television. At the centre of the arrangement, three circular coffee tables of varying heights overlapped slightly in an artful cluster. Beneath the wide, three-way 10-foot window sat a long, curved chaise lounge with only one armrest, strange in shape but somehow striking in its beauty. Even the rooms that only got a light touch-up looked incredible. Whether reimagined or simply refreshed, the manor had transformed into something genuinely special. It finally felt like a place worth living in, not just a manor, but a home. To celebrate the weeks of challenging work (and all the stress that came with it), Henry and Isabelle treated themselves to a well-earned Indian curry and a bottle of red wine. The kind of wine that both knew could easily turn into three if they were not careful. "Can you believe it love? We did it." Henry vocalized, pulling Isabelle into a hug and planting a kiss on her lips. Isabelle stayed close, her arms still around him as she glanced around the room, smiling with pride and admiration. "All we need now is Chase." she mumbled Looking at the door half expecting Chase to walk in at any moment. "Where is she anyway?" Isabelle asked, a hint of concern threading through her voice. Henry just shrugged, reaching for his phone. "I'll give her a call." About five minutes later, Henry lowered the phone. "Well? Is she okay?" Isabelle asked, giving him a little poke. "She's fine." Henry spoke with a nod. "She just popped into the café with Hugo. She will be home in an hour or two." After hanging up on her dad, Chase sat in the café feeling a sudden wave of guilt washing over her. She had lied well, even though it was half-lie it still felt like a betrayal. She was at the café, but she was not with Hugo. She was alone. And she did not even know why she could not just say that. It was not like it was weird for her to be alone. She used to go to cafés by herself all the time. It had never bothered her before. If anything, she liked it. The solitude, the hidden buzz of other people's lives around her, the way she could disappear into a book or her thoughts with no expectations. She swallowed the last sip of her vanilla latte; the bottom always had the most flavour she thought. Just as she was about to bite into her cinnamon roll, her phone buzzed in her jacket pocket. She pulled it out, glanced at the screen, and immediately dropped the cinnamon roll onto the table. She answered the call as fast as she could. "Emily?"

CHAPTER FOURTEEN
THREE-TWO-ONE

1800

Miss Fawns and butler Brown stood side by side, each handing out '*broadsides*' single sheets of paper printed with the songs to be sung during the ceremony. Lady Catherine took a deliberate step forward but suddenly froze in place. Her posture stiffened, her back straightening as she lifted her chin just a fraction, nostrils flaring slightly, as if trying to catch a faint, elusive scent drifting in the air. Her features tightened, the change subtle but unmistakable, a shadow of unease flickering across her otherwise composed countenance. She turned her nose, narrowing her eyes. "I can smell lavender... is it sprayed on these papers?" Miss Fawns glanced at Lady Blackthorn and calmly replied, "No, ma'am. It must be lingering on me. It is the perfume I placed on Lady Arabella." Lady Catherine's lips curled into a smile, slow and easy. She did not notice the way Miss Fawns was watching her so closely.

"Very well." Lady Catherine said, nodding ever so slightly. With an air of practiced grace, she turned and moved smoothly toward her seat, every step thoughtful and poised. Miss Fawns continued handing out the remaining broadsides, but her eyes chased Lady Catherine just a moment longer. Something about that smile had been far too pleased, too knowing. It made the hairs on the back of her neck stand up. Still, Miss Fawns returned to her duties. The ceremony was about to begin.

Present day

"Emily!" Chase whispered urgently into the phone, her voice barely a hush. She could not afford to speak any louder, the murmurs and clinks of the coffee shop filled the air, and anyone nearby would surely overhear. To any outsider, her frantic tone would seem utterly strange, her word tangled with fear and urgency, impossible to fully understand. "Chase, I'm so sorry I've been ignoring your calls." Emily's voice came through, breathless and urgent. "But there is something important you need to know. Something I cannot keep to myself any longer is there any chance we could meet somewhere… isolated?" "Are you okay?"

Chase asked immediately, her worry threading through her words. "And of course, just tell me where you are. I am not from around here, so I do not really know many places." Emily did not answer the first question. Her voice dropped a little. "We can meet at the college library it closes at ten tonight, but I know the code to get in." She added, a faint spark of her usual self-flickering through her words. "It was one of the first systems I ever hacked when I started." Still, beneath the surface of her voice, there was a weight, a heaviness that learned there was something more she needed to say, and soon. They agreed to meet at half past ten. Chase would sneak out of the manor and get a lift from Hugo, who they called afterward to loop in. Once the call ended, Chase sat frozen at the café table, her mind racing. *What could Emily need to tell her that could not wait until morning? What had happened to her since that night to make this so urgent?* Chase's anxiety had spiralled beyond control. She needed to get home; she needed to slip back into the fragile mask of normalcy. To pretend everything was fine. To smile. To act like nothing had changed. But something in her gut told her tonight was going to change everything. Chase arrived home just as her father was taking out the rubbish. True to form, he was meticulous, carefully sorting recyclables from general waste, making sure every bottle, paper, and plastic ended up in the right bin. It was a stark contrast to her mother who tended to toss whatever was closest into whichever bin was nearest, ignoring Henry's precise system entirely. Chase knew better than to mix plastics with glass or toss general waste in the wrong bin. She still remembered the environmental course back in high school, how they drilled into her the importance of protecting the planet. She could not stand the thought of innocent animals or the earth suffering just because someone was too careless or lazy to separate a wine bottle from a plastic bag. "Hey Sweetheart! your mothers in the kitchen making food." Henry called out cheerfully as she walked up the driveway. "Don't worry, she's only reheating last night's leftovers." Henry added with an amused grin. "Hey Dad. Oh, thank God, you had me scared for a second." Chase replied, laughing as she caught up with him at the front door. Together, they stepped inside the manor, the warmth of the house wrapping around them, a moment of lown and comfort amid the aggravation that had been building all day. Chase hung her jacket up by the front door, as she did every evening out of habit, then made her way to the kitchen to greet her mum. "Chase, how was your day? Any news on your friends' families coming over for the charity event?" Isabelle asked while stirring the reheated leftovers in a large sharing bowl. Chase blinked at the salad bowl sitting in the centre of the table. *'Why not just serve everything on individual plates?'* The thought flickered briefly in her mind, but she did not have the energy to start a ten-minute debate about tableware. Some things just were not worth the effort right now. "I've asked them, but I haven't heard anything back yet." She replied. "I'll double-check for you later." With that, Isabelle took the bowl from the counter and placed it in the centre of the dining table in the hall. The family gathered around for tea, each of them scooping food from the bowl using large salad tongs because of course, which is what was closest at hand. The best part There was not a single leaf of salad anywhere. It was cottage pie, or at least, it had been. Now it looked more like a thick stew, the layers of potato, meat, and gravy all melted together from being reheated and stirred one too many times. No one questioned it. Not even Chase. At this point, it was just another normal night in a house that had slowly forgotten what normal even looked like. Everyone chipped in to clear the table and do the dishes. Once Chase had finished drying the last one, she politely declined to watch the movie her father had picked out either Godzilla or Dawn of the Dead, both of which she had seen countless times with him. She was sure she was not missing much. "Night Mum. Night Dad. I am turning in early, it has been a long day." Isabelle and Henry called goodnight back as Chase walked out of the living room. On her way upstairs, she quickly grabbed her jacket off the hook. In her room, she waited for Hugo to give the signal. He was supposed to throw something big enough onto the driveway to trigger the motion sensor lights. The spotlight would reflect off her wardrobe mirror, alerting her. It would not startle her parents since the front of the house was not visible from the living room. After what felt like days, Chase finally received the signal she had been waiting for. A sudden bright light flared in the corner of her wardrobe mirror, shimmering with an eerie glow as it caught the moonlight through the window. Startled, she leapt out of bed, moving silently down the creaking stairs. With cautious steps, she slipped through the front door into the wintry night air. She ran to Hugo's car and hopped into the front seat. "Hey." she said, her voice carrying a bit of awkwardness. "Girl, listen. I am sorry I have been such an ass. I do not actually have a problem with you, and I do not think Emily does either. We were just… both a little creeped out, that is all. But none of this is your fault. You came to us for help, we could have said no, but we did no." Hugo said, his voice softer now, trying to ease the tension hanging thick between them. "It is okay. It has just been hard not being able to come to either of you." Chase replied with a sad smile. "Right, let us head to the library. Emily's already there." She said, trying to shift the mood away from the awkward silence. Hugo shot her a smirk. "You could've done your hair, you know." He teased, adding a little banter to lighten the atmosphere. Chase giggled, and just like that, some of the weight between them lifted as they headed off toward the college. They finally arrived. The car park was empty, and the college loomed in the darkness, looking more like an abandoned hospital than a place of learning. "There's Emily." Hugo framed, nodding toward the front door, his eyes sharp with relief. He and Chase got out of the car and jogged over to her. "Hey Diva." Hugo grinned, pulling Emily into a quick hug. Chase stood back, watching her friend, someone she had not seen in what felt like forever. Emily looked a little thinner than usual, her eyes shadowed with fatigue, but otherwise, she was still the same old Emily. "Chase!" Emily shouted, wrapping her in a tight hug. "I've missed you." "I missed you too" Chase spoke, smiling. As always, Emily took charge. With a few quick taps and her fingers dancing expertly over the keypad, the door lights flashed green, signalling their entry. It worked, Chase thought. "Right, be careful they have security lasers." Emily said, trying to suppress a grin. Both Hugo and Chase looked at her, eyes wide. "I'm only messing." Emily chuckled, a playful sparkle returning to her eyes. "This place is so old, I'm honestly surprised it still has electricity." She turned and led the way toward the college library. They made their way inside, the familiar scent of aged paper and polished wood welcoming them. Settling into their usual corner, right where they used to gather during break times, they sprawled out on the worn, comfortable bean bags, the quiet hum of the library wrapping around them like a protective cloak. For a moment, it felt familiar... but the mood shifted fast. Chase felt it right away something was off. This was not just a casual reunion. Emily had something to say, and whatever it was, it felt urgent. "Emily... why are we here?" Chase asked, trying to keep her voice calm and not come off too pushy. "Chase, ever since that night... I...I have not been able to sleep. I...

could not eat either. I was a complete mess." Emily confessed, her eye's searching Chase is with a mix of fear and desperation. "I was having nightmares about what I saw at your manor. I had to do something, anything to get it out of my head. So, I started digging. I needed to distract myself, so I began researching the history of Blackthorn Manor, hoping to find something that would take my mind off everything." Chase frowned. "I tried that. I did not really find much." "Yes, but Chase… I am an I.T. expert. I can find things no one else can." Emily placed a steady, reassuring hand on Chase's knee, her voice calm but determined. Hugo sat unadornedly beside them, his eyes flickering nervously around the dim library, clearly unsettled by the fact they had broken into the college after hours. Emily pressed on, pulling a sheet of paper from her bag. "Look, I printed this off." She announced, holding it out to Chase. Chase grabbed the papers as fast as she could. She had to know what Emily had found. Her eyes raced over the pages that Emily had printed off:

(1945 - Local Girl of Eleven Years Vanishes from Blackthorn Estate; Search Continues)

**(1920 - Tragedy Strikes: Twin Boys Meet Grim
End in Blackthorn Manor's Tower)**

Chase's stomach twisted painfully as she read
on, hardly daring to believe the chilling stories
laid out before her.

**(1883 - Dreadful Discovery: Remains of
Housemaid Recovered from Blackthorn
Manor's Lake)**

She swallowed hard, her eyes widening when a
name caught her breath, one she knew all too
well:

**(1820 - Calamity at Blackthorn: The Ill-Fated
Wedding of Sir Edward Blackthorn and Lady
Arabella Nightshade)**

Chase froze in place, her breath catching in her
throat. She jabbed her finger at the page, eyes
wide as she looked frantically between Hugo
and Emily. "Look! Nightshade! that is the name
I made up for that teacher remember?" Her
voice trembled. "And now it is connected to the

house I am living in. That cannot be a coincidence. It just cannot." Hugo looked like he had seen a ghost. Even Emily after all her research had not noticed the connection until now. Chase continued to read, her eyes scanning the page until they landed on the most recent entry:

(1950 - Berty Walker, aged eighteen, the last remaining heir to Blackthorn Manor and Estate, has formally relinquished all claims to the property. The decision has sent a wave of dismay through the village, with locals expressing deep concern over the future of the historic estate.
Many are now left wondering who, if anyone - will step forward to preserve the legacy of Blackthorn and its sprawling ancestral grounds.)

"This is it! This is who we need to talk to." Chase promulgated, shoving the article toward Emily. "Yeah, and how exactly do you expect us to find someone who hasn't been seen in seventy-five years?" Emily shot back. "Not to mention he'd be, what, ninety-two? Ninety-three? He might not even be alive." "Emily if

anyone can track someone down, it's you!"
Hugo said, his voice more confident now,
finally feeling like he could contribute
something useful. "I'll try my best." Emily
passed with a small smile. "But I'm going to
need a coffee. And a snack. That always helps
me use my clever side." Chase laughed under
her breath, and she and Hugo headed off to find
some food and drinks, leaving Emily alone in
the library sleeves rolled up, eyes glued to the
computer digging deeper into the mystery of
where Berty Walker might be. On the way
back to the library with three coffees and three
Mars bars double packed a small victory. A
strange noise echoed behind them in the empty
hall. "Rats." Hugo muttered, scrunching his
nose in disgust. Chase slowed her pace, glancing
over her shoulder with a creeping sense of
doubt. Something about it did not sit right with
her. An outsize, crawling feeling crept up her
spine. "Wait here. I need the bathroom." Chase
said, shoving the chocolates into Hugo's hands.
Hugo stood awkwardly, feeling exposed and
vulnerable under the flickering, sickly lights.
He told himself it was normal for an old
building. Still, the uneasy silence pressed
against him like a weight. Chase sat on the
toilet, elbows resting on her knees, trying to
shake the nervous flutter in her stomach. The

lights flickered again. Once, then twice. She sat bolt upright, heart hammering. Meanwhile, back in the library, Emily scribbled in her notebook. The sudden flicker snapped her pencil in half with an edgy jolt. She gasped, clutching the broken piece. All three of them, scattered, isolated, and tense, were on high alert, unknowingly fuelling the presence of whatever unseen thing had stirred in the haziness around them. And then, without warning. The lights went out. Hugo dropped the coffees with a crash and bolted. Somewhere behind him, a laugh high-pitched and inhuman rushed past his ear, freezing him mid step, forcing him to rethink every direction he could run. Chase leapt from the toilet, her heart racing as she sprinted toward the door. In the cracked mirror beside her, she caught a flicker of movement, a shadowy figure darting just behind her. She did not dare look again, fear tightening its grip as she ran forward. She just ran faster, smashing straight into Hugo. "Hugo?!" "Chase?!" They grabbed onto each other instinctively, their grip tight with panic. For a heartbeat, they stayed frozen, clinging together on the floor. Then in unison, they scrambled upright, hearts pounding. The sound came next footsteps. Slow. Planned. Then faster. A biting, charging sprint that made the most awful cry through the darkness like a beast let loose. Hugo grabbed Chase's arm and yanked her forward without thinking. In the library, Emily backed toward the door, muttering, "No, no, no not again..." Her eyes squeezed shut, one hand trailing the wall, desperate to find the exit. A book fell from a shelf right in front of her with a thud. She flinched, nearly stumbling. Still, she kept moving, faster now, heart dropping. "Three." a voice whispered right behind her. Emily froze; every muscle locked tight. "Two." Panic surged, she bolted forward, but the door seemed to stretch farther away with every step. A cold breath, demanding and rancid, brushed her hair, curling around her ear like a serpent. Summoning every ounce of will, Emily forced her eyes open. Inches from her face were eyes! black empty, and soulless, above a gaping maw of rotten, jagged teeth twisted into a nightmarish grin. "One!" The thing screeched, its voice tearing through the silence like a scream from the depths of hell. The books around her exploded from the shelves, hurling through the air like missiles. Thick spines and flapping pages came at her from every direction. She ducked instinctively, arms raised, as one grazed her shoulder with a painful thud. Then the shelves themselves gave way. One by one, they toppled over in a deafening domino crash, the sound vibrating through the floor, thunderous and violent. Just before the final bookcase could come crashing down on her, a hand shot out and grabbed her arm, yanking her hard through the doorway. She stumbled, hitting the floor with a gasp as the towering shelf slammed to the ground behind her, splintering on impact. Everything blurred: running, screaming, falling until chilly air slammed against them. They stumbled into the car park, gasping, shivering, free. Behind them, the old college doors creaked shut with a long, groaning moan. Chase collapsed to her knees, struggling to catch her breath. Hugo leaned heavily against the wall, pale as if the very faintness were still clinging to him. Emily stood frozen; her eyes locked on the dark, looming building like it might suddenly lurch toward them. After a long moment, she finally spoke, her voice trembling but trying to sound upbeat. "Guys." Emily said, forcing a shaky laugh, "I know what just happened was… well, frankly terrifying. But I have some good news." Chase and Hugo looked up at her, wide-eyed. "I found him I found Berty Walker." Without thinking, Chase and Hugo ran to Emily, pulling her into a tight hug. "You did it!" Chase cried. "I knew you could." Hugo added breathlessly Emily smiled, her hands still shivery. "He's alive. He's living in a care home... only thirty miles from Blackthorn." They all agreed, tomorrow morning, they would make the trip. Just a short road trip, they told themselves. Thirty miles was not far. Not really. "And we'll be back just in time for your mum's charity event." Hugo said as he drove them home. But none of them noticed the shadow that lingered out of one of the college windows - watching.

CHAPTER FIFTEEN
TO LOVE AND TO CHERISH

1800

The ceremony was nothing short of splendid, almost otherworldly in its beauty. Down the aisle, delicate lily petals were strewn with care. Upon the back of each chair, white roses and sprigs of purple heather had been fastened with satin ribbon, the vivid violet striking boldly against the pale silk. Above them, lengths of fine white cloth fell from the rafters, billowing softly like restless spirits. The guests adorned in their finest silks and impeccably tailored coats, sat in hushed expectancy. Their faces glowing warmly in the golden light cast by the hanging lanterns. At the altar stood the bride and groom, hands entwined, their eyes locked with a tenderness so profound it felt as though the very room around them might ignite with the power of their love. At the very back, Miss Fawns pressed a gloved hand to her brow. A sudden wave of dizziness washed over her, and she fought the rising panic within. "Beg your pardon." She yauped hastily to Butler Brown her voice scarcely more than a breath. She fled the hall, head bowed low so as not to cause a scene. The butler frowned, glancing after her for a moment but soon turned his attention back to the glowing couple before him. Miss Fawns staggered through the dim corridors; her footsteps unsteady and vision blurring at the edges. Every step felt heavier than the last, her breath flat as if the air itself had thickened. At last, she reached the servants' quarters and collapsed onto one of the narrow beds, the thin mattress creaking beneath her weight. A young maid appeared in the doorway; her apron crooked from how quickly she had rushed in. She hesitated, eyes wide, uncertain whether to speak or run for help. "Miss Fawns you do look poorly." She said feeling sorry for the ill looking woman before her. "I am all well." Miss Fawns snapped, though her voice betrayed her with a faint tremble. She straightened herself with as much dignity as she could muster. "Should you not be attending the ceremony?" she added, her tone regaining some of its usual edge. The maid hesitated, but a glance at Miss Fawns' stern gaze sent her scurrying away. Alone at last, Miss Fawns carefully loosened the laces of her dress, her skin damp with fever sweat. The room seemed to tilt and sway, the sounds around her growing muffled and distant, as if she were sinking beneath a vast, dark sea. Butler Brown suddenly appeared beside her, his face drawn with worry and concern. "Shall I fetch the doctor, Miss Fawns?" "No." Miss Fawns managed, her voice no more than a whisper. "Pray, do not trouble him. I... I shall be well soon enough." She turned her face away, as though the shame of being seen in such a weakened state was unbearable. Despite her lone protests, Butler Brown slipped away, and moments later, the heavy door creaked open. A hushed voice drawled from the shadows, "She is here, Doctor." Miss Fawns turned her head feebly toward the doorway. A figure moved swiftly into the room; a tall man, his face obscured by the shadows. "Dear…dear." he said softly to himself. "What a state we find ourselves in." He knelt beside her, his touch cold as he pressed a hand to her forehead. Miss Fawns shuddered. "You appear to be poisoned." He announced after a brief examination. His voice was rigorous with grim certainty. "Poisoned?" she exhaled, her words sticking painfully in her dry throat. The doctor gently took her hand, lifting it into the fading light that filtered through the narrow window. Her once-delicate fingertips, normally so pale, were now mottled with deep bruises, an unsettling bloom of black and purple spreading beneath the skin like ink in water. A sharp, broken sob tore from her chest. "You must rest." The doctor said, forcing a tight smile. "I will leave you a tincture…but whether it will help remains uncertain." Miss Fawns wanted to ask how he had arrived so swiftly, who had summoned him, and why no one had respected her wish to be left alone. But before the words could form, darkness crept over her vision, and she slipped helplessly into its embrace. As the doctor gathered his case, he allowed himself a final glance down at her prone form. His lips curled into a thin, knowing smile, a smile without warmth, without pity. And then he was gone.

"I, Edward Blackthorn, take thee, Arabella Nightshade, to be my wedded wife; to have and to hold from this day forward, for better, for worse, for richer, for poorer, in sickness and in health, to love and to cherish, till death us do part, according to God's holy ordinance; and thereto I plight thee my troth."

Edward spoke clearly; his voice steady as he gazed deep into Arabella's eyes. He slipped the delicate wedding band onto her slender finger with hands that trembled ever so slightly, the weight of the moment pressing heavily upon him. Around them, the guests smiled warmly, their faces glowing with genuine joy and hope for the couple's future. The air was thick with whispered congratulations and the soft rustle of silk and lace. But Lady Catherine remained untouched by the tender words and soft glances exchanged between bride and groom. She sat perfectly still, her face a mask of cold reserve, every muscle tightened with quietude disapproval. In the depths of her heart, she was certain, Arabella was unworthy of Edward, and no amount of ceremony could change that bitter truth. Now it was Arabella's turn.

"I, Arabella Nightshade, take thee, Edward Blackthorn, to be my wedded..."
She faltered; her words unable to come out. A sudden hush fell over the room, the murmuring guests turning to whisper behind gloved hands. Edward gave her a small, gentle nudge, his voice soft and filled with concern. "Everything all right, my love?" He whispered, his eyes searching hers for reassurance. But when Arabella slowly turned to face him, a sudden chill gripped Edward's heart. A thin rivulet of blood slipped from her nose, stark against her pale skin. Arabella's eyes, once bright and alive,

were now distant, unfocused as if she were staring through him, beyond him, into some dreadful place unseen by mortal eyes. With a soft, startled gasp, Arabella collapsed. Edward's arms shot out instinctively, catching her before she could fall hard against the cold stone floor. He cradled her unsteady form with desperate, shaking hands. "Arabella!" he cried out, his voice breaking with panic and raw fear. A single tear slipped from Arabella's wide, frozen eyes. Then the coughing began harsh, racking and with it came a terrible flood of dark blood, staining her dress a sickly reddish-brown. "Somebody fetch the doctor!" Edward shouted, his voice hoarse with panic, echoing through the great hall as he stumbled forward. Sir Howard, rushed to his side, trying to support him. But Edward hardly noticed, his gaze was fixed in horror upon the woman he loved, whose life was spilling out before him. From across the hall, Lady Catherine slowly rose, lifting a delicate lace handkerchief to her eyes as though to dab away tears. Yet, no real moisture stained her carefully painted cheeks. Inside, a cold, satisfied smile played at the corners of her lips. With calculated grace, she made her way toward Edward. "Dear child." She squawked, "you must come away. The doctor will require space to work." Edward hesitated, torn between duty and despair. Finally, with great reluctance, he allowed himself to be led away, his eyes never leaving Arabella's still form as the guests watched in frozen terror. Lady Catherine, Edward, Sir Howard, and a handful of close friends and relatives were gathered in the drawing room. Some paced anxiously in restless circles, while others sat rigidly, heads bowed in quiet prayer or ultraheavy silence, weighed down by dread. Edward sat apart from them all, wringing his hands nervously. His body was tense, restless, but his lips remained tightly sealed. A thousand terrible thoughts raced through his mind, *'what had happened? How could this have happened? Why Arabella?'* The haunting image of her still, pale form, lying broken in a pool of blood, seared itself behind his eyelids with every blink. He felt as if he might go mad from helplessness. "I must go to her." Edward said suddenly, his voice thick with anguish and desperation. His eyes, filled with raw pain, locked onto those around him, pleading silently for understanding. "Son, no." Sir Howard said firmly, stepping into his path and placing a steadying hand on his shoulder. "You'll do no good in there. Let the doctor work, he mustn't be distracted." Edward shook his head, tremulous, but Sir Howard's heavy hand on his shoulder anchored him to the room. Across the way, a friend of Lady Catherine's leaned close to whisper, "Oh, I do hope she pulls through." She worried, eyes flitting nervously towards the closed doors. Lady Catherine, dabbing again at her delicately dry eyes with a handkerchief, the picture of composed sorrow replied, "Yes... only God can protect her now." She replied smoothly, her tone enlaced with just the right amount of solemnity. She took a slow sip of wine, the rim of the glass briefly obscuring the thin, satisfied smile tugging at the corners of her mouth. Seeing her dear boy in such obvious distress did cause her a twinge of regret but it would pass. Edward was still young. He would recover. He would choose...better. And Arabella Nightshade whether by fate or by careful arrangement would soon be nothing but a sad memory. The drawing room remained silent, the surroundings filled with dread, every unspoken thought hanging between them heavier by the second. Even the ticking of the longcase clock seemed hesitant, each second stretched unbearably long. Suddenly, the door creaked open. The eyes turned as the butler stepped inside, he bowed stiffly, hands clasped tightly before him. "Miss Nightshade has been placed in her bed. The doctor requests only Sir Edward, Lady Catherine, and Sir Howard to join him." Edward did not wait. Brushing past butler Brown, he ran from the room, his heart pounding so loud it drowned out all else. Lady Catherine and Sir Howard followed at a brisk walk, their faces masks of grim composure. Edward flung open Arabella's door and froze. There she lay, pale as winter frost, her skin almost translucent in the dim light. Yet even now, especially now, she was achingly beautiful. Her dark lashes shining across her face, her lips slightly parted as if caught mid-whisper. Edward dropped to his knees beside her, the world narrowing too only this, only her. He seized her cold hand in both of his, cradling it as though he could will warmth back into her fingers with the sheer force of his love. "Arabella, please..." His voice cracked. "Please don't leave me. Please come back. It is your Edward." He whispered, tears spilled freely down his cheeks. The doctor stood nearby, silent, allowing Edward this moment of desperate devotion. Lady Catherine and Sir Howard entered the room moments later, their footsteps muffled by the thick carpet, their expressions grave as they took in the scene. "Doctor?" Sir Howard said gruffly. "What is her condition?" The doctor exhaled slowly, his face hardened and unreadable, like it had been carved from cold stone. "She suffers from a deep swoon, likely induced by poison." He uttered gravely, his words slicing through the room like a blade. "Poison?" Edward repeated, staring at him in horror. "Who would do such a thing?" "I cannot say for certain." The doctor continued in a low, grave tone, each word spartan with dread. "But the discoloration of her blood... and the darkening around her throat... strongly suggest a toxin has poisoned her veins." The doctor's voice was low, clinical. He spoke not to comfort, but to inform, to prepare. His words were precise, heavy with finality. "There is little more I can do. If she wakes… it will be a miracle. If not…" He left the rest unsaid. With his report concluded, the doctor adjusted his coat, placed his hat solemnly upon his head, and gave a stiff nod before stepping serenely out of the room, his footsteps vanishing down the corridor like the last hope slipping away. A hush settled. "Let us give Edward his space." Lady Catherine spoke, placing a gentle hand on Sir Howard's arm, her voice sounding something between propriety and mute satisfaction. And so, Edward and Arabella were left alone. The once bright room had gradually dimmed as the sun set, shadows stretching and slithering across the walls like silent, watchful witnesses. This was not the way their first night together was meant to unfold. Darkness and fear had stolen the joy that should have filled the space. Edward bowed his head over her still hand, feeling the rotundity of the universe press down upon him, and whispered promises only the dead might hear.

CHAPTER SIXTEEN
FLASH BACK

Present day

It was the morning of Isabelle's charity event; everything had been planned down to the last detail. The interior design, the layout, the timings... Isabelle had orchestrated it all with meticulous care. At five AM, she dragged herself out of bed, still dressed in the same clothes she had worn the night before. Exhaustion had overtaken her after hours of completing last-minute preparations, leaving her no energy to even change. She had collapsed onto the mattress without ceremony, sleep swallowing her whole the moment she hit the bed. Yawning, she shuffled to the bathroom, her body still tough with sleep. She turned on the shower, letting the water run until steam curled against the mirror and warmth filled the air. As she began to peel off her clothes, her earrings clinked softly in the sink, tiny sounds in the lonesome morning. With a tired swipe, she smeared away the remnants of yesterday's makeup, the dark smudges a reminder of how hard she had pushed herself. Leaning closer to the mirror, Isabelle studied her reflection, frowning at the dark circles under her eyes. How am I going to make myself look human today? she thought. She opened the mirrored cabinet and grabbed her daily vitamins; Omega-3, Turmeric, Mint oil tablets, and Sea Moss. Isabelle loved trying new supplements, anything that promised to make her feel better, younger, different. She threw them all back in one go the pills clicking against her teeth, then closed the cabinet door and faced her reflection once more. Her eyes were shadowed, her skin dull with exhaustion. With a weary sigh, she stripped off the last of her clothes. Her bra clung damply to her skin, twisted and uncomfortable. She winced as she peeled it away, silently vowing never to fall asleep in one again. She stepped into the shower and let the scalding water pour over her, embracing the heat as it coursed down her body, washing away the grime, the load, and, just for a moment, the cachet of everything else. If she did not come out looking like a cooked lobster, it was not hot enough. She lathered her hair with coconut oil shampoo, working it through the strands until the scent filled the steamy air. Then came the conditioner, silky and soothing, followed by a generous scrub of coconut butter across her skin. As the warm water rinsed it all away, she finally began to feel human again, clean, grounded, and just a little more like herself. As she turned toward the glass door to step outside, something caught her eye. A shape. Faint. Human. It hovered just beyond the pane, barely visible in the grey wash of early morning light, like a smudge on reality. Easy to miss, impossible to ignore. Isabelle felt like someone had walked over her grave, she froze. Then She blinked hard, wiping the steam from her face with her wet shaking fingers. She looked again, but the shape was gone. A shaky laugh slipped from her lips. *'Maybe it was nothing. Just a trick of light. Get a grip, Isabelle.'* Isabelle thought. She grabbed three towels, one for her hair, one for her top half, and one for her bottom, and moved into her dressing room. In the freestanding mirror, she caught a glimpse of herself drying off. Her hand absently brushed the long, thin, purple scar that cut across her tummy. The sight of it sent a sharp ache deep inside her. No matter how much time had passed, that scar still throbbed in ways no one else could see. She stared at her reflection, momentarily lost, as the room around her seemed to pulse with a quiet, lingering memory…

In Isabelle's mind, the years melted away.
Twenty years ago, she and Henry had just
moved into his tiny apartment. She was
pregnant, and they were blissfully happy, giddy
with dreams of the future. That afternoon, they
were on their way to find out the baby's
gender. On the drive, they stopped at a nearby
café to satisfy Isabelle's latest craving: walnut
and cheese twirls; the hot, flaky kind that
melted on the tongue and left a buttery sheen
on her fingers. She tore into them eagerly in the
car, crumbs tumbling down her coat and
peppering Henry's seats. He said nothing, just
smiled as he watched her, amused and solitary
in love. *'Today is a good day, he thought.
Nothing can ruin this.'* Later, after the scan,
they sat together in the parked car, glowing
with joy. The image of their baby; tiny, perfect,
real, still lingered in their minds. Isabelle
clutched the ultrasound photo to her chest, her
eyes glassy with happy tears, while Henry
reached over to squeeze her hand, his heart full
and wordless. "I can't believe we're having a
baby girl." Isabelle whispered, squeezing
Henry's hand. Henry could not even speak. His
heart felt like it might burst; he was going to
have a little girl. But words were not necessary.
Isabelle already knew, their eyes meeting in

perfect understanding. "I think we need to celebrate." She beamed. "I'll call my mum, maybe they'll come over for tea." Henry smiled, warmth in his eyes. "Call your parents too." He stated gently. "We can tell them together." Isabelle's face faltered. Her parents had not forgiven her for walking away from law, a betrayal they pinned squarely on Henry. She smirked. "My mother and father? In the same room as you? Yes, that will be the day." "Just call them." Henry said, laughing. Then... Isabelle's smile crumbled. Her eyes widened, filling with sudden horror. She grabbed on to the car seat tightly, then screamed... "WATCH OUT!" Henry jerked the steering wheel, but it was too late. The world exploded around them. The tires shrieked against the road, a desperate, high-pitched scream that tore through the air. The car lurched, then spun violently, out of control. Metal groaned and twisted. Glass exploded into a spray of glittering, deadly shards. For a split second, the world became noise, chaos, and light. Everything tilted, a sickening roll, and then they were airborne, weightless for one impossible second. Isabelle's body was ripped from her seat, thrown sideways through the shattered window. The night swallowed her whole. She hit the road with bone-cracking force, a brutal slam of flesh against unyielding concrete that winded her. Her body tumbled and rolled, scraping raw against the cold asphalt, finally skidding to a violent halt almost ten feet away from the twisted wreckage. Inside the mangled car, Henry dangled upside down, his seatbelt the only thing preventing him from crashing into the warped dashboard. His face was pale, streaked with sweat that was dripping into his deep cuts, his eyes looking out the window at the upside-down world with shock and pain as he struggled to steady his hands. Blood gushed from his forehead, splashing across the sagging airbag. The smell of smoke and burning rubber filled his lungs. The world spun. The world screamed. And then, nothing. Hours later, Isabelle's eyes fluttered open. Her vision was a blur of colour and light, and everything around her seemed underwater, muffled, warped. A tall, dark figure loomed over her, blurred at first, like a shadow pulled from a nightmare. As her vision slowly adjusted, the shape sharpened. It was Henry, his face streaked with tears; a blood-stained bandage wrapped haphazardly around his head. Relief and anguish warred in his eyes as he looked down at her. Through the haze of her hearing, she made out a sound, her name, but it came out warped and strange, like "Ishbelsh." Henry. It was Henry. Isabelle blinked, her vision swirling as she looked down at herself. She was lying in a hospital bed, her foot stiff inside a white cast. Her arms were bruised and marked with puncture wounds, IVs snaking in, cuts healing beneath pale skin. The sterile smell of the room pressed in around her, grounding her to this harsh reality. Pain throbbed through her body, but not from her injuries. It was her tummy. A deep, raw ache settled within her, A wrongness that seemed to seep into her bones. She shifted slightly and the unmistakable wetness between her legs sent unwelcome fear all over her. She did not need anyone to tell her what it meant. Silent tears slipped from the corners of her eyes, running down her cheeks. Henry's voice cracked through his sobs. "Darling, I'm so sorry. I am so sorry." He wept, the words falling out he grabbed her hand as carefully as if she might break apart. His tears fell, tracing thin lines through the blood and grime on his face. "Please forgive me..." His voice broke completely. Isabelle looked up at him with shining eyes, filled with a deep, aching sympathy. She lifted her battered hand as much as she could and placed it gently on his, forcing a small, broken smile through her tears. Moments later, a nurse and a doctor entered the room, their faces portraying guilt and sympathy. The doctor spoke softly, but the words hit like gunfire. Shattering whatever hope Isabelle had left within her. "I'm sorry to inform you both... when Miss Willow arrived at the hospital, we had to take her straight to the emergency surgery. Where we were left with no choice but to perform an emergency C-section." The doctor paused, his voice intensive with sorrow. "There was no heartbeat. The baby was... deceased. The injuries sustained in the collision were too severe." The world seemed to stop. A raw, animal sound tore from Henry's throat, half scream, half sob. Isabelle cried out too, clutching at her tummy, her heart shattering into pieces that would never fit back together again. Grief flooded the room, drowning them both. And nothing, not even time, would ever wash it away.

Back in the dressing room, years later, Isabelle blinked at her reflection. Her eyes were wet with fresh tears. The past rushing back in sharp, unforgiving waves. The memory of that awful day, the crash, the loss, still burned behind her eyes. She realized, with a pronged pang, that this was the first time she had ever allowed herself to remember it all, in such vivid, painful detail. For a long moment, she simply stood there, swallowed by the thought of those memories. Then, with a small, almost imperceptible shake of her head, she forced herself back into the present, steadying her breath, reclaiming control. She picked up the towel again, slowly continuing to dry her body, forcing herself to keep trying to focus on the day ahead, the event she had planned for weeks, the small anchor she could almost reach to help her keep her feet on the ground. Choosing an outfit was the easy part, she had already bought one specifically for today's event. Something elegant but comfortable. Now, all that remained was the small yet daunting task deciding which shoes matched best and what hairstyle would pull the whole look together. it seemed such a simple task, part of preparing for any event. But with her emotions so close to unravelling, even these small decisions felt strangely impossibly hard. One step at a time, she reminded herself, a mantra to steady her frantic resolve. One foot in front of the other.

CHAPTER SEVENTEEN
"YOUR NEXT"

Present day

Chase, Hugo, and Emily were on their way to the care home, hoping to speak with the former owner of Blackthorn Manor. Chase glanced over, lowering the music "I wonder if he's even going to remember anything useful." Chase announced sounding a bit sceptical. No one spoke in that second, all that was heard was the engine of the car. Hugo just shrugged. "It's worth a try." Emily chimed in, her voice loud with optimism. As they approached the tall, rusted iron gates that guarded the entrance to the care home, Hugo rolled down his window. He pressed the call button mounted on the weathered brick wall. A crackle came through the speaker. "Hello, Bluebird's Care for Life, Kelly Westworth speaking. How can I help?" Hugo gave Emily a gentle nudge to catch her attention. She leaned forward from the middle seat, bringing her self-closer to the speaker. "Hi, yes, we're here to visit Berty Walker." She called out clearly. There was a short pause.

"May I ask who's calling?" Kelly asked politely through the intercom. Thinking quickly on her feet, Emily smiled politely and replied. "We are college students working on a history project about Blackthorn Village. We were hoping to interview Mr. Walker for some firsthand stories." Emily added. Another long pause stretched out after her words. the three friends exchanged uneasy looks, whispering nervously while they waited anxiously for a response. Then click, the demanding gates groaned and began to creak open. Emily dropped back into her seat with a relieved breath as Hugo slowly guided the car forward, careful not to hit the still-widening gates. The care home loomed ahead, "Right, let's do this!" Emily said brightly, bouncing a little with excitement. Chase smiled to herself, admiring how fearless Emily seemed, especially after everything she had been through. Behind them, Hugo muttered something mousy under his breath as he locked the car door. "Vous allez tous me tuer." He grumbled with a tired sigh; you are all going to be the death of me. Chase narrowed her eyes suspiciously and turned back. Towards him. "What did you just say?" She called over. Hugo finished locking the car and straightened up, flashing a wide, innocent grin. "I said hold on!" It was clear he was not going to start arguing, especially not in front of a care home. Not here. Not today. The three of them headed toward the entrance. Chase pulled open the door, and they were at once hit by a strong smell, a mix of pungent cleaning products and, as some might say, the unmistakable scent of old people. At the reception desk, Chase was already talking to a tiny woman with thick glasses, curly white hair, and a flower-printed blouse. "Sorry girl, I don't know what you're talking about." The woman said brightly, her voice strong but confused. Emily was just about to step inside when another woman appeared beside them. She wore a crisp white uniform, perfectly pressed, and a name tag that read Kelly _'Westworth–Senior Carer.'_ Her expression was balmy but alert, as if she were used to unexpected visitors and knew exactly how to handle them. Kelly swooped in smoothly. "Agnes, it's almost time for tea and biscuits. Why don't you come with me?" she said kindly, taking the woman's arm. Hugo gave a small cough, trying, and failing, to hide a laugh bubbling up. Emily caught it too and grinned, nudging him playfully. But Chase was not having it. She spun around sharply, eyes blazing, and shot them both a glare so serious it could have stopped time. "How was I supposed to know she was a resident?" Chase hissed, clearly embarrassed. Emily could not resist; she shot back Chase's words with a teasing grin, perfectly mimicking the tone: "Sorry girl, I don't know what you're talking about!" Hugo let out a full belly laugh, nearly doubling over. Chase rolled her eyes dramatically and watched as Kelly gently led Agnes down a hallway and out of sight. A few seconds later, Kelly returned, with her warm smile. "Sorry about that. Agnes has been one of our longest residents." She said kindly. She likes to believe she works here, so we let her help with little 'jobs'. Keeps her spirits up." Kelly explained. The group nodded, a little sheepishly. "Now." Kelly continued, "You're here to see Mr. Walker, right? You're in luck, he's up in his room." She waved a hand for them to follow. Trailing quietly behind Kelly, they took in the care home's calm surroundings. The walls were painted a gentle cream, softening the harshness of the fluorescent lights above. Along the corridors, framed art prints added splashes of colour, landscapes, abstract designs, and gentle scenes that seemed chosen to soothe and comfort. They passed by a sitting area, or perhaps a games room, its decor striking in its simplicity: sleek white walls and furniture contrasted with plush cushions in deep black and royal purple. The chairs were arranged in small, inviting clusters, perfect for intimate conversation or mousy moments of rest. The whole space felt calm and cared-for, yet carried a faint, bittersweet sense of time slowly passing. It was beautiful, Warm, and welcoming. "Berty, you have visitors." Kelly voiced softly, stepping into the room. She handed Emily a small device with a button on it, marked Room 49. "If you need anything, just press this." Kelly said, handing them a small, worn call button. "It'll alert the nurses immediately." With a reassuring nod, she turned and walked away, leaving the three friends standing still in the hallway. They exchanged a nervous glance, the silent, unspoken question hanging between them: *'Who is going first?* Chase swallowed and stepped forward. "Hi Berty. I am Chase." She said gently. The old man remained seated; his gaze fixed blankly on the flickering television screen. It was impossible to tell whether he was deliberately ignoring them or simply unaware of their presence. Chase took a deep breath and tried once more; her voice steady but carrying an edge of urgency. "I'm living in your old home — Blackthorn Manor." At the sound of those words, Berty's head turned sharply. His gaze locked onto Chase's with unsettling intensity, making her shift uncomfortably on her feet. "I... I have been experiencing some strange things in the house." Chase said softly, lowering herself to meet Mr. Walkers gaze. Her voice dropped to a near whisper, as if sharing a secret. "There is a woman who appears to me, sometimes just a glimpse, sometimes more. I know it probably sounds crazy, but... judging by the way you are looking at me right now, I have this feeling you know exactly what I mean." Berty's eyes narrowed, confusion flashing across his face. "You've seen her?" he rasped. Chase nodded. "That's not possible..." Berty muttered, his eyes narrowing. "She appears only to those who share the blood... the blood of..." He stopped abruptly, still staring at Chase as she were the only soul in the room, ignoring Hugo and Emily standing just behind. "Blood of what?" Chase urged. "Please, I need to know." Berty leaned closer. His voice dropped into an effortless tone that for some might fined uncomfortable. "The blood of her enemy." He spoke. "The Blackthorns." The air seemed to thicken. "But I'm not even a Blackthorn." Chase protested, her voice changing with a sudden surge of panic. "This is not something only I am seeing, she has shown herself to my friends as well. We are not imagining this." Berty nodded once, slowly, his eyes embedded in Chases giving off a look of a man who is living in hell.

"Yes... but only when you're near." Chase's heart raced. "You need to leave, right now!" Berty suddenly shouted, his voice rising and cracking with raw terror. "I'm not safe with you here! Please…just go…LEAVE!" Chase tried to calm him down, speaking in soothing tones, but it was no use. Berty's body stiffened, and then, chillingly, his eyes rolled back, turning a sickly grey. When he spoke again, it was not in his own voice: "You're next." The words slithered through the room like dark poison, freezing Chase in place. Suddenly, Emilys panic took over. Without hesitation, slammed the emergency button. Sending an alarm off to make the nurses aware that the room needs assistance. With in moments, Kelly burst into the room, her face tightening and changed colour seconds after seeing the horror when she saw Berty lying there still. "Hold it down!" Kelly shouted, commanded firmly. Taking Emily's hand to guide it. The alarm changed, a shrill noise filling the halls. Nurses in grey uniforms rushed in. Before they were shoved out of the room, Chase caught a glimpse of Berty's body. Stiff. Lifeless. His face frozen in a look of pure fear. A young nurse appeared almost instantly, her expression peaceful and collective as she motioned them to follow. Without a word, she led them down a quite hallway and into a small waiting room tucked away at the end. The door clicked shut behind them. The room was white, very white, with about six chairs, three each side of the room with one water fountain in the corner, and a few magazines. An old clock ticked on the wall, sounding louder than it should have done. No one spoke. There was nothing to say yet. Chase just stared blankly at the wall. Hugo fiddled anxiously with the tassels on his jeans. Emily's eyes darted between the clock and the floor. Twenty long minutes passed. Finally, the door creaked open, the sound startling the group. It was Kelly. She stepped in slowly, her eyes flicked over to all three of them; Chase, Emily, and Hugo as they all rose to their feet ready to hear the news, "How is he?" Chase asked, hoping to hear some good news, but knowing deep down that was not going to be the case. Kelly stared at them, her face drawn and pale. "I'm so sorry." She declared softly. "Berty suffered a heart attack. He…he…he has passed away. I am sorry you kids had to witness this. Please, let me call someone to come and collect you." "No, it's okay." Hugo said quickly, surprising even himself. "We'll manage. Thank you." Chase said, steadying her voice even though her insides was ready to burst out. Kelly gave a small nod, stepped aside as she held the door open for them. As they walked toward the exit, Chase glanced up at the reception desk. They are sat Agnes. She was not watching the television, nor staring into space like some other residents. No, her eyes were fixed directly on Chase, bovine and steady, like she had been expecting her all along. A strange knowing smile appeared on her mouth creepily wide; it was not friendly. It was not unkind, either. It was something else entirely, it was like she seemed to say, "I know what's coming." Chase looked away as fast as she could, she did not want to prolong the sight of the smile, she wanted to just leave, get out of the building, never to return.

The car journey home felt endless. All three friends were buzzing with shock, trying to piece together what had just happened. "Heart attack?" Emily scoffed, breaking the ponderous silence. "That wasn't a heart attack." Chase kept her gaze locked on the blur of trees and houses flashing past the window, but her mind was far from the passing scenery. Inside her head her thoughts spinning as fast as the world outside. "He told me." Chase muttered, her voice low. "Only Blackthorn blood would grant her appearance, the woman of revenge. But... I am not a Blackthorn. It doesn't make any sense."

Hugo cleared his throat "I'm sure there's some explanation." He said, his tone was hopeful, maybe even a little desperate, as if saying it aloud might somehow make the strange events less real. "Hugo!" Chase snapped; her face still turned away from them. "A man just died, right in front of us, and not from age, or sickness." She paused as she looked up into the sky. "But from fear. Sheer, consuming fear. I've never seen anything like that before." She swallowed hard, the metallic taste of panic thick in her mouth. Her next words came out, sad, scared. "He was murdered... by whatever's out there. And it's after me." Those words sounding more powerfully dangerous as they came out. Hugo gripped the steering wheel tight, swallowing some sticky saliva, which was stuck in his throat. Emily looked down at her hands, unable to look at Chase. All that Chase could see was the memory of Berty's grey, lifeless eyes and those chilling words. "You're next." Echoed inside her skull. *How was she supposed to pull off the charity event now? How could she possibly keep up the facade of normalcy when everything around her was crumbling, falling apart piece by piece?* Chase pressed her forehead against the cool, smooth glass of the car window, hoping the chill would soothe the wild tempest raging inside her chest. But no matter how hard she tried to steady her breathing, the raw, painful truth clawed mercilessly from within. Relentless. Unstoppable. and impossible to ignore.

CHAPTER EIGHTEEN
THE PLOTTING CONTINUES

1800

It had been three days since the tragedy at Blackthorn Manor, the day that should have been a celebration of Edward and Arabella's wedding. The manor was drowning in an endless sea of flowers and sympathy cards, well-wishers sending their prayers for Arabella's recovery, though her condition remained unchanged. Still lost in a deep, unmoving darkness, Arabella lay silent in her bed, her breathing shallow and barely perceptible, so still she might have been mistaken for one who had passed beyond the veil of life itself. Miss fawns on the other hand was fully recovered but she could not help but think *'why me and not Arabella.' Sir* Edward was no longer the man he once was. Gone was the thoughtful, soft-spoken gentleman the household had known. In his place stood someone darker, his temper quick to ignite, his moods shifting like storms across the moors. The maids and footmen had learned to tread carefully, their once-cheerful chatter replaced with hushed whispers and nervous glances. They spoke only when addressed, moved silently through corridors, and flinched at the sound of raised voices. Only two dared to approach him without hesitation: Miss Fawns, the housekeeper whose dull strength had been a constant presence in his life, and Butler Brown, stoic and steady, who had once taught young Edward how to tie his cravat. They had practically raised him, filling the hole left by distant parents and the cold discipline of aristocratic expectations. Their connection with him ran deeper than duty, it was rooted in love, in shared memories, and in the sorrow of watching someone they cared for unravel. "Sir, would you like a tea?" Butler Brown asked carefully, stepping into the drawing room. The room was dim and grinding with the scent of the endless flowers, lilics, roses, lavender. Edward found a small comfort. It allowed him to hide, to retreat into something that felt almost peaceful. "I'll have a scotch." Edward rasped, barely lifting his head. He looked worn, almost unrecognisable, his hair a tangled, wild mess, his clothes hanging loosely and dishevelled, and his face gaunt and hollow, carved deeply by grief. Despite it being barely past eleven in the morning, the scent of strong liquor clung to him, evidence that he had already begun to drown his sorrows. "Do you think that's wise, sir?" the butler asked cautiously, his tone soft and intended, fully aware that even a gentle question might ignite Edward's volatile temper. "I asked you for a scotch, not a lecture." Edward snapped, his voice sharp enough to cut. The butler bowed his head and silently left the room. Edward stared into the empty fireplace for a long, brutal moment, his gaze vacant and distant. Then slowly, his eyes dropped to the full glass clutched tightly in his hand. A wave of disgust twisted inside him, not directed at the butler who was probably hurt quietly nearby, but at himself. Frustration and self-loathing churned beneath his skin, burning hotter than the flames that once danced in the hearth. With a sudden, violent burst of rage, he threw the glass with all his might into the hearth, where it shattered against the cold bricks, shards scattering across the floor. The flames roared to life, bright and violent, and Edward sat there watching them, the reflection of the fire flickering in his haunted eyes. Elsewhere Lady Catherine wandered slowly through the manicured gardens, savouring the rare, gentle warmth of the spring afternoon. The sun filtered softly through the branches, casting dappled darkness across the gravel path. By her side, her trusted friend Doris Mossford walked gracefully, their skirts rustling softly as they brushed against the neatly trimmed, winding hedges that framed the garden like living walls. The two women moved in comfortable silence. "Sweet friend, how is Sir Edward faring?" Doris asked softly. Her voice was delicate, all most musical, but carried concern and empathy. Lady Catherine pursed her lips, barely hiding her disdain. "He is grieving for his lover." she remarked with little sympathy, her tone clipped and cold. "But enough is enough. Months have passed, and still, he mopes about like some forlorn poet. He forgets himself, his name, his station, his responsibilities." She slammed her cane deep into the path "Drinking will not bring Arabella back. It will not save her memory, nor will it save him. He must return to his duties; Blackthorn cannot afford a lord who sulks in shadows and whispers to ghosts." Doris gave a small, knowing nod but quickly changed the subject. "I am hosting a small gathering at Mossford House." She said, pausing mid-walk to await Lady Catherine's response. Before Lady Catherine could find the words to decline or change the subject, Doris continued without hesitation, her voice smooth and confident. "My niece is arriving today from

Scotland." She said, her eyes sparkling with subtle pride. "Her late husband, Lord Frederick, was tragically killed in a hunting accident last autumn. Since then, she has inherited his vast estate and considerable fortune... making her one of the wealthiest women in all of Scotland." Doris turned her head to Catherine, gauging her reaction carefully as they continued their slow walk through the blooming garden. Lady Catherine paused, lifting her chin and spurting her gaze skyward. A brief glimmer of curiosity and calculation flickered across Lady Catherine's eyes, betraying her otherwise composed demeanour. "Of course." She replied smoothly, her tone carefully advised yet edged with subtle enthusiasm. "I shall attend, Doris. I would not miss it for the world." She allowed a faint, polite smile to touch her lips, already imagining the potential advantages such a meeting could bring. Doris smiled triumphantly as Lady Catherine turned to her with a graceful nod. "Shall we continue our walk, Miss Mossford?" "We shall, Lady Blackthorn." Doris replied, she gracefully looped her arm through Catherine's as they wandered deeper into the manicured gardens. Doris, ever the diplomat, leaned in slightly and added in a more hushed tone, "Perhaps some gentle encouragement is all Sir Edward needs. A reminder of what still awaits him here, of what is expected of a man in his position." Lady Catherine agreed and on they both walked. Miss Fawns made her way through the servants' quarters, heading toward the kitchen to deliver the evening's change of plans. She found the cook in the bustling kitchen, halfway through slicing an onion. The knife paused mid-air as he turned to face her, eyes curious yet tired from the day's labour. Miss Fawns wasted no time, her voice brisk and authoritative. "The Blackthorns will be attending Miss Mossford's gathering this evening." She announced firmly. "There will be no need for dinner service tonight." The cook huffed loudly and slammed his knife down onto the chopping board. "I've already prepared the main dish! What do you expect me to do with all this food on such short notice?" he barked. "Give it to the staff." Miss Fawns said simply, her tone cantered and even, unfazed by the cook's muttered frustrations or the slick clatter of his knife against the board. "I doubt Lady Blackthorn will even notice." She did not wait for an answer. With the same composed authority she always carried, she turned on her heel and walked out of the kitchen, her skirts swishing softly as she went. Behind her, the cook muttered under his breath, but he did not argue, he knew better. Her steps quickened down the hall. Though her body was still fragile from the poisoning, her mind had been sharper than ever since she recovered. When she first returned to duty, she had quickly learned of Arabella's condition, the young lady trapped in a silent, unmoving darkness, and it had not taken Miss Fawns long to piece the truth together. She was no fool. A wise, observant woman, nothing escaped her notice. The butler had mentioned a peculiar story: Lady Catherine requesting polish to clean her own ring, a task so trivial, so common, it was entirely beneath her usual airs. The household had whispered about it for days, unable to understand why she would bother with such a thing when she had an entire staff at her beck and call. But Miss Fawns had remembered that day in unsettling detail. She had been in the dressing room, tidying up after Lady Catherine's departure for her afternoon tea. Everything had been done as usual; linens straightened, hairpins gathered, gloves removed for the delicate handling of the crystal perfume bottles. All but one. The polish bottle itself. The single glass bottle with, if she can remember rightly had a warning label on, maybe skull of such form? Miss Fawns had picked it up with bare hands, her gloves still folded neatly on the vanity. At the time, it had seemed harmless. But now, considering the butler's story, it felt calculated. And when Lady Catherine had paused, noticing a familiar scent on her, Miss Fawns understood the dreadful truth. The perfume. That had been the weapon. Miss Fawns adored Arabella with all her heart. It brought her deep pain to see the once-vibrant young lady lying so still, like a tragic statue, lost in a darkness that no one could reach. It was time for Miss Fawns to tend to her. She entered Arabella's silent bedchamber and set to work, washing her gently, with slow, careful movements, hoping, praying, that somewhere inside, Arabella could still feel the kindness and love in her touch. Gathering a basin of warm water and a soft cloth. She washed Arabella gently, her movements slow and careful, as if she might bruise her with anything firmer. With every stroke, she whispered apologies into the quiet, apologies for not doing more, not seeing sooner, not stopping what had come. "I'm so sorry, my lady." Miss Fawns whispered as she dabbed Arabella's forehead with a warm, soapy cloth. "If I had known what was in that perfume... I would have thrown it away without a second thought. What a terrible, wicked thing to do to such a young woman, so full of love." She swallowed down the lump rising in her throat, blinking away the tears that threatened to fall. Her fingers lingered for a moment longer on Arabella's cool skin, as if holding on might somehow pull the girl back from the edge of whatever limbo she was caught in. The sharp ringing of a bell shattered the tender moment. Its shrill chime echoed through the corridor like a crack of thunder, abrupt and commanding. Miss Fawns flinched. She did not need to check; it was Lady Catherine's bell. Precise, insistent, and always impatient. With one last glance at the sleeping girl, Miss Fawns stood, smoothing down the front of her apron. She drew in a slow, steadying breath, willing herself to bury her sorrow beneath the mask of composure she wore so well. Lady Catherine was calling. And when Lady Catherine called, she expected obedience. When she entered Lady Catherine's bedchamber, the mistress was already tapping her foot impatiently. "Sorry my lady." Miss Fawns said calmly, "I was attending to Lady Arabella." "Lady Arabella?" Lady Catherine sneered, her voice dripping with cruel amusement as she turned. "Would it not be simply Arabella now? Lady is a title reserved for women of importance, of status, of worth. And at present, she is none of those things. She is but a sleeping girl, silent, still, and utterly useless." Miss Fawns clenched her fists at her sides, the insult burning through her. But years of service had taught her the art of restraint. Miss Fawns had endured far worse than sharp words and icy tones. She had learned long ago that dignity was not always found in defiance, but in poise, in calm, in knowing when the squelch spoke louder than any reply. Without responding to the venomous comment, she lifted her chin and asked smoothly, "Will it be the blue or the red frock this evening, my lady?" Her voice was perfectly professional, devoid of emotion, as though the jab had never landed. Lady Catherine, apparently satisfied with Miss Fawns' silence and the deference it implied, gave a lazy flick of her hand toward the bed, where two immaculate gowns lay side by side, one a cool sapphire blue, the other a rich crimson silk that caught the light like spilled wine. "I shall wear the red tonight." She declared, as though it were a royal decree. Miss Fawns gave a small nod and moved toward the bed, her fingers already reaching for the crimson fabric, her mind slipping into the familiar rhythm of duty, even as her heart remained back in that quiet, shadowed room where Arabella slept on, untouched by the noise and vanity of the world outside her door. "As you wish, my lady." Miss Fawns uttered, her voice steady, but inside, a fierce promise was growing. She would not let Arabella suffer alone. And she would not let Lady Catherine's evil go unanswered. Sir Edward stood at the bottom of the grand staircase, barely sober, swaying slightly where he waited beside his father. His cravat was loosened, the collar of his shirt crumpled, and though he wore the formal attire expected of him, it hung on him like borrowed clothes, ill-fitting and apathetically arranged. His eyes, once alight with mischief and charm, were now void, blackness sunk deep into the hollows beneath them. Whatever spark had once lived there had long since been smothered. Beside him, Sir Howard kept a stiff posture, hands clasped behind his back, jaw clenched in silent disapproval. He did not look at his son, nor did he speak; his disappointment was already written plainly across his face. From above, the sharp sound of Lady Catherine's cane stretched through the grand hall, each deliberate strike against the marble stair an announcement of her arrival. The modish clicks of her heels trailed a cold percussion behind the intimidating tap of the cane. She descended with regal precision, her ruby gown trailing elegantly behind her. Her eyes scanned the scene below, pausing briefly on Edward, lips pouting ever so slightly at the sight of his unkempt appearance. But she said nothing, at least, not yet. The performance was about to begin, and even grief, it seemed, was no excuse for disarray. In contrast to her red down she layered a crisp white overcoat, the colour of blood and bone, striking, theatrical, deliberate. The fabric clung to her tall frame with regal authority, a warning more than a statement. Atop her powdered hair sat a grand white feather plume, rising like a challenge to the heavens, and with each calculated step down the stairs, the plume swayed and danced. The delicate strands caught the air with eerie grace. Edward refused to look at her. The last woman he had watched descend these stairs had been Arabella, radiant, full of life, mere moments before she was cursed into eternal stillness. The memory twisted like a knife inside him. Sir Howard, ever the dutiful husband, stepped forward with practiced grace and offered his arm to Lady Catherine. She accepted it without a word, her spine stiff with pride, her expression unnoticeable beneath her evil strategized face. Together, they moved in perfect sync, as they always had, two figures bound not by love, but by reputation and obligation. He guided her down the stone steps of Blackthorn Manor, past the assembled staff who stood in silent rows, their heads bowed in reverence or perhaps fear. The gravel crunched softly beneath their feet as they approached the waiting carriage, its polished black surface gleaming under the overcast sky. Without a glance back, Lady Catherine allowed herself to be helped inside, her eyes fixed on some distant point beyond the gates, as though the house behind her no longer concerned her. Sir Howard followed, pausing only briefly to offer the footman a curt nod before the door closed with a quiet click. Moments later, the carriage wheels began to turn, rolling them away.

The ride to Mossford House was a prison of forced politeness. Sir Edward sat stiffly opposite his parents, his posture rigid, as though he were made of stone. His gaze was fixed on the world beyond the window, though he saw none of it, only a blur of green hedges and grey skies. Across from him, Lady Catherine's voice droned on, sharp and tireless, listing gown designs, prestigious guests, and advantageous marriages as if they were pieces on a chessboard. He could barely hear her. The words slid past him like wind against glass. His mind was elsewhere caught in the stillness of that cursed manor, where Arabella had last smiled at him, where time had broken apart like shattered crystal. As soon as the carriage rocked to a halt before the grand estate, Edward leapt down, barely waiting for the footman to open the door, striding toward the entrance without a backward glance. He needed a drink, desperately. "Sir and Lady Blackthorn!" Doris Mossford greeted them warmly, bustling toward them with a wide smile that hardly hid the need to impress. "How delightful you both look this evening. Come, the ballroom is this way, everyone is primarily eager to see you." Lady Catherine accepted the praise with a tight smile, leaning heavily into her husband's arm, more for control than support, though she leaned into him as if the effort of being gracious in public required physical reinforcement. "We must not keep them waiting." Lady Catherine said crisply, looking towards the hallway leading to the ballroom. As they succeeded Doris through the grand hallway, Sir Howard remained silent beside her, ever the escort. Behind them, Edward drifted like a ghost, his steps hollow, his expression vacant. He moved through the ballroom like a shadow, present in body but utterly detached, lost in a world none of the elegantly dressed guests could begin to fathom. The laughter, the music, the clinking of crystal, it all blurred around him, a cruel contrast to the chaos inside his mind. The night dragged on endlessly for Sir Edward. Faces

blurred past him, hands gripped his with false
warmth, voices cooed and moaned platitudes
about poor Arabella, spoken in the same tone
one might use for someone already buried. Each
remark landed like a blow. Each sympathetic
look felt like a betrayal. Meanwhile, Lady
Catherine was radiant. The gathering had gone
precisely as she hoped. She floated from guest
to guest, accepting condolences and
compliments in equal measure, cloaked in a
performance of graceful sorrow and dignified
strength. She spoke of Arabella with the careful
cadence of a seasoned actress, neither too
mournful nor too joyful, just enough to evoke
admiration. She basked in the attention, while
her son-her grieving, broken son, was paraded
about like some tragic relic, something to be
pitied but not utterly understood. And no one
seemed to notice that the real Edward
Blackthorn was already fading. "Lady
Catherine, may I introduce Lady Maple
Robertson, my niece." Doris stated proudly.
Lady Maple was a striking young woman, the
kind who turned heads the moment she
entered a room. Her golden blonde hair had
been swept up into an intricate style, soft curls
tumbling artfully to frame her delicate face.
Her eyes, a piercing shade of blue, held the
smooth certainty of someone used to

admiration. Pale, porcelain skin gave her an ethereal glow beneath the chandeliers, and she carried herself with the effortless grace of nobility. Her gown, a rich buttery yellow, shimmered faintly as she moved. The fabric clung perfectly to her slender, statuesque frame, every seam designed to flatter and highlight her refined figure. A subtle train swept behind her, and tiny pearls along the bodice glinted with each step. She wore little jewellery, but having the advantage of not needing to wear any as her confidence was an accessory itself. "How do you do, Sir and Lady Blackthorne?" Lady Maple said, offering a graceful curtsy. "Please, there is no need to curtsy to us; it is we who ought to curtsy to you." Lady Catherine said, eager to flatter her. "Have you met my son, Sir Edward Blackthorne? I think the two of you would get along simply fine." Lady Catherine said with a rehearsed charm, her eyes scanning the room expectantly. She paused, her smile faltering slightly as she failed to spot him. The carefully curated moment was slipping through her fingers. "I beg your pardon." She added quickly, directing a polite nod to Lady Maple. "Do excuse me for just a moment." Without waiting for a reply, Lady Catherine turned sharply, her gaze sweeping across the ballroom with increasing irritation. Her heels clicked briskly against the marble floor as she disappeared into the crowd, her white plume bobbing furiously with every determined step. "Have you seen Edward?" she asked one of the footmen who had accompanied them to the gathering. "Yes ma'am, he left some time ago. I thought you were informed my lady." The footman gave nervously, feeling the weight of her stare. "He left? Why didn't you stop him?" Lady Catherine's voice cracked sharply, her eyes blazing with fury. "Fetch me a carriage at once, I am returning to the manor immediately!" She hurriedly made her farewells, spinning a story about an untrained maid nearly setting the manor ablaze. "You simply must come for dinner one evening." Lady Catherine said graciously, her voice smooth and inviting as she smiled warmly at Lady Maple. "It would be a pleasure to host you at Blackthorne Manor." "Certainly, Lady Blackthorne." Lady Maple replied with a grateful, genuine smile. "I would be honoured to accept your invitation." With a final nod, Lady Catherine gave a delicate curtsy and then turned away, her thoughts already racing toward finding Edward once more. On the carriage ride home, Lady Catherine was seething with anger at her son for humiliating her in front of important company. "How could he do this to his own mother?" she fumed, glancing at Sir Howard, who was fast asleep beside her. "This Arabella needs more than sleep…" Lady Catherine muttered to herself, but bit her tongue before she said more, plotting darkly in her head.

CHAPTER NINETEEN
SÉANCE

Present day

"Henry, there's a smudge on that glass. I told you not to hold them with your fingers inside." Isabelle snapped, her voice tight with urgency as the clock ticked closer to the start of the event. Henry, ever calm under pressure, after looking over his shoulder, wiped the smudge away with the bottom of his T-shirt. He knew full well she would scold him for using anything other than the designated microfiber cloth, but in that moment, speed outweighed protocol. The doorbell rang. Isabelle made a beeline for the front door, pausing briefly as she passed the hallway mirror to check herself. She straightened her posture, her fingers brushed through her hair, smoothing down a flyaway strand. She checked her lipstick, subtle, but still perfect, and flashed her most charming smile, until she opened the door. But the moment she opened the door her smile dropped. "Oh... it's you. Come in, guests will be arriving any minute." she said quickly, stepping aside. Chase stood on the doorstep with Hugo and Emily at her sides. "Mum, these are my friends." Chase began, but she did not get the chance to finish. Isabelle had already swept into action, ushering all three teenagers inside with a kind of practiced urgency, as though shielding them from something just beyond the doorstep. She closed the door firmly behind them, the lock clicking into place with finality. "Emily, Hugo, is it?" she brought out briskly, turning to them with a poised smile. Her voice was warm, but her posture was unmistakably formal; shoulders squared, chin slightly lifted. She extended a hand to Emily first, then to Hugo, her grip unexpectedly firm, the kind of handshake that said, '*I am not easily impressed, but I am watching.*' "Yes Mrs Willow." They answered in unison, cheerful and polite, though Emily's eyebrows twitched ever so slightly at the tightness of the greeting. Chase hovered awkwardly beside them, caught between teenage embarrassment and the gnawing feeling that her mother's politeness was less about hospitality and more about control. As the duo accompanied Chase into the kitchen, Emily whispered, "Your mum is such a boss, I love it." "Embarrassing, more like." Chase muttered under her breath, shooting a sideways look towards her mother, who was now reorganizing a stack of mail with the intensity of someone preparing for a government audit. Emily stifled a laugh, elbowing Chase gently. "Come on, she is iconic. Total boss energy." Chase just rolled her eyes, though she slid a small side smile. "Yeah, well, try living with iconic." "Hi Dad." Chase said as they stepped into the kitchen, dropping her bag on the floor. Henry turned from the counter, where he was halfway through buttering bread for some sandwiches. "Shhh." He whispered. "You'll awaken the dragon." Henry whispered with a playful grin, putting a finger to his lips. "I heard that!" Isabelle called from the hallway. Henry winced, then whispered to the teens, "Too late. She is up." Laughter broke out in the kitchen. Chase glanced around at the decorations and food, the artfully arranged table, the little touches that made the house glow with warmth and style. She would not say it aloud, but for a moment, she felt quietly proud of her mum. One by one, the guests began to arrive. By then, everyone had settled into their roles for the evening. Henry had appointed himself the official drink pourer, manning the makeshift bar with the flair of a seasoned bartender and the grin of someone who was clearly enjoying himself far too much. A tea towel was slung over one shoulder like he was in an old British sitcom, and he kept cheerfully announcing things like, "Gin or sin folks? Pick your poison!" Chase and Emily were making laps around the living room in matching makeshift uniforms, a last-minute idea that had quickly become the highlight of the evening. Dressed like old-fashioned footmen, complete with thrifted waistcoats and fake monocles, they glided between conversations, offering polished silver trays stacked with perfectly triangular finger sandwiches. "Cucumber or egg, madam?" Emily asked one amused guest in a mock-butler accent. Chase added, "Or both, if you're feeling rebellious." Then gave an exaggerated wink before hurrying off with a theatrical swirl of her tray. At the entrance, Hugo played the perfect gentleman, taking coats with a graceful bow. "Welcome." he said warmly, "Make yourself at home. Drinks are just through there, and the staff, as you will see, are unusually enthusiastic tonight." A few guests laughed as they handed over scarves and coats, clearly charmed by the whole thing. Even Isabelle, peeking out from the hallway with a wineglass in hand, had to admit the kids were pulling it off better than she had expected. Henry raised his glass in a small toast to himself behind the bar. "If this whole charity thing doesn't work out." He called out, "I think we've got a future in themed events." Isabelle, as the evening's main host, floated from group to group with graceful ease, charming everyone she spoke to. The charity event was in support of the town's local history, so Isabelle had opened most of the house for guests to explore, carefully sectioning off private areas with red rope and elegant "no entry." Signs. She and Henry had spent the better part of the week gathering various old belongings, things they no longer used or wanted, and old furniture, vintage books, old photos, costume Jewellery and more. They were displayed around the rooms with small cards inviting guests to place silent bids. It gave the home a lived-in, yet curated museum-like quality. "This place is stunning Isabelle. You have done such a marvellous job, you can still feel the life this house has lived." One of the ladies from the town council remarked, admiring a vintage clock on display. All around her, the house pulsed with life. Laughter rang out in gentle waves, overlapping with the steady hum of conversation and the occasional burst of storytelling from one corner or another. Glasses clinked, silverware tapped against China, and somewhere in the dining room someone was attempting to balance a tiny canapé on top of a wine glass *for science.* 'The lighting was soft and golden, spraying a cozy glow over the carefully arranged decorations and curated displays. The scent of warm bread and red wine drifted lazily through the air. Isabelle paused near the hallway, one hand resting on the back of an armchair, her gaze sweeping across the scene. Her home, her carefully built, lovingly kept home, was alive with laughter and warmth. It was not perfect, not by any stretch, but it was real. It was full. It was hers. She saw Henry at the bar, pretending to juggle lemons to entertain a group of guests. Nearby, Chase and her friends were still weaving between conversations with trays in hand. Emily beaming, Hugo offering polite nods, and Chase, though slightly flushed, clearly enjoying herself. A soft smile tugged at Isabelle's lips. The noise, the mess of half-full glasses and napkins on end tables, the echo of shoes on hardwood, it was all beautiful to her. Her heart swelled with pride and something serener, deeper: gratitude. She glanced down at the charm bracelet on her wrist, the one she had not worn in years. She rubbed one of the silver links gently between her fingers. *'Yes she thought, this is how it is meant to be.'* Chase had run out of sandwiches, so she made her way back to the kitchen, weaving through the crowd. On her way, she glanced at the assortment of items laid out for the charity auction: family relics, antiques, and forgotten odds and ends. That is when something caught her eye. Her heart skipped a beat. Sitting mildly among the mismatched collection of donated trinkets and forgotten heirlooms was the black box, the very one that had disappeared from the tower room weeks ago. It sat there like it belonged, tucked between a chipped porcelain vase and an old leather-bound book, its matte surface slightly dusty, its corners worn with age. But Chase knew better. That box had not been resting for years. It had moved. It had been hidden. And now, inexplicably, it had returned out in the open, like it was waiting for her. Her pulse quickened. She looked around the room, scanning faces. A couple sipped wine near the window. A group of older guests purred over a brass candlestick. No one seemed to notice her. Moving swiftly, Chase stepped forward and scooped up the box with both hands. Its solidness was a familiar dread. She clutched it close and slipped into the hallway, barely brushing past a man admiring the ornate wallpaper and a woman squinting up at one of the oil paintings. as she hurried away, the sounds of casual chatter and laughter fading behind her. Upstairs, she rushed into her bedroom, twisting the lock, locking the door behind her. She caught her breath as she placed the box on her bed, it looked so ordinary now, resting on her duvet cover. She fumbled for her phone, ready to call Emily and Hugo. She hovered over the call button but then stopped. They were downstairs helping her mum, working hard to make the night a success. She did not want to spoil the evening over what might just be an old family heirloom. Chase hesitated, then slowly slid her phone back into her pocket. She turned to the box and sat beside it on the bed, the mattress dipping beneath her weight. The black box resting on her blanket like some forbidden artifact. She lifted the lid slowly, half-expecting something to leap out, but inside, it was exactly as she remembered. The photographs were there, aged and delicate, their sepia tones soaked with time. Some were curled at the corners, others cracked down the middle, and all of them had that same eerie stillness, like the people in them were waiting. Last time, the tower had been too dirty and dusty with cobwebs and all-round creepiness, to let anyone study anything closely. But here, in the familiar warmth of her own bedroom, with soft music drifting up from the living room below and the gentle clink of wine glasses, she felt a little braver. She picked up the top photograph carefully. It showed a young woman standing in a garden, her expression caught between a smile and something colder, almost like she had been interrupted mid-thought. Chase turned it over. Faint writing marked the back in looping, old fashioned script: Arabella nightshade. Downstairs, laughter rose between Isabell's work friends and partners. Holly cracking a joke, David's booming response. Isabelle had been so excited to have them all over. It was the first time she had hosted something this relaxed in years, and the wine had flowed freely. Becky was stretched out on the sofa by now, shoes off, glass in hand, while Tanya and Holly swapped stories about Isabelle's legendary fundraiser mishaps. As the last guest left only leaving Isabelle's friends behind, Isabelle closed the door with a satisfying thud, then turned and surprised Hugo with a warm hug. "Thank you." She spoke genuinely. Then she made her way over to Emily, who was helping Henry, gathering empty glasses. Isabelle placed a gentle hand on Emily's shoulder. "Thank you too Emily, for all your help, you have been wonderful. But do not worry about tidying up anymore, you and Hugo should find Chase. I have not seen her in ages." Emily nodded gratefully and nudged Hugo to follow her. Isabelle watched them disappear up the stairs before turning back to the others. With a grin, she picked up a bottle of champagne and held it aloft. "Well then." She said, eyes sparkling, "Let's celebrate." She popped the cork, the sound echoing through the now-quiet house, and laughter followed as glasses were raised.

Later that evening Henry looked up just as the lights flickered out in the rest of the house. "It's okay." He commented, already moving. "Must be a power cut. I will go check the fuse box." David stood up to follow him. "I'll give you a hand." In the candlelit dining room, Isabelle turned to the others. "There are more candles on the table. Let us light them, just until the power's back." Tanya, Holly, and Becky tailed her, striking matches and illuminating the room one small flame at a time. The glow was haunting across the walls, making shapes people could associate with ghosts. Henry and David returned a few minutes later, their faces a mix of frustration and resignation. "No luck." Henry sighed, running his fingers through his invisible hair. "It is not the fuse this time, it is something bigger. Probably needs a professional to look at it." Becky, already a few glasses deep and delightfully tipsy, raised her eyebrows with excitement. "You know what this calls for?" she said in a spooky voice, wiggling her fingers dramatically. Everyone turned to her, waiting. "A séance!" she finished, eyes wide with playful mischief. The room fell into a brief, uncertain silence. Chairs shifted. Glasses clinked faintly against the table. Then Isabelle let out a breathy laugh and rolled her eyes, shaking her head like a woman resigned to madness. "Oh lord." She said, half-laughing. "Why do I feel like I'm going to regret this?" Becky clapped her hands once, clearly delighted. "Come on, it'll be fun!" They were just starting to pull their chairs in around the table, rearranging half-melted candles and joking about who should lead the ritual, when the old front door gave a long, slow creak putting a stop to any conversation present. Holly and Tanya, who were closest, jumped and let out startled screams and curses, instinctively grabbing at each other. All heads turned. Standing in the doorway, framed by the dim hallway behind them, were Chase, Hugo, and Emily. "What's going on?" Chase asked, eyeing the adults seated around the table. "Shhh!" they hushed her quickly, a little tipsy but welcoming. "Chase sweetheart, we're going to play a little game." Isabelle said with a mysterious smile. "Take a seat kids, unless you're too scared?" Henry added with a taunting smile, his tone teasing. Emily rolled her eyes playfully and nudged Hugo, who muttered something under his breath in French and sank into the nearest chair. Chase watched without a word, her arms still tightly crossed, the box resting silently in her lap beneath the table. With a shuffle of chairs and murmurs of half-laughter, everyone found a place. Nine people now sat around the table, the flickering candles reflecting in each eye. On one side sat Henry, Isabelle, Hugo, Emily, and Tanya. Opposite them sat Becky, Chase, David, and Holly. The air was different now, with an energy none of them could perfectly name. Emily's eyes swept the table, then drifted toward the centre where the candles flickered unevenly. Her face a picture of a frightened girl. Something about the arrangement, the dim light, the circle, the way no one was really laughing anymore, itched at the back of her mind. She blinked once. Twice. Then her eyes widened, and she leaned closer to Hugo. "This is a séance." She whispered, barely audible, as if even the word might stir something awake. Chase's head snapped toward her. "What?" Emily nodded slowly, her voice lower now, more certain. "Look around. The candles. The silence. The way everyone is holding hands." Her gaze flicked to her left, where Tanya was already reaching out. Chase looked down, suddenly noticing the subtle shifting of bodies,

the quiet hush that had fallen over the room.
Her pulse quickened. Hugo tilted his head, still
trying to mask his nerves behind a crooked
smile. "You're joking, right?" But no one was
laughing anymore. A breeze ghosted through
the room, rustling the flame of a candle. Chase
tightened her grip on the box. No, no one was
joking. Chase opened her mouth to protest,
words about how this was a terrible idea
forming on her tongue, but then she hesitated.
A restless knot tightened in her stomach, a
mixture of fear and curiosity. Just maybe, this
was the way to get the answers she so
desperately needed. "Everyone, hold hands."
Becky said, her tone suddenly serious, too
serious. The playful spark was gone, replaced by
something practiced, focused. It was clear she
knew what she was doing. Chairs shifted as
people adjusted in their seats, reaching out to
hold each other's hands, to complete the circle.
Emily hesitated only for a second before her
hand was now holding Hugo's and Tanya's. Her
palms were damp. Chase placed the black box
down under her seat. Becky closed her eyes and
proceeded. "Dear spirit, or spirits." She began
solemnly. "Please move among us and speak
through us. We welcome you with open minds
and hearts." The words seem to stay in the
room like glue. No one spoke you could not

even hear breathing. Hands tightened instinctively. Emilys eyes darted towards the ceiling and then back to the door. She leaned into Hugo slightly "Did you feel that?" she whispered. "Feel what?" Hugo whispered back. "A change. Something is in here with us." Emily continued to look around the room. "This is stupid." Tanya muttered, her voice was a hint of fear. But just as she was about to rephrase it, the candles blew out with a sudden gust of wind. Everyone recoiled, their hands breaking apart. "What the hell was that!" Hugo exclaimed half rising from his seat. Emily grabbed onto Hugo's arm. "Hell no." Holly muttered under her breath. "That was not a draught was it? It could not be. All the windows are closed." Isabelle said waiting for some sort of response for reassurance that would put her mind at rest. Still. Quiet. Nothing. Then one by one, they hesitantly rejoined hands. "If that was you?" Becky averred into the dark, "Please send us another sign." The candles reignited, one by one, in front of their eyes. No one could deny it now. This was real. Suddenly, the table began to tremble. Glasses tipped and clinked. The dangling lights above swung violently, casting shadows that danced on the walls. "I don't think I like this anymore." Hugo said, beginning to stand. But all the chairs scraped forward and locked tight under the table, trapping everyone in place, except Becky's. Becky slowly rose to her feet... and then kept rising. Her heels lifted off the ground. Her arms pendulous at her sides, limp, as if she had no control over her own body. Her head tilted back slightly. She was floating. And when her eyes opened. Everyone stared in silent horror as Becky hovered above them, her eyes black as coal, scanning each person as though judging them. Then Becky's head jerked to the side with a violent snap. She stared right into Chases soul. "You." The voice bellowed low, cold, and not Becky's. It was a deeper, older, and ancient. "You murderer. Your blood, your family line, you all deserve to perish." Chase's voice dry and shaky. "Who are you?" "You know who I am, sitting there with a heart of stone!" Henry stood. "Leave her alone!" With a flick of her hand, without even turning, Becky sent Henry flying. His chair hurled across the room. He collided with the wall, the impact echoing through the room before he crumpled to the floor, unconscious. A piercing chorus of screams erupted, Isabelle, Tanya, Holly, Emily, and Hugo all cried out in shock and alarm. But Chase remained seated, staring back. "Arabella." Chase concluded. At the mention of the name,

the candles flared bright, wild, and angry. A
window shattered, like deadly confetti. Wind
howled through the house, shaking the
furniture. "How dare you speak to me so
casually! It is Lady Arabella!" The temperature
dropped. Everyone could see their breath in the
sudden chill. Chase did not have time to react.
She was lifted into the air by her throat with
invisible hands, trying to get some air within
her tight squeezed neck, as well as kicking
helplessly. Chases eyes bulged. Her vision
blurred. Then, as if thrown, she crashed to the
floor. Her body slamming with a thud. Rising
off the ground in a strong demeanour Chase
looked up at the floating body. "I am not a
Blackthorn. I am not who you want!" Chase
cried out. "Becky, I know you are still in there!
Please help!" Holly shouted. But the voice only
grew angrier. Holly began to convulse against
the table, banging, again, blood spraying until
she collapsed, her head resting lifelessly on the
wood. Isabelle sobbed in horror. Tanya fainted.
"You have the dark blood in your veins." The
spirit growled at Chase. Emily, through tears,
screamed out, "Oi! Bitch! Remember me!?"" The
spirit turned to her. "Oh yes… puppet girl. I am
sorry I did not finish you off." Suddenly,
without warning, the tassels on Hugo's jeans
twisted violently, snapping to life as if yanked

by invisible strings. They shot through the air like serpents and coiled themselves tightly around Emily's neck. She let out a strangled cry, her hands flying to her throat as she staggered backward, eyes wide in panic. The cords constricted mercilessly, digging into her skin. Her face flushed red as she struggled, clawing and twisting, desperate for air. "Emily!" Hugo shouted, lunging toward her, but a force threw him back against the wall, pinning him there with invisible heed. Chase's heart lurched. She could only watch for a second, just a second, before something heroic took over. "Please!" she screamed, stepping into the centre of the chaos. "It is me you want! Take me, not her!" There was a sharp, unnatural stillness. Then, snap. The tassels released their hold and dropped lifelessly to the ground. Emily crumpled to the floor, gasping and coughing, her fingers shaking as they scraped at her neck. Hugo rushed to her side, arms wrapping around her as she wheezed for breath. The room seemed to pulse with malevolent satisfaction, as if whatever dark entity had caused the attack had gotten exactly what it wanted: fear, suffering… and a promise of more to come. Chase was yanked into the air again. David lunged forward, grabbing Becky's ankles, but his wrists snapped back with a sickening crack, bones jutting through skin. He screamed in agony. Then Chase felt something in her pocket, a tiny glass bottle. She did not remember putting it there, but she acted fast. She threw it with all her strength at Becky's hovering form. The bottle shattered on the table. The sharp overwhelming scent of lavender filled the room. Becky let out a scream, raw, primal, and piercing, that shook the walls, and in a blink, the lights flicked on, and she dropped from the air, collapsing unconscious onto the floor. She lay sprawled across the floor, her limbs limp, her eyes shut tight, her chest rising only slightly. The room around her buzzed with electricity. For a long moment no one spoke no one moved no one did anything.

CHAPTER TWENTY
"EDDIE"

1800

The long, winding ride back to the manor had cooled Sir Edward's drunken haze, but not the storm churning within his heart. The cool night air had sobered him enough to walk straight, but his thoughts remained tangled, laborious with guilt and memories he could not outrun. Inside, the corridors were silent, save for the faint creak of the floorboards beneath his steps. shadows danced across the walls, from the flickering lamps, twisting into shapes that mocked him. Every corner held a ghost; every second he felt lost. Then he saw her. A lone figure stood in the dim light at the end of the hallway; a lantern clasped tightly in her hand. Petite. Poised. Still. Her hair, dark as night, tumbled down her back in loose waves, catching the lantern's glow like strands of midnight silk. She did not move. Did not speak. Just stood there. An unexpected presence in a place he thought empty. *'Wait a minute'* he thought. *'Arabella?'* His body lurched forward before his mind could process what was standing before him. In an instant, his arms wrapped around her slender waist from behind, pulling her close into him, desperate and unthinking. He buried his face in the curve of her neck. Breathing her scent in, clinging to the impossible hope that it was truly her. Startled, she stood still, the lantern slipped from her grasp and clattered to the floor. Breaking the glass broke dimming the flame and plunging them into warm, velvet darkness. "Sir Edward…" She whispered her voice full off fear and confusion. "Shhh." He whispered, his voice low and aching, like something fragile barely holding together. "It's only me… my darling Arabella." His hand rose with reverence, trembling slightly as it reached for her. He traced the curve of her jaw with a featherlight touch, as if afraid she might disappear. His fingertips brushed against her lips, lingering there, hesitant, worshipful, memorising the shape of her in silence. The maid, caught between fear and desire, stood motionless, her body wavering against his. "I've dreamt of this." He hollered, brushing her hair aside to press a kiss to her neck. "Of you. In every room. Every shadow." She turned to face him, lips parted, eyes wide. "I… I am just a servant, my lord." "You are not just anything." He breathed. "You

are here. You are real. And I need to feel
something real." He kissed her then, not with
restraint, but with hunger. A kiss filled with
grief, with longing, with mistakes he could not
undo. His mouth found hers like it was the only
thing he was certain of, steady and sure. And
she, unsure but drawn to him all the same,
parted her lips with a dead sigh, letting him in.
There was no rush, no urgency, only the quiet
ache of something long held back, finally
released. He pressed her back against the old
wooden bench, the lantern's glow flickering
across the room, eliminating firelight over bare
shoulders and quivering hands. She was not
Arabella, she knew that, but in his arms, under
the pudginess of his yearning, she felt like
someone who mattered. And for one fleeting
night, that was enough. "Say you want me." He
whispered, his voice thick with wine and want.
"I... I do." She breathed, her voice barely a
sound. She did not know if it was the truth or
the dream she had been aching to live. His
hands roamed slowly, reverently, as though
each inch of her was a prayer answered. Fingers
slipped over silk and laces, pulling each layer
away like unwrapping a secret he was not sure
he had the right to touch. She breathed in deep
as his mouth found the delicate skin of her
throat, her head tipping back, surrendering to

the heat of him, as his fingers found the curves he ached to worship. Her corset came loose beneath his teeth, the garment falling away as her hands fumbled with the buttons of his waistcoat, desperate to feel him, his skin, his heat and the thud of his heart beneath her palms. With a low groan, he gathered her into his arms, lifting her and carrying her to the bed like something sacred. The sheets cool against flushed skin, and there, in the hush of the manor, they lost themselves. His body claiming hers with desperate tenderness, hers arching to meet him, her moans muffled in the crook of his neck. They were lost to the night. Their rhythm was slow at first, a dance of exploration and trembling confession, but it built with every gasp, every whisper of "yes.", "please." And "do not stop." Sweat gathered between them. The headboard gave a soft creak with each movement. When they finally sank into each other, spent, tangled, and breathless, their skin was warm and slick with shared heat. For a long moment, the only sound was their breathing, and the softened, steady rhythm of two hearts beating close.

Lady Catherine arrived back at the manor in full fury. She jabbed Sir Howard in the shin with her cane to rouse him from his sleep and stormed up the front steps, her overcoat billowing dramatically in the wind. The moment she reached the doors; she swung her cane at the startled servants who hurried to open them. She stopped in the entryway, her face flushed with rage, the house seeming to freeze around her. Without a word, she turned and walked down into the servants' quarters, her heels clicking sharply on the stone steps. She flung open the door to Miss Fawns' modest room. "Miss Fawns!" Her voice was not hands down a yell, but it carried through the corridor like a thunderclap. Miss Fawns startled awake, fumbling to light her lantern to full flame. "Oh my… Lady Catherine?" Miss Fawns sat up quickly, pulling her covers closer around her nightgown. "What are you doing down in the servants' quarters at this hour?" Lady Catherine crossed the room and took a seat at the foot of Miss Fawns' bed. She exhaled deeply; her expression magnified with exhaustion. "Oh, what an unpleasant evening I've had." She said, lifting her hand to her forehead as if to steady herself. "I have been utterly humiliated, Miss Fawns, by my selfish son." "I'm terribly sorry, my lady." Miss Fawns said softly, pulling on her night coat as she stepped out of her bed, her eyes still heavy with sleep. "Would you like some tea, or perhaps something stronger?” “Sherry.” Lady Catherine replied without hesitation, her voice clipped but weary. “A small glass.” Miss Fawns nodded and moved with easygoingness through the dim corridor to the drawing room. She lit a single lamp and poured the amber liquid with practiced hands, the scent of it curling faintly into the air. Lady Catherine sat stiffly on the chaise next to miss fawns window waiting for her to return with a stiff drink, her expression composed but tight, like a mask stretched too thin. As Miss Fawns returned with the glass, she began to recount the evening, every insult, every misstep, every humiliation, with unchangeable detail. Her tone wavered between wounded pride and bitter fury; each word edged in ice. Miss Fawns said nothing, only listened with quiet attentiveness. She stoked the fire with care, the embers flaring in response, and gently draped a shawl over Lady Catherine’s lap. Outside, the wind rattled the windows, but within the drawing room, the quiet between them was familiar, companionable in its own way. One spoke, the other soothed. A ritual forged through years of knowing one another. “I will go look for Sir Edward, ma’am.” Miss Fawns said at last, offering a small nod before turning toward the door with her lantern in hand. She ascended the grand staircase carefully, one hand gathering the hem of her night coat to avoid tripping. The corridors lay quiet, dusk stretching long and deep around her. As she passed the guest rooms, she heard a rustle, a movement behind one of the doors. Frowning, Miss Fawns opened it and raised her lantern. The lantern's glow fell across a bed, the sheets shifting with unmistakable movement beneath them. She pulled the covers back in one sharp motion, revealing one of the young maids lying atop Sir Edward, their bodies tangled and breathless in the dim light. The sight hit her like a sudden blow; the quiet betrayal laid bare in the soft glow. "What in God's green earth is going on here!" she cried. The maid shrieked, scrambling to cover herself with the blanket from the floor. "I'm so sorry!" she stammered, bolting out of the room before Miss Fawns could say another word. Sir Edward lay sprawled across the bed, a lazy smile playing on his lips. "Miss Fawns." He slurred with a crooked smile, "how lovely of you to see me to bed. It has been years." His eyes twinkled with mischief, even through the haze of drink, as if trying to mask something deeper beneath the jest. He was unmistakably intoxicated. Sighing, Miss Fawns fetched her discarded night coat and gently draped it over him to preserve what modesty remained. Then, with a mother's patience, she helped him to his proper bedchamber, steadying his stumbling steps. Once he was tucked in, she brushed his hair back from his forehead, her fingers lingering a moment longer than necessary. Her gaze softened as she looked down at him, no longer a man, but the boy she had once soothed through fevers and night terrors. "I'm sorry, Eddie." She whispered, her voice barely audible over the crackle of the dying fire. She used the name she had called him since boyhood, the name that belonged to simpler days. "You deserve better than this." Her throat gripped tight, but she blinked the sting away. She sat beside him in the dim light, the room hushed and still. Her hand rested lightly on top of the covers over his arm, a gentle anchor in the dark. Slowly, his breathing deepened, steadied, until sleep claimed him. With a sigh, she reached over and turned the flame down low, casting the room in a soft, auspicious glow. Still, she stayed a while longer, keeping watch in silence, just as she always had. "Sir Edward is asleep, ma'am." Miss Fawns said gently as she returned to the drawing room. Lady Catherine, seated by the fire with her sherry glass empty, gave a distracted nod. "Hmm… Miss Fawns?" "Yes, my lady?" "Any news on Arabella?" Lady Catherine asked, tipping back the last of her sherry, her tone almost casual, though her eyes betrayed a flicker of unease. Miss Fawns hesitated for only a moment. "We will have to wait and see what the doctor says tomorrow. For now, all we can do is pray." Lady Catherine gave a tight nod, as if satisfied with that answer. But Miss Fawns knew the truth, even if she would never say it aloud. She knew Lady Catherine was at the root of all this. Sir Edward's growing dependence on drink… Arabella's fragile condition… even the maid, now ruined and soon to be cast out without a reference. All casualties of Lady Catherine's need to control what she could no longer command. And yet, there Miss Fawns stood, still loyal, still silent, serving the woman who had destroyed so much in her desperation not to lose her power. "Please return to your sleeping. I will see myself to bed." Lady Catherine commanded, her voice sharp and cold, leaving no room for argument. "Very well, my lady." Miss Fawns replied with a slight, respectful curtsy. "Thank you miss fawns you have always been very loyal to me." With that clothed she turned on her heel, the lantern's light faintly illuminating the corridor as she moved down with temperate steps. Miss fawns smiled as she watched her lady walk away, it has been a long time since she has seen a

glimpse of her old friend *'catherine wrenford'*
and it will be a long time until she will see her
again. Lady Catherine continued, her heels
tapping sharply against the marble floor. But
just as she reached the hallway to her
bedchamber, she veered off, taking a detour
with determined steps. She moved like a
shadow through the inactive manor, until at
last she arrived at the room she sought. She
slipped inside, pausing just beyond the
threshold. The room was dim, lit only by the
faint glow of moonlight filtering through the
curtains. There, lying motionless upon the bed,
was Arabella; pale, delicate, and utterly
helpless, as if drained of all life and will. Lady
Catherine approached slowly, her footsteps fair
but purposeful. Her eyes scanned the girl's face
with a strange mixture of admiration and
disdain, as though she both envied and resented
the fragile beauty before her. For a moment,
something subtle flickered across her features, a
silent judgment, or a reluctant respect, before
the mask of cold control settled back in place.
"Oh, sweet girl." She said in a syrupy,
patronizing tone, "if only you had chosen a
different man." She reached out and gently
brushed a strand of hair from Arabella's face,
her touch deceptively tender, almost maternal.
For a fleeting moment, there was softness in her

eyes, a ghost of affection that might have once been real. But it vanished as quickly as it came. Her expression hardened, the warmth draining from her features. Her mouth tightened into a bitter, rigid line, the edges pulling down as if to hold back something unsaid. Her hand stayed in the air, paused longer than necessary, before slowly pulling back, as unwilling to show any gentleness. Whatever trace of kindness had flickered just moments before, was gone, replaced by a cold, unyielding resolve that settled over her like a veil.

CHAPTERTWENTY-ONE
ROWS OF BLACK

Present day

Chase slowly stood, her body trembling as she took in the utter devastation surrounding her. Hugo and Emily were doing the same, their expressions vacant and shocked, still trying to process the horror they had just witnessed. David was lying on the floor, writhing in pain, his tears mixing with the blood on the floor. Tanya remained collapsed, unmoving, while Isabelle clung to Henry, her tear-soaked face a portrait of anguish. Henry was still unresponsive, his body limp in her arms. Holly's head, covered in blood, rested motionless on the table. Becky, barely coming to, groaned as she tried to sit up amidst the chaos. The room was a loathsome scene of panic and death. Hugo was on the phone, his voice shaky but urgent. "Hello, please help us." He pleaded. "We've been attacked... there are bodies on the floor..." His words were fragmented, but they carried the weight of desperation. When the police arrived, they

were just as stunned as everyone else. The
scene was chaotic, surreal, like something out
of a terrible dream. After a quick assessment,
they called for backup. Sirens wailed in the
distance, growing louder by the second, until a
stream of patrol cars arrived and more officers
flooded into the area, their radios crackling,
boots pounding against pavement. Then, like a
nightmare tearing into reality, Emily's parents
appeared, her mother's scream rising above the
noise, raw and desperate. "My daughter! Let me
through!" She lunged toward the cordoned-off
area, eyes wild with fear, but an officer stepped
in front of her. His arms were outstretched,
firm yet steady, trying to calm her without
force. "Ma'am, please let us do our job." Emily's
father stood frozen behind her, pale and silent,
his hands clenched at his sides, as though he did
not know whether to fight or fall apart. But
then, through the doorway, Emily appeared,
her figure small and unsteady, her face pale and
streaked with tears, lips quivering as she took in
the scene. "Mum!" she cried, her voice hoarse
and broken as she ran forward, feet barely
touching the ground. Her mother let out a
strangled sob and rushed to meet her, gathering
Emily into her arms with the desperation of
someone who had feared the worst. She wept
openly, clutching her daughter as if she might

vanish again. Emily's father stood behind them, stiff with emotion. Though he kept his composure, his fingers twitched slightly at his sides before he stepped in and wrapped both in his arms. His face remained stoic, but his eyes gave him away brimming with feeling, dark with everything he had not said aloud. Nearby, even the officers glanced away, giving the family a sliver of privacy in the middle of the chaos. "Please…" Emily whispered through her tears. "Can we take Hugo home?" Her mother nodded, her arms wrapping tightly around Emily, and within moments, they were gone, driving away from the nightmare that had unfolded. Chase, unaware of her friends' departure, stood beside her mother, who was still grieving over Henry, who was now being loaded into an ambulance. The cold, harsh reality of the situation pressed down on everyone, its burden almost unbearable. David was carried away next, his body limp and motionless, coursed closely by Tanya, who lay still and unmoving. Then came the hardest sight of all: the fourth stretcher. This one was different. Swathed tightly in a body bag, it drew the light away, dimming the atmosphere as it was wheeled out. Holly: gone, sheltered, and lifeless, was taken away, leaving an emptiness that no one could fill. Behind the stretcher, Becky stumbled forward, her grief raw and overwhelming, a storm raging inside her chest. She screamed, a sharp, heart-wrenching sound that broke the uneasy calm, sounding into the daylight like a physical blow, the pure anguish of a soul torn apart. Chase looked down at her phone. 1:30 AM. The screen lit up her hands in a sterile blue-white glare that made her skin look almost unfamiliar. The world around her felt muted; voices blurred, motion sluggish. A police officer stepped toward her and Isabelle. His face was drawn, eyes smart beneath the brim of his hat. "Please, come with us." He said quietly. "We will take you to a safe house. It is not safe here anymore." Chase lifted her gaze to meet his, then turned to her mother. Isabelle's mouth tightened, her posture stiff with tension. She gave the slightest tilt of her head in unspoken agreement. No need for questions. The officer led them toward a waiting vehicle. Chase shadowed, glancing over her shoulder once. The house stood quietude behind them, its windows blank, its silence thick with everything that had happened. Then she turned away. Isabelle stared at him with a mixture of defiance and exhaustion. "I will not leave my home." She said sharply. "Miss, your home is a crime scene." The officer said clearly, his gaze

focused and resolute. "You're not safe here."
Chase turned toward her mother, tears sliding
down her cheeks, her chest tightening with fear
and doubt. The reality of the situation washed
over them like a wave, leaving a hush filled
only by their shared pain. Isabelle's hand
reached out, shaking slightly, seeking comfort
in the small, delicate connection between them.
"Please Mum, let's just go with them. I do not
want to stay here tonight. I cannot…" Her voice
broke, desperate, afraid of what the house had
become. Isabelle's hard expression softened as
she looked at her daughter. Her shoulders
slumped, realising that her role as a mother had
to come first. She sighed, finally letting go of
her pride. "Oh baby, I am sorry. Of course." Her
voice softened, dropping to a quieter tone,
almost weary and resigned as she turned to face
the officer. "Take us away. Just… take us
somewhere safe." The next morning, Chase
stirred awake on the sofa, her neck stiff and her
limbs effortful. She must have drifted off
sometime after arriving at the safe house. The
silence felt thick. From the kitchen, she could
hear her mother's voice, natty and frustrated.
Isabelle was still in the clothes she had worn
the night before, wrinkled and stained, her hair
pulled back in a messy knot. She paced the
floor, phone pressed tightly to her ear, dark

circles framing her weary eyes. Each step was restless, reflecting the unease that hung in the air. Her voice, though remote, carried the burden of worry and frustration as she spoke in hurried bursts. Chase slowly sat up on the edge of the bed, rubbing her face in slow, tired motions, trying to loosen the lingering fatigue. She rose and wandered into the small kitchen, the soft creak of the floor beneath her feet. Her fingers trailed along the cool countertop before coming to rest on the coffee machine tucked away in the corner, a small source of solace. She poured two cups, the warmth comforting against her trembling hands. When she handed one to her mother, Isabelle gave her a tired smile and mouthed, "Thank you." But then her voice broke again, tense and intimidating. "For God's sake!" she swore into the phone, her patience wearing thin. "Can someone just tell me something, anything? "Everything okay, Mum?" Chase asked silently, her eyes searching her mother's face for any sign of relief. "They keep putting me on hold." Isabelle snapped, her fingers tightening around the phone like it were slipping from her grasp. She let out a frustrated sigh and lowered the phone, her voice an unstable beneath the pressure of anger and helplessness. "No one will tell me anything. It feels like I am hitting a brick wall." Her voice cracked, raw and fragile beneath the fury. "It's driving me mad." Chase stepped closer, her hand brushing gently against her mother's arm. "We will get answers Mum. We must not give up we just need to keep trying." Isabelle's eyes shifted with a mix of exhaustion and resolve. She gave a slow tilt of her head, but her grip on the phone stayed firm, as if letting go meant giving in to the unknown. "Mum... did you get any sleep at all?" Chase asked, her concern growing. "I couldn't." Isabelle replied, her eyes shimmering with unshed tears. "I just need to know how your father is doing. I cannot... I cannot find peace until I hear something." Chase reached for her hand, giving it a gentle squeeze. "We will hear soon. He is strong. He is going to pull through." Isabelle nodded but said nothing. Her eyes drifted toward the window, distant and weighed down by thoughts she would not voice. Suddenly, her phone rang, breaking the stillness. She snatched it up like a lifeline. "Hello?" she answered, breathless, voice shaking with hope and dread. Chase watched her mother closely from across the kitchen, gripping her coffee cup so tightly her knuckles turned white. Isabelle's face changed in an instant, her expression falling, eyes widening with horror. She looked up at Chase and slowly shook her head. Chase stood frozen, her heart pounding in her chest. "Mum?" she whispered. Isabelle did not speak. The phone slipped from her hand and clattered to the floor. She dropped with it, her knees buckling beneath her. "Mum!" Chase rushed forward, dropping down beside her. "What is it? What did they say? How's Dad?" Her voice wavered, breaking with fear. Tears streamed down her cheeks as she grasped her mother's shoulders, shaking her gently but urgently, searching for any sign of hope. Isabelle's eyes met hers, glazed and unfocused, and for a moment, Chase thought she saw a trace of something unexpressed, something too much to carry. Isabelle turned to her, tears pouring freely down her cheeks. She cupped Chase's face in trembling hands, trying to steady her voice through the heartbreak. "They said... they said your father is brain dead." The words hanging in the air like a death sentence. Chase let out a guttural cry, collapsing into her mother's arms. "No, no, no, Dad!" she sobbed, her voice breaking apart as she clung to Isabelle. "He cannot be... He cannot be!" Isabelle wrapped her arms tightly around her daughter, holding her close, rocking her gently as she had when Chase was a small child, offering what little comfort she could during heartbreak. Her own tears slipped down, silently now, blending with

Chase's as they shared the unbearable burden of their loss, their bodies shaking together in hushed sorrow. There was nothing else to do, nothing else that could be done......

TWO WEEKS LATER

Chase and her mother sat side by side in the back of the car, both dressed in black. Isabelle wore a delicate mesh veil that concealed her reddened, tear-streaked eyes, a fragile barrier between her pain and the world outside. Her fingers shook slightly as she gripped the fabric of her dress. Chase, quieter in her grief, pressed a tissue to her cheeks, carefully wiping away the tears she refused to let spill freely. Her jaw was set, but the regard in her eyes revealed the storm inside. The car moved steadily through the day, its low hum filling the fierce stillness between them. Outside, the world was bright and calm, but inside, grief wrapped around them like a cold, unyielding cloak. As the car neared the tall town church, a crowd came into view, some standing in small groups, speaking in hushed tones, others moving slowly toward the wooden doors, and a few openly wiping away tears. The murmurs and soft sobs floated on the air, a sombre soundtrack to the grief that filled the space. The presence of the gathering settled deep within Isabelle, making it hard to breathe. "I can't do this." She whispered, voice barely audible, more to herself than anyone else, but Chase was right there beside her. "Mum, we have to." She said gently, her voice steady despite the ache beneath it. She reached out, taking her mother's hand in hers, offering a firm, unexpected comfort. "We have to stick together." Isabelle's fingers curled slowly around Chase's, a faint warmth returning to her touch. For the first time in hours, a fragile hope stirred between them, a promise to face whatever lay ahead, side by side. When the long black limousine pulled up and the doors swung open, Chase and Isabelle stepped out into a sea of waiting arms. Faces filled with sorrow and sympathy surrounded them, offering hugs, kisses, and respectful nods. The air was thick with unexpressed condolences, yet amidst it all, there was a strange, solemn beauty to the gathering. It is beautiful, Chase thought, *'even during such pain. Half of these people did not even know us. But today, they are all here... grieving with us. Together!'* Inside the church, there was a harrowing feeling in the air. Everyone sat dressed in black, rows and rows of black. At the front stood two coffins. One was a polished oak casket with white flowers resting on top, and beside it sat a photo of a smiling woman: Holly. The other coffin was darker, a deep brown, with a floral arrangement shaped into the words "Dad & Husband" in red and white roses. His portrait stood next to it, a picture taken the day before they left their old apartment, all of them smiling together. Chase and Isabelle sat at the front, facing their family members' coffins. The church doors opened once more, heels clicking sharply as Becky entered, her steps slow and drained. She looked hollow, her face blank and distant, like someone who had been emptied of all feeling. Without hesitation, she took a seat near the front on the left side. Chase's eyes swept the room, briefly landing on two of her friends sitting near the back. They offered her a quiet wave of sympathy, their expressions soft but cautious. She returned a faint smile, barely more than a twitch at the corners of her lips, but it was enough to show she noticed, even though the heaviness settling over her made it hard to feel anything at all. The pews around her were filling slowly, the soft murmurs of whispered condolences barely breaking the oppressive salve that hung in the air. Behind Becky, sat Tanya and David. David had both arms in casts. They did not look toward Chase or her mother, not once, their faces distant, lost in their own grief and memories. As the ceremony neared its close, the priest's voice softened as he called Isabelle forward to speak a few words on Henry's behalf. Isabelle took a steadying breath, her hands shaking slightly as she wiped away the tears threatening to spill. With a lull resolve, she lifted her veil, forcing herself to meet the eyes of those gathered, drawing strength from the room's solemn attention. "My dearest Henry." She began, placing a hand gently on his coffin. "I have never met someone with so much love and joy. It breaks my heart to be standing here today, not with you, but for you, in the worst way. I will always love you, my Henry." She choked back a sob. "I might have lost the love of my life, but my daughter Chase has lost her father. And for that… I am so sorry. Chase, my darling, I love you." Tears welled up in Chase's eyes, blurring her vision. Around the room, many others wiped away their own tears, their faces etched with sorrow. The speech was brief, but every word carried a deep, undeniable impact that settled over everyone present. Isabelle pulled a necklace from her pocket, the one he gave her when they first met, and gently placed it on top of the coffin before returning to her seat. It was Becky's turn to speak for Holly. She slowly made her way to the altar and turned to face a crowd full of tear-streaked, broken faces.

"Holly wasn't just a woman I loved." She began, her voice soft yet firm, carrying a calm strength that demanded attention. "She was a ray of sunlight on this earth; bright, warm, and full of life. Her laughter could fill a room, and her kindness touched everyone she met. She did not deserve the fate she has been damned to, the cruel end that stole her away from us far too soon." Becky's eyes swept across the room, then locked onto Isabelle's. "What happened on that dreadful night… forget what the papers say." She said, her voice steady and clear, filled with a peacefulness gravity that glided in the air. "It was not some burglary gone wrong. Only a few of us here know the truth. Dark truths that linger in shadows, hidden from the world's eye. From now on, we will never underestimate the real dangers, the ones you cannot see, the ones that slip through the cracks and haunt us still." She paused, her gaze falling on those who had been there that night. Then gently, Becky picked up the framed photo of Holly, a soft smile crossing her lips. She pressed a gentle kiss to the forehead of the glass before setting it down with deliberate care, her eyes never leaving the empty surface. "It's funny really, if you stop to think about it." She said, her voice shifting, now colder, edged with something sharper, almost bitter. "Two people lost their lives that night. And yet, the one person, the one this nightmare truly targeted, is sitting right here, untouched, without a single scar to show for it. It makes you wonder… why some survive, and others do not." Her voice rose, anger cracking through the calm. Suddenly, Isabelle rose swiftly from her seat, moving quickly toward Becky with concern etched across her face. She reached out gently, trying to soothe her shaken friend, whose breaths came in shoal and uneven. Tanya tagged close behind, matching Isabelle's urgency, her own expression tight with worry. Together, they guided Becky toward the sturdy wooden doors, pushing them open to the cool daylight outside, hoping the fresh breeze might steady her rattled nerves. But as Becky passed Chase, she did not say a word. She just stared. Eyes filled with hurt, something twisted, something vengeful. Chase closed her eyes, trying to hide herself as she sobbed. Her heart ached fiercely. Becky's words cut deep, sharper than any blade, because they held a painful truth she could not deny. Her father and Holly were both gone… and somehow, it was because of her. Without thinking, Chase stood up and bolted for the doors, pushing past her mother, Tanya, and Becky. She did not look back. She did not stop. She just ran, straight out of the church, ignoring her name being shouted behind her. Emily and Hugo exchanged a quick look before hurrying after her. Moments later, they too stepped outside, moving toward the sunlit path. "She went that way." Isabelle said, pointing down the bright trail. She knew, without a doubt, that if Chase were going to open up to anyone right now, it would be Emily and Hugo. Those two who had always stood by her side, offering balmy understanding when words failed. They were the ones who knew her fears, her hopes, and the delicate pieces she struggled to hold together. In a moment like this, their presence felt like the only safe harbour she could seek.

CHAPTER TWENTY-TWO
"11:20"

1800

Arabella awoke in her bed to find her wedding gown already laid out, waiting for her like a silent invitation. She rose, inhaling the warm breeze drifting in from the open window, the sun releasing a reassuring glow outside. Miss Fawns was already there, waiting patiently to help her dress. Her gown had been fastened, her hair swept neatly into place, and her shoes were already secured on her feet. Everything was in order. She was ready. With a radiant smile, Arabella stepped onto the landing, pausing at the top of the grand staircase. Below, the guests gathered in muted elegance, faces upturned in silent admiration, their expressions oddly frozen in time. The chandelier above glinted off her earrings. She began her descent. Her gown whispered along the steps, the delicate fabric trailing behind her in soft, liquid folds. It fluttered gently with each step, graceful, fluid, and alive. And yet, no one else moved. The other women's gowns hung still, their curls untouched by even the smallest breeze. Not a fan stirred, not a single flicker from the candle sconces lining the walls. Only she moved. Arabella barely noticed. She felt light, untethered, as though the air parted just for her. She was the centre, the star, the pulse in a room otherwise drained of breath. She felt beautiful. Chosen. At the bottom, a handsome man extended his hand to receive her. That moment lived in her memory like a dream softened by time, hazy, like an old painting left too long in the sun, its colours faded but its beauty still intact. And sweet. Unmistakably sweet. Now she stood before her love, Edward. His face too, was blurred at the edges, as though seen through mist, but the warmth of his presence anchored her. She felt safe wrapped in something steady and enduring. Vows were exchanged. Words that once passed between them like breath, sacred and soft, spoken not just to each other but to something eternal. But just as Arabella began to speak hers, a darkness fell. The flowers scattered at her feet, petals browning and curling as though touched by decay. Decorations sagged and withered, succumbing to rot before her eyes. The once celebratory air thickened into something foul. Around her, the guests began to change. Their fine clothing shredded and faded into dusty rags. Skin sagged or vanished altogether. Eyes were missing, empty sockets gazing blankly. Noses collapsed; mouths weeping open in silent screams. Some faces were half-gone, blackened as if consumed by fire or a black hole. A nightmare crowd of hollow figures stood before her, watching. She turned to Edward, his body was collapsing inward, drying out like a withered leaf. Arabella screamed and ran, hands clawing at her, long bony fingers tearing into her arms as she passed. She burst through the doors and into the open air. But the outside was no refuge. The clouds had turned a deep, unnatural black, and the wind howled, whipping her long black hair across her face. Her dress was torn to shreds, thrashing violently in the gale. She turned back toward the house. But the house was gone. Nothing remained, just emptiness, endless and absolute, stretching out in every direction. It swallowed the walls, the sky, the ground beneath her feet, until even the memory of form began to dissolve. There was no colour, no sound. Only the vast, consuming hush. And in that emptiness, a single figure approached. Lady Catherine, she stood untouched by the storm. Not a single strand of her glossy, silver hair betrayed the fury of the wind. Her dress, a cascade of heavy silk, sinking perfectly in place as spun from midnight itself. The jewelled headpiece resting on her brow caught the sporadic flashes of lightning, glinting like cold fire, an unvarying crown amid the chaos. It was as though the storm dared not touch her, and the wind curved silently around her as if in respect. Arabella's breath hitched as she stared, rain lashing her skin and hair into a wild frenzy. Her fingers flew to shield her face, but even through the sting and the blur of rain, she could not tear her eyes away. Lady Catherine's steps were slow, reasoned, each one careful as if she carried a insupportable burden on her shoulders, or the secrets of the night. She closed the distance until only a whisper of air separated them. Her face remained serene and self-composed like the eye of a hurricane. But beneath that mask of control, there was a deep-rooted strength, a formidable seriousness that brooked no argument or weakness. In that moment, Lady Catherine was not just a woman. She was the storm's true master, its silent, unshakable heart. Arabella suddenly could not breathe. She collapsed to her knees at Lady Catherine's feet, gasping for the air that had vanished. Panic filled her lungs instead. Lady Catherine stood above her, lips curled into a cold, cruel smile. Her laughter rang out, low at first, then rising, echoing unnaturally through the collapsing scene around them. Arabella's vision blurred at the edges. The world tilted. Darkness crept in, swallowing light and sound like pulling her under. And then, nothing. The tempest's roar faded away, leaving behind an oppressive silence. The manor seemed to pause, as if suspended in time, waiting for something unseen to unfold.

Miss Fawns entered the drawing room with soft, wishful steps, her presence steady and assured. The polished wooden floor beneath her feet gleamed faintly in the dimming glow. Sir Edward sat near the tall window, the evening gloom gathering around him. In his hand, he held a delicate China cup, its contents dark and rich, far stronger than mere tea. His gaze scanned the newspaper, brows drawing together as though seeking answers hidden within the print. There was a weariness about him, as though invisible burdens pressed down upon his spirit. By the fire, Lady Catherine remained motionless, her silhouette outlined by the flickering flames. She turned the fragile pages of an ancient book, each movement meticulous and slow. Her expression was composed, almost detached, but beneath that silent exterior lay a fierce presence, an unspoken authority that filled the room like the lingering scent of smoke. The lull stretched on, filled with unvoiced thoughts and distant memories, as if the tempest had only been a prelude to a deeper, more unsettling peace. "Lady, Sir... I am sorry to bother you." Miss Fawns said with a becalming ease "but the doctor is here." Both Lady Catherine and Sir Edward rose at once, setting their things aside and following Miss Fawns to the door. "Ah, Lady Catherine." The doctor greeted warmly, taking her hand and placing a kiss upon it. "Sir Edward." He added, offering a firm handshake. "We're so happy you came." Edward said quickly. "Yes. Very." Lady Catherine dittoed, her tone more reserved. Miss Fawns led the trio up the stairs toward Arabella's room. Just before she reached the door, the doctor paused. "If I may." he told, "I would prefer to examine the patient alone. I tend to think more clearly without distraction." Lady Catherine nodded at once. Sir Edward hesitated at the beginning, torn. Every part of him screamed to stay by her side, but if the doctor could help Arabella, even in the smallest way, he would do as asked. With visible reluctance, he stepped back. The doctor entered the room, his expression blank, offering no hint of hope or certainty. His footsteps were slow, each one thudding dully against the floor as the door eased shut behind him. The moment he stepped closer, the truth hit him like a cold wave. Arabella's skin had turned an eerie shade of blue, her once warm complexion now pale and hollow, drained of all vitality. Her eyes stared blankly, as if the life had slipped away unnoticed, leaving behind only a fragile shell. He leaned in carefully, a sharp tightness gripping his chest. His fingers shook as they searched for a pulse, the faint rhythm of life he so desperately wanted to find. But there was nothing, no heartbeat, no warmth. The quiet around them deepened, closing in from every side. The reality was undeniable, a cruel and merciless truth that settled like a stone within him: Arabella was gone. She was dead. soothingly, he made a mental note: *'11:20 AM'* That would be the official time of death. He stepped back out and shut the door behind him. Lady Catherine and Sir Edward stood waiting. Removing his hat and holding it respectfully at his chest, the doctor delivered the news with solemn grace, like someone who had gathered these words many times before.

"Unfortunately... the patient has passed on." Sir Edward did not wait to fully grasp the meaning of those words. Without a moment's hesitation, he pushed past the doctor and raced into her chamber, each step driven by panic and disbelief. The world around him blurred as he reached Arabella's room and flung the door open. He dropped to his knees beside her bed, clutching her delicate form as if sheer will could bring her back. His fingers shook uncontrollably as he shook her gently, his voice barely more than a broken plea. "Arabella, please... do not leave me. Please, wake up." Tears welled in his eyes, blurring the room into a haze of sorrow. The cold quiet of the air pressed against him, mocking his desperate hope. But she remained unmoving, silent and distant, lost to him forever. "Wake up... please my love, do not leave me. I love you; I love you!" he cried, his voice breaking into hysteria. Lady Catherine stepped inside, trying to pull her son away. "Please, Edward..." "Get off me! Let me say my goodbyes!" he shouted at her, not even looking. Lady Catherine and the doctor mindlessly exited, leaving him with her. Sir Edward knelt beside Arabella. The stillness of her face and the unbearable cold of her lips did nothing to stop him. He kissed her one final time. "I love you, Arabella. I will always love you." Later that day, the staff of Blackthorn Manor gathered outside to watch as Arabella's body was carried from the grounds. Miss Fawns sobbed remotely at the back. Butler Brown, standing beside her, passed her his handkerchief. Sir Edward was the first to return inside. He climbed the stairs in inarticulacy, each step barely making a sound against the worn wooden floor. The house seemed to fall into a heartrending stillness around him, the darkness thickening with every slow movement. Without pause, he slipped into the bed that once held the late Arabella Nightshade, the chill of her absence settling in like a ghost between the sheets. In another room, Miss Fawns lay awake, her eyes fixed on the firelight flickering and writhing across the cracked ceiling. The flames twisted like restless spirits, erupting distorted shapes that flickered and vanished in the wavering light. The room felt colder somehow, despite the hearth's warmth. She tried to push away the relentless swirl of memories and regrets crowding her mind, but they clung stubbornly, whispers of secrets best left buried, of choices made in darkness. The heaviness pressed upon her, making it hard to breathe. Sleep refused her, slipping further and further away as the night stretched on. *How could I let this happen? Why didn't I save that poor girl?* She had served Lady Catherine for years, long enough to know the cold, cruel edge that lay beneath her graceful exterior. But never, not once, had she thought her capable of breaking her own bloods heart with murder *'murderer'* the word rang in her thoughts again. That is who I take orders from. But she could not leave. Her life was bound to this house, woven into every creaking floorboard, every murmuring corner. This place was all she had left. And if she walked away now... she would lose everything. Besides, *'who would care for Sir Edward?'* Her dear Eddie, delicate and broken, needing her more than ever. A sudden knock at the door jolted her from her spiralling thoughts, quick and urgent against the deep quiet. She sat up, startled. "Who is it?" "It's me, miss." Came a soft voice from the other side. Miss Fawns exhaled, trying to gentle her racing heart. "Come in, child." As the young woman stepped into the glow of the candlelight, Miss Fawns rose slowly from her chair, her spine straight, her expression sharp. "And what brings you here at this hour?" she inquired coolly, her voice tight with restrained irritation. "I... I beg your pardon Miss." The maid stammered, her voice unsteady, the words catching awkwardly in her throat as she struggled to speak. "Is it forgiveness you seek?" Miss Fawns interrupted, her voice clever and invariant. "Or perhaps you think I will speak for you to keep your position?" The girl faltered, her hands shaking slightly as she struggled to meet Miss Fawns' steady eyes. "I...I understand Miss... I am truly sorry." She drawled, her voice faint now, tinged with uncertainty and remorse. "All I ask is that you might consider giving me a reference. That is all." Miss Fawns regarded her in silence for a long moment, the conciliate stretching between them, thick with unspoken judgment. Miss Fawns' face darkened. "How dare you come to my chamber in the dead of night to make such a request." She said, her voice rising just enough to break the tranquil, edged with frost, sending a chill through the room. "No respectable household should ever be burdened with the disgrace of employing a woman of… such a reputation." Her eyes narrowed, cold and immovable, as if daring the other to speak. The meaning behind her words hung in the room, thick and unmistakable. The maid's eyes brimmed with tears. She curtsied hastily, murmuring something incoherent, and fled the room, her footsteps light and frantic against the wooden floor. Miss Fawns closed the door with a firm hand, the latch clicking sharply in the silence. She stood motionless for a moment, the candle issuing long shadows across the chamber. Then she returned to her bed and sat down, hands folded tightly in her lap. And there, in the solitude of her quarters, the composure she had worn like Armor began to splinter. Tears slipped silently down her cheeks.

She did not sob. She simply wept, quiet, broken, and ashamed.

CHAPTER TWENTY-THREE
MURDER SCENE

Present day

Chase had been running for what felt like forever, her lungs burning, her heart pounding in her ears. She had not meant to end up here. Not at the manor. Not this place. And ultimately as the vast silhouette rose before her, she realized how near she had come, closer than she intended, close enough to see the police tape still clinging to the gate, fluttering faintly in the wind like a warning long forgotten. Not the safe house. Not the cramped apartment she shared with her mother, where the walls were thin and the nights felt longer than they should. This was different. It carried a kind of cargo that settled in her ribs, a pressure she could not unqualifiedly shake. Home. If it could still be called that. The word no longer felt right in her mouth, too brittle, too full of memories that no longer belonged to her. She stood frozen at the edge of the property, unsure if she had come looking for answers… or ghosts. She ducked under the tape without thinking and ran inside. It was freezing. The broken window in the dining room still had not been boarded up. Cold air poured in, swirling through the silence like something alive. Chase stepped into the dining room and froze. The scene had not changed. Shards of glass still glittered across the floor like slivers of ice, catching the light in sharp, unnatural angles. Blood stained the carpet in a wide, rust-coloured smear, dried, sunken into the fabric, and impossible to ignore. The air felt stale, untouched since the chaos. Even the chairs remained askew, as if the people who once sat in them had vanished mid-sentence. She swallowed hard, her footsteps hesitant as she moved further into the room. Each movement felt too loud, too real, as though she were disturbing something that should have been left undisturbed. She turned to leave but paused. Something shifted in the air. A pressure. A coldness. Like the moment just before a storm breaks. She turned back, heart thudding. The room… had changed. The shattered glass was gone. The bloodstains vanished. The carpet was clean, thick, and new beneath her shoes. The long dining table was restored, polished wood gleaming beneath an

ornate chandelier, every candle lit and
flickering steadily. Silverware was laid out in
perfect symmetry and untouched dishes
steaming as if the meal had just been served.
The dining room no longer looked like her
own. The mess was gone. Everything was
pristine, but old. Very old. Chase stepped into
the hall, and her breath hitched. The manor
had changed. It was not just the furniture or the
lighting. It was everything. The air felt denser,
assimilated with the scent of beeswax, old
wood, and something faintly floral, like rose
petals left to dry in a locked drawer. The
wallpaper had shifted to a darker shade, rich
with intricate patterns that had not been there
before, curling at the corners as though the
walls themselves were exhaling age. The light
overhead flickered gently, golden and low,
more like candlelight than any modern fixture.
It was like stepping into another century. A
stillness rode over everything, thick and
expectant. No murmur of electricity, no quiet
mechanical rhythms. Just the soft creak
beneath her feet and the awareness of her own
breath, superficial and quick. Older. Grander.
But deeply, unmistakably wrong. A painting on
the far wall caught her attention. She did not
recognize it. A woman stood poised in the
frame, staring straight ahead, her gaze

unnervingly clear, as if she saw far more than she should. Chase took a slow step forward, her skin prickling. She was not alone here. Not really. Then a maid swept past her. Straight through her. Chase did not move. She hardly breathed. The woman continued down the corridor, disappearing through a door that had not been there moments ago. It shut behind her with a soft click, the sound somehow louder than it should have been in the thick air. Chase turned slowly, her eyes darting over her surroundings. Everything looked real, too real. The fine grain of the wood panelling, the muted glint of brass handles, the faint impressions of footsteps worn into the carpet runner. The manor had not just changed… it had awakened. Another figure emerged at the top of the stairs: a young maid, no older than Chase, carrying a silver tray and moving with careful, rehearsed grace. Her expression was tense, her eyes cast low, avoiding the portraits lining the walls as though they watched her. She passed within arm's reach, Chase could see the small tear in her sleeve, the smudge of ash near her collarbone. Still, no sign that anyone saw her. Chase's pulse quickened. She backed away, her shoes making no sound, as if the floor had forgotten she was standing on it. She was a ghost here. Or worse trapped in someone else's memory. She must be the head maid, Chase thought, her eyes following the woman. Then, footsteps. A distinct tapping sounded through the hall steady and slow, like the subtle beat of something ancient and practiced. Chase turned. At the top of the grand staircase stood a woman of terrifying presence. Her gown was deep velvet, sweeping the floor behind her. An overcoat trimmed with gold and a cane like twisted thorns climbing up from the earth. A towering feather arched from her hat, swaying in a breeze that somehow did not touch anyone else. Chase ran after. She had to. She felt obliged to follow the mystery women out of curiosity. The air around her felt charged now, thick, like the moment before a thunderclap. Her ears strained for movement, for breath, for anything. Nothing. Just the faint echo of her own pulse thudding in her ears. She leaned forward slowly, just enough to peek past the corner. The hallway was still. Empty the mystery women was not to be seen. But the quiet did not feel safe, it felt watchful. Chase stepped out cautiously, one foot at a time. the tail end of the mystery woman's black skirts vanishing around the corner at the far end of the hallway. She had not disappeared after all. Chase hesitated. Every instinct told her to turn back, to find the front door and get out. But something stronger held her there, a pull she could not name. A need to understand. To see where the woman was going… and why. Approaching the grand staircase she placed her hand on the banister, its polished wood colder than it should have been, and began to climb. One step at a time. Each footfall silent, but in her mind, every motion screamed. Something was waiting at the top. And Chase was walking straight into it. But she did not call out. Instead, she walked across the landing, past the great chandelier in the centre, and disappeared into a room. Chase moved quickly but cautiously, her footsteps light and careful. She recognized the door ahead; it was her bedroom. Or at least, it should have been. Something about it felt off, as if the room itself had shifted in time or memory. The wood was darker, the brass handle tarnished, and the faint scent of lavender that once filled the air was gone, replaced by something colder, more distant. Her hand shook slightly as she reached out to touch the door. She eased it open just enough to peek inside. The woman was inside, her voice low and gentle as she spoke to a figure lying motionless in the bed. Chase moved closer, her footsteps barely disturbed the dense quiet that filled the space. Her pulse quickened, sharp and insistent beneath her skin. A girl lay there, young, pale, exquisitely delicate, like a porcelain doll untouched by time or pain. The faint rise and fall of her chest was barely perceptible, as if she were suspended between worlds. Then, a name flashed in Chase's mind with sudden, shattering clarity. Arabella Nightshade. Recognition crashed over her like a cold wave, rooting her to the spot. The air around her seemed to tighten, thickening with an invisible presence, watchful, expectant. Chase's blood ran cold. This was no ordinary memory. This was a secret, long buried, alive again. She watched in horrified silence as the woman bent down, lifted a pillow, and without a flicker of doubt, pressed it hard against Arabella's face. Chase's hand flew to her mouth, stifling a scream that clawed its way up her throat. Her mind screamed for her to run, to fight, to do something, anything. But her body betrayed her. She was rooted to the spot, as if invisible chains held her in place, trapped in this cruel moment frozen in time. Arabella's body tensed beneath the weight, faint muffled sounds escaping. The silence that followed was suffocating, heavy and absolute. A fierce, rapid thudding filled Chase's ears, each beat echoing like a warning. Tears welled in her eyes, but she forced them back, swallowing the overwhelming surge of helplessness. A cold knot of dread tightened in her stomach. This was not just a memory, this was a nightmare replaying itself, and she was trapped, forced to witness the horror again and again. Beneath the covers, Arabella flinched once. Then again, a faint tremor rippled through her. And then, exactly settled. The woman stepped back; her movements eerily composed. She gently fluffed the pillow and, with unsettling allay, arranged it neatly behind Arabella's head, as if nothing had just transpired. A silence filled the room, pressing down like a hidden command. Then... she turned. Her eyes met Chase's. And then, she smiled. A soft, knowing smile, one that carried a calm finality and hidden secrets. She gave a gentle nod, a wordless farewell that swam in the air, thick with meaning. And then, she vanished. Chase blinked. And when her eyes opened again, Arabella was there. Inches from her face. Pale. Expressionless. Her eyes wide and unblinking, locked onto Chase's with a hollow intensity that made the world tilt. Chase stumbled back with a scream, the sound ripping from her throat before she even realized she was making it. Her heart slammed against her ribs, breath catching as she scrambled away from the apparition that had not been there a second before. Arabella did not move. Did not blink. Just stared. As though she could see straight through her. And then, Suddenly, a firm hand gripped her arm. "Chase!" "Chase!" The voice was desperate, urgent, pulling her back from the edge of that haunting memory. Everything snapped back. The cold was gone. The candles were gone. She was in her bed. "Chase!" Emily's voice shouted from the other side of the door. Chase bolted upright, breathing hard, heart racing. She ran to the door and yanked it open, letting Emily and Hugo inside. "Girl, we've been calling you for twenty minutes!" Emily's voice wavered with panic, her eyes wide with worry. "We heard screaming… strange noises. But your door was locked." Chase blinked, still shaken, struggling to push the nightmare from her mind. "I…I didn't hear anything." She stammered, voice barely steady. Emily stepped closer, searching Chase's face. "You do not look all right. Please, talk to me. What is going on?" Chase swallowed hard, the words catching like a knot. For a long moment, silence collapsed between them, thick as fog. Then Emily reached out, gently touching Chase's arm. "You're not alone." Hugo looked at the doorknob. His brows knit together. "There's no lock on this door…" Chase sat down on the edge of her bed, motioning for Emily and Hugo to do the same. Her eyes were wide, serious and haunted. "I need to tell you something." She said, her voice low, full of urgency. "I think I know how Arabella Nightshade died." Emily and Hugo exchanged a quick glance. "How?" Hugo asked cautiously. Chase took a breath, steadying herself. "I saw it happen. Just now. It was not a dream." Her voice shaky with the burden of what she had witnessed. "It was like Arabella showed me. Like she wanted me to see it." Emily's eyes widened, the colour draining from her face. "Murdered?" she breathed, her words barely escaping her lips, as if saying them aloud might make the nightmare real. "Yes. Murdered." Chase reached into her drawer and pulled out a photograph, an old black-and-white family portrait from the 1800s. She pointed to the woman standing stiff and proud in the centre. *'Lady Catherine.'* "She was there." Chase whispered, her voice shaking. "I think she did it. She killed Arabella." Hugo leaned in, his brow knitting together deeply. "Wait…are you saying this woman… actually murdered Arabella? And why would she show you this? Why you?" Chase shook her head, frustration and fear warring in her eyes. "I do not know. It is like she wanted me to see it, to know the truth. But it feels like a warning… or maybe a curse." Hugo's gaze darkened, his voice low and serious. "If this woman was involved, things are a lot more complicated as we thought. We have to be careful." Chase looked down, fingers slightly over the worn edge of the photo. "I think Arabella wants revenge." Chase said slowly, each word weighed down by something deeper. "On the entire Blackthorne bloodline." Emily blinked, clearly trying to make sense of it. "But that does not explain you…Chase. You are not part of the Blackthorne family." Chase did not answer. Her mouth opened slightly, but no words came. Instead, she looked away, eyes fixed on the far wall as if it might offer her an escape. Emily's voice softened. "Chase… is there something you're not telling me?" The question slung between them delicate and dangerous. But then something clicked. A sudden realization crossed her face, as if a hidden piece had just fallen into place. "I think I know why." She said softly, her words almost a murmur, meant more for herself than anyone else. Without hesitation, she rose, breaking the shattering uneasiness that postulated in the room. "We should probably head back to the wake." She said, her voice steady but carrying a hint of nerves. Emily and Hugo looked stunned, still processing what they had just heard. Neither spoke, but both slowly rose to their feet, the anxiety between them uncertain. Chase crossed the room and opened the door for them, her fingers still clutching the old photograph like a lifeline. Its worn corners dug into her palm, grounding her, anchoring her in the swirl of confusion. She glanced back into the room one last time, her thoughts swirling in a restless whirl. "I know why." She whispered again, a low whisper. But whatever the truth was, it hovered just out of reach, a secret she was not ready to face. Not yet.

CHAPTER TWENTY-FOUR
PAST TRUTHS

Present day

The wake was in full swing. People were laughing too loudly, drinking too freely, and helping themselves to the endless buffet like it was any other party, not the aftermath of two funerals. Chase stood near the edge of the room, taking it all in. She spotted her mother in deep conversation with Becky, Tanya, and David. Part of her wanted to go over, to be near them, but the other part, the louder part, worried it would only upset Becky. She could not face another confrontation. Instead, she wandered. Across the room, Emily and Hugo loaded their plates with miniature sausage rolls and funeral sandwiches, the kind of dull, forgettable fare that seemed as lifeless as the gathering itself. They exchanged wary side-eyes over half-sipped glasses of wine, each pretending to enjoy the bitter taste, their smiles tight and strained. Then a hand landed lightly on her shoulder. "Hey... I am sorry about your dad." Chase glanced up to see a tall man, sharply dressed, maybe in his mid-thirties. Handsome, in a kind of clean-cut, he-owns-a canoe kind of way. "Thank you." Chase replied silently. "I'm sorry let me introduce myself properly." He intimated, holding out his hand. "I'm Jess." Chase raised her eyebrows. A guy named Jess. She loved a gender twist on names. Her own name, after all, was traditionally male. It was like meeting a stranger who already understood her on a cosmic level, someone whose presence felt strangely familiar, as if their souls had brushed against each other in another time or place. There was an unspoken connection, quiet yet profound, weaving itself between them in an instant. "Hi Jess. I am Chase." she said softly, her voice steady but carrying a hint of warmth that reached beyond the simple introduction. She shook his hand and gave him a smile, that warm buzz of distraction softening her for a moment. "I was just about to start collaborating with your father." Jess continued, his tone casual but sincere. "I'm a drama teacher." Chase blinked, caught off guard by the unexpected news. And just like that, the low hum of excitement that had surrounded them suddenly faded away. Something about it, maybe the forced enthusiasm, maybe the theatricality of the whole scene, just gave her a creeping discomfort she could not dismiss. "I'm sorry." She said quickly, stepping back, her voice tight and brittle. "I have to go." Before he could find the words to respond, her eyes darted to a half-finished glass of whisky resting on a nearby table, someone else's careless drink, and without pause, she grabbed it and swallowed it in one long, burning gulp. The fierce burn spread down her throat, momentarily dulling the restless tension inside her. The spice hit her throat like fire, her eyes watering instantly, but she did not stop. She needed to feel anything else. "Chase." The voice caught her off guard. She turned, pulse jumping ever so slightly, some part of her braced to see Jess standing there again. But it was not him. It was Becky. Her expression was soft, remorseful. Chase could see the weight in her eyes. "I'm sorry about earlier." Becky said, voice gentle. "I was going through a lot of emotions… I should not have taken them out on you. Please, will you accept my apology?" Becky's said with genuine remorse, eyes searching Chase is for any sign of forgiveness. Without hesitation, Chase stepped forward and wrapped her arms gently around her, offering comfort where words fell short. "Of course I forgive you." She whispered softly, tightening the embrace as if to seal away the pain between them. For a moment, neither of them spoke. The speechlessness between Chase and Becky pulsed with all the words neither could bring themselves to say. Then came the uneven sound of heels against hardwood. Isabelle appeared behind them, gripping her handbag tightly, as though bracing herself. Her cheeks were flushed a deep rose, and her lipstick had smudged slightly at the corner of her mouth. She was smiling, brightly, if a bit too much, but her eyes did not all focus. "Chase love… It is time we head home." She said, her voice feathered with the looseness of too much wine. She gave a small, unsteady sway, as though the room shifted beneath her. She looked between Chase and Becky, pausing as if unsure whether she had just interrupted something or wandered into a moment she did not recognize. Chase turned to her mum, not even slightly annoyed. Isabelle deserved this. She had been holding herself together for weeks, barely sleeping, barely functioning. If a little wine was what it took to finally give her a break, then so be it. "All right." Chase said with a tired smile, looping her arm through Isabelle's as they stepped out into the crisp night air. The world outside felt oddly still, like a stage after the curtain had dropped, with everything waiting to be packed away. "I am going to order Chinese when we get home. What do you say to crispy duck rolls and chicken in plum sauce?" Isabelle brightened, cheeks still rosy from the wine, her steps a little more grounded now. "God, yes. And sesame prawn toast. Something messy and comforting. We deserve it." "You deserve a feast." Chase said with a gentle laugh. "We both do." They walked a few paces. "Do we still have those weird fizzy drinks in the fridge?" Isabelle asked. Chase smirked. "Only the lychee ones. The rejects." "Perfect." Isabelle said, bumping her shoulder lightly against Chase's. "Tonight, even the weird ones are welcome." "Don't forget the wontons." Isabelle grinned. They both laughed, just a small, shared moment between mother and daughter. And for the first time in days, maybe weeks... Chase did not feel so alone. Back at the safe house, Chase was in the kitchen preparing the Chinese food, a job her mum usually insisted on doing. But tonight, Chase wanted her to rest. Isabelle deserved it. As she stirred the boxes and carefully plated the food, Chase couldn't help but picture her dad in their old kitchen, the way his cheeky grin would light up the room, the awful old-school music blasting through the house like an unstoppable force, pulling everyone into an impromptu dance whether they wanted to join or not. He would be cooking with an easy confidence, cracking jokes that made them laugh until their sides ached, and once the meal was done, he would insist they all sit together to watch some black-and-white film he adored, filling the room with nostalgia and warmth. The memory tugged at her heart and made her smile. She handed her mum a plate piled high with Chinese takeaway and settled into the opposite sofa, the cushions sighing beneath her. The scent of plum sauce and fried dough hung in the air, mingling with the faint trace of white linin from a long-cold candle on the windowsill. Chase twisted her fork through a piece of chicken, not hungry, but needing something to do with her hands. Across from her, Isabelle tucked her legs beneath her, already picking at a crispy duck roll. Then carefully, Chase asked, "Mum… am I adopted?" The words hung there. Isabelle froze. For a second, Chase regretted saying anything. *What was I thinking?* she thought. *We just buried Dad. Mum's half drunk. This is not the time.* Isabelle did not say a word. She picked up her plate and peacefully left the room. Chase sat there in the hush. the warm smell of crispy duck and plum sauce surrounding her like a memory she could not touch. She finished her food slowly, her stomach full of more than just duck, and eventually drifted off to sleep on the sofa.

The next morning, Chase woke to the sunlight creeping through the curtains. She rubbed her tired eyes and stretched, her body aching from the unexpected nap. That is when she spotted her empty plate still resting on the floor. Gently, she picked it up and made her way toward the kitchen, a small flicker of hope stirring inside her, she could wash up, and, just maybe, find a way to make peace with her mum. When she entered, Isabelle was already there, sitting quietly at the kitchen table, a steaming cup of tea cradled in one hand, the newspaper folded open in the other. The soft rustle of the pages was the only sound in the room. Chase tiptoed around her, unsure if she should say anything yet. She washed her plate in tranquillity, made herself a coffee, and was about to head back out when Isabelle spoke. "I wish your father were here to help me with what I'm about to tell you." Her expression was difficult to read, tired, but steady. The kind of look someone wears when they have practiced their words too many times and still do not know if they will come out right. Chase said nothing. Just waited. "I should've told you a long time ago." Isabelle insinuated, her voice soft but certain now. "But I kept thinking… if I waited, it might never matter. That we could leave it all behind." She looked at her daughter, her eyes glassy with something between guilt and hope. "But it does matter. It always did." Isabelle did not look up right away. Her fingers gripped the teacup tighter. "There was an accident." She began, her voice breaking slightly as if dredging up a painful memory. "It happened years ago… I lost a baby. The doctors told me afterward that I might never be able to have children again." She paused, tears gathering at the corners of her eyes, glistening like delicate glass. "Your dad and I wanted a child more than anything." Isabelle began, her voice wavering just enough to show her emotion. "So, we searched, through every agency, every hope, every restful prayer. And the moment we saw your little face, we knew. You were not our blood, but you were, and always would be, ours. Our daughter in every way that truly matters." Chase blinked hard, swallowing the tightness lodged deep in her chest. The room seemed to close in, the meaning of those words settling over her like a plague. She wanted to believe it, needed to believe it, but the question hovered stubbornly at the edge of her mind *'Who am I really?'* "We raised you with love. And we always hoped that one day, when the time was right, we would tell you the truth. I just… I did not think it would be like this." Isabelle looked up at her daughter, her eyes shining with unshed tears, filled with a mix of regret and love. "Don't you ever, for one second, think we loved you any less than if you'd come from me." She rendered softly, her voice thick with emotion. "You've always been our daughter, no different, no less." Chase reached across the table and took her mum's hand. "Thank you." She verbalized; her voice unsteady. "You and Dad will always be my real parents. But… I do need to find my birth parents. It is important." Isabelle nodded, holding back fresh tears. "Of course, love. I would not expect anything else." They stood and hugged, holding each other tightly. For the first time in a long while, Chase felt grounded. As they gently pulled apart, Isabelle brushed away a stray tear and offered a warm, weary smile. "We have a big day ahead tomorrow, anyway. Moving back into the manor." Chase nodded slowly. "Yeah. Let us just hope it is ready for us."

Later, as she slid into the worn booth across from Emily and Hugo, she offered a quiet, heartfelt thanks. "Thank you for coming." It had been ages since the three of them had set foot in Sit & Sip, yet the little café felt the same, from the handwritten chalk menu scrawled on the blackboard to the lopsided fairy lights that twinkled unevenly overhead. Emily grinned, breaking the comfortable stillness. "It is fine. Besides, I have been craving one of their brownies forever. Honestly, they are the best in town." Hugo nodded in agreement, stirring his coffee absentmindedly. "Sometimes, it is the trivial things that remind you of normal, you know? Like this place." Chase let out a small, tired smile. "Yeah. Normal feels far away lately." The three friends sat together in calm companionship, the familiar hum of the café wrapping around them like a delicate refuge from the turmoil beyond. "I prefer the blondies." Hugo chimed in, already eyeing the glass display. Chase smiled at their easy banter, feeling a small warmth amid the uncertainty. Then she took a deep breath, steadying herself before sharing what had been weighing on her heart. She told them everything, the moment she discovered she was adopted, the devastating news about her mum and dad's life altering car crash, and the persistent, nagging feeling that something about her past had always been just out of reach. Now, with everything unfolding around her, she knew she could not face it alone. She needed their support, their strength, to help her find her birth family and uncover the truths she had longed to understand. "Wow." Emily said, gently. "Chase… I am so sorry." "Don't be." Chase replied, shaking her head gently. "I have always known I am… different. I do not look like either of them, they are nothing like me. But that does not change how I feel. They are my parents. The people who raised me, who love me. That is what matters." She gave them both a warm smile, but it was edged with something heavier, unsure and unrecited. The conversation between them stretched like a thin line, strained with anticipation. Then suddenly, Hugo leaned forward, his eyes wide with a mix of surprise and curiosity, as if he had just pieced together a crucial part of the puzzle. "Wait…if you are adopted, then… oh my god…You could be part of the Blackthorne bloodline." Chase blinked. Emily sat upright as well, her brow creased deeply, the pieces suddenly clicking into place. "That would explain everything." Emily said quietly, her tone edged with unease. "Why you're being targeted… attacked…" Chase's eyes darkened, her voice low and thoughtful, as if the words were meant for her alone. "And why she said I had the blood of a murderer." Her voice seemed to resonate softly among them, carrying a subtle gravity. For a moment,

they all remained motionless, the café's
background noise fading as the significance of
that possibility settled deeply within each of
them. The world beyond felt distant, as if time
itself had slowed. Then the waiter arrived,
setting down plates piled high with warm,
gooey brownies and blondies. The rich,
comforting scent of chocolate filled the space,
inviting and familiar, but none of them reached
for their treats just yet. Their thoughts were
tangled in matters far more pressing than any
dessert. Instead, they learned in closer, voices
hushed. They wondered how they might begin
tracing Chase's birth records, where to even
start looking in the maze of paperwork and
time. *'Were there names, old files, or adoption
records tucked away somewhere, hidden in
forgotten drawers or dusty archives?'* The
uncertainty pressed down on them, but the
search had to start somewhere. And if any of
those records led back to Blackthorne Manor.
Chase and Isabelle stood still, both staring up at
the looming manor. The last time Isabelle was
here, she lost the love of her life, and a dear
friend. The last time Chase had been here, she
uncovered something terrifying about the
ghostly woman known as Arabella Nightshade,
a secret that still lingered in her mind, sending
shivers down her spine. It was strange how a

single place could carry such significance, an atmosphere dense with grief, fear, and memories that seemed to seep from the walls themselves. And yet from the outside, it looked harmless, just bricks, windows, and rooms. Ordinary. Innocent. Chase adjusted the strap on her shoulder, grabbed her suitcase, and began walking toward the front door. Isabelle followed in tranquil step behind her. The moment they crossed the threshold, a wave of nostalgia washed over them, as if the years had folded back on themselves. The air still carried that unmistakable scent, aged wood mingled with the faint trace of lavender polish, a memory paused in time. The walls remained unchanged, and the furniture stood unmoved, soft observers of countless forgotten moments. Yet beneath that comforting familiarity, something had altered. The energy felt subdued, as if the house itself were suspended in apprehension, dimmer, more oppressive, wrapped in a soft veil of stillness. The floor beneath their feet gave a faint groan, an unexpected sound in the hush. Faint murmurs seemed to curl at the edges of their hearing, as though the house was murmuring secrets it had long concealed. It was not until they reached the kitchen that the full burden of that change settled over them, pressing down like a hidden truth waiting to surface. The familiar kitchen, once alive with activity, now felt empty and distant. The stale air carried a chill that seeped into their bones, and the slightest movement of darkness flickered just beyond the edge of sight. Chase swallowed hard, sensing that this was only the beginning. This room would never be the same again. No Henry standing by the stove, cracking cheesy jokes. No dancing to awful old tunes. No warm plates passed around, or flickering candles at dinnertime. Neither of them dared step into the dining room, even though they both knew it had been cleaned. Scrubbed spotless. Still, some stains do not come out with bleach. The air felt dense with memories, as if the room itself carried murmurs of what had happened there. They lingered just beyond sight, traces of the past that no amount of cleaning could erase. Isabelle quietly slipped away to check the post that had piled up in their absence. A stack of envelopes sat waiting. Among them were dozens of condolence cards, *sorry for your loss* scribbled in ink she could not bring herself to read. Then she found something else: A cheque. Twenty thousand pounds, raised from the charity night they had carefully organized. On top of that, an extra ten thousand generously donated by the town itself. Altogether, a remarkable total of thirty thousand pounds. On paper, a success. But in her hands, it felt more like a reminder. Of tragedy. Of how one night meant to bring people together had nearly destroyed them all.

CHAPTER TWENTY-FIVE
RATCHET SECRET

1800

It had been a few months since Arabella's death, though for some, it felt like only yesterday. The manor was no longer the same. The light that once bathed its halls had vanished with her passing. Arabella may have only been part of the family for a brief time, but within that brief span, she lifted the spirits of all who lived and worked within the estate. Tasks that once felt burdensome seemed lighter in her presence. Miss Fawns who used to attended to Arabella the should of bee new lady of the manor, one who, to her stupefy surprise, treated her not as a lowly servant but with genuine respect, as an equal almost reminded miss fawns of lady catherine at that age. This woman had been raised amidst wealth and privilege, yet she was refreshingly unpretentious, never allowing her status to cloud her judgment or diminish the value of those around her. In her presence, Miss Fawns felt a rare sense of dignity and understanding, something she had not experienced in many years within the grand halls she served. The butler, Mr. Brown, remained fixed in his old-fashioned ways, his loyalty firmly rooted in the Blackthorn family. He rarely grew close to newcomers. And yet, over time, Arabella's smile and gentle manner had begun to thaw the frost around his heart. Sir Edward had known many attempts at love in his lifetime, but none had struck him as deeply as Arabella. She had been *HIS* Arabella. Now, she lived only in memory, spoken of in the third person, never again to laugh, to speak, to share in the room. After Arabella's funeral, Sir Edward planted a tree in honour of his almost-wife, a living tribute to the woman who had changed his life. Around its base, a circular bench wrapped gently like an embrace, and a small brass plaque was fixed into the wood. It read: "Here shall I grow, here shall I watch, here shall I keep loving. Here I lay my roots only to be free. I am only but a thought away and will always be part of you all." The words were beautiful, poetic even, and on further inspection they held a sorrow that clung to the soul. A once-vibrant young woman, so full of warmth and light, was now part of the earth. A memory. A tree. Yet those who lived and worked at Blackthorne Estate found a strange comfort in passing beneath the great white cherry blossom tree. When in full bloom, its branches bowed under the root of delicate petals, clustering so densely that it seemed to hold a drifting cloud, soft, radiant, and suspended in a timeless pause. The gentle rustle of blossoms in the breeze like a quiet lullaby, offering a fleeting sanctuary from the estate's lingering gloom and unvoiced secrets. For a moment, beneath that ethereal canopy, the burdens of the past felt lighter, and even the darkest memories seemed softened by the tree's silent grace. It had to be white. Sir Edward had insisted, no other colour would do. White had been Arabella's favourite. He remembered the moment clearly, during one of their walks through the ever-flowing fields. He had asked her what her favourite colour was, and she had replied: "I love white. There is something peaceful about it, so pure, so untouched. It feels honest, like it has not been marked by the world yet. White radiates through me. It is like standing in front of a blank canvas, full of possibility. I get to decide what goes on it. I get to choose who I become." What made that moment even more special was that they had been standing, unknowingly beside a great white cherry blossom tree, its petals drifting around her like snow caught in the soft afternoon sun. Sir Edward remembered watching her then, how the light played across her face, how she seemed almost part of the tree itself, delicate and luminous. And in that still, radiant moment, he knew, without question or pause, that he had found something extraordinary. He did not just want her love. He needed it, like air in his lungs, like roots in the earth. Sir Edward visited the new planted memorial tree, frequently, especially when the craving for drink overwhelmed him. It had become his place of both mourning and escape. In the first month after Arabella's death, Sir Edward unravelled. Grief clung to him like a second skin, intense and unrelenting. He withdrew from everything, refusing to tend to the estate's affairs, refusing even to step beyond the manor's doors. Days blurred into nights. He barely ate, barely spoke. The man once known for his poise and eloquence now wandered the halls like a ghost. His father, Sir Howard, quietly resumed the running of the estate. It was not unfamiliar territory; he had done so for many years before handing the reins to his son. And now, without protest or the hint of a complaint, he simply stepped back into his role, as if the grief had been folded neatly away. Lady Catherine, however, embraced the return to order with a quiet hunger. She had always found power intoxicating, like a fine perfume she could never tolerably resist. Control suited her. Thrived in her hands. Yet even she, in her cold and calculating way, did not wish to see her only son destroyed by grief. So, she intervened in her own fashion. Night by night, she began slipping a blend of sleeping herbs into his evening drinks, nothing drastic, just enough to cloud his thoughts, soften his grief, and zone out the storm inside him. A gentle nudge toward peace. No one questioned Sir Edward's sudden retreat from the world. They spoke in hushed tones of his mourning, of a broken heart too shattered to mend. It was Lady Catherine who crafted the story, soft and vague enough to be believable. She told the staff and villagers that he had fallen ill, that the burden of heartbreak had sapped his strength and left his constitution delicate. Perhaps, she suggested with a faint, knowing smile, the sorrow had compromised his immune system, a poetic kind of curse, born not of magic but of grief so profound it seeped into the very marrow of his bones. And in that time, those Georgian years where sentiment and superstition often held equal burliness such a tale was more than enough. Of course, the staff at Blackthorne Manor knew the real reason for Sir Edward's decline, whisky. The man had clung to it like a drowning soul gasping for air, desperate and unrelenting. It was not sickness that had hollowed his face or dimmed the light in his eyes; it was grief, steeped deeply in drink, wearing him down from the inside out. Lady Catherine, for all her subtlety, had not made much effort to hide her calm inquiries. She had asked the housemaid to fetch herbs reputed to help with sleep; valerian, poppy, chamomile, but she never seemed to sleep long herself. It was poor Edward who unknowingly bore the effects. Each evening, his drink was quietly mauled with a carefully informed blend of calming herbs, just enough to blur the penetrating edges of his anguish and usher him into a delicate, sedated state. He never suspected the source of this slow unravelling; it was his own mother's hand at work. She would sit beside him in the dim light, her presence both soothing and controlling, offering silent comfort while silently steering him away from the harshness of the world. With patient eyes, she watched as he slipped further from reality, sinking deeper into the haze she had woven around him, a delicate trap disguised as care. The staff, though silent, were not blind. They exchanged glances in the kitchen and whispers in the corridors. They had seen the whisky bottles disappear, the heavy-lidded stares, the sudden bouts of calm. They knew. They always knew. In the servants' quarters, down in the kitchen, Miss Fawns was busy passing along the Blackthorns' request for the evening's dinner. The chef, who despised last-minute demands, grumbled under his breath; the kitchen's orders had already been placed, and obtaining new ingredients on such short notice was no easy task. It usually meant sending one of his sous-chefs scurrying across the village in search of supplies. Fortunately, on this occasion, the pantry was well-stocked with everything needed. Just then, one of the maids hurried into the kitchen, breathless and flushed, her footsteps echoing on the wooden floor as if she had been running from some urgent threat. "I'm so sorry to barge in Miss Fawns." She panted, struggling to steady her racing heart. "There's a woman waiting out back, she's asking for you, discussed it's important… urgent even." Miss Fawns let out a soft huff of annoyance but wiped her hands on her apron and made her way to the rear door. There, standing in the fading light, was a face she recognised immediately. "Have you banged your head? What are you doing here?" Miss Fawns hissed in a faint voice, careful that no one nearby could overhear. Without waiting for a reply, she hurriedly ushered the woman inside, her footsteps echoing sharply as she marched her down the narrow, dimly lit corridor. They stopped at a small box room where Miss Fawns kept the household duties meticulously organized. The room was modest and unadorned; a worn wooden table scarred with years of use, a single sturdy chair, and piles of scattered papers that hinted at constant, smooth labour. On the table rested a solitary photograph, its edges faded with age. It depicted an older woman, her expression stern and resolute, her features strikingly similar to Miss Fawns, as if a distant reflection caught in a glass. Closing the door firmly behind them, Miss Fawns seated the visitor in the chair, then poured two cups of black tea into dainty China cups, handing one to the woman before taking a seat herself. They sat facing one another, each holding their cup, the concern between them almost visible in the dim lantern light. "Right girl." Miss Fawns said at last, her voice cutting through the air with a sudden sharpness, pleached with impatience and authority. She fixed the former maid with a steady gaze. "Are you going to tell me exactly why you've come all this way, breathless and frantic, or must I be left to piece the story together myself?" She reached out and turned up the lantern, shooting a stronger glow across the cramped little room. The woman gulped in panic now rethinking her choices of seeking Miss Fawns help, "I know we didn't get off to the best of starts." The woman began cautiously. "You can say that again." Miss Fawns muttered under her breath. "Yes, well... I'm not here to ask for my job back." The woman bent her head, her hands trembling slightly as she raised her teacup to her lips. She barely dared to look at Miss Fawns. It did not take Miss Fawns long to realise the true reason for the woman's return. It was not money she was after, or at least, not only money. The truth sat there, plain as day, in the curve of her now obvious belly. *'Sir Edward Blackthorn's child'.* "Please." The woman added quickly, "I don't want your pity. But I cannot raise this child alone. I have no job, no income..." Miss Fawns' face drained of colour, her usual composure unravelling as horror and shock tightened every line of her features. For a moment, she simply stared ahead, the burden of the news pressing down on her like a tangible force. Then, slowly and with purpose, she set down her teacup, the soft clink of porcelain against wood echoing through the quell room. "I see." She said, her voice low but firm, tinged with a suspension. "And what exactly, would you suggest I do about it?" "If I must." The woman discussed, sitting up straighter now, her eyes hardening with determination as she drew in a steadying breath. Courage blossomed within her like a relaxed flame, pushing back the fear that had gripped her moments before. "I'll be forced to tell the Blackthorns myself, whether they want to hear it or not." "You will do no such thing!" Miss Fawns snapped, rising to her feet so that she towered over the seated woman. "You will not bring scandal upon this family, not after all they have endured, not while I still have breath in my body." There was a moment of peacefulness, and terribly dangerous. "Leave it with me." Miss Fawns said at last, her voice low and uniformed, carrying a subtle but undeniable edge beneath the quiet. Her gaze locked onto the woman's, steady and assured. "You will have a cheque in hand by the end of the week. Consider it done." But the woman, emboldened now, pressed further. "I don't believe a cheque will be enough." She said, her voice trembling with a false sweetness. "This child will need a father... he will need more than money to survive." Miss Fawns' eyes narrowed. "Is that a threat, Miss Rachet?" she asked coldly. "Let us hope it does not come to that." Miss Rachet said coolly, rising with a graceful yet witting motion. "I will see myself out. Thank you for your time, Miss Fawns. I have no doubt our paths will cross again, sooner than you expect." And with that, the woman swept from the room, her presence hanging in the air like the scent of something long burned. Miss Fawns stood motionless for a moment, then slumped against the edge of the table, one hand pressing tightly to her chest as though trying to contain the frantic hammering of her heart. *'What was she to do now? How could she possibly untangle herself from this mess, this dumb, calculated threat of desperation?'* The walls seemed to inch closer, the air growing difficult to draw in. With stiff, unsteady limbs, she lowered herself into the nearest chair. Her mind raced with a thousand possibilities, each one more impossible than the last. The well-ordered world she had worked so hard to maintain was beginning to fracture, and all she could do was sit there staring into the mounting uncertainty. *'I do have some savings, she thought grimly, but they will not be enough to keep the Ratchet woman at bay.'* Yes, she would call her that now: the *'Ratchet woman'* a devil's tongue wrapped in a cruel smile, if ever there was one. Miss Fawns allowed herself a small, bitter smile in return, the kind born from weary endurance and silent defiance. The week that followed was among the harshest Miss Fawns had ever endured, each day stretching endlessly beneath a shadow she could neither escape nor ignore. Every glance, every conversation with the Blackthorns weighed heavily on her, the secret threatening to spill from her lips at any moment. One morning, as she attended to Lady Catherine, the restrain nearly gave her away. "Is everything downright all right, Miss Fawns?" Lady Catherine asked, catching her reflection in the mirror as she pinned up her hair. Miss Fawns froze for half a second, then smiled stiffly. "Oh…yes my lady. Of course." She replied, her voice smooth and respectful. "I was just thinking about the summer fair coming up in the village, the bustle, the crowds… it's always quite the event." Lady Catherine laughed softly, turning on the stool to face her. "The summer fair? I never took you for that sort of woman Miss Fawns." She teased. She was right, of course. Miss Fawns had always loathed the summer fair. The shrill cries of children running amok, the press of sweaty bodies jostling through the lanes, the stink of spilled beer and roasted meats hanging thick in the atmosphere. There were pickpockets among the crowds too; quick, dirty hands snatching purses from the distracted rich. It was chaos disguised as celebration, and she had no patience for it. But now that it had been spoken aloud, now that she had agreed, however reluctantly, she was committed. It was yet another small cost in the growing ledger of sacrifices she made to keep certain truths buried. By week's end, she boarded the creaking transport into town, each rattle of the wheels beneath her seat tightening the knot in her stomach. When she finally stepped off, the change in the climate was immediate, dense, sour, and implicated with coal dust. The lower streets stretched before her like a bruise. Children with grime-streaked cheeks kicked stones near broken fences. Women hunched over market stalls with babies on their hips and exhaustion in their bones. Men leaned against crumbling brick walls, their eyes empty, their mouths slack with too much drink and too little hope. The smell, unmistakable and unforgiving, clung to everything: sweat, smoke, and sewage. A flicker of something old stirred in her chest. Not disgust. Not fear. Something stiller. A pang of memory, sharp and aching. She had walked these streets once. Worn those same hand-me-down shoes until the soles gave out. Waited in line for bread, her tiny fingers numb from cold. Her parents had done what they could, scraping by, working late, sacrificing everything just to put one warm meal on the table each day. It had never been enough, not really. But it had been something. And somehow, through will and stubbornness, they had survived. Pulling her shawl tighter around her, Miss Fawns made her way down a dark, cold, and damp alleyway. There, amid the crooked fence posts and threadbare washing flapping in the dull breeze, Miss Fawns spotted the *'Ratchet woman'*. She was struggling to peg a damp, still-dirty dress onto a sagging line, her fingers red and raw from scrubbing that had done little good. "You came then." Miss Rachet said, her voice thick with suspicion and something close to triumph, eyes narrowing beneath greasy strands of hair. "I didn't have much of a choice." Miss Fawns replied coolly, her tone clipped, her posture rigid. She kept her distance; arms folded tightly across her chest as if the air itself might stain her. "Don't flatter yourself." "You'd best step inside." The woman said, stepping aside to let her pass. Miss Fawns hesitated, then moved forward, wrinkling her nose as she entered the small, squalid home. The place was filthy, the stench so foul it nearly took her breath away. "I know it's not much." Miss Rachet voiced softly, resting one hand protectively over her swollen belly, her voice tinged with both weariness and fierce determination. "But it's a roof over our heads, and sometimes, that's all you can hope for." Miss Fawns forced herself to still be composed, though her spine was stiff with pressure and her jaw clenched tight enough to ache. "Miss Rachet." She said at last, her voice still but edged with strain. She reached slowly into her coat and withdrew an envelope, its corners slightly worn from being handled too many times. "In my hand is a cheque. One I never intended to write. I have had to use my life savings to cover this." She held it out, but not overall far enough for the woman to snatch it. "So, understand me clearly, this is not generosity. It is necessity." She thrust the envelope into the woman's grasp. "I hope you know…" Miss Fawns added, "that we are very grateful for your... discretion. And I trust there will be no hard feelings." The *'Ratchet woman'* smiled thinly, slipping the envelope carefully into her worn coat. "Of course. Incredibly grateful. No hard feelings at all." She said, her tone sweet. They parted ways at the edge of the alley. In Miss Fawns' mind, the matter was finished; she would never see that woman again. But in the *'Ratchet woman's'* mind, as she slipped the envelope deeper into her dress, a different thought lingered: This is far from over.

CHAPTER TWENTY-SIX
MAN TOWER

Present day

Chase and her mum now fully invested in the search for Chase's biological parents, sat close together in a quiet corner of the college library, accompanied by Hugo and Emily. Emily was hunched intently over a computer screen, her fingers flying across the keyboard with determined urgency. Her eyes scanned every line of text, every search result, desperate to find the faintest thread that might lead them closer to the truth. Meanwhile, Hugo lounged near the reception desk, throwing a casual smile and trading light-hearted jokes with the young man behind the counter. His charm was a calculated distraction, buying them precious minutes in the cramped, hushed space where time was running out. The college had a strict two-hour access limit, since the library only had five computers, but Hugo's charm seemed to be buying them a little more time.

Meanwhile, Chase and Isabelle sat at one of the tables, flipping through records of old adoption agencies near the town where Isabelle had once lived. Isabelle frowned at the papers. She could not remember the name of the agency, only that she had seen it once in a newspaper advert years ago, which she ripped out and made the call that changed everything. "I think I might have something." Emily brought out suddenly, her eyes still locked on the screen. "If what you're telling me is right." Emily said, her voice quickening with focus as she scrolled through the dense pages of search results, "then there were three major adoption agencies that leaned heavily on newspaper adverts to reach people. It was not just a strategy; it was their main lifeline. That has to mean something. We might be able to trace them through old archives or classifieds." She leaned closer to the screen and read out the names: "One; The Family Pairing Association Group. Two; Jewels' Children. And three; Match Made in Heaven." Isabelle leaned in, studying the names, but none of them rang a bell. "It was so many years ago." She said, frustrated. "I couldn't say for sure." Just then, Hugo returned, his eyes wide and serious. "I think it's time to go." He said subtlety. Without asking questions, Emily quickly printed out the list and the group gathered their things. "I've got a stew simmering if you kids want to bring this back to the manor." Isabelle offered once they reached the car park. Everyone nodded in agreement. Emily and Hugo climbed into Hugo's car, while Chase slid into the front seat of her mum's. Engines started, and together they drove back to the manor, taking the next step toward uncovering the truth. In the passenger seat of Hugo's car, Emily sat hunched over a bundle of printed documents, the papers soft and worn at the edges from how many times she had flipped through them. Her eyes scanned the bolded headers, three agency names circled in red ink, over and over, as if repetition might unlock something hidden. She turned one sheet in her hands, the corners curling slightly beneath her grip. "I hope it's one of these three." She proclaimed under her breath, her words low and threaded with a quiet urgency. "I really do. Because if it is not… I do not know where we go from here." Outside, the world blurred past in streaks of green and grey, the fading sun casting long twilight across the dashboard. Hugo glanced at her and nodded in agreement. "Oh, by the way." Emily said, punching him playfully on the arm, "Why did you want us to leave so quickly?" Hugo grinned, his cheeks flushing pink. "I think... I have a date." He admitted.

Emily's smile widened. "It's about time! I always catch you staring at him when we are in the library." She teased, making Hugo blush even deeper. Meanwhile, in Isabelle's car, the conversation was much heavier. "Mum, I'm sorry I'm putting you through this." Chase said quietly, staring out of the window. "It must not be easy." She meant it from the bottom of her heart. After all, her real mother, the one who had cared for her, fed her, loved her through eighteen years, was sitting beside her now. The woman they were trying to find was a stranger, tied to her only by blood. "Don't be daft sweetie." Isabelle said warmly, reaching over to squeeze her hand. "I would want to know too." Isabelle said softly. "And I can only apologise for keeping it from you for so long." She paused, her gaze drifting for a moment before meeting Chase's eyes again. "If I could go back in time." She added with a faint, wistful smile. "We would have told you the moment you learned how to tie your shoes. Right there on the hallway floor, laces tangled, beaming like you had conquered the world." Her voice caught slightly, not with sadness, but with the burden of all the moments she had carried in silence. "You deserved the truth. You always did." Chase glanced over at her beautiful, kind-hearted mother and offered a soft smile, feeling some of the ache in her chest begin to ease. She truly was the luckiest girl in the world to have a parent so full of love and understanding. Even after the loss of her father, Isabelle's heart had not hardened, there was still so much warmth in her, so much care. As they pulled up to the manor, both cars rolled to a stop side by side. From one vehicle, Hugo and Emily stepped out: from the other, Chase and Isabelle. Without exchanging a word, the four of them walked toward the front door, their footsteps falling coordinated. As soon as Chase stepped inside, the rich, warm smell of home-cooked food hit her. She normally hated the smell of her mum's cooking; it had always bothered her in a way she could not explain. Maybe she had been too harsh before, back when her dad was still around. He had this way of making her feel truly seen. But now, all she had left was her mum... and the mere idea of losing her was unbearable. "It smells divine in here." Hugo said, swinging his bag onto the kitchen counter. It was strange really; how fast Hugo and Emily settled into the manor. Despite all they had faced here, the fear lurking in every corner, the gloominess that seemed to breathe, the near tragedies that had tested their very souls, they kept coming back. As if the pain itself were a magnet, pulling them closer, and the manor's tangled history gave that pain a weight and meaning they could not find anywhere else. Somehow, in all of that mess, it had become a kind of home. The four of them sat around the dining table, a soft hush settling over the room. It felt strange, almost eerie, to be sitting here again. The last time they had gathered in this very dining room, they had been brutally attacked by her... The ghostly woman. Arabella Nightshade to be exact, though no one dared speak her name aloud. "This is lovely Mum. Thank you." Chase said, chewing a tender piece of beef, the flavour instantly reminding her of tranquil times. "Yes, thank you." Hugo and Emily echoed, layering their manners over Chase's in unison, each offering a grateful smile. "No problem at all. I am just glad you are enjoying it." Isabelle replied, her cheeks tinged with pink from all the compliments. She fussed with a napkin at the edge of her plate, not meeting their eyes. "Your father was always the one in the kitchen. He could whip up a feast without even trying. Honestly, I half-expected this to end in takeaway. But look at me!" she added with a small laugh. "Not one fire, not even a smoke alarm." Chase smiled, a mixture of amusement and affection curling in her chest. For a fleeting moment, it felt like a piece of normality had returned. Once the plates were nearly cleared, Isabelle set down her cutlery with a soft clink and looked around the table. "So… after we've all finished eating." She began, "I thought we could head to the study and start digging into those adoption companies. Thanks to Emily, we already have a solid starting point." Chase blinked, mouth still half-full of food. "Study room?" she asked, curiosity edging through her words. Isabelle smiled. She had forgotten to mention the surprise. While they were away at the safe house, she had spoken to the restoration company, the ones helping to repair the damage done by the haunting. She explained how she had asked for the old tower room to be converted into a study; a lull, cozy space where she could retreat and find some peace. A little sanctuary that reminded her of her late husband. As Isabelle spoke, the chatter around the table gradually faded into a thoughtful hush. Then, one by one, smiles began to bloom, softening the room with a shared sense of hope and comfort. Chase stood up, walked over to her mother, and wrapped her in a hug. "That's a perfect idea." She whispered. Chase, Emily, Hugo, and Isabelle made their way to the tower room. They walked down the long hallway, toward what used to be a dark hole in the wall, now replaced with a clean white door, finished

with a golden handle. Chase glanced at Hugo
and Emily, remembering the last time they
were here. For Emily, it had been a nightmare,
the spot where she was attacked by what she
could only describe as a possessed Pinocchio.
"I... I do not think I can do this." Emily
proclaimed abruptly, her voice faltering as she
came to a sudden halt. Both Chase and Hugo
froze, momentarily forgetting Emily's well-
known fear of spiral staircases. The narrow,
twisting steps stretched upward like a silent
challenge, the dim light folding around them
like a subtle threat. Chase looked over at Hugo,
then back at Emily, her brow creasing with
concern. "Hey, it is okay. We will take it slow.
You are not alone." Hugo gave a reassuring nod,
stepping a little closer as if to shield her from
the daunting climb. Emily swallowed hard, her
eyes flickering upward toward the spiralling
steps before her, the familiar tightness growing
deep inside her. "Emily, you can do this." Chase
said softly, reaching out and gently taking her
hand. "You have got us, all three of us, right
here with you. If it makes it easier, just close
your eyes. We will guide you every step of the
way." Emily took a deep breath. Then, with her
hand firmly clasped in Chase's, she allowed
herself to be guided up the narrow, winding
staircase. It was over in mere seconds, but when

she opened her eyes at the top, a calm pride swelled within her, she had made it. Chase finally took in the room properly, and her jaw nearly dropped. It was nothing like the old, dusty attic she remembered, the one cluttered with forgotten junk, heavy with the smell of damp and thick shadows that seemed to press in from every corner. Now, the space felt almost transformed, lighter, as if some invisible burden had been eased. Soft rays of sunlight filtered through clean windows, illuminating the worn wooden floor and the carefully arranged belongings. Now, it was a sanctuary. A man cave, or a man tower, if the shoe fits in honour of Henry. Sunlight poured through a wide window, bathing the space in gold. Beneath it sat a plush, velvet chaise longue, perfect for stretching out while admiring the view. In one corner stood a bookshelf, only half full, almost pleading for Chase to add her own stories to its empty spaces. She could already picture her history books artfully arranged there, each spine a window to another time. Across the room sat an old wooden desk, worn but sturdy, topped with a vintage typewriter, a treasured find from the manor's renovations, waiting patiently to be brought back to life. The centre of the room was warmed by a beautiful, mustard-yellow rug, soft and fluffy underfoot.

Near the back of the room stood a compact fridge, its quiet hum blending with the soft ambient light. Inside, rows of fizzy drinks shimmered alongside vibrant cans of Porn Star Martinis, their bold labels promising a taste of something daring. Next to it, a polished wooden wine rack showcased an elegant selection of red, white, and rosé bottles, each waiting patiently to be uncorked. Above, crystal-clear wine glasses and slender cocktail flutes hung with precision from a gleaming rack, catching stray rays of light and expelling delicate reflections on the walls. Across the room, a plush, inviting sofa curved gently, accompanied by a low coffee table adorned with a few well-thumbed magazines and a small vase of fresh flowers. Nearby, a sleek, ultramodern coffee machine stood ready for action, flanked by a three-tiered drawer bursting with a colourful variety of flavoured pods, a promise of warm, aromatic comfort with every brew. To Chase, it was perfect, without a doubt the best room in the entire house. "This room is something else Mum." She aired turning with a bright smile toward Isabelle. "I cannot believe it. It is gorgeous." Slowly, everyone settled in, the room quickly filling with the easy comfort of feeling at home. Chase and Emily curled up on the small corner sofa, sipping vanilla and cinnamon coffee from the machine. Hugo sprawled on the chaise longue, taking selfies that made him look like royalty. And Isabelle, smiling, poured herself a glass of red and settled into the spinning chair beside the typewriter, the perfect spot to listen and still be part of the conversation. "Let's begin." Isabelle asserted, spinning around in the chair and pulling a sleek silver laptop from one of the desk drawers. Chase watched her mum expertly sip wine with one hand and type with the other, a true vision of multitasking that made her laugh quietly to herself. "Right Emily, give me one of the adoption names. I will see if I can find anything. I have some old notebooks in my bag too, filled with passwords and notes I used to write down so I would not forget." Isabelle said, eyes on the screen. "Let's start with The Family Pairing Association Group." Emily said, handing over the printed list with a hopeful glance. Isabelle's fingers moved swiftly and confidently across the keyboard; her eyes focused as she typed in the company name. The soft clatter of keys filled the mitigate room. Beside her, Chase sat curled up, flipping through one of her mum's worn notebooks. The pages, filled with neat handwriting and faded notes. "Nothing's coming up." Isabelle said with a sigh, placing her wine glass gently on the floor and frowning at the screen. "I can't see anything in here either." Chase said, flipping through the pages. Then she paused, eyes catching something. "Ooo, what is this? It is written in French… and there is a little heart drawn around it." "Let me have a look." Hugo said, leaning over and taking the notebook from her. He read the passage aloud, a smirk spreading across his face before he suddenly burst out laughing. "Oh god, what is it?" Isabelle asked, suddenly nervous. Hugo cleared his throat. "À. mon amour de rêve, s'il te plaît, prends ceci comme une invitation à être ma petite amie. J'ai besoin d'embrasser tes lèvres à nouveau, et cette fois avec du sens et non du sexe ivre." Then he translated it in English for the rest of the room: "To my dream love, please take this as an invitation to be my girlfriend. I need to kiss your lips again, and this time with meaning, not just drunk sex." The room fell completely silent, and then everyone erupted into laughter. "Give me that!" Isabelle exclaimed, snatching the notebook away, her cheeks flushing a deep shade of hot crimson. "I was young!" she defended quickly. "Your father wrote that in my notebook, fully knowing I did not understand a word of French. He wanted me to take it to my French teacher just so I would be mortified. He did it after I turned him down once, typical of him! it is a good job I didn't take that to my very attractive French teacher." Isabelle laughed, shaking her head. "Probably another reason your father wrote it." Everyone chuckled softly, but Isabelle's smile faltered, a shadow of sadness flickering across her features. Chase caught the change and quickly chimed in, "Well, I think it's romantic." She said warmly, offering her mum a gentle smile, hoping to lift her spirits. Isabelle jerked her head, collecting herself. "Right then. Emily, what was the second adoption agency name?" They began their search again, focusing on Jewels' Children. "Nothing." Isabelle purred after a while, frowning at the screen. "Nothing here either." Chase muttered, flipping through a stack of worn notebooks, frustration flickering in her eyes. "What a weird name for an adoption agency." Hugo remarked, his head dangling upside down over the back of the chaise longue, a teasing grin tugging at his lips. Emily sat up straighter, a flicker of hope in her voice. "Hopefully we get somewhere with the last one… Match Made in Heaven." This search took longer. There was so much information to sort through. "Oh my God." Isabelle whispered, her hand covering her mouth. "What? What is it? Let me see." Chase demanded, leaning over the laptop with a mix

of curiosity and growing unease. The group
huddled closer; eyes fixed on the screen.
Emily's fingers hovered over the keyboard
before she clicked a link and began to read
aloud, her voice steady but platted with
disbelief:

'Match Made in Heaven? Or Match Made in Hell?'

"Several bodies were discovered hidden within the crumbling walls of the former orphanage. Approximately sixteen sets of children's bones were unearthed after a sudden leak revealed decades of unspeakable horror. The unnamed owner of the facility has been charged with sixteen counts of murder and over fifty counts of child abuse."

"sacré bleu." Hugo muttered, visibly shaken.
The article was dated 2010. "I hope this isn't the
place I was from." Chase snarled, her voice low.
Isabelle had gone quell. She had managed to log
into an old website using one of her saved
passwords. "I'm sorry darling." Isabelle said
softly, finally turning the laptop screen toward
Chase. Her voice wavered just slightly, as if
carrying the weight of years kept hidden. "This

is the agency; this is where your father and I adopted you from." Chase stared at the screen, her breath catching as a profile came into focus.

Sex: *Female*
Health: Healthy
First Name: *Unknown*
Last Name: Blackthorn
Description: *Baby girl, approximately three months old. No visible injuries. No signs of illness.*

Beneath the details was a chilling note, written in faded, shaky letters:

"Please take diligent care of her. She will only be a curse to us."

Chase's eyes stayed fixed on the words, the meaning of the message settling over her like a cold stone in her chest. Chase sank slowly onto the sofa, her limbs slack and unresponsive, eyes locked on a distant point that held no meaning. Emily and Hugo flanked her quietly, their presence steady but filled with a shared understanding of the crushing reality that had just unfolded. Across the room, Isabelle stood motionless, her wine glass quivering lightly in her grasp. Her eyes shimmered with unshed tears, glowing with a delicate sorrow, yet not one tear dared to fall. "She will only be a curse to us." Chase whispered, repeating the words from the note left with her as an infant. The sentence predicated in the air like a noose tightening around them all. She was a Blackthorn. Whoever had abandoned her at that orphanage had not done so blindly, they knew something. Something about Arabella. About the past. About her. Chase's fists clenched at her sides, nails biting into her palms. A strange mix of anger and dread twisted in her stomach. Her voice cracked through the speechlessness, intertwined with disbelief and rage. "How could someone abandon their baby over some pathetic ghost named Arabella Nightshade?" She said the name in a mocking tone, drawing it out with venom. She should not have said it. The instant the name escaped her lips; the room grew thick with exasperation. Isabelle's wine glass jerked violently from her hand, as though yanked by unseen claws. It crashed against the wall, crimson wine bursting out like a wound, spreading dark stains across the plush mustard rug. A hush fell over the room, broken only by the faint drip of spilled wine and the quickened rhythm of their breaths. Emily screamed and leapt to her feet. Isabelle watched, stunned. Hugo grabbed Chase's hand instinctively, both of their eyes darting around in panic. "I've got a feeling I shouldn't have done that." Chase whispered, her voice shaking. "You think?!" Emily snapped, her voice groomed with fear. The door slammed shut behind them, the sound like a gunshot. They were trapped in the tower room. Hugo lunged at the door, shoulder slamming into the wood with a dull thud. It did not budge. The new door, solid oak, sturdy and reinforced with gleaming brass hardware, might as well have been a brick wall. Then, without warning, the light from outside disappeared. It was as if the sun had been snuffed out like a candle. Darkness engulfed the room completely. They were no longer alone.

CHAPTER TWENTY-SEVEN
LOVE STRUCK

1800

Miss Fawns felt sick to her stomach. What she had done, though necessary to shield the Blackthorne family from scandal, felt like a betrayal. Her loyalty was once unquestionable, yet now it trembled under the amount of secrecy and guilt. Lady Catherine stalked the corridors of Blackthorne Manor with intent, her heels clicking sharply against the polished floors. Her hawk-like gaze swept over every surface, hunting for the slightest trace of dust or disorder. Nothing escaped her scrutiny, not the arrangement of the silver candelabras, nor the symmetry of the floral displays brought in earlier that morning. She was preparing for the ball to be held the following evening, the first grand event since Arabella and Sir Edward's wedding. And, more significantly since Arabella's tragic and untimely death. Months had passed. In Lady Catherine's eyes, the appropriate time for mourning had come and gone. She had worn the veil, received condolences, and tolerated whispers behind gloved hands. Enough. Now was the time to reclaim what mattered most: dignity, control, and the family's place at the pinnacle of society. She swept past one of the maids, who knelt on the floor, polishing tirelessly until her knuckles were raw and reddened. "Have you seen Miss Fawns today?" Lady Catherine asked sharply, her voice edged with impatience as she loomed over the girl without meeting her eyes. The maid glanced up briefly, dabbing sweat from her brow with the back of her hand. "She stepped out this morning my lady." She replied quietly, her tone cautious yet respectful. "I see. And does one happen to know where she travelled at such an hour?" Lady Catherine inquired, her gaze now drifting to the window. "No, my lady." The maid said nervously, rising to stand. "There is no need to stand. The floor will not clean itself." Lady Catherine said, turning and gliding away, her heels echoing down the hall, leaving the maid staring after her before silently returning to her task. Outside, Sir Edward sat beneath the white blossom tree, the one he had planted in Arabella's memory. Its delicate petals fluttered in the breeze, some catching in his hair, others drifting onto the open pages of his sketchbook. The book rested on his knee, a half-finished rendering of the Blackthorne estate slowly taking shape in soft graphite lines. Sketching had once been a boyhood joy, something he had long abandoned when the substantiveness of duty and expectation pulled him elsewhere. But now, it was the only thing that quieted the noise in his head, the only act that brought a semblance of peace to his otherwise restless mind. Each line on the page felt like a tether, to memory, to grief, to her. He raised his thumb to the horizon, measuring angles and distance, when a familiar figure appeared at the edge of the garden path. "Mother you should not be out here alone." Edward called, his voice gentle, knocked with mild surprise. Lady Catherine did not slow her pace. "I am not alone." She replied briskly. "You are here, are you not?" Her tone was as sharp and composed as ever, but Edward could hear the hush intensity beneath it, the need to appear unaffected and untouchable. "I suppose you are right, as always." He said with a faint smile, setting his sketch aside. "What can I do for you mother?" She held her chin high, eyes forward. father and I are hosting a ball tomorrow night." Edward stiffened, a flicker of discomfort crossing his features. "So soon?" Lady Catherine's tone was firm and resolute. "I know it may seem premature." She said crisply. "But you cannot abandon your duties. The family's reputation depends on appearances, no matter the cost. If we delay further, we risk losing respect. The Blackthorns do not fade into obscurity, Edward." "But…" "No buts." She snapped. "I will not hear another word. The ball will be a triumph. Please, do not embarrass your parents. "As she passed, she dragged a gloved finger across his sketch, smudging the delicate lines. Edward turned back to the drawing. His jaw clenched, and after a pause, he tore the page in two. "I'm sorry you had to witness that, my love." He whispered to the white blossom tree, as if Arabella herself still lingered among its branches. "Mother has lost what little heart she had left." Sir Edward turned his head to watch his mother vanish into the distance. She was out of reach now, both in distance and in spirit. With a weary sigh, he lowered his gaze to the white blossom petals at his feet. Meanwhile, Lady Catherine ascended the steps of Blackthorne Manor. Her posture was rigid with her as spine straight as ever. As she reached for the gleaming brass handle, something flickered at the edge of her vision. A movement, quick and intentional. From the corner of her eye, she caught sight of a shadowy figure skirting the edge of the hedge line, attempting to slip past unnoticed. Whoever it was moved with the cautious, calculated steps of someone who did not wish to be seen. Lady Catherine froze, her hand hovering mid-air. Her eyes narrowed, lips tightening into a thin line. "Ah, Miss Fawns." Lady Catherine bolted without even turning. Her instincts were sharp she knew it was her. "Good evening my lady." Miss Fawns stammered, rooted to the spot like a schoolchild caught sneaking in past curfew. "Please, don't mind me, I was just returning from an errand." Lady Catherine regarded her for a moment, then slowly turned to face her fully. "I see." She said coolly, her voice carrying an edge that made Miss Fawns's heart quicken. She gave Miss Fawns a long, assessing look. "May I be so fortunate as to know the nature of this errand?" Miss Fawns hesitated. "Well, you see my lady, I was visiting my cousin… she lives down by the old farm." Lady Catherine's gaze travelled downward, her expression sharpening. "Oh, dear Miss Fawns, it seems your errand involved trenching through mud?" Miss Fawns glanced down at her muddied hem and boots, her heart beginning to race. "Yes well… the weather has been cruel to the land. The floods have ruined all the crops and swamped the pens. It is dreadful really." The lie flowed easier now. In truth, the hovel she had visited earlier could pass for a farm, at least to someone like Lady Catherine who had never set foot in a real one. That was why the lady suddenly shifted her tone. "How unfortunate." Lady Catherine articulated, tapping a finger thoughtfully to her lip. "I had hoped to find a farm nearby; fresh eggs and pigs would have been most welcome." Miss Fawns offered a small, strained laugh. "I'm afraid this one wouldn't be much use to you, my lady." Lady Catherine tilted her head ever so slightly, a smile flickering at the edge of her lips; controlled, polite, and not entirely warm. "Very well." She spoke. "I suppose I could not trouble you for a moment in the drawing room. I find myself in need of your assistance." Miss Fawns straightened her expression composed. "Of course, my lady." She replied clearly, her voice loud enough to carry, ensuring any nearby ears would take note. She watched as Lady Catherine ascended the steps and vanished into the manor, the powerful doors closing behind her with a mollify click. Miss Fawns remained for a moment, her gaze drifting briefly toward the darker edge of the garden. As soon as the door closed behind her, Miss Fawns let out a massive breath. She scanned the grounds, no one in sight. The tight grip of anxiety started to loosen within her ribs.

"Miss Fawns!" The sudden shout from behind jolted her so sharply, her heart nearly jumped into her throat. "Oh, Sir Edward! You gave me quite a fright." Miss Fawns exclaimed, turning to find his familiar, kind face illuminated by a gentle smile. "I am terribly sorry." he said with a soft chuckle. "I did not mean to startle you." They fell into step beside one another, heading toward the servants' entrance. Their pace was unhurried, easy, marked by the quiet comfort of long acquaintance. Sir Edward asked, offhandedly, about preparations for the upcoming ball. And Miss Fawns, despite her usual discretion, found herself answering him truthfully. She spoke of Lady Catherine's grand plans, the meticulous attention to detail, the unspoken rules governing his attire and behaviour, and even mentioned, somewhat hesitantly, the young woman his mother intended to present to him for the first waltz of the evening. Under normal circumstances, Miss Fawns would never have spoken so freely. But after her anxious encounter with Lady Catherine…and fully aware of the cruel things the woman had done to Arabella, Miss Fawns no longer cared for caution or restraint. "Thank you Miss Fawns." Edward said softly, his voice warm with genuine appreciation. "I can always count on you to look after me." He bent and kissed her hand, an old-fashioned gesture that warmed her heart. She smiled and entered the servant's wing, removing her mud-streaked overcoat and handing it to a passing maid with a request to have it washed. Then she slipped into her tiny office, unlocked the drawer she kept for emergencies, and poured herself a small glass of sherry. She needed the moment to steady herself. After taking a small sip of sherry, Miss Fawns slipped into a fresh dress and sturdy boots. With purposeful steps, she made her way swiftly toward the drawing room, her mind focused and determined. She opened the door and spotted Lady Catherine standing rigidly by the window, staring out into the gardens. "My lady." Miss Fawns said softly, announcing her presence with quiet respect. Lady Catherine did not turn. She remained motionless, her gaze fixed on the window, hands clasped tightly in front of her. "Miss Fawns." She said at last, her tone like frost on glass. "I do not wish to be rude, but when I request your assistance, I do not expect to be kept waiting." The room felt colder for a moment, as if the air itself had taken on her disapproval. "Yes, my lady. Understood." Miss Fawns replied, knowing any excuse would fall on deaf ears. Lady Catherine only heard what suited her. "Shall I make you some tea?" she offered, trying to shift the atmosphere. Lady Catherine finally turned and gave a stiff nod, then moved to sit in a highbacked chair near the fire. The flames lit up her sharp cheekbones and glinted off her cold eyes. "I asked you here because I am growing concerned about Sir Edward. He has become far too attached to that tree, and I… I can not reach him." Lady Catherine confessed as she accepted her tea, her voice salty with frustration. "With respect my lady, I'm not sure what help I can offer." Miss Fawns replied honestly, a hint of genuine puzzlement in her tone. Lady atherine's eyes narrowed slightly, her voice tightening with bitterness. "I do not believe that. He has a softness for you. You practically raised him." "My lady." Miss Fawns replied with arcadian grace, a small, polite smile tugging at her lips. "I serve this house. I did not raise anyone. You and Sir Howard have done a remarkable job with him." Her voice was steady, respectful, yet carried a hint of genuine affection beneath the formality. Lady Catherine's eyes darkened. "I saw you both speaking outside not long ago. The smile on his face… it was one I have never received. He trusts you." Miss Fawns felt the walls closing in. "If I may speak freely, my lady… I can explain what we discussed." She said carefully. Lady Catherine waved a hand.

"Very well." Miss Fawns hesitated, then sat down across from her. She spoke in a hushed tone; her voice barely audible above the crackling fire. Lady Catherine listened in taciturnity, her eyes locked on the flames, expression unreadable. Whatever Miss Fawns said, it was enough to make Lady Catherine's fingers constrict around the delicate teacup, knuckles paling with the pressure. When Miss Fawns finished speaking, the room was swallowed by a dense, oppressive stillness. Lady Catherine refused to meet her gaze; her eyes fixed on some distant point beyond the walls. "Miss Fawns." She stated slowly, "you are not to speak of this to anyone. Am I clear?" "Yes, my lady." Miss Fawns replied quietly, rising from her seat with calm poise. Lady Catherine did not spare her even a glance. Instead, she stared deeper into the flickering fire, as if willing its flames to consume some unbearable truth. Words between them were few, almost non-existent, as the older woman prepared for bed. The quiet that settled over the room was tense, charged with meaning, almost deliberate in its presence. Miss Fawns found herself stealing glances toward the mirror, catching fleeting reflections of Lady Catherine's pale, unreadable face. The expression never wavered, still, composed, and utterly cold. Miss Fawns found herself wondering, as she often did, what did happened to Lady Catherine on the night of her sisters flames to make her this way. Miss fawns remembered a time her and lady catherine use to be friends not just a maid and lady. But with everything that happened in Lady Catherines life it must have turned her into a woman so distant and heartless. But then again, she understood. Wealth and status, when left unchecked, had a way of eroding love, warping reality. It was one thing Miss Fawns did not envy about the Blackthorne family, their endless performance, the hollow formalities that masked an aching absence of warmth and genuine connection. After attending to Lady Catherine, Miss Fawns slipped away restfully, making her way back to the servant's quarters.

The following morning, Miss Fawns returned to Lady Catherine's room and was surprised to find her already awake, seated at her dressing table, hands folded in her lap, spine straight as a rod. "Miss Fawns do come in." Lady Catherine said, her voice oddly calm. "My lady." Miss Fawns said softly, bowing her head in a small, respectful curtsy. Lady Catherine turned slowly to face her, catching her own reflection in the mirror. The image looking back was older than usual, worn and pale, the piercing edges of her usual composure softened by a rare and profound fatigue. Her voice was quieter than before, almost vulnerable. "What we spoke of yesterday evening." She confessed. "I find I cannot get it out of my head. It haunts me." Miss Fawns stepped a little closer, her expression gentle yet undeviating. "My lady, I give you my word. Not a soul will ever hear of it from me." She said reassuringly, her tone steady as a rock amidst the swirling uncertainty. They both knew the conversation was far from over, but for now, they would let the secret rest. There were pressing matters that could not be ignored, the grand ball was set for that very evening, and the manor still buzzed with preparations. Every detail had to be perfect. Miss Fawns listed the names of the arriving guests, described the arrangements, and informed Lady Catherine of the food, the wine, the live musicians, and every detail down to the polished silverware. The day moved forward like clockwork, a carefully staged performance returning to routine. Elsewhere in the manor, Sir Edward sat quietly as the head butler shaved his jaw. He said little. His mind, however, was racing with thoughts of Miss Fawns, of what she had told him, and of what he now knew he must do. The manor transformed as dusk fell. The ballroom glittered in gold and silver, draped in luxury. Statues: elegant and towering, resembling ancient Greek gods, lined the corridor leading to the ballroom. In the grand stairway, a newly installed five-tier marble fountain sparkled under candlelight, water cascading like silk. Outside, along the stone steps, a rich black and gold carpet led the way beneath great ornamental lions, white and regal, guarding either side. By evening, the guests began to arrive. Live chamber music floated warmly through the grand halls of the manor, weaving a delicate tapestry of sound that softened the edges of the evening. The gentle melodies of violin and piano entwined, filling the space with an air of refined elegance and voicelessness celebration. Footmen, impeccably dressed in crisp uniforms, moved with practiced grace among the clusters of guests, balancing silver trays laden with sparkling champagne flutes and artfully arranged hors d'oeuvres. Their movements were seamless, almost choreographed, as they navigated the crowded rooms without disturbing the flow of conversation. Laughter bubbled up here and there, light and carefully foresighted, mingling with polite conversation that hummed like a gentle current beneath the soaring melodies. Soft whispers of gossip slipped through the air, blending with the clink of glasses and the rustle of silk gowns and polished shoes. The manor itself seemed to pulse with expectancy, its grand chandeliers venting a warm, golden glow over the scene. Yet beneath the surface of this carefully crafted gaiety, hints of unease and secrets hovered, concealed behind poised smiles and genteel laughter. Lady Catherine descended the grand staircase with the perfection of a monarch entering her court. Her arrival hushed the room instantly, conversations faltering and eyes turning toward her as if drawn by an unseen magnet. Draped in a magnificent ruby and gold gown, an heirloom from her youth, freshly tailored to perfection and still breathtaking, the fabric shimmered in the flickering glow of the sconces like flames caught in silk. The gown hugged her figure with regal precision, every fold and seam crafted to command attention. Her posture was impeccable, spine straight and chin held high, radiating an authority that brooked no challenge. Soft gasps and murmurs of admiration rippled through the assembled guests as she reached the bottom of the stairs, her presence filling the vast hall like a force of nature. As always, Lady Catherine was the most exquisitely dressed woman in the room, a living testament to elegance, power, and control, just as she had always intended. Sir Howard stood beside her in a dignified tuxedo, his son Sir Edward looking equally stately, though far more sombre. Then the doors opened once more, and a hush fell over the guests. Two women entered, immediately drawing every gaze in the room. Doris Mossford, draped in sumptuous emerald velvet carried herself with polished grace, a composed smile playing on her lips. Beside her stood a striking young woman clad in a grand black and white gown; dramatic, refined, and impossibly elegant, as if she had stepped straight from a painting. Lady Catherine's eyes narrowed ever so slightly as her gaze settled on the newcomer. It was Lady Maple Robertson. Just as she had hoped. "Lady Catherine." Doris called, approaching with a wide smile. "You never fail to astonish. You look absolutely divine." Doris said, her voice carrying a note of genuine admiration. "Like an oil painting." Lady Maple added softly, bowing her head with effortless grace. Lady Catherine, lips curving into a rare smile, extended her hand. "Lady Maple, my dear. A dream in person." She would ensure this night was nothing short of a triumph. For her son. For the family. For the enduring legacy of Blackthorne Manor, which she would defend and uphold at any cost. And no ghost of Arabella Nightshade, not even in memory, would be allowed to ruin it. Lady Catherine grabbed her son's arm with purpose. "Dear Edward, I must introduce you to someone I believe you'll find most agreeable." She said, pulling him along before he could protest. Sir Edward allowed himself to be led forward, each step weighted with reluctant inevitability. Miss Fawns had warned him of what was to come, but knowing did little to ease the tightening grip in his heart. His memories of Arabella lingered constantly, casting a presence over every moment. The idea of meeting another woman, no matter how carefully chosen or well-intentioned, felt like a subtle betrayal, as if by moving forward, he was abandoning the past they had shared. A bitter pang settled deep within him, mingling with the polite smile he forced onto his lips. Duty pressed down with relentless poundage, reminding him that some sacrifices were unavoidable, no matter how painful. But as they approached Lady Maple and Doris Mossford, something shifted. Regret lifted from his shoulders the instant his eyes met Lady Maple's. Her features were striking, refined and graceful, but it was the gentle warmth in her gaze that softened the ache nestled deep within Edward's chest. For a brief moment, he felt something unfamiliar: a flutter of shyness, as if meeting her had quietly unsettled him. "My lady." He said, taking her hand gently and offering it a subtle gesture to dance. Lady Maple bowed her head in acceptance, and the two moved onto the floor to begin the waltz. From across the ballroom, Doris Mossford and Lady Catherine stood side by side, quietly admiring the fruit of their matchmaking. "It appears Sir Edward has taken a liking to her." Doris said, eyes following the couple. "I do believe you're right." Lady Catherine replied with a pleased smile. "I think I shall find a drink. Care to join me?" She gave Doris a small nod, signalling it was time to grant the pair some privacy. The evening unfolded just as Lady Catherine had hoped. Sir Edward and Lady Maple moved with effortless grace across the floor, and with every spin and step, their bond deepened. "You're altogether the dancer, Sir Edward." Lady Maple said, her voice light, her gaze playful. "Well." he replied, twirling her with one hand. "When one lives in a place like this, one learns quickly. A thousand balls will do that to a man." They spoke with a natural ease, exchanging stories of their childhoods and the lives they now led. Lady Maple confided unobtrusive how she had lost her husband in a tragic hunting accident, a sudden, devastating blow that had reshaped her world. The revelation struck a deep chord within Edward, as he too, had borne the intense burden of loss, his bride cruelly taken from him by poison on their wedding day. In that moment, their shared sorrow bridged the space between them, weaving a quiet connection that neither needed to voice aloud. It was a delicate, tenuous bond, one born of grief and loneliness, which drew them closer, offering a tentative comfort in the face of their lingering pain. Around them, the music continued to play, the polite buzz of the ball swirling like a distant whisper, while Edward and Lady Maple found themselves settled united by their pasts. And somehow, in the flicker of chandeliers and whispered violins, they both began to believe in love again. Later that night, Sir Edward walked Lady Maple to her carriage beneath a moonlit sky. "Lady Maple." He clothed softly. "I didn't think I could feel anything like this again… not until tonight." Lady Maple leaned gracefully from the carriage window; her eyes locked onto his with a quiet intensity. "Sir Edward Blackthorn." She memorized softly, a gentle smile playing at her lips, "it was a pleasure. I do hope this is not the last time we speak." Her words sailed in the evening air, a tender promise that lingered long after the carriage began to pull away. The carriage began to move, and Edward stood still, watching it disappear into the night, the echo of possibility lingering in the air. Sir Edward could not get Lady Maple out of his mind. Her face, her voice, the way she had looked at him, it all lingered like a song he could not stop humming. He had only just met her, yet it felt as though he had known her longer. *'Was it foolish to feel this way after a single evening?'* Perhaps. But something about her had awakened a part of him he thought had died with Arabella. The idea of another night passing without her felt unbearable. *'Could he genuinely love again? And so soon after losing Arabella?'* His heart quietly whispered yes, even as his mind grappled with the big load of guilt. Still, despite the turmoil, one undeniable truth appeared, he found himself wanting to marry her. Meanwhile, Lady Catherine lay in her bed chamber, staring at the ceiling with a rare sense of satisfaction. Lady Maple: refined, wealthy, and well-bred, was everything she had envisioned for her son. Finally, a match worthy of the Blackthorne name. Edward had smiled tonight, truly smiled, and that was all the proof she needed. It had taken relentless effort, countless sacrifices, and secrets buried deep beneath polished surfaces, but it had all been worth it. She had carefully orchestrated this path for him with uniform precision, and she would allow nothing to unravel her plans. As her eyes closed briefly, one final thought solidified in her mind: Lady Maple will be his bride. I will see to it.

Present day

Chase stared into pitch blackness. She knew something was about to happen, it was only a matter of time. *'Who would Arabella choose? Who would the ghostly woman haunt, or worse… possession?'* Her thoughts twisted into terrible shapes, each one darker than the last, as she imagined the horror that was about to unfold. Around her, the finite breaths of her friends punctuated the tense quiet, delicate and strained. She could feel her mother's subtle panic ripple through the calm, a trembly presence barely contained. Her own heartbeat pounded like a relentless drum in her ribs, plummy with the dread that coiled tighter with every passing second. Beneath it all, the atmosphere thickened with the unmistakable scent of death; dense, metallic, and ancient, clinging to the room like a malevolent shadow. Then, the cold came. It was not the sort of cold that could be cured with a coat or with a hot tea and blankets. No, this was unnatural. It sank into her bones like rot. Solid. It was suffocating, a crushing moment that seemed to stop her blood from flowing, as if her limbs had been drained of life and no longer belonged to her. Like she was naked in a void, pierced over and over again by invisible icicles. Chase began to shiver violently, not from fear, though fear clawed at her like an animal, but from something deeper. Something wrong. Something that whispered, she is coming. Isabelle slowly sank back into her seat, not even checking if the chair was beneath her. Her mind was not with her body; it was fixed on the glowing orb floating across the room. It hovered in the distance, though Isabelle could not totally tell were. Everything around her dissolved into darkness, thick and impenetrable, swallowing all sense of space and time. Only the orb remained visible, a soft, pulsing light that swayed gently, first up and down, then side to side. Its movement was hypnotic, almost mesmerising, drawing her deeper into its silent rhythm. "Can you see that?" she whispered, barely moving her lips, speaking to whoever might be near her. "See what?" Emily's voice drifted in, a soft murmur that wrapped around Isabelle's ears like a whisper from every direction, disorienting, close, like an echo bouncing endlessly in a hollow chamber. Isabelle told nothing. She did not have to. The truth had settled deep within her now, undeniable and clear. Whatever she was seeing, the glowing, swaying light, was meant for no one else. It flickered just beyond the reach of others' eyes, a secret only she could perceive. Hugo sat on the floor, knees pulled tight against his forehead, eyes squeezed shut as if willing the world away. He rocked slowly, a steady, rhythmic motion, trying to drown out the whispers with a low, desperate hum. The sound thrummed deep in his throat, a fragile shield against whatever unseen presence leaned closer, first to his right ear, then his left. Each time, a cold breath grazed his skin, invisible yet invasive, sending shivers that crawled beneath his flesh. Still, the humming was not enough. He paused briefly, just long enough to catch a single word whispered into the silence. "Death…" Then, the word came again, this time drifting softly into the opposite ear, as if the darkness itself were speaking in haunting echoes. "Death…" The whisper came again. And again. The same word, softly hissed, slicing into his mind from both sides like icy needles. Death A word he had heard a thousand times before, but never like this. Never with such overload. Never with such intent. Terror took hold of him so completely that he did not notice the warmth spreading beneath him. He had wet himself. Emily stood rooted in the centre of the room, clutching a jagged shard of broken wine glass, flung from Isabelle's hand just moments before. Her fingers clenched so tightly that blood welled up and trickled in thin rivulets down her wrist, the crimson stark against her pale skin. Yet, the pain had not registered. Not yet. Her adrenaline surged fiercely through her veins, drowning out every sensation, every rational thought. Time seemed to slow around her, the turmoil blurring into the background as her mind focused on the sharp edge pressed against her palm. Her breath came quick and uneven, pulse racing like a frantic drumbeat beneath her ribs. She felt simultaneously suspended and utterly exposed, as if the delicate thread holding her together could snap at any moment. She had taken off her shoes. Barefoot, she could feel the edge of the rug beneath her toes, which is how she knew she was standing dead in the middle of the room. The darkness was absolute. Then she heard Isabelle's voice again, but it was not vaguely right. "If you come closer, you can see it." The voice whispered, too calm, too slow. It was Isabelle's voice, but not pretty. Something twisted beneath the familiar tone, a dark undercurrent that sent a chill crawling down Emily's spine. She took one cautious step

forward, and then it happened. A hidden sliver
of glass, biting and merciless, sank deep into the
sole of her foot. The more weight she bore, the
wider the cruel cut tore through her flesh. She
opened her mouth to scream. But no sound
escaped. Silence swallowed her voice whole.
The reserve was more horrifying than the pain.
Her voice had been taken, stolen from her
throat like breath sucked from a flame. She was
trapped inside her own agony with no release.
Blood now covered her feet. She was still in
silent pain.

CHAPTER TWENTY-EIGHT
SINKING BODY

1800

Another month had passed at Blackthorne Manor, and in that time, much had changed. Sir Edward and Lady Maple had been courting frequently, their every meeting woven with subtle smiles, lingering glances, and conversations charged with great ease and hints of something deeper blossoming between them. Arabella, once the ever-present shadow of his grief, had begun to recede into the past, still tenderly remembered, still mourned, but no longer holding his heart captive. Lady Catherine, for her part, had taken a pronounced liking to Lady Maple, far more than she had ever shown Arabella. It was not merely Lady Maple's poise or noble breeding that captivated her, but what Maple represented. The truth was clear: Lady Catherine needed Lady Maple far more than Lady Maple needed the Blackthorn legacy. For Lady Maple Robertson was one of the wealthiest women in Scotland, her fortune rivalled only by her mystery. Yet she had told Sir Edward nothing of her inheritance. She wanted him to desire her for who she was, not for the gold-laced future she carried in her name. While both Lady Catherine and Sir Howard were keenly aware of her financial worth, Maple had made it clear: *she* would be the one to reveal the truth, and only when the time felt right. Miss Fawns had been carrying an agonizing burden since the night of the ball, though her troubles did not stem from the event itself. No, her torment was rooted in the scandalous aftermath of Sir Edward's reckless behaviour, behaviour he had no memory of. That night, in a haze of grief and confusion, Sir Edward had mistaken a maid for Arabella. What followed was an act of passion that should never have occurred. Miss Fawns had tried to forget it, bury it deep beneath duty and routine. But forgetting was impossible. Only two people shared the momentousness of that secret with Miss Fawns: the maid herself, crude, demanding, and wholly without shame, and Lady Catherine. Miss Fawns had nearly forgotten she had confessed it in a moment of desperation during her interrogation in the drawing room. At the time, she had hoped that sharing the truth with Lady Catherine might lift some of the burden, but it had only deepened her dread. Lady Catherine's silence on the matter was far more terrifying than outrage or judgment. And now the maid, '*that ratchet woman,*' had returned again and again, demanding hush money. She had drained already every penny of Miss Fawns' wages, and to meet the growing demands, Miss Fawns had even once resorted to stealing from her Ladyship's belongings, an act that made her stomach twist with guilt. But now since lady catherines knowing it was her who paid the '*rachet women*' for her silence. The child had been born just days ago. Miss Fawns had learned this through a terse letter left under her pillow. Enough was enough. Miss Fawns fastened her cloak, her jaw set with determination. She would visit the woman, this final time. Something had to change. The secret had taken everything from her and now burdened on her lady She would plead, she would bargain, she would *do* whatever it took… but she could no longer live under the shadow of this threat towards her lady. And the manor, her livelihood, her soul, it was all at stake now. Trudging down the familiar muddy path, Miss Fawns clutched her shawl tighter around her shoulders. The rain had long since stopped, but the air still smelled of rot and damp leaves. She soon found herself standing outside the same broken-down house she had visited once before, the home of the wretched woman. The sight had not improved. The crooked garden gate collapsed at the faintest touch, splintering at her feet. She stepped over it and ducked beneath filthy bed sheets and clothes hanging on sagging lines, brushing against her face like unwelcome hands. Just as she raised her fist to knock, the door suddenly burst open. A man, grimy and dishevelled, reeking of stale beer, shoved past her without so much as a glance. The intolerable scent of unwashed skin and sour ale glided in the air like a thick fog. He disappeared into the tattered sheets ahead, and Miss Fawns, her heart pounding fiercely, stepped inside silently, closing the door behind her with careful stillness. From somewhere deeper within, a baby's desperate cry shattered the oppressive stillness. Guided by the sound, Miss Fawns moved cautiously through the dim space, her breath catching as she passed the sitting room. There, sprawled across the grimy wooden floor, lay a woman, naked, one leg bent with her foot barely touching the floor, her arms stretched above her head and bound tightly to a rough wooden pole by coarse, unforgiving rope. Her face was pale and drawn, streaked with dirt and tears, but her eyes burned with a fierce stare. "What? never seen a naked woman before?" The *'ratchet woman'* sneered, completely unfazed by her state. "Oh my." Miss Fawns whispered, hurrying toward her to undo the bindings. "Leave it." the woman barked. "My man is not finished with me. He will be back soon." Miss Fawns froze, her hands midair. Her stomach turned, not just at the image, but at the realisation that this woman had *chosen* this life. Not out of desperation, it seemed, but out of something darker. Something twisted. "And your baby?" Miss Fawns snapped. "You'll be no use to her trussed up like a beast." "She will be just fine." The woman muttered, her voice disturbingly calm. "She's learning already crying gets you nowhere." The baby wailed again, louder now. Miss Fawns stormed past her, into the dim room where the infant lay on the floor, swaddled in a rag that could barely be called cloth. Filth lined the edges of the room, and the air smelled of Mold and decay. Kneeling, Miss Fawns gently lifted the child and held her close. "There now, hush… everything is all right." She whispered softly, rocking the baby with surprising tenderness. When the cries softened, she placed the child carefully on a cleaner patch of cloth. Returning to the doorway, Miss Fawns carefully avoided meeting the naked woman's fierce gaze. Her voice wavered slightly, but she kept her chin lifted, steadying herself with every word. "I came here today to tell you this must end. No more threats. No more demands. You have already had your money." From somewhere behind her, the woman let out a low, guttural laugh, rough and bitter. "And who do you think you are, to issue commands? You? Or the Blackthorn family?" Miss Fawns took a slow breath, feeling the weight of the room pressing down. "Neither. But I serve the house, and I will not stand by while you ruin what little dignity remains." Miss Fawns remained silent. "I agree this has gone on long enough." The woman continued, her voice lilting with mockery. "I do hope Sir Edward wanted a daughter." Miss Fawns' pulse thundered against her ribs as the man lurched forward, blocking her path. She instinctively took a step back, but the cramped room. left little space to retreat. His eyes locked onto hers, dark and unfocused, flickering with menace. The baby's cries seemed distant now, swallowed by the oppressive weight pressing down on them both. Miss Fawns swallowed hard, forcing herself to stay sunny despite the turmoil gathering before her. "Please." The said quietly. "This has to stop." But the man's only response was a guttural growl as he reached out with shaking hands. "I'll see myself out." Miss Fawns uttered sharply, not daring to look back. "Oh miss, why don't you..." She shut the door on whatever vile suggestion he was about to utter. Outside, she finally exhaled. The sky above was grey, low, pressing in around her. She had done what she could, but it was not enough. She needed help. She needed Lady Catherine's influence, her power, to turn the tide. As Miss Fawns neared the manor, anxiety knotted her gut tighter with every step. The imposing silhouette of Blackthorne Manor rose ahead, cold and unyielding. It no longer felt like a sanctuary, but a cavernous beast, its jaws ready to snap shut or engulf her in flames. Still, she moved forward, resigned to face whatever fate awaited. Inside, Lady Catherine sipped her afternoon tea with practiced elegance, a neat pile of telegrams resting nearby. Sir Howard, her husband, lounged opposite her, partially obscured by his newspaper, savouring a rare moment of respite. The room was steeped in a delicate calm, as if the walls themselves paused in alarm, awaiting news that could shatter the careful balance of power and propriety. Miss Fawns's footsteps were quiet but determined as she entered the drawing room. The burden of what she had witnessed pressed down upon her, and despite her composed façade, her mind raced with the implications. Whatever she discussed next would change everything, for the family, for herself, and for the dark secrets lurking just beneath Blackthorne Manor's refined surface. "Sir Edward and Lady Maple have announced their wedding date Howard." Lady Catherine said, eyes not leaving the telegram she held. Sir Howard let out a low hum of acknowledgment without lowering his paper. Lady Catherine smiled to herself, unconcerned by his indifference. "We are going to be the wealthiest family in England, aside from his Majesty, of course." She knew he was not really listening, but it felt good to say it aloud anyway. These little victories, spoken into the room, made her plans feel real. Sir Howard finally set down his paper. "I do hope you'll keep out of Edward's way this time." Lady Catherine paused, her teacup hovering just below her lips. Her husband's tone was quiet but firm. He did not know everything, not about Arabella, not the whole truth, but he knew *her.* He knew she was not one to lose sleep over the dead. "I will do no such thing." She replied coolly, sipping her tea with poise, though her mind already stirred with ideas. She had no intention of being sidelined. There were always ways to involve oneself in a marriage, especially when wealth and reputation were at stake. Outside, Miss Fawns stopped at the dreadful oak door, her hand resting on the cool brass handle. She took a deep breath, steadying herself against the growing knot of anxiety in her stomach. The moment she had been anticipating, and fearing, had finally come. With careful control, she stepped forward. "I beg your pardon, my lady." Miss Fawns studied unnoticeably, her tone respectful yet earnest. She dipped into a graceful bow before Lady Catherine, her eyes meeting the ladies. "Might I have a moment of your time?" Lady Catherine glanced at her husband, noting that Sir Howard had not even acknowledged Miss Fawns' presence. With a soft sigh, she set her teacup down on the table and slowly rose from her chair, using her cane for support. Without a word, she followed Miss Fawns through the manor, down to the servant quarters. Miss Fawns led her to the small, tucked away room she liked to call her "box office." It was quiet, secluded, a perfect place for secrets. As they stepped inside, Lady Catherine looked around with mild curiosity. "Still the same as the last time I saw it, Miss Fawns." She announced, lowering herself into a chair. "Yes well my lady, I have always held a fondness for the charm of simpler things." Miss Fawns remarked, reaching discreetly into the folds of her dress to reveal a small, well-hidden bottle of sherry. The faint clink of glass as she produced it was almost inaudible, yet it caught Lady Catherine's attention. A brief, almost imperceptible smile flickered across her lips, a rare crack in her otherwise composed demeanour, hinting at a grudging respect. Without waiting for permission, Miss Fawns carefully poured the amber liquid into two crystal glasses, the rich colour catching the dim light of the room. She handed one glass to Lady Catherine with a steady hand. Lady Catherine accepted it with practiced elegance, her fingers curling around the stem as she raised the glass to her lips. She took a slow sip, her snappy eyes never leaving Miss Fawns. "Miss Fawns, to what do I owe the honour of your visit this evening?" Her voice was smooth, carrying just enough curiosity to mask the guarded wariness beneath. "There's no easy way to say this, my lady..." Miss Fawns paused, then continued carefully. "But the woman we do not speak of, she has lost her mind. Completely." She went on to recount her visit that morning, what she had seen, what he had heard, and how the woman continued to demand money in exchange for silence. Her threats had not stopped. If anything, they were escalating. Lady Catherine listened in total stillness. Her face was unreadable, carved from stone. "You see, my lady." Miss Fawns said, finishing her story with a deep breath, "I had no choice but to come to you for help." "This will certainly not do." Lady Catherine replied after a pause, her voice crisp. Miss Fawns was not sure what that meant, *'was she angry? Disgusted? Amused?'* "I would like to meet this girl." Lady Catherine declared at last, rising from her chair with slow, purposeful grace. Her gaze fixed on Miss Fawns, steady and determined. "The mother of my grandchild." Miss Fawns stayed where she was, a flicker of disbelief, and something darker, passing over her face. "Do you truly think that's wise, my lady?" She asked cautiously, her voice carefully controlled but edged with concern. Lady Catherine's eyes narrowed, a cold fire gleaming behind their polished surface. Her tone dropped to a sharp, final edge, leaving no room for argument. "Do not question my authority." She said, her words clear and uncompromising. "She shall be invited to luncheon tomorrow. Is that a task beyond your abilities Miss Fawns?" The prominence of the command settled over the room, inescapable. "No my lady, I will ensure it is done." Without another word, Lady Catherine turned sharply and swept from the room, her cane striking a steady rhythm against the cold stone floor, each step deep like a verdict. Miss Fawns let out a breath she had not realised she had been holding and sank heavily into her chair. A restless heat surged through her, tightening her limbs with nerves and unuttered fears. Her fingers shook as she reached for the bottle, pouring herself another glass of sherry. The liquid burned warmly as it slid down her throat, grounding her momentarily. Forcing her hands to steady, she lifted her quill and carefully dipped it into the inkwell. The hush of the room seemed to press closer as she began to write, her script flowing with urgency and a hint of unease:

Dear Miss Rachet,

The Blackthorne Manor requests the honour of your presence for luncheon tomorrow afternoon. We wish to discuss the future of our newest family member, should you choose to accept.

Signed,

Lady Catherine Blackthorne

Miss Fawns carefully folded the letter, pressing it flat before sealing it with a warm, crimson wax stamp. Without a moment to lose, she hurried through the dimly lit corridors toward the servants' dining hall. There, she spotted one of the younger footmen busily clearing away dishes, his movements swift but distracted. "Richard is it?" she called softly, her voice carrying a note of urgency that made him glance up immediately. "Yes, ma'am?" he responded, pausing his work to give her his full attention. "I have a task for you. Wine and chocolate in return." She said, holding up the sealed letter. "I need this delivered by hand to an address in town discreetly." Richard did not hesitate. He took the letter and nodded. "Consider it done." Miss Fawns watched Richard's retreating figure disappear into the shadowed hallway, a stinging pang of unease twisting in her gut. Tomorrow held more than just formality, it held risk, and consequences none of them could fully predict. It was the next day and in the drawing room, Lady Catherine sat perfectly poised, every inch the image of refined control. She had arranged the small table for two with exacting care: the tea steeped exactly right, releasing a fragrant steam that curled upward like soft murmurs; the cakes were daintily arranged, their pastel colours almost too perfect to eat; the cucumber sandwiches were trimmed with painstaking precision, each crust removed and aligned to suggest effortless grace. Her choice of chair was no accident, it softened her stern silhouette, making her seem less imposing, more... accessible. Yet beneath the serene facade, her patience was thinning, stretched taut as the ticking of the antique clock grew louder, each tick echoing like a countdown. Then, the soundless was broken by a fast knock, its sound clear and purposeful. "Yes?" Lady Catherine's voice cut through the stillness, carrying a keen edge of expectation. The door opened. Miss Fawns stepped in, chaperoned by a woman in a worn but clearly her *'best'* grey dress, clean, but faded at the seams. A dress chosen with purpose, though not enough to disguise the woman beneath it. "My lady, allow me to introduce... Miss Rachet" Miss Fawns told politely, then left the two alone, closing the door behind her. She lingered just outside, wondering why the child had not come too. "You must be the famous Miss Rachet." Lady Catherine said, gesturing to the seat opposite her. "It's good to see you again catherine it's no shock to me that you have no idea whom I am." the woman replied, sitting down without hesitation. "Lady Catherine." She corrected. Miss Rachet simply stared at her, unblinking. "Let's not sit here and play tea party... *Lady* Catherine." She uttered, drawing out the title like a challenge. "Indeed." Lady Catherine replied coolly, abandoning the pretence of friendliness as she straightened her back and returned to her usual regal posture. "It has come to my attention." Lady Catherine began, her tone controlled but resolute, "That you are the mother of my son's child." "My child." Miss Rachet shot back, her voice sharp with a fierce edge. "I came here for her future, not to be insulted." Her eyes glinted with suspicion, hard and fixed, daring Lady Catherine to challenge her. Between them, the atmosphere grew serious, like a pot simmering, its contents barely contained and ready to boil over at the slightest spark. Their conversation shifted, circling the delicate subject of the baby's future: the possibilities, the expectations, the promises of financial support. Yet beneath the formal words, an undercurrent of hostility and distrust pulsed, threatening to erupt at any moment. Then, Miss Rachet rose abruptly from her seat. "Excuse me." She brought out brusquely, and without waiting for a response, she turned on her heel and strode from the room, Miss Fawns close behind to guide her departure. Lady Catherine was left alone once again, the stillness wrapping around her like a shroud. She wasted no time. With the grace of long practice, she twisted the ornate head of her cane, revealing a hidden compartment within. From it, she withdrew a tiny glass vial, its contents gleaming amber, the colour of honey warmed by sunlight. Without a moment's pause, she carefully uncorked the vial and tilted it, allowing the liquid to slip silently into the slender flute of fruit wine set before her, the glass reserved exclusively for her. As the honey-coloured liquid mingled with the wine, Lady Catherine's lips curved into a faint, inscrutable smile. The trick, she knew, was in perception. She tucked the empty vial back into her cane, twisted the cap shut, and by the time Miss Rachet returned, all appeared normal once more. "Thank you for your patience." The woman said as she resumed her seat. "I believe we have come to an understanding." Lady Catherine replied with a gracious nod. "Shall we toast to it?" Miss Rachet hesitated only a moment before reaching, not for the glass nearest to her, but for the one across the table, Lady Catherine's original glass. Just as Lady Catherine had planned. The older woman deliberately averted her eyes, adopting an air of casual distraction that concealed the raw cunning beneath. She let Miss Rachet linger in the false comfort of victory, convinced she had slipped free of the web woven around her. Their glasses lifted in unison, the faint clink of crystal cutting through the thick silence like a soft murmur of challenge. Lady Catherine's lips lifted into a smile, cool, controlled, and edged with something darker, an implicit vow that the true game had only just begun. Beneath the refined surface, a whirlwind of intentions churned, each hidden move bringing her closer to the outcome she desired. "To the future." She discussed. "To the future." Miss Rachet echoed and drank deeply. A few restful minutes passed. The glasses were empty, the wine almost gone. Then came the cough. At first, just a cunning sound, dry, abrupt. But then another, deeper. And another. Until Miss Rachet was clutching her throat, hacking violently, her body trembling. Miss Fawns stood frozen, horror anchoring her to the spot as Miss Rachet's convulsions grew more violent. The sickening sound of choking filled the air, sharp and ragged, mingling with the low, guttural gurgles that resounded unnervingly in the confined space. Lady Catherine remained seated, her face the picture of calm control, though her eyes gleamed with a cold satisfaction. Slowly, intentionally, she lifted her glass and took a small, dutiful sip of the wine, as if savouring the moment. Miss Rachet's struggles weakened, her body shaking uncontrollably as the poison took hold. Finally, she collapsed forward, lifeless, her bloodied face pressed against the gleaming

floor. Miss Fawns' inhalation caught sharply, a
chill crawling down her back as the full impact
of what had just happened settled upon her. She
reached out to Miss Fawns, fingers twitching,
desperate, pleading. But Miss Fawns could not
move. She stood there, locked in a nightmare,
her eyes flicking between the horror unfolding
at her feet and the woman sipping wine at the
table, so calm, so utterly composed. Lady
Catherine delicately placed a crustless sandwich
between her lips, chewing as if she were
attending an afternoon play, rather than a slow
and gruesome execution. The choking grew
louder. Blood splattered from Miss Rachet's lips,
staining her once-grey dress, which now
bloomed red across her chest and lap. She
collapsed forward, dragging herself an inch
across the floor, then another, until her
strength gave way. With one final, gasping,
guttural breath, her body convulsed, then
stilled. Her head lolled sideways, cheek pressed
to the blood-slick floor, her arm outstretched as
though in final protest, reaching for a mercy
that never came. Silence returned to the room.
Lady Catherine placed her glass down with a
soft *clink*. She dabbed the corners of her mouth
with a silk napkin and looked up at Miss Fawns.
"Well." Lady Catherine said, her tone calm and
detached, "I dare say the wine was a touch

strong." Miss Fawns stepped back slowly, her legs unsteady, a tightness of fear coiling deep within her stomach. "She… she's dead." Miss Fawns mumbled, her voice barely audible, trembling with shock and disbelief. "No." Lady Catherine sheared, standing up with the poise of royalty, "she has been *dealt with*. There is a difference." The night was silent, the air damp with mist as Lady Catherine and Miss Fawns dragged the bundled body out to the rear gardens. The old sheet, soaked through with blood, left a dark trail behind them like a slug of death. Together they reached the edge of the lake, moonlight glinting off the rippling surface. Without a word, they heaved the body forward. A sickening *splash* broke the stillness, followed by the slow rise of bubbles as the corpse sank. The sheet unfurled beneath the water like a ghost being swallowed whole. Lady Catherine stood upright, brushing invisible dust from her gloves, her eyes cold and unblinking as she watched the last air pockets pop on the surface. "Miss Fawns." She put into words calmly. "See to the floor being cleaned." She turned without waiting for a reply, her cane tapping rhythmically against the stone as she walked away into the darkness. Miss Fawns stood still at the lake's edge, her breath smooth, her hands trembling at her sides. Her eyes remained fixed on the water, trying to convince herself that what had just happened had not. But it had. *It had.* "What have I done…" she whispered, barely audible over the faint lapping of the lake. Then, as if struck by a sudden, slick pang, she remembered, the baby. "The baby." She said aloud, her voice stronger but cracking with urgency and fear. Lady Catherine paused, just long enough to offer a reply without turning her gaze. The faintest hint of something unreadable flickered in her eyes before she spoke. "Get rid of it." She articulated, each word a dagger. "I do not care how. See to its death." And then Lady Catherine strode forward, slipping away into the manor's looming shadows, her figure swallowed by the dim corridors like a ghost retreating into the night. Miss Fawns remained still; her eyes locked on her own reflection dancing on the water's surface. Her face was ashen, the pale hue casting her features in stark relief. Her wide eyes shimmered with shock, and her lips parted slightly, as if seeking words, or breath, which refused to come. The gentle ripple distorted her image, twisting it into something alien and terrible, something both monstrous and unwillingly complicit in the dark deeds unfolding within those walls. *'Two deaths now,'* she thought, the forceful burden of guilt and fear settling deep within her. Two women claimed by Lady Catherine's cold, unrelenting hand. And soon... an innocent child might be caught in the same merciless snare. The manor's silence closed around her, stifling and complete. Somewhere beyond the heavy curtains and cold stone walls, the cruel game continued, and Miss Fawns knew with a sinking heart that she was now entwined in it, whether she wished it or not. She turned from the lake and headed slowly back toward the manor; her legs weak beneath her. She had a decision to make. One that could save a life or take another.

CHAPTERTWENTY-NINE
MIRROR MAN

Present day

The room blinked into harsh, artificial brightness. Everyone squinted, blinking rapidly. And then they saw her. Emily. Face down. Motionless. Blood pooling beneath her. Isabelle was the first to move. She sank to her knees, her hands shaking uncontrollably as she gently rolled the body over. Chase's scream tore through the still air, raw and desperate. Emily's eyes stared blankly back at them, empty, unseeing, frozen in a silent plea. A jagged shard of glass protruded abnormally from her throat, a cruel and twisted mockery of a necklace, glinting coldly in the fading light. She must have been holding it. When Hugo struck her, she had stumbled, fingers clutching desperately, but the glass had found its mark, slicing deep into her neck. Hugo stared down at his shaking, bloodied hands, then shifted his gaze between Emily's still form and the horrified faces of Chase and Isabelle. His chest rose and fell in ragged gasps, each breath thick with shock and mounting despair. His lips parted to speak but no words came. He could not breathe. He was drowning in air. Chase's fingers clutched Hugo's arm like a lifeline, her other hand trembling as she wiped the slick tears from her cheeks. Her breath came in ragged gasps, each word torn from a torso tight with panic. "We have to get out of here."

She choked, voice cracking like brittle glass. With a desperate shove, she threw the overweight door wide open. The stale air of the room was instantly replaced by the cold, suffocating chill of the dark stairwell. Without a second thought, Chase plunged into the spiral staircase, pulling Hugo behind her. They did not walk. They fell. Tumbling, crashing, bodies slamming hard against cold stone steps, skin scraping and knees buckling under the relentless descent. The sound of their panicked thuds echoed, mingling with a low, distant whisper that seemed to seep from the very walls. At last, they reached the bottom. But instead of relief, a paralyzing quietude gripped them Isabelle stepped over both helping each one up. Chase's chest heaved as she stared into the shadowed abyss beyond the last step. The lights were off. Everything was wrong. The landing stretched out endlessly, longer than memory allowed walls seeming to pulse and breathe, warping in the extraordinarily little light. The familiar doors lining each side had vanished. Replaced by murky voids that consumed sound and hope alike. Just a smooth, endless hallway. "What the hell…" Chase whispered, her voice barely holding together. She stepped forward cautiously, fingertips gliding over the walls, seeking any hint of a seam, a frame, a hidden passage, Nothing. No fractures. No doorways. No way out. "Not possible." Isabelle whispered, her voice hollow. Hugo just stood there. He looked like a ghost of himself, wide-eyed, blank, utterly drained. The blood on his hands had dried, but the horror clung to him like wet skin. Then, without warning, he sprinted. He glimpsed an opening, a fleeting mirage of space, and he lunged toward it. "No, Hugo!" Chase screamed, lunging for him. Isabelle reached out too. But he was too fast. Too far gone. "Come back! It is not safe!" Isabelle cried. "Hugo!" Chase yelled again, desperation cracking her voice. But he did not stop. He did not turn. He did not even look back. He vanished. Just like that. One moment, he was standing there, solid, real. The next, nothing but empty air. Gone. Like the hallway itself had yawned open and swallowed him whole, leaving behind only a hollow stillness that closed in on them from all sides. Chase and

Isabelle greyed their fingers together tightly, white-knuckled and shaking, as if that slight grasp might hold back the creeping darkness. Their screams tore through the void. "Hugo! Hugo!" but the endless corridor devoured their voices, twisting them into fractured, ghostly wails that ricocheted like lost souls trapped in an endless chasm. The walls seemed to contract, their forms deepening, writhing and alive. The air grew dense, cold, and suffocating with something unseen, watching, waiting. And somewhere in that oppressive gloom, the silent had claws. Something was behind them. Watching. Following. But whenever one of them dared to glance back, there was nothing, only the same endless corridor stretching into oblivion. The darkness writhed at the edges of their vision, slipping away like something alive, just beyond reach. The corridor began to shrink. The ceiling lowered. The walls pressed in. Soon, they were forced to crouch, then crawl, on their hands and knees like trapped animals. The air was growing thinner with every breath. Their backs scraped against the ceiling. Shoulders dragged against the walls. "Mum, please… let me go first." Chase panted, her breath ragged, her eyes stinging with sweat. "I am your mother. I go first. I will protect you." Isabelle said, her voice steady but wavering beneath the calm, like a fragile flame battling a rising gust. "Here, take my shoelace. Tie it tight around your wrist. So, no matter what happens, I will know you are still by my side." Her fingers shook ever so slightly as she knotted it, but the fierce determination in her eyes burned brighter than any fear. Chase obeyed with trembling fingers, getting married tight as Isabelle wiped the damp strands of hair from her forehead. Together, they crawled, inch by suffocating inch. The hallway had become a coffin-shaped tunnel. Arms pinned to their sides. The floor slick with sweat and something else, something cold and sticky. Chase shut her eyes. It felt easier that way. Suddenly, bang! She smacked into the soles of her mother's boots. "What is it?" Chase gasped, heart hammering. Isabelle tilted her head toward something just ahead. "It's a door." She said, voice dazed with disbelief. She reached out, fingers tremulous, and pushed it open. A sudden, harsh light poured through the opening. Isabelle slipped through first, moving cautiously like a shadow stepping into the daylight. Chase fumbled at her wrist, quickly untying the shoelace, then scrambled in after her, heart pounding like a frantic drum. They pushed themselves up slowly, muscles aching from the crawl, eyes adjusting to the brightness.

The oppressive burden that had settled in the air dissolved and replaced by a brittle quiet, as if the darkness itself had been torn away, leaving behind something cold and hollow in its place. They were in a bedroom. Chase's bedroom.

Not Chase's bedroom. Everything looked the same, yet something was unmistakably wrong. Off. Decayed. Haunted by time's cruel hand. Chase's breath caught in her throat. "This isn't my room." She whispered. Her voice barely made it out. "This is… Arabella's room." The same four-poster bed. the same faded wallpaper. Chase had seen it before, in the vision. This was the room Arabella died in. "Is that…" Isabelle whispered, her voice staggery as her eyes fixed on the antique, floor length mirror. Chase watched her mother's gaze. There, in the mirror's reflection, stood Hugo. Alone. Pale. Stricken with terror. His eyes darted wildly, searching, trapped between worlds, desperate for escape. "Hugo!" Chase screamed, lunging toward the mirror with desperate urgency. Her palms slammed against the icy surface, leaving faint prints on the glass. "Hugo! It is us! We are here!" But the reflection did not change. No flicker of recognition. No sign that he even heard. He was trapped, locked behind the mirror's cold, relentless surface, a silent prisoner caught in a world just out of reach. Then Isabelle saw her, the woman. A tall, pale, ghostly figure drifted silently from the murk behind Hugo. She moved with an unnatural, glacial slowness, her tattered gown dragging across a floor that seemed to dissolve beneath her feet, like she was gliding between two worlds, neither fully here nor there. Her face was a hazy blur, drained of all warmth or humanity, but her eyes… those hollow sockets oozed thick, black tears that spilled like ink, pooling and twisting as if alive. The tears left a dark stain, spreading down her cheeks in slow, sinister trails that whispered long-buried griefs. A coldness radiated from her, a silent warning of something broken and malevolent lurking just beneath the veneer, something that did not belong in the living world. "Chase…" Isabelle whispered in horror. Chase screamed Hugo's name, fists pounding desperately against the cold glass. "Behind you! Hugo, please!" But he did not flinch. Did not even turn. He was frozen, trapped in a silence she could not break. Until suddenly, his eyes snapped upward locking onto theirs. A flicker of hope ignited. He saw them. A faint, delicate smile cracked his lips. He lifted a shaky hand and took a hesitant step toward the mirror, fingers stretching out as if to break the barrier that held him captive.

But it was already too late. The ghost's skeletal hand wrapped around his head. Her fingers, too long, too thin, wormed into Hugo's eye sockets. "No!" Chase shrieked. Hugo writhed in silent agony, his body twisting and thrashing, but no sound escaped his lips. Trapped within the mirror's cold prison, his screams were swallowed by an endless, deafening silence. His blood sprayed behind the glass like ink in water. Chase collapsed into Isabelle's arms, sobbing uncontrollably. Isabelle held her daughter tightly, shielding her eyes, but neither could look away. The ghost pulled. Hugo's eyes bled glossy, black tears that traced shimmering trails down his hollow cheeks. His face, vacant and contorted in silent agony, turned toward them one last time, reaching blindly, desperately, as if begging for help he could never grasp. Then her hand returned. A final, lingering squeeze. A horrible, squelching crack. His skull collapsed. His body dropped. A limp, broken heap. And then… The woman looked at them. Right at them. Her cracked lips peeled back into a smile, wide, unnatural, and soaked in menace. It stretched too far, revealing teeth sharp and jagged like broken glass. BANG!…Her fists slammed relentlessly against the mirror's icy surface, each strike ringing out like a gunshot in the dense silence. The glass groaned and fractured beneath her fury, cracks spiderwebbing outwards with a sinister, crawling life of their own. BANG!... BANG!... BANG!... The mirror shuddered, shards vibrating on the edge of collapse, as if the very barrier between worlds was about to shatter. Her snarling face pressed closer, pale and warped, eyes weeping thick, oily streams that pooled and dripped down her face, black rivers staining the glass like ink spilled from a cursed soul. A chilly wind seemed to hiss from the broken mirror's cracks, carrying with it a murmur of ancient rage and unspeakable torment, as if the darkness beyond was clawing to break free. "GO!" Isabelle screamed, yanking Chase's hand with desperate force. They lunged toward the bedroom door and ripped it open, but the world twisted beneath them. Chase stumbled forward, only to find herself swallowed by darkness, standing alone in the tangled gardens behind the house. Towering hedges loomed like ancient sentinels, their gnarled branches clawing at the starless sky. The maze twisted and shifted as if alive, the narrow paths folding in on themselves, closing off any chance of escape. The damp earth beneath her feet felt cold and unforgiving, while faint murmurs drifted through the dense gloom, voices that brushed against her ears like the memory of a scream. High above, Isabelles destination through the door led her clung to the jagged ledge of the old stone tower, its rough edges digging into her skin with each quivering grip. Her lungs caught mid-inhale as she peered down into the silver glow of the moonlit maze, where Chase wandered like a ghost, swallowed by dusk and swallowed whole by fear. The hush around her was unnatural, broken only by the rustle of leaves and the relentless thud of her heartbeat. Time seemed to stretch, each second a cruel eternity as mother and daughter remained trapped in their separate prisons, bound by dread and the cruel grip of the endless labyrinth.

1800

The infant lay still in the centre of the cold, filthy room, motionless and pale like an old porcelain doll, abandoned by a long-dead family, forgotten by time. It was a sight that turned the stomach, a cruel contrast to the innocence of new life. Miss Fawns knelt beside the child, her hands trembling as she lifted the small bundle from the floor. Her breath caught in her throat; she was prepared to reveal the lifeless face of a babe stolen too soon. But as she

slowly peeled back the soiled cloth, two bright
blue eyes met hers. The baby lay silent,
unnervingly still, its gaze as steady as a windless
summer lake, without even the faintest ripple.
A single tear slid down Miss Fawns' cheek,
glistening in the dim light. She knew what
Lady Catherine demanded of her. And the very
thought of it shattered something inside her.
She carried the child through the fog-drenched
grounds, holding it tightly to her chest as if
shielding it from the night itself. The mist
curled around her like fingers, clinging to her
dress, muffling her footsteps in the damp earth.
At last, she reached a narrow stone bridge, slick
with moisture and old moss. Beneath it, the
black river raged, its waters wild and hungry,
churning with a current so fierce it seemed to
growl. It was not just water; it was something
darker, something ancient, a force that
devoured whatever touched it. One glance into
that swirling void, and she understood: if she
let go now, if the baby fell, it would vanish
without sound or trace. No cry. No splash.
Just… gone. Swallowed whole, like it had never
existed at all. Her hair whipped about her face
in the bitter wind as she raised the baby above
the railing, the child now squirming gently,
then crying, a sharp, innocent wail that tore
through the silence like a blade. Miss Fawns

froze. The baby's cry was haunting, like a plea from another world. With a choked sob, she pulled the child back to her chest, clutching it tightly, whispering apologies into its soft cheek. "I am sorry... I am so sorry…" Turning on her heel, she fled through the darkness, heart pounding. She ran until she found a cottage at the edge of the village, its lantern barely flickering behind frosted glass. She laid the baby gently on the doorstep, swaddling the child in every scrap of cloth she could find. With a final, urgent knock, whetted and pleading, Miss Fawns vanished into the shadows of the night. Back at the manor, Lady Catherine stood at the drawing room window, gazing out across the gardens as she so often did. Her posture was rigid, arms folded loosely, her expression unreadable. She spoke without turning. "Has the matter been dealt with?" She knew precisely who lingered by the door. "Yes, my lady." Miss Fawns replied, her voice low. "But if I may speak freely… I would rather not discuss it." Lady Catherine pivoted slowly, her eyes keen and inscrutable as they settled on her loyal servant. The emptiness lingered between them, thick, laden with things left unverbalized. Then, with a slight, elegant tilt of her head and the faintest curl of her lips, she spoke softly, "Very well As you wish." She turned back to the window, her hands clasped now behind her back. "Sir Howard has requested the Scottish whisky be brought out for the evening. We are celebrating Lady Maple and Sir Edward's engagement." The topic shift was swift and deliberate, a clean break from the foul business of the day. "Yes, ma'am. I will inform Butler Brown at once." Miss Fawns replied, curtseying with habitual refinement before swiftly slipping out the door. She moved with such haste that she did not allow herself a single moment to dwell on her true feelings, nor on the image of the elegant, smiling Lady Maple, nor the unsettling thought of her becoming the future mistress of Blackthorne Manor. Lady Catherine and Sir Howard had spared no effort ensuring the evening ahead was executed to perfection. A Scottish menu had been requested, along with the finest whisky and a selection of rare wines. The dining table was draped in crisp linens and set with the manor's finest silver, silent proof of Blackthorne's enduring grandeur. Throughout the halls, the mournful wail of bagpipes would rise and fall, a haunting blend of tradition and celebration. Doris Mossford and her husband were also expected; the closest remaining family Lady Maple had left. Their presence was a particular delight to Lady Catherine, as Doris had long been a cherished friend. Lady Maple arrived precisely on time, flanked by Doris and her stiff-backed husband. Sir Edward and Lady Catherine stood in the grand vestibule to greet them. "Sir Howard is just finishing a letter to Lord Channing, rather important business." Lady Catherine announced, extending her gloved hand in greeting. "I'm glad to hear Sir Howard will be joining us, Lady Catherine." Doris's husband replied, his voice muffled beneath the heavy curtain of a thick, tobacco-stained moustache. His lips barely moved as he spoke. At that moment, Butler Brown appeared with perfect timing, bowing deeply before ushering the guests toward the drawing room for wine, while the final preparations were made to the dinner table. "I was positively gay with delight when I read of your engagement, Lady Maple." Lady Catherine said, her voice a velvety blend of charm and appropriate cunning. "Such a fortunate match, for both parties, I'm sure." She watched the younger woman closely, noting the faint stiffness in her posture, the way her smile hesitated for just a breath. There was something about Lady Maple that fascinated her, flawless poise, effortless beauty, and yet... a subtle unease that clung to her like a shadow. Beneath the polished exterior, Lady Maple carried the unmistakable trace of longing, an aching need she tried so hard to hide. Not borne of lack, but of uncertainty, of never truly feeling safe, of knowing that her place in society, though gilded, was still fragile. Despite her wealth, she sought something more enduring: permanence. Protection. A name that could not be stripped away. And Lady Catherine? She had all those things to offer. But nothing came freely. No security without strings. No alliance without control. Lady Maple did not know it yet, but she was already caught in the web. She needed someone new to mould, someone young and pliable. A woman who would not challenge her word, who would mistake her manipulation for affection, if *'manipulation'* were the proper word at all. "Mother please." Sir Edward said sharply, clearly uncomfortable with the lavish attention. "No, no it is quite alright." Lady Maple brought out, her tone smooth and intentional, every syllable cloaked in elegance. She smiled at Sir Edward, gentle, deferential, then turned that same smile upon Lady Catherine, though now it lingered just a moment too long. "I am truly honoured." She said, her voice like warm porcelain. "I very much look forward to becoming part of this family… and part of this remarkable manor." The words lingered between them, soft but unmistakably pointed. Her gaze drifted across the grand walls, the ancestral portraits, the velvet-draped corners where dusk seemed to settle like breath. She was not merely admiring the estate; she was assessing it. Mapping it. As though she were already weaving herself into its story, anchoring her future to its foundations. There was grace in her expression, but beneath the glow something colder stirred. Something inconspicuously possessive. Lady Catherine saw it. Lady Catherine returned her smile, but behind her eyes something far colder lingered. It was not love she offered the young bride-to-be. It was ownership. The meal and evening unfolded like a well-rehearsed play. Conversation flowed as smoothly as the wine, the atmosphere around the table was nothing short of splendid. There was not a whisper of awkward stillness nor the flicker of a brewing debate, a stark contrast to the last time Sir Edward had introduced a future bride at this very table. That night had been tense and unnatural. Silence had lingered like a fog, broken only by the clinking of glasses and the excessive pouring of alcohol. Tonight however, proved how pleasant an evening could be when the mother-in-law was in favour of the match. The addition of bagpipes, a thoughtful gesture orchestrated by Lady Catherine herself, touched Lady Maple deeply. The mournful yet proud notes transported her back to the Highlands, to memories of a marriage long past and a life once lived among mountains that stretched into eternity, beside lochs that mirrored the sky. But this, this would be her new home now. Blackthorne Manor, though grand and steeped in centuries of history, bore none of the wildness of distant lochs or untamed waters. Its sprawling grounds were hemmed in by carefully clipped hedgerows and towering ancient trees whose gnarled branches whispered secrets on the wind. The manor's waters were confined to still, glassy garden lakes, placid and controlled, like a polished mask concealing what lay beneath. Nearby, the villages moved with quiet, comforting rhythms: shopkeepers opening their shutters, children's laughter drifting through cobblestone streets, and the soft toll of church bells marking the passage of time. To the casual observer, this was peaceful isolation, the very picture of rustic English charm. But to a woman who had once known the bone-deep loneliness of truly forgotten places, Blackthorne felt like a city, a crowded, breathing entity, thrumming with life and danger both visible and unseen. Lady Maple smiled softly, sipping her wine as the

music played. This was not the life she had
before, but it could be the life she needed.

FINAL CHAPTER
PART I
ARABELLAS REVENGE

1800

The wedding had been a success. There was no interruption, no heartbreak, no poisoning, nothing to ruin the day. Sir Edward and Lady Maple were now happily married, their vows spoken beneath the high arches of the old chapel, and the moment sealed with kiss and fitting approval. Lady Maple, now officially a Blackthorne, had stepped gracefully into her new title, becoming the new Lady of the Manor. She took on the role once held by Lady Catherine, along with all the expectations, responsibilities, and arcadian influence that came with the name. Lady Catherine had always been destined to still be the true Lady of the Manor. Titles could shift, faces could change, but control was something she never relinquished. And now, through her new daughter-in-law, she would no doubt continue to pull the strings, quietly, persistently veiled in charm, manipulating her just as she had so many others before. The guests had all departed. The grand halls now echoed with absence. It had been, on the surface, a day of great fulfilment, for appearances, for legacy, for power. Though the hour was still early in the evening, just past five o'clock, it felt as though an entire lifetime had passed. In the drawing room, the newlyweds sat alongside Lady Catherine, Sir Howard, and Doris, all enjoying celebratory wine and fine Scotch. Butler Brown entered quietly and offered Lady Catherine a discreet nod. She rose with grace. "I would like to raise a toast." She began, lifting her glass with slow elegance, her eyes settling first on Sir Howard, then drifting toward the newlyweds. Her smile lingered with pride. "My only son, now married and ready to take his rightful place as master of the Manor. It fills me with joy to see him stepping into this role with strength and dignity. And his wife, Lady Maple, who will stand beside him not only as his partner but as his guiding hand, graceful, wise, and ready to meet all that lies ahead." She paused, allowing the moment to settle over the house like a warm breeze. "We Sir Howard and I, would like to offer a small gift in honour of this marriage, a gesture of our love, and a symbol of our hopes for the life they will share.

May it be long, may it be peaceful, and may this house thrive under their care." She swept the skirts of her gown to the side and gestured toward Butler Brown. "If you would all be so kind as to follow." They stepped through the front doors and out into the garden, the soft crunch of gravel underfoot was the only sound for a moment. The evening breeze was crisp, carrying the faint trace of roses, faded, but still woven through the hedgerows. They walked the winding path toward a familiar clearing, once a place of retreat for Sir Edward. At the top of the garden stood a newly erected statue: Sir Howard handing a key to Sir Edward, a symbolic passing of legacy. Yet something felt amiss. Something that once made this place peaceful and beautiful was no longer there. Sir Edward turned slowly, searching for the source of the change, the thing that tugged at the edges of his memory. But it was Doris who saw it first. "The white blossom tree." She asserted softly. "It has been cut down." Edward snapped his head in the direction she was looking. The sight struck him like a jolt, he stopped breathing for a moment, and a wave of shame washed over him for not noticing sooner. *How could he have missed it?* "Who did this?" he demanded, fury rising like a tide. "Who ordered this?" "We had to make room for the statue."

Lady Catherine replied coolly. "The tree was overgrown. It overshadowed everything, including the meaning of this gift." She knew it would wound him. She also knew she did not care. It was the final remnant of the woman she had so deeply despised, and she had finally rid herself of it. Before Sir Edward could voice his grief, Lady Maple stepped in, placing a calming hand on his arm. "Your mother and I made the decision together." She said gently. "We thought it best. We did, however, preserve Arabella's plaque." She stepped toward the darkened stump, her heels clicking softly against the stone path, and beckoned him to join her. The plaque had been carefully mounted into the flat top of the tree's remains, weathered, but intact, its inscription only visible when one stood directly over it, as if the memory it carried was meant to be discovered peacefully and intimately, by those who chose to look. Clever. Out of sight, out of mind. This appeased Edward, or at least, he pretended it did. It was, after all, his wedding day. He could not be seen mourning another woman before his new bride. He turned to his mother and father, forcing a smile. "Thank you for this tremendous gift. What a fine sculpture." Lady Catherine smiled in return, a well-rehearsed expression, polished through years of social grace and subtle manipulation. It was the kind of smile that looked warm from a distance but, up close, revealed nothing at all. Beneath it lingered something far colder, something calculated. She had played her part perfectly. As always. Sir Edward and Lady Maple remained by the statue; their figures half lit by the fading afternoon light. They spoke in hushed tones, their heads close, lost in whatever private words passed between newlyweds. Lady Catherine, Doris, and Sir Howard turned from the garden path and began the slow walk back toward the manor. The breeze had changed; it was no longer gentle. It swept through the grounds with a sudden sharpness, tugging at cloaks and brushing against exposed skin. It was far too cold now, too biting for their thin, delicate faces, which had grown unused to anything unpleasant. "My dear wife, how radiant you look this evening." Sir Edward said, taking both of Lady Maple's hands in his. He looked into her shining eyes with tasteful reverence, a softness in his expression that spoke of true affection. Lady Maple returned his gaze with a gentle blink, her smile delicate and radiant, capable of stirring even the most guarded heart. "My wife." He gasped again, as if savouring the word on his tongue, letting its meaning settle into his bones. "I shall never tire of saying that." He leaned forward and pressed a slow, tender kiss upon her pouted, glossy lips. For a moment, time seemed to still around them, the world narrowing to that single, delicate touch. But just as their lips met, the atmosphere shifted, in an almost imperceptible change. The clouds rolled swiftly across the sky, shrouding the warm orange glow of the sun. The heavens turned a brooding grey, and the still afternoon air gave way to a sudden, biting wind that stung the skin and swept through the gardens like a warning. The moment shattered. "Shall we head back?" Sir Edward asked, glancing about with unease. "I think it wise, dear husband." Lady Maple replied, gathering her skirts tightly to guard against the chill wind that teased the fabric. They walked side by side, arms linked, stepping away from the now-shadowed path. As they disappeared into the garden's soft, misty veil, neither noticed the ghostly figure that appeared from the fog. A faint, flickering outline of a woman, motionless and silent, watching their retreat with unblinking eyes. The felling of the white blossom tree had awakened something long buried. In its roots, a boundary had been broken, a portal between life and death, disturbed by meddling hands. And when their kiss sealed the bond, it became the final key, unlocking something long buried, something that should have remained forgotten. Arabella had returned. But she was no longer the Arabella Sir Edward once knew, no longer the woman he loved, pitied, or mourned. She had transformed into something far beyond human, A ghost. Not just any ghost, but a vengeful spirit, restless and unforgiving, bound by rage and unfinished business. Arabella appeared from the fog, but before her form could fully take shape, the newlyweds drifted back within the manor's walls. The great manor had fallen eerily silent. Not a footstep echoed; not a breath stirred the drapes. The servants had all been dismissed for the evening, granted rare reprieve. Lady Catherine, ever the embodiment of propriety, had withdrawn to her bedchamber, her curt "Good night." Repeated twice, to fill the lingering stillness. Miss Doris had already slipped away to her own quarters, ever eager to escape the burden of celebration and company. Lady Maple and Sir Edward shared but a brief, meaningful look before ascending together to the master chambers. There, at last, they would consummate their bond, unseen, unguarded, and free from prying eyes. This left only Sir Howard in the drawing room, alone but content, settled deeply into his worn leather chair. The soft glow of the fire flickered across his features as he cradled a glass of fine whisky, its golden liquid catching the light. A cigar smouldered slowly at his side, its faint smoke curling upward and blending with the stilly silence of the room. He read whatever it was he fancied now, something dry and dense, filled with dense prose and little emotion. The kind of book that required patience and thought, much like Sir Howard himself. In this calm solitude, surrounded by the presence of history and fading light, he found a rare moment of peace. The whisky he sipped was old, decades aged, saved for this very occasion, his only son's wedding... his own quiescent retirement. At last, the burden of duty could pass to Edward, and Sir Howard could tend to gentler matters: leisure, letters, and less watchful eyes. As he turned a page with a satisfied sigh, his elbow knocked the whisky bottle. It teetered, then tumbled from the table, spilling its reverberative contents across his trousers and soaking the pages in pungent spirit. "Damn it!" He barked, reaching instinctively for the bell cord, only to remember: no staff tonight. He had insisted they take the evening off. With a low grunt, he sank back into his chair, hoping the warmth of the fire would chase away the dampness clinging to his skin. He lit a fresh cigar, brushing away a few stray embers that had settled on his waistcoat with effortless ease. Then, without warning, a sudden coldness began to seep through the room, the atmosphere thickening with menace that went unacknowledged. The zephyr turned dense. Ghastly. As though someone had stepped into the room behind him. Sir Howard stiffened, a sudden prickling crawling along his nerves. For a fleeting moment, unease gripped him, but he quickly shrugged it off as nothing more than the fog of too much drink and too little rest. Unbeknownst to him, behind his chair, shrouded in traces and smoke, stood the faint silhouette of a woman. Her form barely distinguishable, like mist clinging to shape. The whisky bottle, which had settled upright near the fireplace, suddenly tipped over once more, as if pushed by some unseen force. It rolled slowly, unnaturally, its movement purposeful and unsettling, until it came to rest spilling its golden contents toward the waiting fire. The flames flickered and danced eagerly, stretching out like hungry tongues to catch the creeping stream of alcohol. The liquid hissed as it met the heat, feeding the fire and causing it to flare with sudden, wild brightness. Sir Howard swore under his breath, retrieved the bottle, poured the final drops into his glass, and then tossed it carelessly across the room with a muted clink. He sighed softly and leaned back into the chair, but now… she was closer. The figure stood just behind his chair, so near she could have whispered into his ear. Her hands rose, gaunt, pallid, barely corporeal, and with that gesture, a violent gust tore through the room. Papers took flight. Curtains flailed. The fire roared to unnatural height, its flame deepening to a blueish hue before flashing crimson. Sir Howard froze. His glass hovered before his eyes, suspended mid-air and turning gently like a pendulum caught in a silent stillness. Silence settled over the space, thick and insufferable, as if the very air had stopped moving. He found himself utterly powerless, unable to speak, unable even to blink. Every instinct screamed for him to move, but his body remained locked in place, trapped by some invisible power holding him fast. And then, the glass shot forward, crashing into the fireplace. Suddenly, a flash erupted, a burst of flame so fierce it shot from the fireplace and struck him squarely in the chest. The fire hungrily seized his whisky-soaked clothes, igniting them instantly. Within moments, he was engulfed in roaring flames, with the power to move his body again he staggered backward with wild, desperate flails of his arms. No screams emerged from his throat, only a dry, rasping breath as his flesh blistered and cracked. His skin peeled. His face warped. The fire danced over him like a living creature, devouring all it touched. He collapsed to the rug in a fit of spasms, shuddering, twitching. Then silence. The flames, as suddenly as they had come, extinguished. And with the last flickers of life leaving his scorched body, Sir Howard opened his eyes, wide, unblinking, to behold the figure standing over him. Arabella. Arabella hovered silently above Sir Howard's liquefied remains, the flesh and bone distorted into a unsightly puddle upon the floor. Her hollow eyes glowed faintly in the darkness, the remnants of vengeance clinging to her spectral form like frost. Without a sound, she drifted backward, gliding through the wall and vanishing into the shadows beyond the crime scene. Elsewhere in the grand manor, the fire in the grate crackled softly, jetting a rose-coloured glow across the room where Lady Maple and Sir Edward lay entangled in the opulence of his four-poster bed. The velvet curtains swayed gently with the breeze, the scent of lilacs and candle wax mingling in the air. Their bodies pressed close beneath the silken sheets, warmth passing between them like whispered secrets. Sir Edward leaned in, brushing his lips against

Lady Maple's ear, his voice husky with longing. "I want all of you." He pronounced, his hand tracing a slow, thoughtful path along her waist, down her side, until it found the place that made her breath hitch and her back arch in pleasure. Lady Maple breathed out quietly, a gentle moan slipping past her lips. "You have all of me." She whispered in return, lifting her arms slowly above her head, her fingers trailing gently through the soft waves of her loose curls. Her eyes fluttered closed, surrendering to the moment, while a tender smile curved at the corners of her mouth, delicate, yet charged with restful desire. It was a smile that spoke of trust, longing, and the intimate connection growing between them. Sir Edward disappeared beneath the sheets, his kisses trailing downward like a storm gathering strength. Lady Maple's sighs grew louder, her fingers curling into the embroidered pillows as wave after wave of sensation rippled through her. The room was alive with the soft rhythm of breath and subtle movement, the ancient bed groaning gently beneath their weight. Every shift, every brush of skin against skin, was an intimate gesture, a delicate dance of desire and longing made flesh in the quiet sanctuary of night. Hours later, Lady Maple and Sir Edward lay side by side, sprawled beneath the tangled sheets, their bodies still echoing the warmth of shared closeness. Their skin glistened with sweat, hair tousled in every direction, as the last embers in the hearth flickered low. Lady Maple sat up slowly, flipping her hair over one shoulder with a languid grace. "That was… magical." She whispered, pouring a satisfied smile toward her husband. She leaned down to press one more lingering kiss on his lips before rising from the bed, entirely bare. She moved with playful elegance, hips swaying, twirling briefly in the dim candlelight as if performing just for him. Sir Edward watched, enraptured by her beauty, his new wife, radiant and free. She settled at the dressing table, brushing her hair with long, deliberate strokes, smiling at him through the reflection in the mirror. "Every night." Sir Edward looked softly. "Will be as magical as the next." Just as the words left his lips, a violent gust blew open the balcony doors with a loud crash, sending curtains billowing and startling them both. They laughed nervously, a shared moment of surprise, but Sir Edward's laughter quickly died. In the mirror, only in the mirror, stood a woman he recognized. Pale, delicate, and shimmering like mist. Arabella. Lady Maple, still brushing her hair, appeared completely unaware. Sir Edward sat upright; his face

drained of colour. "Maple… do you see that?"
"See what, love?" she asked, her voice faltering
as she paused. "You are scaring me." He did not
answer. His gaze was fixed on the reflection, on
those familiar, haunting eyes. He whispered the
name like a curse. "Arabella…" Lady Maple
froze, her body stiffening as a flicker of
confusion clouded her features. Gradually, that
confusion twisted into a simmering anger,
tightening her jaw and narrowing her eyes.
"My name is Maple, Edward! After such a
dream of a night, I would prefer to be called as
such, not the name of some ex-lover!" She
snapped. Wounded pride flashed in her voice.
She stood abruptly, throwing on her nightdress
with a huff, and stormed out onto the balcony.
She stood there, arms crossed tightly over her
chest, staring up at the vast night sky above. A
sudden tightness gripped her chest, filling her
with a fragile hope and an ache that would not
fade. She hoped, no, she was almost certain,
that Edward would follow her out here. That
he would close the distance between them,
wrap his arms around her protectively, whisper
soft apologies that would melt away the
concern, press a tender kiss to her shoulder, and
promise, with all the sincerity she longed to
believe, that he would never mention that
name again. But Edward did not move. He

stood rooted in place, eyes wide, as the apparition slowly turned away from the mirror and began to glide toward Lady Maple. "I forgive you." Maple whispered, her voice barely more than a breath, softening with an ache of compassion. She turned around, expecting to find her husband's steady presence behind her. Instead, she came face to face with a breathtakingly beautiful woman, ethereal and almost translucent. Arabella. A scream tore from Maple's throat. Her entire body went rigid with terror. "Edward!" she cried, her voice quivering. "What is happening?!" But Sir Edward could not speak. His mind went completely blank, swallowed by a sudden, overwhelming stillness that seemed to press against his very thoughts. Before him stood two women, his past and his present, one alive and radiant, the other long dead, a haunting spectre from a time he thought was buried forever. A stropped constriction gripped his lungs, leaving him momentarily paralyzed. The world around him wavered, and reality fractured into jagged shards of confusion, disbelief, and something darker lurking just out of sight. Lady Maple closed her eyes, praying to wake from the nightmare. When her eyes opened again, Arabella's pale hand was stretched out, her finger quivering as it pointed directly at her. A piercing shriek shattered the chamber, resonating off the walls like a banshee's wail. In an instant, the bedsheet that had been draped over Sir Edward surged upward as if seized by unseen forces, hurtling through the air to engulf Lady Maple, wrapping her tightly in its ghostly embrace like a suffocating shroud. Trapped in the fabric, she screamed in blind panic, stumbling in frantic circles across the balcony, trying desperately to escape. Her bare feet slipped, arms flailing. Each movement brought her closer to the low stone railing. Sir Edward jolted from the bed, finally realising the danger. "Maple!" he shouted. "Wait! Do not…!" But it was too late. With a final misstep, she stumbled backward over the edge. Her scream as she fell pierced the night sky, a sound Edward would never forget. A sickening crack followed as her body hit the ground far below. Sir Edward burst out onto the balcony, breathless, his heart pounding wildly beneath his ribs like a desperate drum. He leaned over the cold brick railing, his eyes locking onto the horrifying sight below. There, sprawled across the stone courtyard, lay her lifeless body, motionless and broken. Her skull was brutally split open, a dark river of blood winding its way slowly across the smooth white stone, staining the once pristine surface with a gruesome, unforgiving finality. A cold wave of shock and despair crashed over him, leaving him momentarily rooted in place, unable to look away from the terrible scene. He screamed. He wept. "Maple! No! Why? Why would you do this?!" Sir Edward remained on the cold stone floor of the balcony, knees raw and bruised, his bare skin pressed uncomfortably against the biting chill of the night. His arms stretched forward, clutching the top of the rough brick railing, fingers curling and digging in as though trying to hold onto the very threads of reality slipping through his grasp. His head lolled low and weary, hair tousled and damp from grief, while his chest rose and fell in uneven, silent sobs that tore at his soul. Naked and exposed to the harsh wind that bit relentlessly at his skin, he felt nothing but the hollow ache of loss. Everything else faded away, only the cruel truth remained: Maple was gone, and with her, a part of himself was lost forever. Behind him, a voice, familiar, gentle, but tanned with sorrow, spoke softly. "Edward… you allowed this to happen. You let your mother be the hand that killed me. And then, without a word, you welcomed another woman into your life, into your heart, while I lay forgotten, cut down, abandoned." He turned his head slowly. Arabella. She was no longer the faint shimmer of a ghost, no longer translucent She stood before him, fully formed, no longer a memory, but something solid, present. Her skin was pale, almost glowing in the moonlight, casting an ethereal sheen that made her seem both divine and dreadful. She wore the blue dress, the one he had always adored. The same dress she had worn the night he first told her he loved her when the world had felt untouched by tragedy. Edward rose to his feet, shaking with a delicate mix of shock and sorrow that threatened to overwhelm him. He moved toward her as if caught in a dreamlike haze, every step slow and hesitant, as though afraid to fully believe what lay before him. When he reached her, he reached out with unsteady hands to cup her face gently, his fingers tracing the faint warmth and delicate softness of her skin. His eyes welled with tears that brimmed and spilled freely, blurring his vision as the crushing burden of loss and heartbreak pressed relentlessly down on his soul. "My mother did this? I… I did not know." He whispered, voice cracking. "Oh, Arabella. My Arabella. I am sorry. I should have done more. I should have saved you. My heart…it has always been yours." She gazed at him with aching sadness, and when he leaned in, she did not pull away. Their lips met in a kiss, slow, longing, bittersweet. The wind stilled. Time seemed to pause. Arabella pulled back first. A single tear rolled down her cheek. She looked at the man she had once loved, and still did, even now. "I do." she whispered, words she had never lived long enough to speak at the altar, words that had once hovered on the edge of her voice in another life. And then, with one swift, almost merciful motion, she placed her hand on his neck and twisted, ending it before he could even exhale a last word. The sound was soft, almost inaudible. His body crumpled in her arms like a marionette with its strings cut. She held him for a breath longer. Then let him fall. Sir Edward's body crumpled lifelessly onto the cold balcony floor, his eyes still open, glassy and shimmering in the pale moonlight. The night air grew still around him, as if waiting in suspended reticence. Above him, Arabella stood silently, a shadow against the dark, her delicate fingers reaching out to brush a final tear from her cheek, a silent farewell to the last flicker of a shattered soul. Her eyes remained fixed on him for a moment, filled with sorrow and something far older, before she turned and vanished into the darkness. "I will always love you we shall be together once again." she whispered. Then she turned and walked slowly back into the manor, her form fading with each step until she was once again a ghost, silent and sorrowful. The balcony doors remained open behind her, the black sky stretching endlessly beyond, and the moon sending out its silver light upon the lifeless body of Sir Edward Blackthorne. Lady Catherine lay perfectly still in her vast canopy bed, her body stiff beneath the pristine sheets, tucked so tightly they might as well have been sewn into place, a shroud masquerading as linen. Her hands rested neatly at her sides, fingers long and loose, arranged with an almost ceremonial care, the picture of noble repose. She looked like a corpse. From the foot of the bed, the covers began to slide, slowly, as if peeled away by invisible hands. Inch by inch, they crept down her body, revealing the pale, liver-spotted skin of her ankles. Then, her foot lifted slightly, twitching. With violent force, Lady Catherine was ripped from the bed. She slammed to the floor with a puissant thud, bones clattering against wood. Her eyes flew open; mouth parted in a ragged gasp as a jolt of pain snapped her fully awake. For a moment, she lay stunned, blinking, against the dim flicker of dying firelight. But something was wrong. Deeply wrong. The room was cold, unnervingly cold, as if the very air had turned to ice. Her breath escaped in soft clouds, misting before her like fleeting shadows.

Though she was alone, a strange presence slithered beneath her skin, crawling with an unsettling sensation, like a swarm of invisible insects stirring restlessly just under her flesh, sending chills racing down her spine. Grimacing, she pushed herself upright, using the bedframe for balance. Her nightgown clung to her skin with sweat. She reached for her cane mounted on the wall, but the moment her hand neared it; the cane began to tremble. Then it launched toward her. It shot off the hook with unnatural speed, forcing her to duck instinctively, adrenaline surging through her veins. The object whizzed dangerously close to her ear, the rush of air like a razor's edge, before driving deep into the wooden floor with a sickening thud, like a spear thrown with lethal intent. The very walls seemed to shudder as the room began to hum, a low, menacing vibration that filled the air and set every nerve on edge, wrapping her in an unsettling, electric trouble. "Who' is there?!" she snapped, her voice knifelike but shaky. No answer. "I know you are here." She growled. "Show yourself!" In the far corner, the darkness thickened, heavier than shadow, alive with venom. It began to stir, congealing into the shape of a woman. Her limbs stretched too far, joints bending the wrong way. Her head lolled to one side at an unnatural angle, like the final slant of a hanged body, swaying in silence. Lady Catherine narrowed her eyes, burying her fear deep beneath a fierce mask of fury that flickered like wildfire across her features. "You dare creep into my chamber and try to frighten me? Me? You will regret…" The figure stepped into the firelight, and Lady Catherine's voice caught in her throat. It was Arabella. But not as she remembered her. Arabella's skin was pallid, grey blue with death, bloated in some places, sunken in others. Her mouth was stretched unnaturally wide, her lips torn at the corners, revealing too many teeth, sharp, cracked, and wet. Black ichor oozed from the corners of her eyes. "You... you are dead..." Lady Catherine stammered. Arabella's voice was no longer her own. It was echoing, warped like a voice underwater. "By your hands, Lady Catherine. By poison. By betrayal." Catherine scrambled backward, hands and knees catching splinters as she crawled toward the door. Arabella stepped forward, her feet hovering inches above the floor, toenails split and black, dragging blood as she passed. "I have returned." The spectre hissed, her face splitting into a smile that cracked the skin of her cheeks. "To take back what is mine." Lady Catherine stumbled to the door, fingers slipping on the handle, slick with sweat. "What do you want from me?" she cried, her voice breaking into sobs. Arabella's head turned, far too far, until it faced her with an inhuman angle, the crack of vertebrae echoing through the chamber like gunfire. "Not what, Lady Catherine... who." Suddenly, the mirrors exploded. A cacophony of shattering glass erupted from the vanity. Hundreds of jagged shards tore through the air like knives. Some embedded themselves in the walls, others embedded themselves in Lady Catherine. She screamed as slivers pierced her cheek, her shoulder, and her leg. One jagged shard drove into her thigh, plunging deep enough to scrape bone. Blood burst in pulsing waves, streaking the walls in dark red arcs. She dropped to the floor, a raw scream tearing from her throat. Arabella glided forward, black veins twitching beneath her translucent skin. Her hair floated around her head like seaweed in black water. Lady Catherine dragged herself to the door, leaving a slick trail of blood behind her. Her fingernails bent and snapped against the wood as she clawed her way to escape. She yanked the door open with fierce force and propelled herself into the corridor, heart racing as she fled into the midnight beyond. But the horror proceeded. She limped through the dark, gasping. The hall seemed longer, narrower, the walls breathing, pulsing inward like a throat preparing to swallow. She reached the top of the grand staircase, the great chandelier above gleaming in the dark. Her hand shot out to grab the banister, but something gripped her spine. She could not scream fast enough. Arabella's unseen power hurled her down the staircase with relentless force. Lady Catherine's body flailed wildly, thrashing against the unforgiving stone. Her skull slammed hard against a step, the sickening crack ringing out. Her left arm bent harshly backward, tendons snapping with a wet, tearing sound. Blood spilled from her mouth as her jaw shattered open. The fall stretched on, endless, a nightmare in slow motion. She came to a sudden halt at the base, her body contorted into unnatural, horrible angles that defied all sense of humanity. Her left leg was brutally torn open, the shattered bone split cleanly in two, jagged shards jutting out through the raw, bleeding skin. Dark blood seeped slowly from the gaping wound, pooling beneath her like a crimson stain. Her right eye hung precariously from its socket, suspended by a single glistening strand of muscle and tissue, flickering with a faint, agonized twitch. The sight was both horrifying and pitiful, an unpleasant testament to the violence that had befallen her. But still, she breathed. "Please..."

she rasped. "Please, I'm sorry..." Arabella descended from the ceiling like smoke, hovering above her broken prey. "Sorry will not bring me peace. Nor will it save you." Catherine was lifted into the air, her bones grinding audibly. She convulsed, blood dribbling from every orifice. Arabella whispered: "The Blackthorns end tonight." Catherine ascended, rising higher, until she hovered at the apex of the grand hall, just inches above the glittering chandelier, her fingertips nearly brushing the vaulted ceiling. Then, Arabella unleashed a piercing scream, an eerie, otherworldly shriek that made the very walls weep and bleed. With a sudden, sickening rush, Lady Catherine plummeted. She crashed through the massive chandelier, impaling herself on the iron and crystal. A spike pierced through her gut, another through her mouth, splitting her face. She hung there, twitching. Then stillness. Her blood spilled in thick, glistening sheets across the marble floor, pooling beneath her like a dark, blooming flower. It crept along the cracks, soaking into the spaces between the tiles with low determination. Torn shreds of her once elegant gown drifted around her like ash, fluttering to the ground in slow, mournful spirals. A single foot gave a final, reflexive twitch... then nothing. Only silence. The grand tyrant of Blackthorne Manor had fallen, ripped open, shattered beyond recognition. Her bones lay twisted, her body broken and bleeding, her death as cruel and unrelenting as the life she had inflicted on others. No dignity remained. No legacy spared. Only ruin, red and still. Arabella hovered above the scene, watching her murderer swing gently on the chandelier, Lady Catherines twisted remains. Her blackened mouth stretched into a wide, satisfied grin, teeth gleaming like splinters of bone in the dim light. And then, without a sound, without so much as a ripple in the air, she melted into the shadows, fading as if she had never been there at all. Her vengeance was complete, and the darkness welcomed her home.

FINAL CHAPTER
PART II
ARABELLAS REVENGE

Present day

The cold outside had grown unnatural, biting and bitter, and Chase's bare feet were nearly blue. The skin on her soles cracked and raw as she stumbled, breath stuttering in foggy gasps. There was no way out of the endless hedge maze. She had tried every path, every turn. It was hopeless. The maze of hedges and memories twisted endlessly, looping back on itself like a nightmare. She was trapped, utterly and irreversibly. Above her, Isabelle clung to the narrow ledge of the tower, her knuckles drained of colour from gripping the slick, icy stone. The wind howled around her, tearing at her clothes, dragging her hair across her face like lashes. Below, the darkness waited. Her eyes were wide, frantic, watching her daughter below. She screamed Chase's name again and again, but the wind drowned her out. It howled like a dying animal, tearing across the manor grounds with vicious gusts. Rain slashed

sideways, and thunder rattled the sky.
Isabelle's-soaked clothes whipped around her,
clinging to her shaking frame. The storm
churned above her, black clouds spiralling like
a celestial drain. The lightning within them
throbbed and flared, casting jagged white veins
across the sky. Isabelle's fingers trembled
against the stone. If she stayed up here, she
would either fall… or freeze, her body
stiffening until the wind claimed it. A few feet
below, an open window yawned in the side of
the tower, narrow, treacherous, but possible.
The only way in. Or out. She looked down. Her
breath hitched. One wrong move, and she
would plummet. But she had no choice. If she
could just lower herself down the slippery slope
without falling to her death, she might make it.
Slowly, she slid down, heart thundering in her
ears. The rain-slicked bricks offered no grip,
only the illusion of safety. Then, betrayal. The
edge crumbled beneath her boots. Isabelle
screamed as her body lurched into open air.
Her fall stopped with a brutal snap; her arm
wrenched violently as her fingers hooked into a
jagged stone. Pain tore through her shoulder,
but she held on, nails splitting against the
crevice. Blood seeped down her wrist where
the stone sliced her skin, but she held on. Her
other hand flailed, searching desperately for

another grip. Below, Chase writhed helplessly, ensnared in a tangled web of thorned vines that twisted and squirmed like living beasts. The nettles throbbed with a malicious pulse, dragging her deeper into their grasp with cruel insistence. Jagged thorns gouged into her flesh, raking her arms and legs with sharp, agonizing bites, like venomous fangs sinking ever deeper. The vines crept up her neck and over her face, piercing her tender skin and drawing dark, hot rivulets of blood from her lips and cheeks. A thick, serpentine vine slithered over her mouth, wrapping tightly and silencing her screams. All the while, through the blur of pain and terror, her eyes locked onto the horrifying sight above, her mother hanging from the tower, swaying gently in the freezing wind. Suddenly, CRACK. A bolt of lightning struck the tip of the tower, lighting up the world in a flash of white. The blast loosened a spray of stone debris, jagged bricks and piercing mortar hurtled downward like cannonballs. Isabelle narrowly avoided the first wave, but the second came with no warning. A brick, hefty and cruel, slammed into her face with a sickening crunch. Her head snapped violently backward, pain exploding behind her eyes. Her fingers twitched briefly, then slackened as her body gave way. Time seemed to slow as she tumbled, the world spinning wildly around her before darkness claimed her. Her body slammed into the cobblestones below with a meaty, bone-shattering thud. Her limbs twisted grotesquely, one arm bent completely backward, her skull cracked open like a melon. Blood pooled instantly beneath her, mixing with rainwater into a thick, pink slurry. Chase let out a muffled, agonized scream. Her mother, her last parent, had just died in front of her, and she had been helpless to stop it. The thorns gradually released their hold, retreating like satisfied hunters pulling back into the shadows. Chase collapsed to her knees for a moment, her face a chaotic canvas of blood and raw scratches, each breath burning in her chest. She forced herself up, wobbling as her legs struggled to steady her on the slick, soaked earth. With a fierce determination, she pushed forward, breaking into a desperate run through the twisted gardens, every step driving her closer to the hill's shadowed peak and whatever salvation, or horror, awaited there. At the summit, she spotted it, a shattered statue leaning precariously next to a gnarled, decayed tree stump. Nestled within the stump's hollow, half-swallowed by earth and bark, lay an ancient plaque, crusted thick with rust and time. With hands slick from blood and trembling with desperation, she pressed her soaked shirt to the metal, scraping away years of neglect until the faded letters began to emerge. The name glared back at her: *'ARABELLA'* Rage boiled through her veins. This was it. The tether. The cursed object. Just like in every horror film, if she could destroy this, maybe, just maybe, she could end this nightmare. She slammed the plaque hard against the rough tree stump again and again, but it was no use. The stubborn metal held firm, refusing to shatter or give way. Frustration burned at her as she realized it was unbreakable. Then Chase looked to the sky. Thunder growled. Lightning split the clouds. She turned back to the stump. Her eyes widened. She knew what she had to do. She scrambled up the stump, hoisting the plaque above her head, her arms trembling with the effort. Her voice tore through the howling wind, a raw, defiant scream swallowed instantly by the raging storm. In that electrifying instant, lightning cleaved the sky and struck. A blinding white bolt pierced the sky, driving down through the plaque, through Chase's body. The force launched her backward, her body contorting mid-air, then slamming into the muddy ground. She convulsed, smoke rising from her clothes. Her skin was blistered, blackened. Her hair partially singed. Her mouth opened, but no scream came. The stale air hung thick around her, carrying murmurs of forgotten pain and hidden secrets. Figures flickered at the edges of her blurred sight; shapes vague but threatening. Each breath she took felt skin-deep, as though the very atmosphere resisted her struggle to awaken. Somewhere distant, a faint, hollow sound echoed, like the slow ticking of time in a place where hope had long since withered. She knew this smell. It was old, sterile, unnatural. A nurse opened the blinds; light seared her eyes. "I see you decided to come back to us Chase." The nurse announced gently, her silhouette hovering overhead. "I know this will take some adjustment, but with our help, you'll be as comfortable and well looked after as possible." She tucked the blanket around Chase with an eerie calm. "You're at Blue Birds Care for Life, one of the best long-term care homes in the region." She continued. "You were in an awful accident… unfortunately, it left you paralyzed from the neck down. And you… unfortunately cannot speak." The nurse's smile stayed plastered on, but there was no warmth in her eyes. "You're safe now." A loud buzzer interrupted them. The nurse frowned slightly. "I'll be right back, sweetheart." Chase lay still, unable to move or call after her. The door clicked shut. A chill swept through the room. Darkness crept along the floor like creeping vines. Her eyes widened as shapes emerged into view, faces. Recognizable faces, their expressions twisted with sorrow and rage, hovered just beyond reach. Silent, they watched her, waiting. The air thickened, pressing in with a coldness that seeped into her bones. Emily. Hugo. Isabelle. Henry. Holly. Burtie. And others, faces she did not know but had seen in old portraits. Maid Ratchet. Sir Howard. Lady Catherine. Sir Edward. Lady Maple. All dead. All standing silently around her bed, their flesh pale and rotted, eyes glassy and unblinking. Water dripped from their hair and stained clothing. Some were broken, burned, their wounds still fresh. Then, a cold hand brushed her cheek. Arabella. She towered over Chase, her eyes black and glistening, void of mercy. Her mouth curved into a smile that spoke of endless hunger, of delight in suffering. A single tear traced a slow path down Chase's cheek, her body frozen, her mind screaming. Arabella leaned in close, whispering in her ear: "Forever... mine." The dead stepped forward, hands reaching, teeth grinning. Chase could not run. She could not scream. She was awake. She was aware. And she was paralyzed...trapped in

a body that would not move, not speak, not
scream. A prisoner behind unblinking eyes,
condemned to feel everything and do nothing.
Haunted by the dead. Tethered to their rage.
Bound to their whispers. The voices would
never stop. The footsteps would never fade.
Cold fingers would always brush her skin.

Never to escape.
Never to die. Never
to be alone!

About the Author

I have always been fascinated by horror, especially the kind that blends the paranormal with suspense. Equally, I've long been drawn to period settings, whether in drama, history, or true events. My greatest joy as a writer is bringing these passions together, shaping stories where past and present collide to create what I like to call a *terrifier of two worlds*. My love of writing began after reading a handful of horror novels just for fun. Before long, I was completely hooked, and with encouragement from my uncle, I began crafting stories of my own. What excites me most is imagining the forgotten lives and dark secrets that linger behind old walls and ruins, and then asking: what if the haunting began here, at the very start? I write by collecting scraps of dialogue, eerie moments, and strange images in a notebook, slowly weaving them into full chapters. My goal is always to give readers that same creeping, goosebump thrill that drew me to horror in the first place. I am currently working on a prequel that explores the Blackthorn matriarch's life, peeling back the layers of history to reveal the darkness that shaped everything to come. And that journey reminds me of one thing: *every past hides another, waiting to be unearthed.*